true calling series ~ book three

LOVE'S TRUE Measure

LORI DEJONG

Scrivenings
PRESS
Quench your thirst for story.
www.ScriveningsPress.com

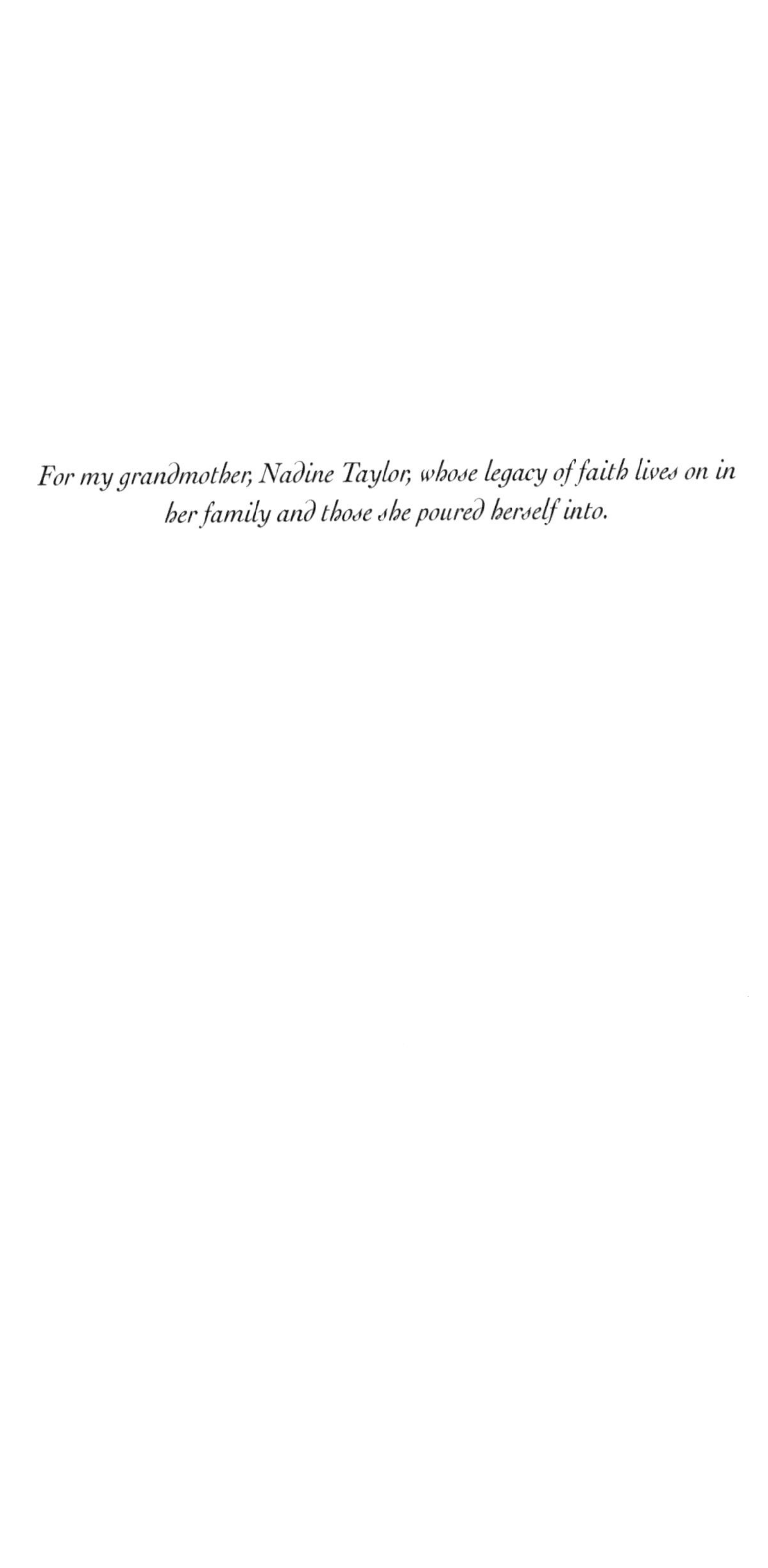

For my grandmother, Nadine Taylor, whose legacy of faith lives on in her family and those she poured herself into.

CHAPTER ONE

Oh, the joys of standing all of five feet, two inches tall. And that only if her ponytail was high enough.

Regretting her choice to grab the last two boxes instead of leaving one for a return trip, Shannon wished the carton on top was as transparent as the glassware inside. Unless she craned her neck to peer around it one way, then the other, the view directly in front of her consisted of the logo on the side of the box.

"Why didn't you have your friends move these with everything else over the weekend, Shan? Then we could be at brunch right now."

Shannon rolled her eyes at her little sister's whining. Okay, so not really *little*, as Delaney had passed Shannon by five inches years ago. At least Delaney could see over her box. "They weren't packed yet. And there aren't that many, Dee. Man up."

"I'm all girl, and you know it."

"Okay. Girl up, then. If you break a nail, I'll pay for your next manicure."

"Don't think I won't take you up on that."

Nearing the front entrance, Shannon smiled at the now-familiar gurgling of the fountain outside the historical building renovated into high-end condos. Such a nice greeting to come home to, even if she had almost passed on the top-floor unit with a loft. A decision she'd come to reluctantly, knowing it made the most sense, even if it meant sacrificing some hard-won self-reliance.

But with everything else on her plate, it would've been unwise, and prideful, not to accept the offer of a free condo for as long as she needed it. Once she earned her master's degree, a full-time position as an adolescent psychologist awaited her. Then she could reclaim her independence.

"Shan, watch out!"

Her sister's warning came a nano-second before the man's voice. "On my way n—*oomph.*"

A jolt knocked her back a step as her load teetered in her arms. A small splash and Delaney's gasp preceded the top box crashing to the ground with the gut-wrenching sound of glass shattering into a million shards.

Still holding the other box packed with plasticware, the epiphany that she should've stacked *that* one on top came a minute too late.

She turned to see a man staring down into the fountain's base, a leather briefcase held in one hand and the other against his forehead. A nicely dressed man, obviously on his way to work. Probably in one of the downtown Fort Worth high-rises only walking distance away.

"You didn't see me coming?"

His arm lowered as he turned a thunderous scowl to her. "See *you* coming? Who carries a box they can't even see over?"

Ignoring his question—because standing at least six foot, he could never understand the struggles of the vertically challenged—she peered into the fountain and sucked in a breath. "Uh-oh. Is that your phone?"

"Yes. With my boss on the other end."

He pulled a wireless earbud from his ear, which explained

how the phone ended up flying into the fountain. *His* epiphany, should he have one, would no doubt be he should've kept it in his pocket instead of his hand.

Except he probably hadn't anticipated being broadsided by a moving carton.

"I am so sorry."

"He probably thinks I got hit by a bus, and this meeting is wrecked." He raked long fingers through thick, wavy brown hair as he stared into the water.

She chewed her bottom lip. She had less than an hour to get to work, a part-time position at the counseling practice where she'd interned last year. Where she'd work full-time once she finished up her grad program.

"If I can't get back to him, this meeting *will* be wrecked, and I'll wish I *had* been hit by a bus." He turned his steely blue-gray eyes to her. "I'll even allow you the honor of pushing me in front of one. You know, to finish the job."

"Yeah, that's not overly dramatic." She set the box on the ground and pulled her phone from her back pocket. "Here. Use mine."

"Thanks." With no hesitation, he took the phone and punched in a number.

"But I need to be at —"

"Hey, Jules, I was on the phone with Alden when I ran into a ... a ..." He looked at her. "Neighbor. I think. Anyway, my phone is currently under water, so if you could have it replaced today, I'd appreciate it. Can you transfer me to Alden, please? Thanks."

He walked a few yards away from the gurgling fountain and traffic passing by on the other side. Shaking her head, Shannon pulled off her tennis shoes and socks.

Delaney set her box on the side of the fountain and took a seat next to it. "What are you doing?"

"Getting Mr. Big Shot's phone. Doubt he's going to roll up the legs of that thousand-dollar suit to go get it." Remorse replaced her indignation. "Sorry. I shouldn't have said that. I knocked it in, I should get it out."

Delaney leaned in, her gaze fastened on Shannon's new neighbor. "Mr. Big Shot is hot," she said in a stage whisper. "And a good dresser." Both very important things on Delaney's list. "If he lives here, I may be coming to see you more often."

"Whatever it takes."

Anything to have more time with her sister. Shannon worried about Dee's college party-girl ways and continued to hope she would accept her weekly invitation to come with her to church one of these days.

She stepped into the fountain and gasped as cold water darkened her jeans up to her knees. She retrieved the phone, shook it out, and stepped back onto the stone pavers.

The man nodded at something *his boss* said but didn't look her way. With nothing to do but wait to exchange phones, she set it next to the fountain and walked over to the battered box on the ground.

The tape had split open on one side, and several newspaper-wrapped bundles lay next to it. When she picked one up, the drinking glass inside collapsed in her hand. The others followed suit, as it appeared none had survived the fall.

She righted the carton and said a silent prayer of gratitude none of the shards had escaped the paper. It was bad enough she'd have to replace all her glassware.

And her neighbor's cell phone. She should at least offer, right? Regardless of his snarly tone?

An unpleasant detour on this late September Tuesday that had started out with such promise. The blue sky dotted with powdery white clouds she'd watched from her new balcony during her quiet time had buoyed her to move the final pieces from her last apartment. Missing her roommates and not in love with the idea of living alone—an extrovert's worst nightmare—she'd sought solace and strength from the one place she always knew she could find it. Hopefully, she could reclaim some of the peace from those early morning moments.

Still holding the phone to his ear, the man glanced up but made no move their direction. She checked her watch. Forty-five minutes to change into something more office-appropriate than wet jeans and a Texas Rangers T-shirt, put on some make-up, and do something with her hair. Not to mention the twenty-minute drive to the office in Arlington.

"I bet he's really smart," Delaney said. "Good-looking, intelligent, designer suit. I wonder if he's married."

"He's too old for you."

"What do you think he does?"

"Probably something corporate. Has the same attitude as Dad and Cam when they're in business mode." Which was pretty much whenever they were awake.

After finishing his call, his brisk stride brought him back over to them. He would be more handsome if he smiled. A smile always improved a countenance, not to mention mood. And his disposition definitely needed improvement.

"Thanks." As he returned her phone, and took his drenched one, he regarded the crumpled box with a grimace. "Sorry about your ... stuff. Sounded ominous."

"Not as big a deal as your phone. When you get a new one, give the concierge the invoice, and I'll reimburse you. I'll let him know to send it up to me. I truly am sorry."

He gave the phone a few good shakes, and water droplets spotted the ground. "Don't worry about it. It's insured, and my admin will have a new one for me by end of business today." He glanced at her broken box again. "I'd offer to help, but this meeting—"

"It's okay. We've got it. I hope your day gets better."

"Can only go up from here."

He turned and walked away, his gait easy and shoulders back. Confidence was not this guy's shortcoming. Chivalry? She'd reserve judgment on that. Chances were slim she'd run into him much, anyway, even if they did live in the same building.

Delaney stood and picked up her box. "Totally hot neighbor."

And totally not Shannon's type. She made a habit of steering clear of corporate hotshots, like her father and brother. If Delaney wanted him, she could have him.

CHAPTER TWO

Five hours into a two-and-a-half-hour drive.

Or so it seemed to Hunter.

He glanced at the sullen teenage girl in the passenger seat. Normally chatty and effusive, Brylie had spoken little in the eight days since he'd been called to Mount Pleasant, Texas, in the middle of the night. Only hours after a car accident had taken their mother.

Now on the road home to Fort Worth, the weighty silence stretched the miles even farther apart, despite the country music wafting through the speakers.

Usually, he'd be on the phone with a client or one of the other lawyers from his firm, getting work done while behind the wheel. Over the last week, however, he'd kept the device on Do Not Disturb to be here for his sister.

Because, truth be told, there was nobody else. He was it. The enormity of which hit him as he stood at his mother's graveside, next to where they'd laid his grandmother four months before. He and Brylie were now the last two of their family still living.

Brylie's no-good drunk of a father didn't count. He'd become a non-entity to Hunter when he abandoned Mom and

Bry because he gave the bottle more value than his wife and daughter.

If only Mom had lived long enough to enjoy her much-deserved freedom longer than twenty-one months.

Now, Hunter's normally pristine BMW sedan traveled down Interstate 30, packed to the gills with all of Brylie's earthly belongings. Or, more accurately, what was left after they'd sold off what little their mother had accumulated in her short but rocky forty-five years.

He'd worked sunup to head-down on his pillow over the last week to clear out Gran's house, leaving this afternoon with a *For Sale* sign glaring at him from his rearview mirror. The only time he'd return to the little town that had raised him would be for the trial of the man who murdered his mother with too many shots of tequila and a pick-up truck.

He chanced another glance at this little girl who owned his heart, because in his mind, she'd always be little. As she had been since leaving Mount Pleasant over an hour ago, she sat silent. Still. Elbow propped on the door, head resting on her hand, staring out the windshield.

His chest tightened. Completely out of his element here, same as he'd been the night of the accident when he walked into the foster home she'd been taken to and she'd dissolved into gut-wrenching sobs in his arms.

He'd never been so helpless or unprepared, with no idea what to do for a girl who'd lost her anchor in the split second it had taken a drunk driver to blow through a red light. The only smidgen of comfort Hunter could take from any of it was that Mom had died instantly. No pain. Now at peace. Reunited with Gran, if her and Gran's belief in heaven proved true.

He cleared his throat of the thickness that had been stuck there the better part of this beyond abysmal week. "Hey, Bry, we have about forty-five minutes before hitting Dallas. You need to stop for anything? Restroom? Something to eat?"

"I'm fine."

He nodded. She was anything but fine. "I'm going to make a quick stop at the Buc-ee's up here. We might want to pick up a few things. I don't ... well, there's not much at my condo. We'll need to do some grocery shopping tomorrow, but maybe you can find a few things at Buc-ee's you like?"

Her shoulders hitched in a shrug. "Maybe."

"Speaking of groceries, why don't you start a list? We can get anything you want. I also have a service that delivers fresh meals during the week. We can go through the list when we get home, and you can preorder whatever sounds good."

She turned to him and narrowed her bluish-gray eyes. Their mother's eyes. The same eyes he saw every day in the mirror. "You don't even cook?"

His gaze returned to the road. "I don't usually have the time, and I can heat them up at the office. They're much healthier than take-out or fast food. I'm sure you'll find some things you like."

She stuck her cheek in her hand again. "Whatever."

His heart grew another crack, and apprehension crawled along his spine. What on earth was he supposed to do with a fourteen-year-old girl? He worked seventy-plus hours a week in a bid to make partner by the time he turned thirty, his goal from the moment he accepted the junior associate position at his firm straight out of law school. Now the youngest senior associate after two promotions, and with only eighteen months to make it a reality, it would be difficult to cut back now.

But he couldn't leave Brylie to her own devices until he got home at nine or ten every night. Or on the weekends when he would spend several hours in the office or in his study at home scouring case law for research on his laptop.

As for a social life, that was usually a Friday or Saturday evening with friends from work either at a club or some sporting event. But he could give that up easily enough to accommodate Brylie. He'd rather spend time with her, anyway, than guys he saw every day already. And there hadn't been a woman in the picture for a couple of years.

Although old enough to be left alone for a little while, living as she was in the grip of grief, she would need someone there for her. Maybe there were after-school programs he could check into. Or she could take the bus to his office and stay there until he was done.

No. That wouldn't work. She'd hate it, and it wouldn't be fair to her. She'd already been yanked out of her home and needed some semblance of stability. Well, maybe not *home,* exactly, because Mitch had moved them every time he lost yet another job. The last year-and-a-half Mom and Bry had lived at Gran's were the most stable she'd ever known.

He had to do better by her than her father ever had.

Moisture blurred his vision behind the sunglasses he'd donned against the late afternoon sun setting in front of him. Yes, she deserved so much better. This sister he'd vowed to protect at any cost, if it came to it, the day his mother and stepdad brought the tiny baby girl home two weeks after his fourteenth birthday.

Now it had come to it. The little girl who'd followed him everywhere the first four years of her life, would barely leave his side every time he'd come to visit, texted him videos and gifs to make him laugh, or would call to *just talk* at least once a week, now needed him like never before.

And as with his goal of being promoted to partner, he would not fail. If only he could figure out a way to accomplish both without sacrificing either.

CHAPTER THREE

This had to be the answer to her prayer.

From her spot on a poolside chaise, Shannon peered over the top of her textbook at the young girl with the long, chestnut-brown hair. Saturday, she'd been curled up with a novel in one of the chairs in the lobby of their building while an early fall rain pummeled the floor-to-ceiling windows. Nobody else around, nobody with her or watching out for her, her countenance matching the weather.

Granted, the building had top-notch security. Its occupants could only get in with a passkey from the garage or the lobby doors, and all guests had to be admitted by the concierge. Only repeat visitors registered with the front desk could enter without being announced, like Delaney. But this girl being there utterly alone hadn't sat right with Shannon.

Yesterday, she and the girl had been in the elevator with three others. Certain one of them had to be a parent, Shannon was surprised when the teen exited on the third floor alone. So, she'd had a talk with God, praying that if there was something she should do, He'd open the door.

And now, there the girl sat by the pool in shorts and a UT Longhorn T-shirt on this mild, early October Monday afternoon, knees drawn up to her chest with her arms wrapped around her shins. Her curtain of hair fell around her as she stared out onto the water with another novel resting beside her. Nobody with her yet again.

The most alone girl Shannon had ever seen.

Why wasn't she in school? Maybe homeschooled? Or home sick? Hopefully, she wasn't ditching. And why wasn't anybody ever with her?

Shannon remembered how it had felt to be utterly alone. Bereft and grief-stricken. Isolated and despairing.

And if she could put a name to the expression on this girl's face, it was despair.

Even though she had more homework than she had time, she couldn't sit by and do nothing any longer. With another silent prayer, she plopped the textbook onto the table beside the chaise, threw her legs over the side, and walked slowly over to the steps at the shallow end of the pool, only a couple of feet from where the teen sat.

She stepped onto the first step and stretched, the cold water causing gooseflesh to rise on her legs. Although still warm enough here on the third of October for shorts, the lower overnight temps had chilled the pool past the comfort zone for swimming.

"Ah, that feels good. Needed to get away from homework for a bit."

The girl's gaze never wandered from the water, but at least she didn't get up and leave. Shannon took that as an invitation to sit.

"I'm new here. Moved in a couple of weeks ago. Have you lived here long?"

The girl shook her head without changing her focus.

"Another newbie. Well, I think you'll like it here. The pool's a little cold now, but there's another indoors if you like to do laps. And a hot tub. We have the fitness center, the theater, a game room, and a rooftop deck with lights. Looks very cool at night." She waited for any kind of response. "Oh, and a library."

The teen's slate-blue eyes came up to meet hers, and a momentary sensation of *déjà vu* swept over her, as if she'd looked into those eyes before. But she'd never met this girl. She was sure of it.

"A library? Where?"

"On the second floor. Pretty decent selection. I was surprised."

"I'll have to go look."

"Yeah." She gave the girl a smile, but nothing was returned. "I'm Shannon. I live on the top floor."

"Brylie. Third floor."

"Beautiful name. Is that a family name?"

Brylie shrugged and turned her attention to the water again. "Nobody's ever said. My brother might know."

"Your brother. Does he live here too?"

That garnered a nod but no other information.

"Is he at school?"

"Working. In the apartment. I got bored."

Working? How old was her brother? "I know the feeling. I live by myself and get bored too. Hence, why I study in other places, like the lobby the other day, and today by the pool. It's such a pretty day."

Brylie looked up and around, as if only now noticing the clear blue sky overhead. "Yeah."

"What grade are you in, Brylie?"

"Ninth. But I'm not in school. Yet."

"Yet." Interesting. "Because you're new here?"

Another nod, with those eyes directed to the water. "I guess I'll have to go at some point."

"Probably. It's kind of the law." She chuckled and was rewarded by the briefest upturn of the corner of Brylie's mouth. "And has to be better than sitting around bored while your brother works."

"He'll be going back to the office next week. Said he got really behind when he came to get me."

Okay, wow, there was a story there. Shannon's psychologist radar went into full alert. Or psychologist-to-be.

"How old is your brother?"

"Um … twenty-eight. We're fourteen years apart, but we've always been close."

"I see. And it's just the two of you?"

"Yeah."

"Where did he have to go get you?"

"Mount Pleasant. That's where I lived the past couple of years. Until …" Tears filled her eyes and spilled down her porcelain cheeks.

"Oh, honey, I'm sorry I upset you. I'm too nosy sometimes. But I'm also a good listener, if I can help at all."

Brylie swiped at her face. "It's okay. Still … hard … hard to believe." The girl turned her tortured expression toward Shannon. "That she's just gone. Went to the store and never came home."

Her? Mom, maybe? Just left the girl to her brother? "You mean, your mother?"

"She was in a car wreck."

Shannon's stomach knotted. "She died."

Brylie nodded, then the sobs came. Shannon scooted over and enveloped the girl in the circle of her arms. "Oh, sweetie. I am so, so sorry. I can't imagine."

Letting the girl cry, Shannon closed her eyes and prayed silently for the right words, for peace on Brylie and her brother. For guidance.

Once Brylie's sobs had quieted, Shannon let her go. How she wished she had the ability to take away this darling girl's pain. But nobody did. Nobody could change what happened to her, go back in time and edit the outcome. It was done. And now Brylie had to live with it.

A feeling Shannon was all too familiar with.

Father, thank You for letting me be here for Brylie. Please use me to help her.

Brylie swept her fingers down her face. "I'm super sorry about that. It hits me at strange times. And Hunter gets all weird when he sees me crying."

Hunter. The brother. She sympathized with him. Some guys had no idea what to do with a woman in tears. Even a pre-woman.

"Nothing strange about it. It's completely normal and nothing to apologize for. If you ever want to talk or cry or just need somebody to sit and be quiet with, I'm in 501. You can knock on my door any time. If I'm not home, leave me a note, and I can get a hold of you later. I can even give you my number."

"My brother will want to meet you first. He's okay with me walking around here, as long as I don't leave the building or go to anybody's apartment."

"Absolutely. He sounds like a good big brother." Except he was working instead of spending time with his brokenhearted little sister.

And how was he handling his mother's death? By working? To numb himself while leaving this precious girl to fend for herself?

Then again, she shouldn't judge. Grief was an insidious creature. Affected people differently. She learned that from her own tragic experience. Caught in her own abyss of sorrow, she'd gone searching for something to fill the void and finally found God, literally hours before she gave up altogether.

Brylie lived in a fog, preferring to be alone. Her brother apparently chose to stay busy.

Yes, she would like to meet this brother. Hunter. Maybe she could help them both.

CHAPTER FOUR

"And you invited this girl over for dinner?" Hunter stared wide-eyed at his sister. "Without telling me?"

"I'm telling you now."

Sadness still clouded Brylie's eyes, but there was a bit of light there he hadn't seen since he'd gone home to visit a month ago. The last time he saw his mother alive in person.

"But you know I don't cook. Do you cook?"

"Just order something like you always do. She wants to meet you so I can go hang at her apartment."

"Brylie." He took a deep breath in and swiped a hand through his hair, leaving it sticking straight up. He would have to take a shower before this ... lady ... showed up at his door. And apparently order something for dinner. "You can't go to people's condos I don't know."

"Duh. Which is why she's coming *here*. For dinner."

"And I'm supposed to judge whether she's okay based on one dinner?"

"You'll like her. She's super nice. She was studying by the pool yesterday, and we started talking. Then she showed me the library on the second floor. She had class this morning, and when I texted to see if she could hang out this afternoon, she said she would be home around four. So, I asked if she could come for dinner."

We started talking. He hadn't succeeded in pulling more than a sentence or two at a time from his usually chatty sister over the past twelve days. But this stranger by the pool had apparently been able to get through to a place he couldn't, because this conversation so far had been the longest he and Brylie had shared in nearly two weeks.

"So, she's in school? Like, college school?"

Her brow furrowed, and she swept a strand of her long hair off her forehead. "She said she graduated already. So, I guess it's like after-college school. At Dallas Heritage University."

Impressive. Even he knew DHU as a well-regarded private university, although he'd done his time in a state school. "Grad school. Probably her master's, then, I would guess."

She snapped her fingers. "Yes. That's what she called it. Her master's."

"Does she have roommates? Live with family? Boyfriend?"

Her ponytail swished across her shoulders when she shook her head. "By herself."

He let out a sigh. "Nothing to do but have dinner with her, I guess." He cocked his head. "There's a library on the second floor?"

She rolled her eyes. "Yes. Kind of an honor system. People can put books in and take books out. How long have you lived here?"

"Eight months. But I haven't been able to take advantage of many of the amenities besides the gym. Too—"

"Busy. I know. Don't you get tired of working all the time?"

He gave her a shrug. "I like my job. It pays well, and the work is interesting. Mostly. And I have goals. I have to put in the time if I want the reward. And the promotion."

She stared at him for a long moment. "The reward is more work?"

Planting his hands on his hips, he had to think about that one. "Well … kind of. But as a partner, I'd be able to delegate work to—" He shook his head. "Never mind." He really didn't need to defend himself to a fourteen-year-old. "Anyway, next time you invite someone for dinner, give me a heads up, okay?"

"Thought that's what I did."

"At least a twenty-four-hour heads up."

"Oh. Okay, sorry."

"No problem. What do you want to order?"

She smiled the first smile he'd seen since her life had turned upside down, and he found himself reluctantly grateful to a stranger. What had this woman done or said that he hadn't?

"Pizza. She likes pepperoni and mushroom."

"How on earth do you know what kind of pizza she likes?"

"We played twenty questions by the pool yesterday. One of my questions was what kind of pizza she liked. So, pizza for dinner."

"Okay, pizza it is. I hate mushrooms, so the lady's getting her very own pie. She can take home the leftovers."

"I'll split a meat lover's with you."

He pulled her in for a hug. "Just like always. Little sister loves her meat lover's pizza. And I love you. You know that, right? I've got you. I don't want you to worry."

"I know. And I love you too. I just—I mean …" She sighed and pulled away. "I know you want to go back to the office, and I'm gonna have to go to that really big high school. But what am I supposed to do until you come home?"

He walked over to the desk he'd moved into the living room in preparation to turn the spare bedroom into Brylie's personal space. "I've got that all worked out." He closed the laptop and turned to his sister. "Mrs. Burleson next door said she'd be happy to have you stay with her if I have to work late."

"The lady with the yappy dog?" Why did her face say that was akin to water torture?

"I'd feel better if you were with someone if I get caught at the office into the evening. And Mrs. B was the first person to welcome me when I moved in. Brought me meals, helped me pick out kitchen stuff. She's been a great neighbor. It's nice of her to offer."

"I'm old enough to stay here by myself for a few hours. Or I could hang with Shannon."

"Shannon, who I don't know yet." He joined her in the kitchen. "Shannon, who goes to school. And works. How else could she afford to live here?"

That posed a whole other question. He knew from his own purchase, these condos in the heart of Fort Worth didn't come cheap. So, how did a student afford it? Was she renting? House sitting? Was she a stellar saver? Maybe she had someone putting her up, which wouldn't be a good influence on his impressionable teenage sister at all.

"She may not even be home when you get out of school."

Brylie's face fell. "True. She does work. Part-time something, until she gets her degree to be … I can't remember. Psych-something. For kids."

His pulse hitched. "Psychologist?"

"Sounds right."

"For kids." That could certainly come in handy about now, if the woman turned out to be above board.

He'd heard Brylie crying several times at night but had no idea how to help her. He could make sure she had a roof over her head, three squares a day, clothes, necessities—although some of those could be awkward—and give her as much of his time as he could.

But having someone who could walk her through this awful time might be just the thing. And from the change in Brylie's emotional state, it appeared this Shannon had a knack for helping kids. "Must be adolescent psychologist. Is that what she's getting her master's in?"

She shrugged. "You can ask her when she gets here. In an hour. So you might wanna do something with"—she gestured up and down—"all that."

He looked down at his seen-a-better-day holey sweatpants and the T-shirt with the jelly smear from the pb&j sandwich he'd downed for lunch while at his laptop. This was the second day he'd worn the same socks, his face sported two days' growth of stubble, and his hair hadn't seen a brush in as long. He missed the high energy of the office, but working from home did have its benefits, as long as he didn't get pulled onto a video call.

Grinning, he threw her a wink. "On it."

When a knock sounded later on the door, he shot a glance at the clock by his bed, still not used to seeing Brylie's purple frog clock instead of his more guy-like black square. That's what happened when a big brother surrendered his room to his little sister until they could procure proper furniture for said sister. But after only four nights on the sofa, a gnarly crick he wouldn't soon be rid of had taken up residence in his neck.

He grabbed a clean polo shirt from the closet and pulled it over his head to wear with his last clean pair of jeans. He'd have to do some laundry soon. The previous hour had slipped away after a work call caught him on his way to the master bathroom for his shower. The call that left him only twenty minutes to prepare for their dinner company.

Brylie's voice blended with another female's while he ran his fingers through his still-damp hair. At least he'd shaved, after Brylie demanded it. Said he reminded her of a hobo, which had him wondering exactly how many hobos she'd come into contact with.

His feet now in clean socks, he stepped into his tennis shoes, opened the bedroom door, and walked down the hall. When he rounded the corner into the living area, he noticed the long, blonde hair first—hard to miss as it cascaded in soft waves down her back—then the petiteness of her frame. A good three or four inches shorter than Brylie's lanky five-foot six, but definitely curvier in all the right places.

"Hey, sorry about that."

She turned, and his breath caught as he stopped short.

Not usually at a loss for words, all he could do was stare at the slack-jawed woman he'd last seen in front of the building two weeks ago to the day. When he'd been a complete jerk for reasons of his own making, not hers, although she'd borne the brunt of his frustration.

Yeah, he wouldn't be surprised if Brylie's new friend simply walked out. And he'd deserve it.

CHAPTER FIVE

Great. Mr. Big Shot Corporate Guy.

Shannon couldn't tear her attention from her host for the evening. The neighbor she hadn't seen once in the two weeks following their unfortunate collision by the fountain. That had suited her just fine.

Her face heated as she silently chastised herself for her uncharitable thought. Followed hard on its heels by the acknowledgment Delaney was right. Shannon's neighbor, big shot or not, was ho—very nice-looking. Even more so with slightly damp hair showing a hint of curl. The light aqua pullover he wore with jeans brought out the blue in his blue-gray eyes.

His eyes. That's who Brylie's eyes had reminded her of that day by the pool—the handsome, if snarly, man by the fountain. He spoke first, taking a few steps closer. "Uh, hi. Again. Or I guess for the first time, since we kind of skipped all that before."

"Hi," was all her short-circuited brain had yet to download to her mouth.

Brylie's gaze bounced between them. "You know each other already?"

"Um …" Shannon cleared her throat. "Not exactly. I kind of ran him over with a box. And drowned his phone."

The girl's eyes widened as her mouth dropped. "Ohhh. *You're* the one?"

Super. He'd told his sister all about the clumsy spectacle she'd made of herself. Maybe she should plead a migraine and make a quick getaway.

Except she wasn't here for Mr. Big—uh, Hunter, was it? She was here for Brylie. A warm flush traveled from her neck up to her face. "Guilty. I really would like to pay for your phone. It's the least I can do."

He shook his head and grinned. Maybe the guy had multiple personalities, because the demeanor of the man standing in front of her now and the one bristling with irritation that awful morning reminded her of those creepy comedy-and-tragedy masks. One smiling, and one that looked like … well, like somebody drowned their phone.

"Not necessary. I could at least see where I was going, if I'd been paying attention."

"Yeah, well, that's a burden we short people must bear. Seems like something or another is always blocking my view."

When he laughed, she couldn't keep from joining him and found her shoulders relaxing after her initial shock.

"If anything, I should reimburse *you* for what you lost because I was distracted, if you'll let me, Miss …"

"Shannon. Trent. And totally not necessary. We'll call it even."

"Miss Shannon Trent. I'm Hunter Kavanaugh. As for that morning, all I can say is I certainly wasn't at my best. I'd left a file at home I needed for a meeting. Otherwise, I wouldn't have even been there. My boss wasn't at all pleased, then my phone … you know. None of which is an excuse for my lack of courtesy, so I hope you'll give me a second chance to make a decent first impression."

She flipped her hand toward him. "No worries. Especially

because I hear we're having pizza from Luigi's for dinner. My absolute favorite."

"Mine too. Tried it my first week living here and have been ruined for anything else."

"Right? I don't know what his secret is, but I'm all in."

As if conjured up by their praise, Hunter's phone dinged with a text alert. "That's the concierge. Bry, I'll go grab the pizza to save the delivery guy a trip up here while you set out some plates and glasses. We'll eat at the table for a change, like civilized folks."

Brylie moved to a cabinet by the refrigerator. "Works for me."

While they waited for him to come back, Brylie pulled out plates and glasses and set them on the table. "This will be the first time we've eaten at the table since I got here."

"At least you can see your table. Mine's covered with research for a paper I'm doing."

"What about?"

"Cultural and Social Influences on Adolescent Development."

Brylie blinked at her. "Sounds … interesting."

Chuckling, Shannon shrugged. "It actually is. Just a lot of information."

Hunter appeared a couple of minutes later carrying two large pizza boxes, which he set in the middle of the table. "One meat lover's, one pepperoni and mushroom."

"That's my favorite."

"So I hear. Figured you could take the leftovers home."

Caught off-guard by his kind gesture, it took a second for her to come up with a response. "I'll be happy to share."

He and Brylie exchanged a look and wrinkled their noses in an adorably similar fashion. "Actually, we're not big mushroom fans. It's all yours."

"Then I should reimburse you."

"Nonsense. You're our guest. Besides, Bry tells me you're a

student and also have a job. Sounds like you could use leftovers with your busy schedule."

That much was true. She could find her way around a kitchen, or more accurately, between her refrigerator and the microwave.

Thankfully, her best friends, Ally and Harper, were fantastic cooks. Since she'd moved into the new place, they'd taken it upon themselves to supply her with meals while she juggled her graduate studies, her part-time job, and captaining the Fort Worth club for ConnectUP student ministries. They were the older sisters she'd always wanted, and she vowed to be as good a big sister to Delaney as they were to her.

"That's very kind. Thank you."

When his phone chimed with an incoming call, he checked the screen and winced.

Brylie stuck a fist on her hip. "Tell me that's not work. We have company."

"Sorry, Bry. I'll make it quick." He tapped the phone and put it to his ear. "Kavanaugh." On his way out of the room, he grabbed the laptop off the desk. "No sir, this is fine."

Shannon's eyes flicked from Brylie to the man disappearing down the hall and into the master bedroom. The door closed, muffling his voice.

What just happened? One phone call, and he'd morphed into the corporate big shot from that first morning. Absorbed in work when his attention should be elsewhere.

Memories assailed her, knotting her stomach and sending her back to a time when she felt small and inconsequential. All because the man who should have been the center of her life instead valued money, status, and work over his family.

The choices she'd made in her quest for acceptance and affirmation had almost destroyed her. She now realized why God had opened this door. And she would do everything in her power to see Brylie didn't walk the same path.

"Unbelievable." Brylie's irritated tone pulled Shannon's

attention. "Here he's supposed to be getting to know you, and he takes a call."

While she sympathized with Brylie's aggravation, and didn't disagree, she decided to make the best of the situation. "It's okay. This will give us a chance to have some girl talk."

The scowl softened on the teen's pretty face. "Sounds good to me. My mom and I would—"

When Brylie's eyes filled and she bowed her head, Shannon reached out to rub her shoulder. "You and your mom would have girl talk?"

She nodded. "It was only the two of us after my grandma passed away a few months ago. We'd cook something together or bring home burgers or pizza and eat on the floor at the coffee table. Things were better after we moved in with Gran. More … peaceful. Just us girls. And Hunter when he'd come visit."

Hmm. So much information in that short statement. So much pain Shannon could feel radiating off this young girl who shouldn't have to carry that weight. Was Hunter helping her at all? Or was he too busy, like right now, when he should be here instead of holed up in his room talking business? Whatever business that was.

"If you want to sit on the floor instead of at the table, I'm all for that. I actually do that at home myself when I want to watch TV while I eat. I have a white couch, so I always eat sitting on the floor."

Light entered Brylie's eyes with her smile. "Okay." She picked up two glasses. "If you want to take the pizzas over to the coffee table, I'll grab the sodas. Unless you'd prefer tea?"

"Soda sounds great." Shannon hefted the two large pizza boxes, snatched some paper napkins from a holder on the kitchen island, and carried her load over to the coffee table. Balancing the pizzas on one arm, she scooted a hardcover book of Texas skylines and another showcasing high-performance cars to the side.

She set the pizzas on the table, then lowered herself to the soft, shaggy rug placed over the wood floor with her back to the espresso-hued leather sofa. Her hostess planted herself across from her, both sitting cross-legged so they could eat pizza right from the box. This was her kind of girl night.

Except for the specter of the man in the other room hovering over them. Apparently, *I'll make it quick* had a different meaning for him than it did her.

Of course, it didn't matter to her if he made the time to get to know her or not. But it mattered to Brylie. So Brylie could come see her at her apartment. Something Shannon would love to be able to do in order to help the girl through this painful time.

Especially once she started school. A new girl in a large, urban high school, dealing with grief on top of the stress of trying to fit in.

Exactly what ConnectUP was all about.

She'd have to find a way to bring that up to Hunter, to see if she could perhaps take Brylie to club so she could meet some really great kids. Even a few from her new school.

After swallowing her first generous bite, she let out a groan. "This is so good."

Brylie covered her mouth. "It's the best. I've only been here five days, and it's the third time we've had it."

"Hunter's not big on cooking, I take it?"

"He uses a meal delivery service kind of thing."

"I see." Shannon had a meal delivery service, too, but their names were Harper and Ally. "I'm not much of a cook myself, unfortunately, but my friends keep me supplied with food. You can come eat with me any time. Especially if your brother's working."

"That would be great. I hope he'll let me. He's a little overprotective."

"Good for him. He should be. You're worth it."

Pink suffused Brylie's face with her shy grin. "Yeah, he's a pretty cool big brother. Just works too much."

"What does he do?"

"Lawyer. Not sure what he does, exactly. Only that he seems to be on the phone or his laptop constantly, even at night. I don't know what it'll be like next week when he goes to the office."

"They didn't give him time off for bereavement?"

"Be-what?"

"Bereavement. Companies will usually give their employees time off when they lose a close family member."

Brylie shrugged. "Not sure. He didn't work the week he was in Mount Pleasant getting all my mom's stuff sold or given away. And for the … funeral."

Shannon pulled another piece from the box. "Were he and your mom close?"

Brylie nodded, swallowed, then took a gulp from her soda. "Very. She was super young when she had him, he was twelve when she married my dad, I think. So, it was only the two of them most of that time."

A chill ran up Shannon's spine. How young? Old enough to keep him, obviously. So, probably older than —

"Mom used to tell me he was a little adult from the time he started school. Took care of her more than she did him."

Shannon pushed aside the fog of sorrow that lived in the periphery of her memories and smiled at Brylie's depiction of a little Hunter taking on the world. Seeing him at his most intense two weeks ago, she could believe it.

"She was a great mom, though. Loved us both like crazy." Brylie's stare went back to her plate. "I really miss her."

"Of course you do. And you will, honey. You'll always miss her, but it's because you loved each other so much."

Shannon's thoughts went to Ally, who'd lost her own mother when she was twelve. Maybe there'd be some way to introduce the two. Ally could help Brylie better than Shannon could, having never lost a parent.

Not that she didn't know grief. They were all too well-acquainted. Most of the time, she could keep the jagged darkness away. Other times, it threatened to swallow her whole.

The bedroom door opened, and Brylie's gaze drifted above Shannon's head a second later. "It's about time. We're almost done."

Hunter stopped at the end of the sofa, peering down at them with a deep furrow in his forehead. "I thought we were going to eat at the table."

"*We* decided we wanted to sit on the floor and eat from the box."

Shannon chuckled. "Like *un*civilized people."

He shot her a grin as he took a seat at the end of the rectangular coffee table. "Whatever works." After grabbing a piece of pizza, he looked at her. "About that call, that was our senior managing partner. I got so far behind last week, I'm playing major catch-up."

Shannon wanted to tell him it was okay. But was it? Would there always be something more pressing, more important ... *bigger* than the time he needed to spend with his little sister? Not only now, but as she made her way through her teens into young womanhood? Where would he be when all of that was happening?

No, it really wasn't okay. Shannon had known from her earliest memories where she fit in the priorities of her father's life.

Brylie deserved better.

If Hunter had hoped for another chance to make a decent *first* impression on Miss Shannon Trent, he'd failed. In epic fashion.

Dinner had been pleasant enough, with the two ladies talking over their pizza while he sat and finished off what Brylie didn't eat of the meat lover's pie. When he wasn't stealing glances at his pretty neighbor, that is. Pretty and animated and quirky and just plain fun. He found himself completely charmed.

And grateful. Tonight was the first time he'd heard his sister laugh since their last video call two days before the crash.

But while Shannon clearly liked his sister, the wariness in her eyes when her gaze would wander to him made it clear he hadn't improved his stance with her from that first ill-fated meeting. If only Alden hadn't picked tonight to call at the dinner hour to grill him about the research he'd been conducting from home the past two days.

Hunter was behind. Not exactly news to him. Things would have been easier had he been in the office, but remote work allowed him to still get things done and not force Brylie back to school too soon. Especially a new one much larger than the one she'd left. Starting high school was harrowing enough. And his sister would have to do it twice in two months' time.

But he had to get back on Monday. He couldn't lose the momentum he'd built up after passing the bar and going to work at the most prestigious firm in Fort Worth. He'd seen others escorted to the door for lesser offenses than falling behind, with nothing more than a banker's box as evidence of their time at the firm.

Clearly, he needed to balance things better than he had tonight.

"Brylie tells me you're a lawyer." Shannon's voice brought him back to the conversation that had been going on for the most part without him. "Where do you practice?"

"Williamson, Sheffield, and Moore. A little over four years now, since I graduated from law school."

"That's a major firm. You like it?"

He hitched one shoulder. "So far. Hopefully on the fast track to a partnership. That's the goal, anyway."

The guardedness he'd noticed when he joined them after his phone call returned as she regarded him. "That's a big goal. Probably means jumping through a lot of hoops."

"Mostly just being on top of things. Dependable."

She nodded, then turned to Brylie. "I should get going. I have some homework to finish up."

She braced her hands on the tabletop and stood to her feet in front of the sofa. The leather sofa that had cost twice as much as the first used car he'd purchased from his own hard-earned savings upon leaving for college. But he could afford it, along with the other designer items with which he'd outfitted his condo. While they may be merely *things* to some, this home and everything in it was a testament to how far he'd come in reaching his goal of being *someone*.

Someone of substance, who worked hard, had a stable career, made good money, had no debt. Someone who had made something of himself after growing up poor and in more towns and rundown rentals he didn't even want to remember.

Except remembering where he'd come from had propelled him to become who he was.

He rose and picked up the one empty pizza box and the other still containing little more than half of the pepperoni and mushroom. "I can wrap this up for you, if you want. To take home."

She lifted her eyes to him, and the deep blue of her irises drew him in again. "No worries. I can take the box. Thank you again for dinner and for letting me keep the leftovers."

"Happy to do it. Do you mind if I walk you home?"

Her grin lit up those dazzling baby blues. "All the way to the fifth floor?"

Smiling back, he gave her a shrug. "It seems like the gentlemanly thing to do." Like not taking a call during dinner. Strike two since their disastrous meeting two weeks ago. He'd do everything he could to not strike out altogether.

Especially seeing how great she was with his baby sister.

Brylie crossed her arms over her middle. "He just wants to grill you before he lets me come over. Because, obviously, you could be an axe murderer."

"He's not wrong to be concerned for your safety, even in a secure building. Let him grill me, discover how boring I am, and then you have an open invitation to come by whenever you'd like. Shoot me a text, and if I'm there and it's okay with your brother, you can come over."

Brylie gave him her best impression of a St. Bernard puppy. The tactic she'd employed almost from the time she could walk, knowing he'd move heaven and earth to make her happy.

He chuckled and shook his head. "Feeling a little outnumbered here. But, yes, if we could talk privately for a minute, I'd appreciate it."

Shrugging, she started around the couch. "We'll take the stairs, then. I need it after all that pizza, anyway."

After giving his sister a hug, Shannon walked through the door he held open for her, and he followed her into the hall, carrying her pizza box.

"Lock the door, Bry," he instructed, waiting outside until the deadbolt engaged.

Several seconds of silence passed as they strolled down the hall. She shot him a smile as he held the door open to the stairwell. "We only have about two minutes before we get to my door, so you'd better get to grillin'."

He returned her teasing grin. "No grilling necessary. I only wanted to thank you for befriending my sister the past few days. I tried to get her interested in some things while I worked, but she got bored real fast. Apparently, I'm not adequately equipped to keep a teenager occupied."

"She loves to read."

"That she does. But not the stuff I have, which is mostly legal thrillers and the not-so-thrilling legal practices and procedures books I kept from law school."

Her giggle sent a tingle down the back of his neck. That was interesting. While definitely pretty, she landed more on the cute and quirky side. Not exactly what he'd call sophisticated, like the women he'd dated.

Not that there had been that many. Relationships, especially of the romantic variety, were a distraction he didn't need while clawing his way to a partnership. There would be time for that. Later. Once he'd met his career goals.

"She may not enjoy legal thrillers, but she has excellent taste in reading material. I introduced her to the *Anne of Green Gables* series by L.M. Montgomery yesterday afternoon, and she said she's already halfway through the first book."

They rounded the landing at the fourth floor and started up the next flight. "Yeah, but I don't want her sitting with her nose in a book all the time. I hope she can meet some kids at the new school to do things with."

"She will. It might take some time, especially considering she's dealing with a lot right now. She may not feel like talking to a lot of people."

"But won't the other kids think she's stuck-up or something if she doesn't talk to anybody?"

At the top of the stairs, she pushed open the door before he could get to it. "I think first you need to encourage her not to worry too much about what other people think. To be true to herself and not try to fit a mold or someone else's opinion of who she should be."

Gut punch. She was right, of course, but with moving around so much during his high school years, he'd done everything he could to fit in. To not look like the kid from the wrong side of the tracks whose stepfather couldn't keep a job because he put more value in the bottle than his integrity. Or his family.

Thankfully, Hunter had been smart and could adapt academically wherever they landed. Got a full ride to college, where he determined he wouldn't waste the opportunity to make something better of himself. Very rarely drank, never tried drugs. Probably took advantage of a girl here or there who was only interested in a good time with no commitment. Always made sure there would be no unexpected surprises and never got himself into any trouble. A win-win all around.

No way could he tell all of that to Shannon, though. She practically oozed goodness and innocence. She'd no doubt blush to the roots of that amazing light-blonde hair if she knew some of the things he'd done.

The silence stretched as they walked side by side down the hall, until she stopped in front of a door with the numerals *5-0-1* above the peephole. So, she not only lived in this rather expensive piece of real estate, she had one of the loft condos he'd passed on to keep his budget in line. He really needed to get her story.

"This is me. You want to come in? Make sure I don't have a stash of firearms or bundles of heroin lying around? A biker dude for a roommate?"

He chuckled. "Funny. No, I'm okay with Brylie spending time with you." His sister at least talked to Shannon. Laughed with Shannon. Apparently confided in Shannon. More than she'd done with him the past four days she'd lived with him. "But don't let her become a pest. I know you have a lot going on, and I don't want her taking too much of your time."

"No problem. Even if I'm doing homework, she can bring hers up, and we'll study together. Oh, and she has my cell number if you need it."

"Great. I'll get it from her. You want mine, just in case?" Didn't hurt for a neighbor to have a way to contact him, right? Especially if she'd be spending time with Bry.

"Sure." She pulled out her phone and punched in the number he gave her. "I'll guard it with my life."

Chuckling, he shook his head. "Doubt it will ever come to that."

She put her key in the deadbolt but hesitated, looking up at him after a moment. "I'm so sorry about your mom, Hunter. Such a tragedy for you both."

Glancing away, he swallowed hard. Tonight would've been his weekly Tuesday night video call with Mom. The second week now it would go undone. Because nobody waited on the other side of the screen.

He cleared his throat, willing back the emotion that threatened. "Thank you. It's been ... rough. Thank goodness I visited a couple of weeks before the accident. But Brylie ... I'm a little out of my depth there, helping her navigate all of this."

Moving her gaze to his shirt, she bit her lip for a moment before looking up at him. "I don't know what your stance is on spiritual matters, but I'm involved with a student ministry called ConnectUP. We meet every Wednesday night with high schoolers in different areas of the Metroplex. If she wanted to go with me tomorrow, it could be a great opportunity to meet some kids from her new school."

Ministry? As in, God stuff? "This is a church thing?"

"It's not through any specific church. Feel free to scroll through our website so you can read our faith statement and what we stand for. It's a great melting pot of kids from all walks of life. Heavy emphasis on fun and community. We don't stuff religion down their throats, but we do talk about how a relationship with God can affect their lives for the better."

So, a church thing. Pretty much. And Hunter had long ago written off anything to do with church. "I don't know."

"It's up to you, absolutely, which is why I didn't say anything to her about it. But even if she hasn't had much exposure to spiritual things, it's a very positive environment. If you'd like to mention it to her, I'll leave that to you. I didn't want to go around you. But if she hangs with me much, she's going to hear about ConnectUP. It's a huge part of my life."

"ConnectUP. Sounds like a dating app."

When she laughed, it was as if fresh air poured into the hallway. "It may not be about dating, but it's all about relationships. Connecting with each other, but ultimately to God. As in, *up*. If you saw our logo, you'd get it."

"Oh, I think I get it." He stared at her for a moment, balancing the pros and cons in his head.

As a kid, going to church with Mom and Gran hadn't been so bad. He always had fun at Vacation Bible School. And there had been some truly nice people at their church in Mount Pleasant who had taken care of a young single mom and her rambunctious little boy.

Until Mitch … the one huge con he couldn't get past. The consummate wolf in sheep's clothing.

"I'll check out your website. She and Mom went to church, so I don't think things of a spiritual nature would be completely foreign to her. She's just never talked about it much with me."

Probably because of his pointed lack of enthusiasm about that sort of thing.

Shannon tilted her head and narrowed her eyes, studying him as if she could see into his soul. Hopefully not, because this lady full of sweetness and light, and apparently Jesus, would not like what she saw.

He scratched his brow. "So, um, okay. Thanks for coming for dinner." He handed her the pizza box.

"Thank you for having me. Good night, Hunter Kavanaugh."

"Good night, Miss Shannon Trent."

She left him with a cautious smile before disappearing through her door. He stuck his hands in the pockets of his jeans and headed to the stairs, his thoughts swirling like a load of laundry in a spin cycle.

No doubt Shannon's Pollyanna outlook on life would be good for Brylie. She was kind, wholesome, innocent. Seemingly untouched by life's cruelties and darkness.

But even as he hoped Brylie might benefit from spending time with their perky neighbor, he would somehow need to keep a safe distance. Miss Shannon Trent didn't need to see too far inside Hunter Kavanaugh.

She was much too good.

CHAPTER SEVEN

"You're sure it's okay with your brother I'm coming today? He may be tired of me since you've already had me over twice this week."

Thursday, Shannon had texted Hunter asking how she could help him out with Brylie next week when school started. He'd responded with an invitation to their place for burgers to discuss it, then she'd stayed to watch a movie with them.

Now she stood beside Brylie in the elevator, excited about a day of furniture shopping on this sunny October Saturday but not at all sure about spending so much time with Brylie's brother. He was distracting. All charming and handsome and confident. He really should learn to tone that stuff down. It made it hard for a girl to think clearly around him.

"Oh, he's cool." Brylie flipped her hand in the air. "Especially 'cause he has no clue about this kind of thing."

"Really? His condo is super nice."

The dark-stained wood floors and cabinetry, shaggy rug, masculine furnishings, and modern décor were a sharp contrast to the light airiness of her more traditionally laid-out condo, with its light floors, white kitchen, and homey vibe. But while her place had her name all over it, his home perfectly suited a young, single lawyer.

"He had a designer do it."

But of course he did. Shannon would've expected nothing less. Either Hunter made big money as a lawyer, or he was living well above his means. Neither scenario appealed in the least.

Wealth—the accumulation of it, the pursuit of it, the possession of it—had only ever brought her pain. And she had no time for a guy who chased after money or lived up to his eyeballs in debt.

Even better reasons to *not* be attracted to Hunter Kavanaugh. The first was made crystal clear to her when he'd left her at her door Tuesday night. He didn't know the Lord. Couldn't share her faith. If she wasn't already frustrated with his skewed priorities—work over everything else—the fact he wasn't a believer not only closed that door but nailed it shut.

Hopefully, spending time with Brylie would provide the opportunity to be a witness not only to the hurting teen but to her brother.

"I'm happy to come along, although I'm not sure how much I know, either."

Brylie gaped at her. "Are you kidding?" The elevator reached the bottom floor, and they stepped out into the lobby. "I absolutely *adore* your apartment. And you said you did it all yourself."

A smile spread on Shannon's face, and it had nothing to do with the sunshine they stepped out into or the gurgling of that infamous fountain. "I'm sure we can find something spectacular for you."

"Awesome." Brylie scanned the area in front of the building. "There he is. He said he'd bring the car around for us."

A sleek BMW sedan pulled into the half-circle drive in front of the building. Again, very pricey but, to her surprise, not overly showy. Black, sedate, classy. She'd half expected him to own a Porsche or BMW sport coupe, but this vehicle still had *success* written all over it.

Like every one of her father's dozen or so vehicles.

She reached for the back door handle as Hunter got out on the driver's side.

Brylie caught her hand. "You sit up front. I'll take the back."

"I don't mind taking the back."

"You heard the little lady." Hunter smiled as he opened the front passenger door. "I'm learning quickly she's in charge."

"At least he catches on fast," Brylie quipped as she hopped into the back seat.

Shannon considered the man holding the door open. This morning, he was in pressed khakis, a navy button-down shirt with sleeves rolled up to just below his elbows, and brown suede Chukka boots. Casual yet refined.

She, on the other hand, had dressed comfortably in a peasant-style dress with wispy long sleeves and a skirt that brushed her thighs an inch or two above her knees. She'd given it a touch of Texas with her cowboy boots and finished it off with the felt Fedora she'd plunked on her head on her way out the door.

"Good morning, Mr. Kavanaugh."

"Good morning, Miss Trent. Glad you could join us on our hunting expedition today."

"For shopping?" She grinned up at him as she stepped into the car. "Didn't exactly have to twist my arm."

Once back in the vehicle, he buckled up and pulled away from the curb. "Any suggestions on furniture stores? I did an online search, but Brylie said you did a great job on your place, so I thought you might have some favorites."

"Price point?"

He shrugged. "High quality over price."

"Gotcha." She mentioned three she'd used to furnish her own home, and they drove to the closest one.

Once there, he took up the rear while she and Brylie perused the bedroom section. As they meandered through the aisles, the teen looked over several "suites" of bedroom groupings from white French Provencial to black, modern, boxy styles.

Coming to a stop, Brylie stuck her hands on her hips and shook her head. "Nothing's really singing to me here."

Shannon grinned at Brylie's turn of phrase but couldn't say she disagreed. If the girl wanted a feel close to what she had in her condo, they would have to go elsewhere.

"If you like my place, that'll be more shabby chic. Different textures, light colors with pops of florals, antique-y or weathered-looking finishes."

"Yes. Exactly what I'd like."

"Shabby?" Hunter's voice sounded behind her. "I don't want it to look like used furniture."

She glanced at him over her shoulder. "Shabby chic simply means comfortable elegance, I guess you could say. Nice furniture you can live in and on. Not like the formal living room at my parents' est—uh, home, where we weren't allowed to be in there except for special occasions or events."

"All right," he said with an eyebrow quirk and a quick tilt of the head. Clearly a doubter. "Guess we'll keep looking."

Back in the car, Hunter checked his watch. "It's almost noon. What do you ladies say we stop for some lunch and fortify ourselves for what may turn out to be a long afternoon?"

Shannon laughed out loud. "I take it a day of shopping is not your cup of tea if you already need fortification."

His chuckle joined hers. "Can't say as I've ever taken much time for it."

"I love shopping. Especially with other people's money."

"Even if you don't get anything out of it?"

"I'm getting plenty out of it. Enjoying a gorgeous fall day with two new friends, getting chauffeured around in this luxury car. All in all, a good day for me."

"Glad to be of service, Miss Trent."

After lunch at a downtown Chinese restaurant, they drove to the next store Shannon directed him to. Hunter's phone rang as they walked in the door, and he pulled it from his pocket.

His eyes met hers, then Brylie's. "I'm so sor —"

"You're kidding." Brylie's impatient tone spoke volumes, and Shannon knew exactly who was on the other end of the line. The boss she wished had stayed at the bottom of that fountain. "On a *Saturday?*"

"I have to take this, Bry. I'll be right back."

"Yeah, sure," the girl muttered as Hunter walked away.

Shannon reached over and put her arm around Brylie's shoulders to direct her forward, hoping to distract her by perusing the many designs the store had to offer.

"I'm sure he's doing his best, Bry." Or at least trying, she hoped. "If this is the schedule he's used to, it may take a while for him to balance everything out."

As long as Brylie came out on the heavy side of that balance.

The girl sighed that *yeah whatever* sigh that came stock with teenagers. But Shannon's heart hurt for her. She'd just lost her mother, had mentioned her father only once, and now her brother couldn't seem to get away from his work long enough to spend a day — on a weekend — with her.

Lord, please let me be right. That Hunter's working on reorganizing his priorities. Because we both know what could happen if Brylie seeks the attention she needs in the wrong places.

Yes, she knew all too well, so she'd stand in the gap for Brylie as much as she could.

Even if it meant setting straight a certain young lawyer.

CHAPTER EIGHT

One step forward, two steps back. Metaphorically speaking, anyway.

Hunter matched his pace to Shannon's as they meandered through yet another store. Things had been relatively silent between them following his nearly forty-minute call.

Brylie had gone to the ladies' room, so if he wanted to get on Miss Trent's good side, it was now. She probably expected an apology, except he hated apologizing. He believed in owning his actions, putting the required thought into his decisions, and proceeding with confidence. His boss calling him on a weekend was out of his control, so an apology would be empty, anyway.

He glanced at her as her eyes raked the showroom under the brim of her hat. "At risk of repeating myself, I'm grateful to have you along today. You've been a huge help."

Her startled gaze snapped up to him. "I don't know how, really. Except to keep her company while you …" She bit her lip.

He nodded. She didn't need to complete the thought. Her opinion of him had dropped another notch. And he couldn't say he blamed her. Not that it could be helped, but she wouldn't understand. Understand he was completely out of his element trying to guide his sister through this season of grief. Especially juggling all of his work responsibilities at the same time.

Like the phone call today. He'd always made himself available to the partners or co-workers who needed his help, no matter the day or time. Until he'd become his sister's guardian, he'd worked most weekends, either at the office or from home. In the study that would now be the lair of a teenage girl.

If she could make up her mind.

Shannon regarded him again, stopping in the middle of a living room set in a nautical motif, complete with anchors embroidered into the pillows and lamp bases in the shape of buoys.

"I'm sorry." Clearly, she had no problem making apologies, yet didn't appear weak doing so. "I didn't mean that. I know you're busy and have an important job. And having your sister full-time now is a big adjustment."

"But ..."

Her focus landed on the circular coffee table made from a ship's wheel with a glass top before returning to him. "She's making a lot of adjustments too. And I'm not sure you're aware, but she's protecting you."

His head popped back. "Protecting me? I thought it was the other way around."

"You're providing for her. But she's not confiding in you about losing her mom because she says you get *weird* whenever you see her cry. She doesn't want to be emotional around you, doesn't want to make things harder on you, because she already feels guilty about you having to take her in."

His chest hollowed as he stared at this pretty, petite woman. A woman with a spine of pure steel, he was finding out.

After leaving her at her door Tuesday night, he'd found his

thoughts drifting from work a few times on Wednesday to the lady upstairs. There was something about her. A spark, a brightness he couldn't put a word to. Couldn't define. It was just ... her.

His resolve that night to keep her at arm's length, however, had been put to the test by her genuine caring spirit. Brylie had begun to come out of her funk with the time she'd spent with their spunky neighbor over the last few days, and he couldn't deny he'd also enjoyed her company, ready laugh, and quick sense of humor. The way she listened. Her infectious optimism.

"I don't want her to feel guilty. I was the one who advised Mom to name me as Bry's guardian should anything ever happen."

Her mouth slackened and eyes grew wide. "Then you need to let her know that. She feels dropped in your lap. Her exact words not even an hour ago while we were waiting for you. I don't believe she was ever made aware this was always the plan."

"Always. Never a doubt in my mind what I wanted to happen once they were free of Mitch. If I never see the man again, it'll be too soon."

"Mitch. Brylie's dad?"

"My stepdad, yeah." Over Shannon's head, he caught sight of his sister walking toward the bedroom displays at the rear of the store. "Super creep, and that's the nice version."

"Is he still in the picture?"

He shook his head. "Not after leaving them high and dry a couple of years ago. Long story I don't want to get into right now, but suffice it to say, Mitch being gone is a good thing."

Her brow crinkled. "Y'all have been through a lot. Have you ever been in counseling? Or has Brylie?"

Counseling. Right. As if he needed counseling. He knew exactly where he was going and what it would take to get there. Had known since high school. Keep his head down, study hard, get a free ride to college, stay out of trouble, get through law school, and work hard to make partner. A nice, concise, straight road. He didn't need a counselor to tell him he was okay. He'd made himself okay.

"I'll take that as a no."

He shook his head again. "I've never needed counseling. And I'm sure Bry's never had it because no way could my mom have afforded it."

"You need it now."

"How's that?" He took a quick peek to make sure Brylie wasn't where she could hear this absurd conversation. He should've apologized and been done with it. How this door got pushed open, he didn't know, but Shannon had barreled right through it.

Her hand reached out to touch his arm, and a warm sensation cascaded down to the tips of his fingers, instantly calming him. "Hunter, I'm not trying to offend you or tell you your place. You're her guardian. Her brother. I know you love her, and she adores you."

She removed her hand, and he resisted the urge to reach for it. Had he missed connection that much? With a woman? A friend?

"And that's why she's protecting you. But she needs someone to help her navigate through everything she's feeling right now. Losing her mother, moving in with you, leaving everything behind, and starting at a new school."

"That's not exactly unfamiliar. Mitch moved them around all the time, which is why I wanted her with me if it ever came to that. Because I'm not going anywhere."

"I get it. And on the external front, that's all good. Stability will be a great asset to helping her heal. It's the internal I'm concerned about. The part of us that governs our character, our values, how we make decisions. Her emotions right now are in a psychological blender, if you will, and she's in desperate need of direction."

He searched the showroom floor and found his sister bouncing on the edge of one of the display beds.

"Even this today," Shannon continued. "She's having a hard time committing because she's not sure who she is right now. She likes my style, but is that true, or is it a way to connect with me?"

He swallowed, letting her words settle between them. "Because you're the only person who's let her cry." Resting his weight on one leg, he put his hands on his hips, his eyes directed to the floor.

Control. Get control. Concentrate on breathing. Even breaths.

Exactly how he prepared for court when he needed to be in control. Without emotion. He needed to be as clear-headed now as he was then. This was his sister. She needed him at his best.

Silence stretched.

"Hunter, I'm—"

"It's okay." Centered again, he let himself look at Shannon. "You think counseling will help her?"

"No doubt. But not only her. You both need help processing the loss, the new circumstances of your lives."

"I've got it handled. But if it would help her, is that something you can advise me about? She said you were getting your master's in psychology."

"Yes, I can help. I did my internship and am working part-time at McCowan, Sanders, and Associates Adolescent and Family Counseling until I get my grad degree and take a permanent position. I can set you up with someone who could talk with her. But I really feel you both—"

"Can you let me know by Monday or Tuesday? I'd like to get her started as soon as possible."

She released a light sigh. Those azure eyes of hers conveyed without question her frustration that he wouldn't go to counseling. But he didn't need it. Why waste good money on something unnecessary?

If it would help Brylie, though, he'd be happy to pay whatever the cost if someone could assist her in navigating this new normal.

"Yes. I'll have a name for you on Monday."

"Sounds good." He gave in and reached for her hand. "And, hey. I really am happy you came into Brylie's life." *And mine* came the unbidden thought. "You've been great with her this week."

"It's been a privilege."

Without him noticing her approach, Brylie was suddenly beside them.

"Are y'all on a date or something?" Her mouth quirked in a grin.

Shannon pulled her hand free and took a step back. "We were just talking, sweetie."

Brylie's expression dimmed. "Oh. About Mom?" When she came to his side and wrapped her arms around his waist, he drew her close with a kiss to the top of her head. How he loved this little girl. "I'm sorry, Hunt. I know it hurts you too."

It did, but he needed to be strong for this one. She was his focus right now. His feelings would order themselves in time. When they found a vacant crevice in his heart to burrow in and hide.

Like everything else had before them.

CHAPTER NINE

"*You're* late."

"Good morning to you, too, Jules," Hunter said to his assistant as he passed through her office en route to his larger one.

"Alden's called three times already."

Hunter glanced at his watch. "It's only 8:45."

"And you're usually here by seven."

A thing of the past, he couldn't help thinking as he entered his fourteenth-floor office with its bank of windows overlooking downtown Fort Worth. A long way from a corner office, but his name wasn't listed at the top of the firm letterhead. Yet.

He set his briefcase on his desk and looked across at Julia, holding out a cup of coffee.

"Your caffè macchiato. Just the way you like it."

Releasing a breath, he smiled and took it. "You're too good to me."

"Right?"

He plopped down and motioned for her to take one of the designer chairs situated in front of his desk. "Alden called me twice over the weekend. What's he needing this morning?"

"It would be easier to tell you what he *doesn't* need. And that would be for you to ever leave this office again."

Sitting up, he set his coffee down and placed his elbows on the desk. "He forgets I'm a parent now, for all intents and purposes, and a single one at that. What am I supposed to do with Brylie while I'm here every waking hour?"

"Hey, you're preaching to the choir. If it weren't for my nanny, I wouldn't be here." She studied him for a moment. "How are you, really? You were so quiet the day of the funeral, which was understandable. But I was worried about you."

The funeral. A day he hardly remembered because of the fog he'd found himself in and the overwhelming weight of his increased responsibility. Making the arrangements had been doable only with the help of Mom's pastor and his wife. The service was nice—what he remembered of it, anyway. And well-attended.

He'd been touched by the number of co-workers and partners who had made the drive—or short flight via the firm jet—to Mount Pleasant from Fort Worth. Julia and her husband even came to the house after the luncheon the church provided, where they spent the next several hours helping him organize Mom's things to give away before they headed home.

"We're settling in. I know Alden would've preferred I be in the office last week, but my sister needed the time before starting school today."

"Oh, absolutely. And you're entitled to bereavement leave. Even if you didn't take it."

"I couldn't see any way to do that and stay somewhat on top of things."

"That's where you were this morning, then? School?"

He nodded. "We met with a guidance counselor last week to arrange her class schedule, but I couldn't just drop her and leave this morning. She told me I didn't need to walk in with her, but I think she was glad I did, at least to the security checkpoint."

"I can imagine. What are your plans for after school?"

"Today, I want to pick her up, so please block out my schedule from 3:30 on. I'll work from home on anything Alden or Gail need done. After today, she'll ride the bus, and a couple of neighbors have said they'd be happy to have her if she wanted to come hang with them until I get home. In case she doesn't want to be alone."

At fourteen, she could certainly stay home by herself. But so soon after losing Mom, he didn't want her spending hours on her own if he got caught late at the office. Between Shannon and Mrs. B, however, she should be well covered. Hopefully, he could organize his work to complete everything that had to be done here during the day and everything else at home later in the evening.

Julia leaned forward and folded her arms on top of his desk. Six years his senior, and with her fiery Irish heritage as evident in her personality as her shoulder-length, ginger-red hair, she early on had assumed an older sister role with him. And he'd never hated it.

"Hunter, you have big goals for this place, and I'm with you all the way. You know that. But you may need to apply the brakes a little. Give yourself some grace. So, you may not make partner until you're thirty-two. Or even thirty-five. It seems like you have more important things to tend to now. There's no shame in taking the time you need for your sister."

Staring into her green eyes, he let his thoughts spin. Put on the brakes? He'd been living and breathing this career since the first day of law school. How could he stop now, so near to the prize? Once he got himself organized between his work life and the home life he'd never had to worry about before, he should be back on track.

He grabbed his coffee and stood. "I hear you. And I'll give it some thought. In the meantime, I need to get to Alden's office."

She rose and met him when he walked around his desk. "I

should warn you Monty's been like a puppy at Alden's heels, picking up the work you haven't been here to do."

His heart sank. "I can't say I'm surprised. He believes he's automatically next in line, even though I post twenty-five percent more billable hours than he does."

"Just telling you what's been going on in your absence." She stopped him with a hand to his chest as he took a step. "Grab the Hinton Logistics file. Alden needs your summary from the last witness deposition."

Nodding, he backtracked to his briefcase and removed the file. "What would I do without you?"

"You'd be half the man you are."

Grinning, he followed her out to her office. He'd missed being in the office with Jules. "Do you sass your husband as much as you do me?"

"More."

"Poor guy."

"He'd be lost without me too. Text me if you need anything."

He left her office and made his way to the elevator and up three floors to the penthouse senior partner suites. All the lower-level offices were nice, outfitted with wood accents, custom light fixtures, designer furnishings, and wood-look tile floors.

But this level was a different world, with its rich, mahogany woodwork, plush Asian rugs situated over dark-stained hardwood floors, and chandeliers to rival the one from *Phantom of the Opera* hanging from the fifteen-foot-high ceiling. Three lavish conference rooms with state-of-the-art tech, a kitchen worthy of the finest Dallas/Fort Worth estates—with a chef to boot—and a spiral staircase leading to a rooftop deck completed this floor.

Someday, there would be a suite of offices here with Hunter's nameplate mounted by the door. He'd grow old working at this firm. Old and wealthy and with a richer legacy to leave behind than he'd been given. His future children would want for nothing.

Alden's assistant waved him through, and he entered the managing partner's office to a burst of laughter from his boss and none other than Monty Montgomery, sitting at the conference table in the corner. The camaraderie between the two was hard to miss.

"Hunter Kavanaugh." Alden stood and reached out to shake his hand. "Glad to have you back." The older but distinguished man covered Hunter's hand with his other. "And, again, I want you to know how very sorry we are for your loss."

"Thank you, sir. I appreciated you coming to the service. It meant a lot to me."

"Of course, of course. Never an easy thing, so we wanted to show our support. I hope things are settling with your sister."

"Yes, sir. We're making our way. Today was her first day at the new school. I wanted to make sure she got in all right, and I'll be picking her up this afternoon."

"Understandable. Maybe after today, she'll be fine, and you can get back to your routine."

In other words, back to his twelve- to fourteen-hour workdays. Unfortunately, that probably wouldn't be happening under this roof. He'd stay as long as he could in the office to be available for meetings or depositions, but any desk work would have to be taken home to finish up there. Not ideal, but at least he'd be in the same place as Brylie.

Monty shook his hand. "No worries if you can't handle things, Kavanaugh. I've got your back."

Right. Enough to stick a knife in it.

"Appreciate that, Monty." Like he would a push off a cliff.

Two hours later, he sauntered to his office to find Julia on the phone.

"Oh, here he is. Let me tell him you're on the line. It's been so nice talking with you. I hope we can meet soon." She listened to the caller for a moment, then laughed. "And you've only known him a week? You couldn't be more right."

A week? His pulse picked up. Had to be Shannon.

"Okay, I'll let him know you're holding. Have a great day."

She put the call on hold and peered up at him. "Shannon Trent. And she sounds like an absolute kick. Has you pegged already."

"Great. If the two of you should ever meet up, I'll have to make myself scarce."

In his office, he hurried around his desk, taking a seat before picking up the phone. "Miss Shannon Trent. Good morning."

"Good morning, Mr. Kavanaugh. How's your first day back?"

"So far, so good." Sort of. Julia's warning about Monty had been spot-on. Another senior associate five years older than Hunter's twenty-eight, Monty hadn't put in the time or the labor Hunter had. Not until recently, when he noticed the interest the partners were showing Hunter, and was now vying for first position in the race to the big promotion.

And if this morning's meeting was any indication, Hunter had lost some ground over the last two weeks. Hopefully, Alden and the others would put more value on good hard work and dependability than the kissing up Monty had done the last two hours.

"And how was Brylie when you dropped her off?"

He propped his elbow on the arm of his chair and rubbed his forehead. At the momentary panic in his sister's eyes standing at that security checkpoint this morning, he'd almost taken her back out to the car. But she assured him she'd be fine, and he left her there.

What she didn't know was he'd sat in the car in the parking lot for twenty minutes before leaving, in case she texted him to come get her. So far, no texts. Hopefully, that meant she'd met some kids and was doing fine.

"She was nervous but put on a brave front."

"I've been praying for you both."

"Thanks." At this point, he'd take any help he could get, even of the divine variety, if it existed.

"I hope it's okay I called your work number. I tried your cell first, but when it went to voicemail, I called the number on the business card you gave me, figuring your assistant would have your schedule."

"No problem. I leave my phone on Do Not Disturb in meetings." Except he shouldn't have today in case the school called. Brylie's number would automatically ring through, even on DND, but not the school. "So, what did you need my schedule for? Another furniture expedition? More romping in the fountain?"

Her giggle bubbled through the line, and the tension in his neck from sitting with Monty and Alden all morning eased. "Not that that doesn't sound like a great time, but I thought I'd see if we could get Brylie scheduled to meet with Gretchen Hill, one of our counselors. I shadowed her for my internship, and she's amazing, especially for grief recovery."

"Let me check." He punched a key on his laptop to bring up his calendar. Julia had already blocked everything out after 3:30 today, added two meetings for tomorrow morning, a witness interview out of the office first thing Wednesday, two more that afternoon. Thursday had been set aside for research, and Friday was packed with back-to-back depositions. "Tomorrow or Thursday after school should work."

"Tomorrow, 4:30?"

"Got it. Will we see you?"

"Yes. I get off at three, but I'll do homework until you get here so I can make introductions."

"I appreciate it."

"No problem, Hunter. I'm so happy you agreed to this."

"I think it'll be good for her. And I wanted to say thanks again for this weekend. I know we took up a lot of your time shopping on Saturday, but I think rollerblading yesterday helped get her mind off starting school today."

"It was a blast. Thanks for asking me to come along."

"Any time. Would you like to come over for dinner tonight? Maybe let her know what to expect in counseling?"

"I would, but I have my ConnectUP leadership meeting. I could come by afterward, though. Around 8:30 or so. Is that too late?"

"Not at all. Plan on it."

"Will do."

"Thanks." He paused for a moment. "Hey, Shan?"

"Yeah?"

"I took your advice and told Brylie it was one hundred percent my idea to have Mom name me her guardian. And you were right. I could see right away she was relieved to know."

"I'm so glad."

"Well, again, I owe you my gratitude. I don't know if I would've ever seen that. And I don't want her feeling like she has to protect me from her emotions."

"I know you don't. But it may take you being open with your emotions to make her feel safe showing you hers."

His emotions? Like … cry? He didn't cry. He never cried. Didn't cry when he got the phone call. Didn't cry when Brylie dissolved in his arms when he picked her up at the foster home she'd been taken to the night of the accident. Didn't cry at the funeral. Or at any point since.

Was he sad about Mom? Yes. But sad didn't equal tears. So, how else would he show Brylie his emotions?

A rapping on his doorframe caught his attention. Julia stood pointing at her watch. "Gail. Five minutes."

Gail Emerson. Junior partner trying a case against a company that supplied faulty rebar for a bridge that collapsed. Thankfully, the only casualties were two trucks and a leg. A grievous injury for that driver, but at least his life had been spared. She'd asked Hunter to sit second chair with her two weeks before his mother had passed, and so far, he'd been able to keep up with the work.

He gave Julia a nod and stood. "Hey, Shannon, I'm sorry. I have a meeting I need to get to. But I have 4:30 tomorrow on my schedule, and we'll see you tonight."

"See you then."

He disconnected, stood, and collected the items he needed for Gail.

The stress from his meeting with Alden had dissipated as he'd talked with Shannon, as if only hearing her voice had been the remedy to his churning thoughts. Much as she had been since stepping into their lives a week ago. A comforting presence amid the kind of emotional upheaval he'd always done his level best to avoid.

But there was no escaping this. Mom was gone. He had sole responsibility for Bry now and a demanding career, both vying for his attention. And Shannon had somehow become his oasis, the place of rest and wisdom and light he'd needed to keep hope in front of him. Hope he could do and be everything expected of him.

"She sounds adorable."

He walked toward Julia, still standing in his doorway. "She's very nice. And just a friend."

With her hands raised, she stepped out of his way. "I wasn't saying anything. Just that I like her already."

Yeah, what wasn't to like?

So far, Hunter hadn't found a thing.

CHAPTER TEN

Shannon looked up from her laptop when the counselor's door opened and Brylie walked out, followed by her handsome brother and Gretchen.

She gave herself a mental kick. She had to stop thinking of Hunter as the *handsome brother*. He was just Hunter. Her neighbor. A new friend. Brylie's brother.

An unbeliever. Workaholic. Materialistic.

Intelligent. Caring. Confident.

A mixed bag for certain, but one she needed to leave closed.

Standing from behind the receptionist's desk, she waited for Gretchen to walk them over.

"Let's schedule Brylie for a weekly visit," the counselor said. "Same day and time."

"I'll make sure it gets on your calendar." Shannon smiled, relieved to hear Hunter had agreed to continue.

With a nod, Gretchen put her hand on Brylie's shoulder. "I'm so happy to know you. I'll see you next week." She extended her hand to Hunter. "Thank you for coming in."

He shook her hand. "Thank you for your time."

Shannon packed up her books and laptop, threw her

backpack over her shoulder, and met Hunter and Brylie on the other side of the counter. "I thought I'd introduce you to my friend Wyatt, then we can walk out together."

"Sure thing." He reached for her backpack. "Let me take that for you."

"Oh." With pleasant surprise, she let the strap slide from her shoulder into his hand. "Thanks."

She led them down the hall to an office at the corner. After a quick rap on the frame of the open door, she poked her head inside. "Have a second, Wyatt?"

The man she'd come to know and respect since her time as a student in his psych classes at DHU stood and waved them in. "Always."

"I wanted to introduce you to my friends."

He came around his desk to meet them. "Wyatt McCowan."

"Hunter Kavanaugh." He shook Wyatt's outstretched hand. "And this is my sister, Brylie."

Wyatt gave her a smile. "Glad to meet you both." He looked back at Hunter, his expression sobering. "Shannon told me a bit about your circumstances. You have my sincerest condolences. I'm sure this has been a difficult time."

Hunter's eyes clouded. "We're taking it day by day right now, making it up as we go."

"Sometimes that's all you can do. And we're here to help you any way we can."

Brylie took her brother's hand. "I like Miss Gretchen. She's nice."

Wyatt nodded. "I believe she'll be a great asset to you both."

Hunter glanced at Shannon. "It's just Brylie who'll be seeing her. I was in there today for the preliminaries, but she'll meet with Bry for the subsequent sessions."

"I see. Well, Gretchen's top-notch."

"We won't keep you," Shannon said. "See you tomorrow."

"Tomorrow." Wyatt and Hunter exchanged another handshake. "Nice to meet you. I'm sure I'll see you again."

If this worked out like Shannon hoped, Wyatt would see a lot of Hunter. If anybody could counsel someone without that someone knowing they were being counseled, it was Wyatt. He'd done it with her. With other students. Their CU kids.

Even his own wife, before she was his wife. As a new Christian, Harper had struggled to be true to the calling God put on her life while not disappointing her career-oriented parents. Even as her boyfriend, Wyatt had encouraged her to stand on her own and trust God with the rest. Now, not only was Harper working alongside her husband in student ministry, but she'd grown closer to her parents than ever.

Shannon prayed Wyatt could connect with Hunter during Brylie's sessions. Hunter had it all together. On the outside. But every now and then, the shield would drop for the briefest of moments, and she could see the pain, the uncertainty, the grief. Being pulled in two vastly different directions and dealing with a significant loss on top of it would throw anybody off-center.

Hunter wasn't immune, no matter how good a game he talked.

Outside the building, they stopped on the sidewalk by the parking lot. "Would you like to join us for dinner?" he asked. "My treat."

"I'd love that, but I'm actually on my way to a fitting for my friend Ally's wedding next month. Then we're all headed to dinner afterward."

"We can at least walk you to your car, then."

Finding herself reluctant to lose their company, she agreed. When she pressed the fob to unlock her doors, the little car let out a beep.

With a chuckle, Hunter gave the vehicle a once-over. "Why am I not surprised you drive a bright yellow Mini Cooper?"

"I have no idea, Mr. Kavanaugh. You think it suits me?" Like his sleek BMW suited him?

"Oh, absolutely." He walked over and opened her door. "Sunny, quirky, fun. Tiny. Definitely suits you."

"I'll take that as a compliment."

"As it was intended."

Brylie's smile brightened. "I love this car. I want one like it when I start driving, Hunt. Only purple."

"No way. I'm getting you something much bigger than this, little girl. Like a tank."

The teen rolled her eyes. "Please don't get me a grannymobile. At least make it a Jeep or something cool."

"Getting a little ahead of ourselves, Bry. We'll talk about it when the time comes."

"Whatever." Brylie enveloped Shannon in a hug. "See you later."

Shannon gave her a tight squeeze. "Later, sweetie."

After taking her backpack from Hunter, she plopped it in the passenger seat and climbed behind the wheel.

Resting his forearm on the roof of the car, he leaned in. "Drive safe, Shan. I have to say, thinking of you in DFW traffic in this little number concerns me."

Her chest filled with warmth that spread to her face. Both Wyatt and Ally's fiancé Zane had expressed the same thing about her driving such a small car on the Metroplex's infamous freeways. But while she appreciated their concern, they were like big brothers to her. In some ways, more than her own flesh and blood brother.

But knowing Hunter cared … it felt different. Weird. Like butterflies tumbling around in her belly.

"I'm always careful. I promise."

"Still, shoot me a text when you get home tonight so I know you're safe."

"Seriously?"

"It'll take you two seconds. *Hi Hunt, I'm home.* Simple as that."

She shook her head, but her grin grew wider. Harper had been the only other person ever to ask her to report in when she got home. Harper, the consummate mom to everybody, even her contemporaries. "Okay. I'll text you."

"Good girl." He shut her door and waved before he and Brylie turned to walk to his car.

A man who wasn't afraid to show he cared and could also fill out a suit quite nicely. Could it get any better than that?

Her heart plummeted. Yes. A God-fearing man in shapeless shorts and a tee would be the wiser choice over a faithless one who rocked a tailored suit.

CHAPTER ELEVEN

Whoever said the thing about silence speaking
louder than words sure had nailed it.

Hunter took the last bite from his baked chicken with rice
dinner and snuck another look at his sister, curled up with a
book in a chair. After a brief hello when he came in after work,
she hadn't said anything.

Nothing of substance, anyway. Only answering his inquiry
about which ready-made meal she wanted him to pop in the
microwave for her. Since then, zilch.

Nada.

He picked up her plate from the coffee table to take to the
kitchen. "You doing all right?"

"Yep."

"How was school?"

"Okay."

He put their plates in the sink and turned back to brace his
hands on the island. "Meet anybody?"

She shrugged and kept reading.

"What do you do at lunch?"

"Eat."

"Glad to hear it. But where do you sit?"

Her sigh preceded the glare she threw his way. "Why does it matter?"

"Just asking, Bry."

"I eat at a table."

He suppressed the urge to sigh himself. This was worse than pulling information from a hostile witness on the stand. "With ..."

"Me, myself, and I." She lifted her book. "And Anne Shirley."

He winced. Third day of school and she still hadn't met anybody? How could that be? She was pretty, bright, funny. Why wouldn't anybody make the effort to get to know the new girl at school?

"Nobody talks to you at all?"

"Well ... there was a girl in Algebra today. Asked if I understood one of the problems, and we worked through it together."

Okay, that was something.

Her face flushed as her gaze fell back to her book.

"Bry? Something else you want to tell me?"

The fingers of one hand flipped the corners of the pages. "You're not gonna like it."

"Try me."

She placed a bookmark in the fold and closed the book before meeting his eyes again. "There was a boy."

She was right. He didn't like it. "And?"

"He came up to me at lunch yesterday. Asked me my name and where I was from." She swallowed. "If I liked to party."

Hunter's stomach lurched to his throat. "Party as in ..." He sincerely hoped it meant something different than it had when he was in school but figured that was highly unlikely.

"As in, was I interested in scoring some weed. Or anything else."

Okay, not exactly what he'd thought the kid meant, but just as bad. "What did you say?"

"I told him no. What do you think I said?"

"And he left?"

Her head moved from side to side.

"Brylie."

"He caught me on my way out today. Told me about a party on Saturday, if I was interested."

He stood up straight. "Shoot, Bry, what'd you say to *that*?"

"I told him thanks for the invite and asked him for a ride."

It was his turn to glare. "Not funny."

"Chill. I told him I had plans already."

His breath left in a *whoosh*. That clinched it. She'd met one girl who spoke to her when she needed something and another kid who wanted to *party* with her. Time for reinforcements.

He hadn't mentioned Shannon's thing because he didn't want Brylie getting all wrapped up in some Jesus group, filling her head with empty promises or fireside *kumbaya* nonsense. Yes, he'd done his time in youth group during junior high. Had almost bought into all of that God-is-good-all-the-time business.

Until the man he'd loved and respected as a father turned out to be nothing but a worthless hypocrite, using the church to find a good woman. Unfortunately, he'd found the best, which had been the worst for Mom.

But after Brylie had gone to bed following their pizza dinner with Shannon, he'd Googled that ConnectUP group.

A safe place for teens to discover their value and identity through connection with others and with the God who created them in His image for their own special purpose.

Reading their mission statement had been the reason for his hesitation. Connection with God. Who gave them a special purpose.

God hadn't given him anything. *He* had decided his purpose. His own plan for his own life. He'd made it happen, with his own grit, sweat, smarts, and dogged focus. Not because a God he still wasn't convinced even existed had paved the way.

But as he'd continued through the website, the photos snagged his attention. Kids playing basketball or volleyball, sitting around a table playing games. A line of girls laughing as they danced. Kids with their arms raised on a roller coaster at Six Flags, showing off colorful holiday socks at a Christmas party.

Kids handing out meals at Thanksgiving. Gathered in a huddle, arms around each other as they prayed. Sitting in circles, some with Bibles open on their laps, some not, yet all eyes trained on a leader. Kids building homes, digging wells, distributing food, and playing soccer in a dirt lot with Guatemalan children. Their first mission trip, the site said.

It's a very positive environment … it could be a great opportunity for her to meet some kids from her new school.

Jesus kids were at least a better bet than drug dealer kids.

"You have homework tonight?"

"Already done."

He started around the island. "Excellent. Let me change, then I want to show you something on my laptop."

Her brows knit together. "Are you sending me to an all-girls school or something?"

He laughed on his way to his room. "Not yet."

CHAPTER TWELVE

*H*er heart swelling, Shannon smiled as she scanned the room. Gymnasium, really, connected to a recreation center right outside the downtown area, central to five Fort Worth high schools. There was no competition or battle lines within these walls. Only community and mutual respect between the various ethnic and socio-economic groups. A couple dozen kids had already arrived and were playing basketball, standing in groups talking, or hip-hop dancing in a far corner.

Her gaze drifted to the door, her pulse jumping when Brylie walked in, her handsome—er, her brother right behind her. Why hadn't Bry texted her if she wanted to come to club? Shannon hadn't even known Hunter talked to her about it.

She jogged over to them. "Hey, there. I didn't know y'all were coming tonight."

Hunter glanced at his sister. "Kind of a quick decision."

Brylie nodded. "Yeah, he didn't tell me about it until about an hour ago. I liked youth group at our church back home, so I figured I'd give it a try."

"I'm so glad." Shannon looked up at Hunter. "Do you want to stay?"

He shook his head. "I'll pick her up later."

"No need. I can bring her home."

With a crinkled brow, he panned the room with his eyes, taking in all the activity.

"We always start with free time—basketball, volleyball, line or hip-hop dancing, table games. Then we have snacks followed by conversation circles divided by gender. We usually have a topic we discuss, but we're very loose, so if there's a particular issue one of the kids wants to talk about, we'll go there. We do use scripture as our base."

"Yeah." He frowned. "I saw that on your website."

Nodding, she pointed to a table with several baskets lining the top. "We have all the kids leave their cell phones in the baskets on silent mode for the duration of the evening. No screen time during club. Face-to-face interaction only. We do have one leader who keeps their cell phone for any emergencies. Number's posted next to the door, so you can get it as you leave. Do you have any questions?"

"I can't think of any."

Shannon pulled her arm through Brylie's. "Come on. I'll introduce you to some of our girls."

"Sure."

Hunter studied his sister. "You're okay?"

"I'm okay." Her answer belied the uncertainty clouding her eyes.

Shannon prayed the evening would go well for Brylie, or Hunter would more than likely not bring her back.

He gave the girl a squeeze on the shoulder. "I'll see you later, then."

Her arm still linked with Brylie's, Shannon led her across the gym. "Was today any better, sweetie?"

"Only if you consider a drug dealer inviting me to a party to sample his product *better*."

"Oh, my gravy. What'd you do?"

"Told him I had plans with my boyfriend. Who plays

football at another school. I know it was a lie, but I figured he might steer clear if he thinks I have a guy who could snap him like a twig."

It might have been a lie, but Shannon couldn't help laughing. "Very creative. But don't be afraid to seek out a resource officer or another authority figure if it becomes a problem."

She'd been concerned when Brylie told her last night she hadn't met anybody yet. A couple of girls had said hello the first day, but when Brylie confided she'd eaten her lunches alone, with only a novel to keep her company, it broke her heart. She'd been praying the Lord would send Bry a friend or Hunter would allow her to come here to meet kids in a more relaxed environment.

Thank You, Lord, for answering that prayer. Although He sure picked a creative way to do so.

"These are some of the girls from my conversation circle." Two of them even went to her church, and she felt certain they would make Brylie feel welcome. "You'll like them."

"Hey, Shannon," the girls said as they approached.

"Hey, y'all, this is Brylie Kavanaugh. She recently moved to Fort Worth and started at Merritt High on Monday."

"*Hola,* I'm Isabella," the pretty, dark-haired girl said. "I'm a sophomore at Merritt. What year are you?"

Brylie cleared her throat. "Um, freshman."

"Oh, cool. This is Ellie, and this is Samantha. They're both freshmen."

Ellie's eyes widened. "I just moved here, too, about a month ago. From Seattle."

Shannon backed up as the girls conversed, and the circle closed up again with the new addition. Grinning, she made her way across the room to where Hunter stood, his hands tucked into the pockets of his jeans.

"She's going to be fine. I'm so happy you brought her."

His gaze moved from his sister across the room to

Shannon. "I probably should've mentioned it to her sooner. I just wasn't sure, with the church thing and all. But you're right. This doesn't feel church-y."

"Nope. Just a bunch of kids looking to connect with other kids and not feel like they have to fit a mold. That's what Wyatt envisioned from the beginning."

"Wyatt? Who I met yesterday?"

"Yes. He founded the ministry with one club in Arlington while getting his doctorate five years ago. Now we have clubs in three states, with new ones set to launch in two more over the next six months."

"Huh. Impressive." His brow furrowed, and he shook his head. "I'm worried about her, Shannon. When she told me the only kid who'd made an effort to reach out wanted to sell her drugs, I figured this was better than that."

"Definitely better here. These kids are amazing." She followed when his gaze moved to the girls still talking in a circle, smiling when Brylie laughed with them.

She turned back to Hunter. "I can guarantee they aren't trying to sell her drugs."

Chuckling, he rubbed his forehead before dropping his hand to his side. "Just don't fill her head with … I don't know. A bunch of rainbows and unicorns."

She put her finger to her chin. "Hmm. I distinctly remember a rainbow in the Bible, but I can't say as I've found any unicorns."

His smile changed his entire countenance, as she'd known it would that first day, when his demeanor manifested more Scrooge than smiley-face emoji. "Heard."

"Rest assured the only thing she'll hear in this place is truth. I promise you that."

He nodded. "Okay. But I think I'll still come pick her up." Bending his head, he pondered the stained concrete floor for a moment. "No offense, but that little car of yours … and my sister …"

Understanding dawned. "Oh. Of course. I totally get it. You feel she's safer in your car. And she probably is. No offense taken."

"Just after Mom and all—"

"Hunter. No explanation needed. We'll be done around nine."

"Nine. I'll be here at nine."

The door opened and a couple came in carrying more plastic bins of cookies. "Hey, I want you to meet some folks." She grabbed the arm of the girl walking up to them. "Ally. Zane. This is my neigh … friend … Hunter Kavanaugh. Hunter, this is Ally Kincaid and Zane Carpenter. They run the missions arm of ConnectUP and rove between the different clubs each week. Tonight happens to be our turn."

Zane shot him his trademark ear-to-ear grin and reached out to shake his hand. "Hunter. Glad to meet you."

"Likewise." Hunter looked at the other girl in their circle. "Ally. The one who's getting married next month?"

Ally's face glowed. "One and the same."

"To this guy? Really?"

Zane howled in laughter. "I like him, Shan. As long as he doesn't make a play for my lady, he's in."

Hunter threw up his hands. "Card-carrying member of the bro club here. Would never cross that line."

Ally's gaze moved between Shannon and Hunter. "How do you know each other?"

Shannon glanced at Hunter. "Oh. I drowned his phone."

Zane cocked his head. "How is that? Exactly?"

"When I was moving in, we bumped into each other, literally, and his phone went flying into the fountain outside our building. Then I met his sister Brylie by the pool, she invited me over for dinner, and that's when Hunter and I realized we'd met before."

Ally nodded. "So, you're neighbors."

"Yes. He brought Brylie to club tonight."

Zane's smile grew. "Excellent. Are you considering becoming a leader? We're always on the hunt for new leaders." He jabbed Ally with his elbow. "Get it? On the hunt? Hunter?"

"Yes, honey. I get it." She rolled her eyes but couldn't contain her giggle. Ally loved Zane's sense of humor. And Shannon loved that her friend had found such an incredible man. "Anyway, we'd love to have you."

Hunter shared a quick glance with Shannon. "I'm just dropping off my sister. Thank you, though. Nice to meet you both." He gave Shannon's arm a brief touch. "See you at nine."

"See you then."

He left, and she turned back to her friends.

Zane's focus remained fixed on the door. "Hope I didn't offend him."

"Not at all. But you should know, Hunter's not a believer. He recently became guardian of his sister after their mother passed, and he brought Brylie because she's having a hard time settling in at school."

"That's something, at least," Ally said. "If he spends much time with you, he'll definitely see the Lord. We'll be praying for him. And his sister. Poor thing. I'll find a way to introduce myself to her, since I know exactly what she's going through, losing her mom so young."

Grabbing Ally in a hug, Shannon's heart filled. "Thank you. That means so much." She pulled back. "And I don't think he meant any offense about you marrying Zane. He was just having fun."

Zane chuckled. "No offense taken. You know how often I told Harper right in front of Wyatt he was marrying up?"

Ally's jaw dropped. "You didn't."

"He knew I was joking. Now, Hunter. He might have hit it on the head. I'm definitely marrying up."

Ally melted against him and slid her arm around his waist. "Not true. And I can't wait to be Ally Carpenter."

"*Ally Carpenter.* I love the sound of that."

Shannon watched them stare at each other for a moment before clearing her throat. "Do I need to be here for this?"

Laughing, the two separated to flank her on the way to the snack table.

"Too bad hunky Hunter isn't a believer," Ally said. "He's a hottie."

"Hey, hey, there," came Zane's protest from Shannon's other side.

"Not as hot as you, of course. Not even close." Ally winked at Shannon. "We'll pray him into the kingdom for you, Shan."

"I'm all for that, but not for me."

Because Hunter had big dreams. Big goals. A big career and a big life. A life she couldn't see herself fitting into.

Just like she hadn't fit into her father's. And she couldn't allow another man with upside-down priorities to rip her life apart.

CHAPTER THIRTEEN

"*H*ave fun, Bry." Hunter hugged his sister at Shannon's door.

"I will." She lugged her pillow, bag, and bedroll into the condo as her hostess stepped out into the hall. "See you tomorrow."

Hunter's heart swelled when the girls already there squealed and grabbed Brylie in a group hug. Eight days since that first ConnectUP meeting, and everything had changed for her.

Who'd have thought?

His eyes snagged on the smiling blue ones trained on him. Of course. Shannon had known. She'd been right about everything so far. Counseling—check. ConnectUP—check. Brylie's new violet and light yellow bedroom motif—check.

He returned her grin. "What?"

She shook her head. "Nothing. I just love watching you watching her. I can't imagine Cam ever looking at me like that."

"Cam. Your brother?"

Her jaw slackened and eyes widened, as if she'd said too much. Except she hadn't really said anything at all. She'd never shared much about her family, only that she was the middle of three.

"Oh. Uh, right. My brother. Three years older, so the situation is completely different."

Nodding, he let his eyes wander inside again, where the girls stood in front of the fireplace posing for a group selfie. "There was never a time I didn't want her around. Weird, I know. A teenage kid completely besotted with his baby sister. But I was. I thought she was the coolest thing. Still do."

"It shows. And she needs to see that."

"Yeah. It's hard, though, you know? To look at her now and not miss the little girl who used to launch herself at me every time I'd visit from school, wherever they happened to be living. She wouldn't leave my side. Even at night. Have you ever slept with a four-year-old right next to you? All legs and arms poking you all night long. But I would've never told her to go sleep in her own bed. I loved spending as much time with her as I could because I never knew when they'd be moving again. If it would be close enough for me to get there very often."

"Maybe you can tell me about that someday. About all the moving."

He shook his head. Last thing he wanted to dump on this amazing lady was his pathetic past. "I'll spare you. And you'll be grateful."

"I'd be grateful if you trusted me with it."

He tilted his head. "I do trust you. You've been a huge help over the past couple of weeks." He gave his head a quick shake. "Wow. Has it only been two weeks?"

"Almost three. And it's been a pleasure."

Had it? Been a pleasure for her? Because it sure had been for him.

The day after that first Wednesday night club, Brylie had gone straight to Shannon's to tell her all about her *amazing* day, then repeated it all to him when he got home from work and

Shannon invited them to stay for dinner. Eating lunch with several of the CU kids, switching one of her electives to mixed chorus at her new friend Samantha's encouragement, being invited to go home with Ellie after school on Friday for their family movie night.

When he'd asked about that later, Shannon assured him the girl's parents were top-notch and he needn't be concerned. So, having the evening free on Friday, instead of blowing off steam with his friends from work, he and Shannon had their own movie night here at her cozy, bright condo, a bowl of popcorn between them on her couch.

And they'd seen each other almost every day since. Their final furniture-hunting expedition last Saturday, soup and sandwiches at his place Sunday evening after the girls returned from shopping for accessories for Brylie's new bedroom. Dinner out Tuesday following Bry's session, and dinner in last night here at Shannon's. He'd never had such a close female friend, besides Julia, and he found himself coming up with reasons to touch base with her, even if only to wish her a good day via text.

"It's been a pleasure for me, as well, Miss Shannon Trent." He swallowed. "Tomorrow will be a month."

Her brow creased. "A month—" Her eyes widened. "Oh. A month since ... the accident. I'm so sorry, Hunter."

"I'm ... fine. But she may ... I don't know. Call me if you need me."

"Absolutely. I'll watch out for her. And she's already made some fantastic friends. They'll be here for her if she has a moment tonight."

"She's been excited about this all week."

"Me too. I love our monthly sleepovers. And we have a lot more room here than in my last apartment."

That tidbit again begged the question, how did she afford this place? Her part-time job couldn't pay much, she was in grad school, and her ConnectUP leadership position was strictly volunteer. The asking price for his smaller, single-level condo had been significantly less than these top-floor condos with a loft, vaulted ceilings, and more square footage.

Was somebody taking care of her? He hadn't asked, and she hadn't offered. But his curiosity had only intensified as their friendship grew.

"Where was your last apartment?"

"Arlington. I roomed with two friends from Dallas Heritage who were also ConnectUP leaders. But after graduation, one got married, and the other took a job in Austin, where she's helped launch two new clubs. Figured I had to move anyway, why not find a place closer to the Fort Worth club. I hadn't planned to live here in The Medallion, but when the opportunity presented itself, it was too good to pass up."

"With no roommates?"

She shrugged. "Most of my friends are from the university and prefer to live closer to campus. Can't blame them. It's not always a horrible commute, but some mornings the traffic is gridlocked on the freeway. So, I give myself double the time to make sure I'm not late "

"I see." Still didn't explain how she went from splitting rent with two other girls to buying this half-million-dollar slice of downtown Fort Worth real estate on her own. Perhaps someday she'd tell him more.

"So, what are your plans tonight?"

"Catching up with some guys from the office. Meeting up in about an hour."

Funny how he wasn't all that excited about it. But with nothing else to do with his evening besides work, he figured why not. He hadn't done anything with the guys since the weekend before he'd been called to Mount Pleasant.

"You're going out, then?"

"To a new club over on Houston. Never been, but I hear it's good."

She peered over her shoulder when the elevator dinged, and two girls emerged carrying bags, pillows, and bedrolls with one of their mothers behind them. Shannon must have left all their names with the concierge because she hadn't received a notification from downstairs that anybody had arrived. He recognized Bry's new friend Ellie but hadn't yet met the other girl he remembered from his sister's first night at CU.

"Hey, girls," she said in greeting. "Go on in and get situated. We'll order pizza here in a few." She hugged the woman who'd come with them. "Emily, great to see you. Looking forward to your date night?"

Emily smiled as she released Shannon. "Definitely. Chaise is dropping the boys at his parents', then a nice, quiet dinner out."

"Sounds lovely."

Emily's gaze moved to Hunter. "Are you Brylie's brother, by chance? You're too young to be one of the dads."

He nodded. "Hunter Kavanaugh. I met Ellie and your husband last week when I picked up Brylie at your house."

"Oh, that's right. I was sorry I didn't get to the door to meet you. We absolutely adore Brylie. She, Ellie, and Samantha have become fast friends."

"They certainly have." So, that was Samantha who came in with Ellie. Brylie talked about both girls all the time, and he was thankful they'd taken her under their wings at school.

"And please accept my condolences. Such a hard thing. If you need anything at all, we're here to help any way we can. Brylie has my number. If you need me to take her for a night or pick her up from school, anything, just say the word."

"Chaise told me the same thing and gave me his cell number. I appreciate you both."

"Of course. It can't be easy being a young professional and suddenly the guardian of a teenage girl."

"It's been an adjustment. But it's all about her. Whatever she needs."

"You're a good brother. And that's according to your sister, so kudos." After waving to the girls inside, she looked back to Shannon. "See you tomorrow at ten. Have fun."

Shannon smiled. "Thanks. We always do."

Emily disappeared into the elevator, and Hunter turned his attention to Shannon. "I should let you get to your party."

"And I should let you get to your friends."

"Good night, Miss Shannon Trent."

"Be safe, Mr. Kavanaugh."

Unable to help himself, he reached out and took a long strand of her light-blonde hair in his hand, letting the silken lock fall through his fingers. "Always."

Leaving her standing at her door, he strode to the stairwell, where he stopped inside and took a deep breath.

Despite his assurance to her, *that* hadn't felt safe at all.

CHAPTER FOURTEEN

*B*ry's upset. Asking for you. Can you come?

The desperation in Hunter's voice the night before replayed in Shannon's memory as she applied the final touches to her makeup Sunday morning. The Friday night sleepover had gone without a hitch, the girls giggling and chatting and snacking into the wee hours. After a quick nap Saturday afternoon, Shannon settled at her table to dive into her homework.

Until the call from Hunter around nine.

Without hesitation, she'd run down to their condo, where she found Brylie curled into a ball on the couch, sobbing.

Her mother had been gone a month. And the reality of a life without ever hearing her mother's voice, feeling her embrace, sharing all of the joys and tears and victories and stumbles of her life had crashed down on her.

For once, the confidence Hunter wore so effortlessly had slipped, and the stark fear on his face when he met Shannon at the door had her heart breaking for them both. For the girl whose world had collapsed, and the man who wanted with everything he was to fix it but had finally accepted he couldn't.

That nobody could. That this was the blatant truth of their lives now. A life without the mother they both adored.

After praying over and holding Brylie until she finally slept, Shannon tucked her in right there on the sofa. But when she stood and encountered the brokenness in Hunter's eyes, her chest constricted, mirroring his pain.

"We were just talking," he'd said in a broken whisper. "She asked about my memories of Mom from when I was little. Told me about hers."

She took him gently by the arm and led him out into the hall to not wake Brylie.

Facing her at his door, he shook his head. "I didn't know what to do. When she melted down, I had no idea how to help her. I was holding her hand. Asking how I could make it better. She asked if I'd call you. I felt so …"

He released a trembling sigh and ran his fingers through his hair. "I've never felt like such a failure. At anything. And this is my sister. The most important thing in my life. I don't want to fail her."

"Oh, Hunter, you're not failing her. Remembering your mother is good. For both of you. She needed this outlet tonight, and it's never a sign of weakness to reach out for help. I don't think she asked for me because you weren't enough. It's because she knows this is hard for you too. And I'm a safe place for her to let down her guard."

She took one of his hands in hers. "I hope you feel that way, as well. That you can let down with me if you need someone to talk to. Or when you don't want to say anything at all."

When his red-rimmed eyes filled, she could do nothing less than offer him the same comfort she had Brylie, wrapping her arms around him and letting him sink against her. He held onto her, so tight, as if he himself needed a lifeline.

And the emotion she fought standing there in his embrace,

letting him draw whatever strength he could from her, released in a rush of tears the second she closed the door of her condo.

Drained. Exhausted. Humbled.

Yet, above it all, grateful Hunter hadn't hesitated to call for help. That he'd put his sister's well-being above his own need to fix it and gave up control of the situation to someone he'd known not quite three weeks.

And as always when she surrendered herself to be the hands and feet of Jesus, she came away blessed.

Speaking of Brylie, she needed to get downstairs to pick her up for church. And get Hunter's fob to his car. He still hadn't relented and let Bry ride in her Mini, instead giving her the fob to his car last Sunday when his sister asked if she could go to church with her, then for shopping after. But Shannon completely understood his reticence. He'd already lost so much. The thought of something happening to Brylie was unbearable.

After one final check in the mirror, she picked up her purse, sweater, and Bible and headed to the stairs. She knocked on Hunter's door, and her words lodged in her throat when the man himself opened it, wearing gray slacks, a white dress shirt, and a print tie hanging loose around his neck.

Was he going into the office? They wouldn't require him to wear business attire on a weekend, would they?

"Good morning," he said as his eyes scanned her from head to toe and back again. "You look beautiful."

"Thanks," was all she could manage as she walked in.

He closed the door and focused on the tie around his neck. "We're almost ready."

Her breath hitched—because, honestly, would she ever grow immune to seeing Hunter in dress clothes? "W-we?"

He looked up at her. "Is it all right if I tag along today?"

"To church?"

"Yeah."

To church? "Absolutely." *Absolutely!*

He dropped the ends of his tie again to perch his hands at his waist. "And thanks again. You know, for last night. The way you handled … all that."

"Thank you for calling me. It's an honor to be here for Brylie. For you both. Whatever you need."

He nodded, staring at her as if he wanted to say more. Instead, he turned his attention back to his tie. "Bry. Shannon's here."

"Coming!" The girl's voice sounded from the other side of the condo now that she'd moved into her own room.

Shannon stepped up and took his finished tie in her fingers, tightening the knot and pressing the ends against his chest, where she might have let her hands linger a bit too long. When her eyes met his, the intensity in his gaze had her taking a step back.

She cleared her throat. "I'll bet it's been nice being in your own bed again."

"It's been great. I appreciate your help in finding her bedroom stuff. No telling how long I would've been on that couch waiting for her to make up her mind."

Brylie walked into the room. "I heard that. And the couch isn't that bad. I slept on it all night." She grabbed Shannon in a hug. "Thank you again for coming last night. It meant a lot."

"Of course, sweetie. Any time at all. Just call."

Brylie pulled away and looked her up and down. "You look nice. Should I put on a dress? I do actually have some."

"You look great, as always."

"At least these are my nice jeans."

"And I love that blouse." The light blue, loose-fitting, peasant-style top would be perfect in Shannon's closet with the rest of her boho-leaning wardrobe. Not to mention the girl's platform shoes, similar to the ones Shannon wore.

Hunter gestured to the door. "Shall we, ladies?"

They filed out of the condo and to the elevator, exiting at the parking garage. The ride to church was short and filled with Brylie's recounting of her week at school. Shannon uttered a silent prayer of gratitude Hunter had reconsidered and brought Brylie to ConnectUP. And that it had made the impact she'd been sure it would.

Inside the church auditorium, Shannon led them to the seats where she always sat with her friends. After exchanging greetings and making any needed introductions, Shannon took a seat next to Harper with Brylie between herself and Hunter. Thankfully.

Because she wasn't sure she would be able to concentrate on the message with Hunter, smelling oh so good—a subtle mix of what she could only describe as sandalwood and something vaguely spicy—sitting right next to her.

Harper leaned in before the worship time began. "So, that's the hottie neighbor Ally told me about."

Shannon's face heated. "He's okay."

Harper chuckled under her breath. "If he's just okay, you need glasses, my sweet friend. Can y'all come with us for lunch after church? We're going for barbecue."

"I'll ask."

Harper nodded, then leaned the other way, into her husband who took her hand. Wyatt and Harper. Ally and Zane. Two couples Shannon deeply respected and somewhat envied. Her own love story hadn't ended happily ever after. Very much the opposite, with heartbreak and tragedy and decisions made in the name of survival.

If she could go back …

The worship band launched into their first song, and heaven itself seemed to fill her soul as she gave herself up to the music, singing and raising her hands to the Lord.

This was her true love story. Her true joy. From a Savior who loved her beyond all measure, with no conditions or rules or expectations. All from a place of grace.

No, she couldn't go back and fix what had gone wrong. Nor would she want to. If she did, there would be a life missing from this earth, and she probably wouldn't be here, in this place, with these people, working in a ministry she loved with everything she was, looking forward to a career committed to helping young people like she had been.

Lost.

Searching for a place to belong.

For acceptance.

When the music ended and the pastor took his place up front, her heart began its earnest prayer that the two people to her side would hear the words, feel the Spirit move, and find their own true love without measure.

From the only One who could provide such a love.

CHAPTER FIFTEEN

*L*etting his gaze roam around the lunch table, Hunter had to admit this was not what he expected when he thought about church people.

Shannon's friends, including the engaged couple he'd met the first night he took Brylie to ConnectUP, all acted like one huge family. A boisterous, teasing, happy family. Even as diverse as they were—Yolanda from Guatemala, her blond, blue-eyed husband Steve, and Mason and Rhonda Carlysle, people of color expecting their first child. And the ginger-haired McCowan brothers—Wyatt and his brother Reed—with their wives and children.

Or maybe because it was only him and Brylie now, Hunter found himself drawn to any semblance of family, especially one as close-knit and enjoyable as this one.

"What kind of law do you practice?" Harper's question brought his focus to the woman across from him.

"Corporate law. In the broad scope, everything from structuring a new corporation to corporate takeovers to personal injury or fraud."

"Sounds like a lot to keep in your head."

"My brother graduated first in his class at law school. He's crazy smart." Brylie threw him a grin and took a bite of her brisket sandwich.

His face heated. "Not important."

"Sure, it is," Shannon said from beside him. "Important and impressive. Where'd you go to school?"

"University of Texas. Both undergrad and law school."

Wyatt's eyes widened. "First in your class at UT law? That *is* impressive."

Hunter was more impressed with how Wyatt effortlessly held a bottle to his four-month-old daughter's mouth with one hand and held a fork with his other, all while balancing her on his lap. The baby girl, introduced to him as Gracie, was as beautiful as a porcelain doll, with pink cheeks, fiery red curls, and her mother's big green eyes.

"Only because I had no life. I lived, ate, and breathed law school. I guess you could say I had an agenda."

And still did. Mostly. His straight road toward his goal might have hit a curve, but he was handling it. With a lot of help from folks like the pretty lady next to him, who had stepped in when he wasn't sure which way was up.

Even last night, when Brylie had come apart, Shannon stood in the breach. Yet even so, there was a Mom-shaped hole in his sister's heart that would always be there.

The same hole that existed inside his.

It had been just him and Mom for twelve years until Mitch entered the picture. Then once his stepfather revealed his true colors, Hunter had done all he could to hold them together. It killed him to leave for college, but Mom insisted. Said he needed to take his God-given smarts and make the world a better place.

He hadn't been sure about the whole *God-given* business, but after this morning's sermon, he certainly had a lot to ruminate on. Although he remembered some from his Vacation Bible School days, the passage the pastor read from Ephesians was new. Something about how God had created everybody as a one-of-a-kind masterpiece to carry out good works He had planned long ago.

For a self-made man such as he'd always considered himself to be, that was a bit hard to swallow. But maybe it was about more than vocation. Pastor Jason had talked a lot about the heart, about thoughts and words and actions. About the care and treatment of others. In that regard, he could certainly understand how Shannon was a masterpiece. She excelled at all the above, in her own special way.

When he drew himself back to the conversation, the group was talking about an upcoming ConnectUP event.

He leaned toward Shannon. "When is this?"

"On Halloween, we hold a Trunk-or-Treat in each of the communities where we have clubs. Folks volunteer to decorate their trunks or the back of their pick-ups, SUVs, whatever, dress up in costumes, and pass out candy to kiddos. We also have game booths and inflatables to keep them entertained."

"How do you get the money to do all that when you don't require the kids to pay a membership fee?"

Wyatt threw a cloth over his shoulder and placed Gracie on her belly on top of it, gently patting her back. "We have sponsors and donors who provide either materials or funds. Parents provide cars, candy, and donations, and several come out to man a game booth. We're centered on kids in ConnectUP, but it's all about strengthening families and parents' connections with their teens."

"How can I help?"

"Any way you'd like." Wyatt kissed Gracie's chubby cheek when the baby let out a healthy belch. "That's my girl."

Harper reached for her daughter. "I'm sure she needs a change."

Ally jumped to her feet. "You stay and finish your lunch. I'll take care of Gracie." Ally took the baby from Wyatt and grabbed the diaper bag hanging from Harper's chair. "Come with Aunt Ally, baby girl. We'll get you all fixed up."

"Thanks, Aunt Al." Harper smiled up at her friend. "I appreciate it."

"I'll take every chance I can to spend time with this little one."

Wyatt picked up his fork and stabbed a piece of brisket. "If you'd like to come out for the event next Monday, you can decorate your trunk and hand out candy, man a booth, direct traffic. Or if you'd like to simply make a donation, that's a huge help."

Hunter looked across the table at Bry. "Let's decorate the trunk and pick out costumes. It'll be fun."

Brylie's face lit up. "That would be awesome. Can we go today to shop for costumes?"

Thinking through the stack of work on his desk at home, he tried to gauge how much time he could still spend out today and have it all done tonight. Yet all that mattered at the moment was the gleeful expectation on his sister's face, regardless how late he might have to stay up.

"Let's do it."

"And Shannon can come too."

Shannon's wide-eyed gaze moved from Brylie to him. "I don't want to get in the way."

"You're welcome to come with us," he told her. "I could probably use some tips, anyway."

"Yeah," Brylie said. "You have such great ideas."

That much was true. Shannon was creative and colorful and fun. While he wouldn't mind spending the afternoon out with his sister, having Shannon along made the idea of shopping even more palatable.

"Okay," Shannon answered with a shrug. "I already have my costume but need a few more things for my car. It's going as a bumble bee, with wings and everything. And I'm dressing as a beekeeper."

"Can't wait to see that. I think my car will go as a BMW."

Brylie laughed. "But we'll decorate the trunk up really good."

That settled, he took another bite of his barbecued pork loin. He'd never been to this place before but would have to remember it. Especially since they delivered.

Zane nudged Hunter from his other side. "You play hoops?"

Hunter shrugged and swiped his napkin across his mouth. "A little. In high school." Between moves, when he could get on a team. "Some college intramural."

"You should come out on Saturday. We're having a CU three-on-three basketball tournament. Students against leaders."

Wyatt nodded. "My brother tweaked his knee, so Zane and I need a third."

Hunter looked at Shannon. "Are you playing?"

She shook her head. "We'll be with Ally on her bachelorette weekend trip to Granbury. Spa day. Lots of shopping."

"Sounds ... fun."

Her laughter brought a smile to his face. "Right. I noticed how much *fun* you had shopping for furniture. I think the tournament will be more up your alley."

With a chuckle, he turned to Zane. "It's okay for me to play even though I'm not a leader?"

"Yep. We have some parents playing."

Hunter quickly ran through the week's schedule in his mind. Gail would be out of town next weekend, and Alden's granddaughter's sweet sixteen birthday bash was Saturday afternoon. Hunter should have the day free and clear. "What time?"

"We start at one and should go until around five, then we're doing burgers and dogs."

"I might be a little rusty, but if you're desperate for a third, I'll be there."

Zane clapped him on the back. "Excellent. Glad to have you."

Hunter glanced at Shannon, grinning beside him, and his heart seemed to press against his rib cage. Spending the last hour over lunch with these people, observing the way they interacted, all of them such a big part of each other's lives, filled him up in a place he hadn't even realized sat empty. And they'd welcomed him and Brylie in as if they were old friends and not merely acquaintances.

Not that he didn't have friends. He had several. Mostly co-workers, considering that's where he'd spent the bulk of his time over the past several years. But nothing like this. There was a bond here, a kinship he'd never seen before, much less experienced.

Something he hadn't even known he'd missed. Until one tiny, spunky lady invited them into her life and showed him what true friendship looked like.

CHAPTER SIXTEEN

"*Y*ou're kidding."

Shannon read back through the text that had come in during club while her cell phone was in the basket with everybody else's. With a shake of her head, she typed a response, then scanned the room for Brylie. She found her speaking with Ellie and Isabella across the room. Their conversation appeared serious, so she decided to clear snack trays instead of interrupting.

And tried not to let that text steal any of the joy from the evening.

"Hey, Shannon?"

She turned at Brylie's voice behind her. "Hey. Your brother texted and asked if I could bring you home. He's stuck at the office."

The girl's eyes widened briefly. "Wow. That's late."

Exactly what Shannon thought. Good thing Brylie had gone home with Ellie after school so they could come to club together.

"Yeah. Must be something big. Especially to be letting me take you home in my car."

"True." Brylie's eyes moved to the floor and back up again.

"But I'm okay with it because I was hoping I could talk to you. Privately."

"Everything okay?"

"Yeah. Just ... what we talked about tonight, about God being close to the brokenhearted. I've been thinking about that."

"Okay. We'll talk when we get to your place."

"I'll help you finish up here."

Shannon locked up after the kids left and returned the key to the rec center desk. Brylie was uncharacteristically quiet on the way home, but Shannon sensed it would be better to leave her to her thoughts.

Once in Hunter's condo, Brylie went to her room while Shannon made them each a cup of hot chocolate. Having spent several evenings here over the past month, she'd grown comfortable in Hunter's kitchen and had even stocked it with some new things. Her favorite hot cocoa mix and caramel syrup, trail mix, microwave popcorn, and other healthy snacks for them to enjoy while working or watching television.

Brylie came back in her flannel pajamas, taking a seat on the couch. Shannon joined her and handed her a steaming mug of cocoa, sipping from her own and letting the teen set the tone for whatever she wanted to discuss.

"I really like ConnectUP." Brylie took a sip and placed the mug on a coaster on the coffee table. "Like, a lot. I'm so glad Hunter finally told me about it."

"Me too. I'm sorry I didn't mention it to you, but I'd just met you both, and I didn't feel it was my place. I hope you understand."

"Totally. Plus, my brother isn't exactly thrilled about religious stuff, which is why I was shocked when he told me Sunday morning he wanted to go to church with us."

Shannon had been a little blown away herself. And now he was going to play in the CU three-on-three basketball tournament on Saturday and come out for next week's Trunk-or-Treat. Unless work got in the way, like it had tonight.

"After what happened Saturday night ... when you came down here so fast, and the way you prayed over me ... I think that got to him. In a good way. I know it did me. I felt this weird ... peace, I guess you could say. I don't know how else to explain it. You kept praying something over and over. About God's mercy. And I could feel it kind of pour over me."

"I'm glad, Bry. Prayer is so important in a believer's life. It's our connection with God, Who loves us without condition. No expectations other than to come to Him with all our joys and troubles. That's it."

"I'm a believer, you know. My mom and I went to church all my life, even when my dad was still with us. Then we went with Gran before she passed away. But I haven't talked with Him much since everything happened. I've been kinda mad. I feel bad saying that, but it's true."

Looking away, Brylie stared at the skyline outside the balcony window for a moment. "I still don't get why Mom had to die, but I don't want to be mad at God anymore. I was talking to Izzy after circle tonight about that, and she said I should talk to you. She called it rededicating my life to God, and I think that's what I want to do. Rededicate my life to God."

Shannon thought her heart might burst. "That's so great."

"I was kinda hoping you'd pray with me. Then maybe you'd help me with some verses to read in the Bible and stuff."

"Of course, sweetie."

Tears filled Brylie's eyes and slipped down her face. "And can we pray for Hunt? I know he went to church when he was younger, until he decided he didn't want to in high school. But until last Sunday, he hasn't been interested in God at all. And I don't want something to happen to him and he not know —"

She brought a hand to her mouth when a sob tore at her throat, and Shannon scooted over to wrap her in her arms. "I know it's hard when the people we love don't know the Lord. My siblings aren't believers, either, and I pray for them all the time. But at least Hunter did go to church with you. Mine have yet to do that much."

Sniffling, Brylie pulled away and swiped her sleeve across her cheeks. "You never talk about your family."

Shannon bit her lip for a second. "I have an older brother and a younger sister. When I was little, I wanted to be around my brother all the time because I was a bit of a tomboy, and Delaney only wanted to play with dolls and do girly things. But as we've grown older, I'm closer to Delaney than Camden. Camden's all about work."

"Yeah, I get that." She brushed at her cheek again. "But I know Hunter's trying. He has an important job. And his bosses have a lot of expectations. It's just hard sometimes, like tonight. I feel bad for him, that he's been at work for over twelve hours already. He has to be tired."

Shannon ached for them both. For the girl who needed her brother … here … with her. And for the man who worked so hard to meet the expectations of those he so wanted to please when he already had the adoration of this sweet girl.

Brylie's mouth tipped up at the edges. "But I'm glad I have you."

Reaching out, Shannon took Bry's hands in both of hers. "And I'm glad I have you. Why don't we pray? You want to start?"

Brylie nodded, and they bowed their heads. "Dear God, thank You for Shannon. And thank You for ConnectUP and my new friends. I know I haven't talked with You a lot over the past few weeks, but I'm not mad anymore. I'm sad I don't have Mom, and I don't know why things happened like they did. But I'm trusting You, that You know best, and that You're taking good care of her. I know You're close to the brokenhearted, so thank You for being close to me. Take care of Hunter, please. And work on him so he'll also come to know You. That would be so totally cool. In Your name I pray."

Shannon swallowed the knot in her throat. "Father in heaven, we're so grateful for Your boundless love, Your grace we don't have to earn, and Your forgiveness that covers all. Thank You, Lord, for my sweet sister, Brylie. For Your Spirit who lives inside of her and has spoken to her, to let her know You're with her and she's priceless to You, a daughter of the King.

"We lift up Hunter. We know he's juggling a lot right now. We pray he'll find balance, but above all, we pray he'll find You. That he'll find his place in Your kingdom, his purpose in Your plan. His peace in Your love. In the name of Your precious Son we pray, Amen."

Brylie leaned in, and, closing her eyes, Shannon put her cheek against the teen's silky hair. She'd grown to love this girl so much in such a short time.

Her eyes opened as tingles of ice spread down her spine. As she had Brylie's brother, she feared. As more than the friend he'd grown to be. More than she should for a man with skewed priorities.

More than she should for a man who didn't believe.

CHAPTER SEVENTEEN

*W*as that … sunlight?

With one eye open and the other still sunk into his pillow, Hunter reached for his bedside clock, his head popping up a second later.

"Ten after nine?" He couldn't remember the last time he'd slept this late, even on a Saturday. But he'd apparently needed it after working well into the evening the past three nights.

Rolling over onto his back, he stared up at the ceiling. The hours he'd put in the past few days had been the norm for him before Brylie, and he'd never had a problem with it. Could stay focused and accomplish whatever had been asked of him. This week, however, he'd found it more difficult. Making sure Brylie was home safely, finding his mind wandering to the ladies hanging out together while he was stuck at the office.

And although he'd tried to talk her into staying at Mrs. B's next door until he got home last night, since Shannon had left for Ally's bachelorette weekend, Brylie assured him she'd be fine on her own.

"I'm not ten, Hunter. I don't need a babysitter."

"I just figured you didn't like being here by yourself since you hung out with Shannon the last two nights."

"That's different. That's Shannon. Not that I don't like Mrs. B. She's super sweet. I even like her dog. But I'm totally okay staying here by myself. I promise I'll keep the door locked and won't open it to anybody but you. Or Mrs. B."

When he'd walked in a little after nine last night, he found Brylie curled up on the couch, group texting with Ellie and Samantha about the show they were all watching at the same time from their own homes. Safe and sound and even made her own dinner. Guess he had to get used to the fact his little sister was growing up.

He stretched and released a sigh. If only he could've seen or at least spoken with Shannon before she left yesterday afternoon. It surprised him how much he'd missed her the past few days. But other than a quick *good night* when he got home Wednesday and Thursday and a polite *thank you* to his *have a great time on your trip* text yesterday morning, they hadn't exchanged more than a dozen words.

Getting drawn into the final stretch of Alden's trial had been unexpected. Thankfully, the trial was mostly wrapped up, with last night's work session dedicated to drafting Alden's closing statement for Monday morning. And today was free and clear to enjoy the basketball tournament, since Alden would be occupied with his granddaughter's day-long birthday festivities.

Once he dragged himself from the warmth of his bed, Hunter slipped a sweatshirt over his pajama pants and pulled on a pair of heavy socks, the best defense against the cold hardwood floors. Scrubbing the last vestiges of sleep from his eyes, he shuffled into the kitchen, where the bowl and spoon in the sink and box of cereal on the counter told him Bry was already up.

Turning, he found the blinds pulled open to the balcony and his sister wrapped up in a blanket in one of the chaises. The morning temps here in late October hovered in the fifties, but the sun shone bright, and the blue sky dotted with white clouds promised the perfect day for basketball outdoors.

At the sliding glass door, he stood and watched her. She sat with her long legs pulled up in front of her, still wearing her PJs with bright pink fuzzy socks, and her generous mop of hair pulled into a large clip on top of her head. Her Bible lay open next to her, and she scribbled notes into a journal propped against her thighs.

That was new. Maybe a ConnectUP thing?

He'd hesitated to mention it to her after Shannon told him about it because he didn't want Brylie getting all hyped up on Jesus stuff that would end up letting her down. But he had to admit, the change in her over the last three weeks had been remarkable. Yes, she still had moments of overwhelming grief, and she was still a teenage girl with all the angst that came along with it.

But she was handling things. She looked forward to school. She hadn't given him any attitude over his work schedule the past three days and had even told him she was praying for him.

He opened the door and stepped outside. The *whir* of the light weekend traffic below blending with a mild breeze made for a peaceful welcome to the day. "'Mornin'."

She looked up over her shoulder. "Hey there, sleepyhead."

"Yeah. Guess I hit my alarm and went back to sleep."

She shook her head. "I went in earlier and turned it off so it wouldn't wake you up. That's why I asked last night if you had work to do this morning before the basketball thing. I wanted you to get some rest after such a busy week."

He took the chaise next to her. "That was nice. Thanks."

"I got you."

"Looks like we've got each other."

Her grin lit up her face. "I like that better."

"Me too." His eyes wandered to her Bible. "Whatcha reading?"

She regarded her journal for a moment. "Shannon gave me

some verses to read about grief and seeking comfort in the Lord. How He provides for us even in our darkest times."

"Hmm."

Her slate-blue eyes studied him. "I truly believe that, Hunt. Remember last Saturday, when I was missing Mom so much and Shannon kept praying that prayer, over and over again? I felt such peace come into me. It wasn't like being tired from crying. It was like …"

Her mouth scrunched to one side, and her eyes gazed up to the sky before returning to him. "Like everything was suddenly okay even though nothing had changed."

Like everything was okay even though nothing had changed.

How could that be? Was it a form of escapism? Of not facing her troubles?

Or was it more? Could there truly be a peace so complete as to cover a circumstance there was no going around?

He scanned the view off the balcony, the trees surrounding the building and the skyline beyond, and let his thoughts meander back to that night. Brylie in tears, him clueless as to how to help her. Then Bry asked for Shannon, who had somehow become a lifeline over the last few weeks.

And she'd come. In two minutes, she was in his apartment, had wrapped Brylie in her arms, rocking back and forth and quietly repeating the same words while he stood behind the couch watching them. It had taken him a minute to realize it was scripture she was reciting. What she believed to be God's direct word.

What Brylie hadn't seen that night was him sinking to the floor with his back against the sofa, his face in his hands to cover the first tears he'd shed following the loss of their mother, desperately trying to pray himself.

But he'd pulled so far away from the God of his childhood he hadn't had any right to ask for anything then. Not when he'd done so many things, made so many decisions that didn't include God, had never intended to include God. So, he'd instead latched onto the words Shannon repeated, over and over, and whispered them to himself.

Until Brylie quieted and Shannon's words reduced to a whisper, still praying. But then he heard his name as well.

And as his own tears dried, perhaps he'd also found a measure of that peace Brylie spoke of.

Is that what had propelled him out of bed and into church clothes the next morning?

He didn't know. Couldn't be sure. And Shannon was out of town.

Turning back to his sister, he reached for her hand. "I can take you to church tomorrow, since Shannon's gone. If you want."

Her thin fingers latched on to his. "Take me? Or go with me?"

He swallowed. Hard. "Go with you."

CHAPTER EIGHTEEN

Hunter waited until Brylie went in with Gretchen before approaching the girl behind the front desk. "Excuse me."

"Yes, Mr. Kavanaugh. What can I do for you?"

"Is Shannon here, by chance?"

"No, sir. She gets off at three."

"Right." Except last Tuesday, she waited until after Brylie's session and went to dinner with them. Maybe the distance growing between them since his late-night work sessions last week wasn't a figment of his imagination. "Would Dr. McCowan have a moment, possibly?"

"I have more than that," came Wyatt's voice from behind him.

Hunter turned and offered his hand. "Good to see you."

"Likewise. Come on back."

Hunter followed him down the hall to his office. "I feel like I should've made an appointment."

"Not a problem. I always have time for friends." He closed the door behind him and gestured to a chair in the corner. "Have a seat."

After settling in one of the comfortable upholstered chairs,

Wyatt took the one adjacent to him and propped his ankle over the opposite knee.

"Thanks again for letting me play with y'all in the tournament on Saturday. That was a blast."

"It was. And you downplayed your skills a bit."

"I'm a big proponent of underpromise and overdeliver."

"You certainly did that. I still can't believe Mason and his guys won the whole thing, though. I'll never live that down."

They shared a laugh as Hunter shook his head. "Yeah, but we made them work for it." He clasped his hands in his lap, one leg crossed over the other. "ConnectUP has been a great help for Brylie. Not to mention Gretchen."

"Gretchen's an excellent counselor." Wyatt inclined his head. "Said you weren't interested in counseling for yourself. May I ask why?"

Hunter's stomach rolled. "I guess I've never seen a need for it. I've always known where I was headed. What I needed to do to get there. I've never allowed anything to derail me from going after my goal."

"And you believe counseling would do that?"

"Counseling makes you look back. I don't believe looking back helps you move forward."

"Ah. Now I see. I would respectfully disagree." Wyatt raised his hands, palms up. "But, then, I'm a counselor." He chuckled and lowered his arms. "Sometimes by not looking back, our past can hinder us from moving forward. We think we're making progress because we're moving, but we're running on a treadmill. We're not necessarily growing or moving past any of the stuff that's wounded or harmed us. It can still hold us back in certain areas of our lives."

Hunter nodded but said nothing.

"Let me ask you this. You say you've always known where you were headed. Where is that?"

"A partnership with my law firm."

"So, in your career."

"Exactly."

"And is that all you are? Your career?"

Hunter's face pulled tight. What was it with these psychologists—or psychologists-in-the-making—and their sucker punches? First Shannon telling him he needed to encourage Brylie to be herself and not change anything to fit in, when that's all he'd ever done in high school. Now Wyatt questioning his life's goal.

"Is that all I am?"

"In your estimation. I already know the answer. Of course you're not. You're a brother, a friend, a son. I know your mother is gone, but you're still her son. She will always be your mother, and you'll always have that love in your heart for her. You'll always have her voice in your head directing you, encouraging you, telling you how much she loves you. That will never change."

The despised tears burned behind Hunter's eyes. Tears he would not give in to.

"But when you think of who you are, is your career all you think about? It appears in the last month or so, following this life-altering event, you've been pushed out of your comfort zone. And maybe being forced to see new facets of your life."

Hunter nodded. "I can't deny that's true. Before Brylie, my career was my life. I worked sixty, seventy, even eighty-hour weeks sometimes. But my goal has always been to be partner by thirty."

"Why so fast?"

"Stability. Job security." The status. The title. Although admitting that out loud sounded arrogant even to Hunter, much less to a godly man such as Wyatt. "I'd be in one place my entire career."

"And that's important to you, to stay in one place?"

With a grin, Hunter pointed at his friend. "See, I should've made an appointment. This has definitely turned into a session."

Wyatt laughed and folded his hands. "I told you that was a pitfall of my profession, that I ask a lot of questions. If you're uncomfortable, we can talk about football. But I'd rather hear more about you."

Swallowing, Hunter stared down at his fingers clasped tightly together. He'd never shared any of this with another living soul. The anger, the shame, the sense of betrayal. Yet here in this office, with this new friend asking the hard questions, he somehow felt safe. Respected, not judged.

He cleared his throat. "My mom married my stepdad when I was twelve." His eyes came up to meet Wyatt's. "She met him at church. It had been only Mom and me until then, but I thought Mitch was great. He'd come to my Little League games and school events, and he even asked for my blessing when he wanted to propose.

"And for a while, things were awesome. Bry was born when I was fourteen, and I was crazy about her. Loved being a big brother. But right about that same time, something happened with Mitch, like a switch being turned off almost overnight. Started going to happy hour with work folks, then he started keeping beer in the house. Then he wouldn't come home until all hours."

Clenching and unclenching his fists, he fought back the anger his memories brought with them. Memories of Mom, worried to distraction, keeping watch at the front window, not knowing where her husband was. What kind of shape or mood he would be in when he finally did walk in the door. Memories of the obscenities shouted at her, the rough treatment. The tears and her apologies for doing nothing but loving a man who didn't deserve her.

"He lost his first job around the middle of my freshman year, and we moved to Austin where he found another one. That one only lasted eight months before we had to move again for yet another job. And so on. Each house was worse than the last, and each job lower-paying than the previous one. Mom would find a new church in every town. Took Brylie with her, of course. She was a toddler then. But Mitch would usually be sleeping one off, so I refused to go. Figured if the so-called man of the house didn't have to go, why should I?

"I guess that's when God and I parted ways. Mom met Mitch at church. A seemingly God-fearing, Bible-believing, family-loving man who turned out to be none of those things. And I was done."

Wyatt nodded, his elbows braced on the arms of his chair and fingers steepled together in front of him. "Completely understandable. We often equate God with the father figures in our own lives. It makes sense you would want nothing to do with a God like that."

Hunter stared at the man across from him. Is that what he'd done? He'd assumed God was like *Mitch*? Two-faced, selfish, uncaring? A God who would abandon those He'd once professed to love?

"And that would also explain why it's so important for you to have stability. Financial and otherwise. But what about in other areas? Have you ever been in a serious relationship?"

"Not serious, no."

"So, focused solely on the career."

"It takes time to cultivate close relationships, especially romantic ones. There's time for that later."

"And what about God now? You've come to church the last two weeks. Took part in the CU basketball tournament and Trunk-or-Treat last night. Are you perhaps contemplating making some room for Him in your life? I know Brylie recently made a commitment in that regard, according to Shannon. Has she shared that with you?"

"A little. What she's reading in her Bible."

"We can learn a lot from the kids in our lives. Their faith often surpasses our own."

Hunter couldn't argue with that, seeing as, at this point, Brylie had all the faith, and he had none.

A beep sounded from the cell phone on the table next to Wyatt, and he picked it up. "That's the receptionist. Brylie's done."

They walked out to the front desk to meet her, and Hunter couldn't help but notice her red-rimmed eyes. Extending his arm, he drew her to his side. "You okay, Bry?"

She nodded against his shoulder. "I'm good."

Wyatt reached out and shook his other hand. "Great talking with you. Let me know if you want to sit down again. Any time at all."

"I will. Thank you."

His arm still around his sister, he led her out the back exit and into the parking lot. It was a silent trip home, both of them lost in their thoughts.

Is that all you are? Your career?

Six weeks ago, he wouldn't have found anything wrong with that. His career *had* been everything to him. He took pride in his profession, his work. His goal and his reputation. His income and what he had to show for it.

But now?

At a stop light, he looked at the girl beside him, staring out the side window. Now he needed to be so much more than his career.

And he had no idea who that was.

CHAPTER NINETEEN

"I'll see you after school tomorrow, Bry." Shannon hugged the girl at her door, happy her brother had relaxed about her being in the Mini.

"Why don't you come in and say hi to Hunter? I know he's home because he texted me right before club."

"I'm sure he's tired. I'll talk to him later." Before she could take a step, however, the door opened, and Hunter stood there in jeans and a UT sweatshirt.

"Hi. I'm Brylie's brother. Hunter Kavanaugh. Figured I should introduce myself."

Barely holding back a grin, she leveled a stink-eye at him. "You're a riot."

His eyes widened as his mouth formed an *O*. "Right. You're the girl from upstairs. Sharon … something?" He smiled, and those butterflies took flight again. Guess it didn't matter how long it had been since she'd spent any time with the man, nor what he was wearing. "Sorry. Couldn't help kidding you. How long's it been? A month? Two?"

"You have a very poor sense of time, Mr. Kavanaugh."

In reality, she'd last seen him two nights ago at Trunk-or-Treat. But after a quick hello to see they were settled at their parking spot and compliment them on their zombie costumes, the busyness of the evening had precluded any subsequent conversation. The previous week, he'd worked late not only Wednesday but Thursday, as well, and she'd made a hasty exit after keeping Brylie company.

The realization her heart had taken her feelings somewhere they shouldn't be, for a man who didn't share her faith, had her discombobulated. His late work hours, then the girls' weekend, had been perfect excuses to put some much-needed distance between them to gather her wits.

Except she'd missed him. More than she should for someone she was only helping out.

Okay, so it was more than that. She considered him a friend. A friend who had burrowed his way into her life to the point of distraction. A distraction she couldn't afford to entertain. Not another man who could rip her life apart with his mixed-up priorities.

She could walk away if she had to, but she couldn't leave Brylie behind. Not if his work was going to take center stage. She would have to figure out how to balance being present for Brylie and keeping Hunter at a friendly but safe distance.

"But you have to admit, Miss Trent, we haven't talked much lately."

"Yeah, I guess we've both been pretty busy."

"Do you have some time now? I have some hot chocolate made, and not the usual stuff. I bought a new mix from that gourmet store down the street, but I've been waiting to try it with you."

What could she say to that? Not only was hot chocolate her number one vice—especially the gourmet variety—he'd waited to try it when they could do so together. "You sure know which buttons to push, don't you?"

He raised his eyebrows. "Is that a yes?"

"Yes. But only for a little bit."

He held out his arm, and she followed Brylie inside, where

the girl immediately made some excuse about homework and closed herself off in her bedroom.

Hunter sent Shannon a wink from the other side of the island. "Finally alone."

Her face heated. "Don't get any ideas, Kavanaugh. I'm here for the gourmet chocolate."

Turning away, she shrugged out of her jacket and laid it across the back of the couch, walked around, and plopped down onto the soft leather. She might not like to consider how much he paid for this luxurious piece of furniture, but she sure did appreciate how it melted around her, as if it had been waiting all day to give her a hug.

"How'd your trial end up?"

"We won. Eighty-five-million-dollar verdict. Wrongful death suit for the collapse of a hotel deck that killed four people. Construction company used shoddy materials and pocketed the rest of the money."

Her jaw dropped as he came around the sofa to hand her a cup of hot cocoa. "Oh, how awful."

"Really awful. Stuff like that makes me so angry."

"I can see why. Do you get a bonus when you win a big verdict like that?"

"Yes. Too bad I have to share it with good ol' Percival Montgomery. It's his fault I got pulled into it to begin with."

"How's that?"

The couch let out a *whoosh* when he settled into it. "Monty dropped the ball on an expert witness, and they had me come in at the eleventh hour to clean up the mess. That's why I had to put in all those extra hours. Takes time to vet and prepare a new expert, and I only had two days. Fortunately, I've built up a stable of engineers, architects, and project managers and was able to find a replacement right away."

"Oh." Wow. He'd been the hero of an eighty-five-million-dollar wrongful death verdict for the families of four people lost because a construction company had decided to cut corners. Maybe she shouldn't have been so quick to judge. "I'm proud of you. That's great."

He tilted his head. "Thanks, Shan. I appreciate that." His focus moved to his sister's door and back to her. "I know last week was an inconvenience, but I hope you know how much I appreciate you for all your help. Seriously, Shannon. You've been amazing, and I could never repay you for how much you've done for us over the last several weeks."

"I would never expect you to. I made two new wonderful friends. That's all I need."

"Friends. Yeah."

When his gaze lingered, she pulled hers away and sipped the creamy cocoa. "This is delicious. I'll have to get the name to pick up some myself."

He took his own sip. "Oh, yeah, that is good." He took another, then held his cup between his hands in his lap. "I had a talk with Wyatt yesterday while Bry was in her session."

Her eyes snapped to his. "You did?" Exactly what she'd hoped would happen—covert counseling.

"I did. And he got me thinking about some things. Friends being one of them. Or relationships, I guess you could say."

Her toes curled inside her boots. Relationships? Where exactly was this conversation going?

"I've been laser-focused on my career for so long that relationships weren't all that important to me, outside of my family. I didn't have time to think about needing anybody in my life because I worked all the time. Even my so-called friendships revolved around work. And I was fine with that. But the night y'all had your sleepover and I met up with the guys, it was … different."

Her hands gripped her mug. "In what way?"

"My friends have been mostly guys from work. We would meet up on the weekends at a club or bar to blow off some steam. Harmless fun. Sometimes a little too much drinking, but

I've never been a big drinker. I usually end up being the designated driver or at least the one to call the ride-shares.

"But that night … it was odd. I got to the club, we threw some darts, talked some shop, danced with some girls."

Turning her attention to the fireplace, she took a sip from her cocoa. Not altogether surprising that he'd met some girls, but the idea of Hunter on the dance floor with a short-skirted beauty caused a ripple in her midsection. What kind of woman turned his head in a club when he wanted company? Tall blonde? Curvy brunette? Spunky redhead?

"But I left around eleven. Stone sober and bored out of my mind. Sacked out before midnight on a Friday night."

Her pulse hitched. He'd been home and asleep while she and the girls were in the middle of their second movie, painting each other's nails. At least when she hadn't been wondering what he was doing, if he was drinking or with … someone.

"I see."

He chuckled. "Glad you do. Cuz I'm a little confused."

She gave it some thought while she sipped her cocoa. "That was the same weekend you came to church the first time, right?"

"Right."

She shrugged. "Sounds like you're seeking deeper connections."

He stared at her for a moment. "You could be right. I had a great time at lunch that day after church, and playing basketball was a lot of fun, even if I could hardly move on Sunday. Still went to church with Brylie, though."

"You did?" Oh, my. How did she not know *that*?

Because she'd been keeping her distance. Her own fault.

"I did. The message this time was on grace allowing us to come boldly into God's presence. From Ephesians three."

"A great message. We watched it online from the Airbnb Sunday morning."

"Did y'all have a good weekend? I wanted to ask about it at Trunk-or-Treat, but things were pretty hectic."

"A wonderful weekend. So much fun. We got manicured and pedicured, exfoliated and massaged. Had a super nice dinner for Ally on Saturday. And I think we hit every store Granbury has to offer."

"Sounds like a great time."

"What else did you talk to Wyatt about?"

His sigh came from a deep place. "It's a little late to get into that, but maybe we'll talk about it sometime. Just a lot of junk from my past."

The junk he hadn't yet confided in her.

Of course, he didn't know about her past, either. But, then, he hadn't asked. He had enough on his plate without her unloading all of her *junk*, as he put it.

Nodding, she picked up her cup and stood. "Speaking of late, I should probably go. Early class in the morning. I'm glad we could catch up, though."

He met her on the other side of the sofa. "Me too." He nodded toward the half-finished drink in her hand. "Take that with you."

"Great. It's probably my new favorite. Thanks for sharing it with me."

"Sure thing. And since Bry's hanging with you after school tomorrow, wanna stay for dinner?"

She grabbed her jacket and bag. "Better yet, why don't you plan to change after work and come on up to my place? Brylie and I will probably already be in the thick of homework, and that way we don't have to pack it up to come down here."

"Great idea. I'll more than likely be doing some research, so it'll be like study hall. What do you want me to pick up to eat?"

"Nothing. Harper dropped off a pan of her chicken enchiladas yesterday with all the sides. It'll take me a week to finish it by myself, so y'all would be doing me a favor."

"Super. It's a date." His eyes widened, probably as much as

hers did. "Um … I mean … dinner. It's … dinner. And study hall. Tomorrow."

"Tomorrow."

So much for keeping her distance, but she couldn't help it. Sitting there talking over gourmet hot chocolate reminded her how much she enjoyed his friendship. And dinner and a pseudo study hall with the Kavanaughs sounded like a great way to spend an evening that would otherwise be just her and her homework.

He walked her to the door. "Oh, I keep forgetting to tell you. That night of your slumber party, when I met the guys?"

"Yeah?"

"I saw that girl you were with the first day we met."

Apprehension crawled up her spine. "When I was moving in? The tall one?"

"Yeah. That one. She came up to me, said she remembered me from that day my phone ended up in the fountain. We talked for a minute, but she was pretty wasted, I'm sorry to say. On my way out, though, I noticed a guy getting handsy with her, so I … uh … offered to call a ride-share for her."

His cheeks colored. "Short story is she declined the offer, so I left. But I've wondered about her, hoping she was okay. Have you spoken to her recently?"

She nodded, wondering what the long story might be. "Saw her last night, actually. Went over there to do homework together." She swallowed against the tears that threatened. "Delaney's my sister. My *underage* sister. Junior at UT Arlington."

His eyes widened. "I didn't know that. If I had, Shan, I would have gotten her out of there. How old is she?"

"Twenty. She'll be legal in a few months, but I guess she got ahold of a fake ID."

"Or has connections somewhere."

"Or that. She doesn't seem to understand how dangerous her lifestyle is."

"Yeah. She leaves herself pretty vulnerable in that state." He planted his hands on his hips and shook his head. "When I think about Bry doing something like that, it makes me want to lock her in her room."

"I hear you. And she won't. As long as she always knows how important she is to you. More than work, more than anything. That's what Delaney's missing. What she's searching for. What I went searching for. Because we didn't get it at home. I finally found it in the Lord, but not before I lost a huge chunk of myself. Unfortunately, Dee doesn't want anything to do with Jesus or church. Nobody in my family does."

His brow creased. "I assumed you'd been raised a Christian."

She shook her head. "Jesus found me despite my upbringing. And just in the nick of time."

CHAPTER TWENTY

$\mathcal{H}$unter stood in the family room of Zane and Ally's new home and took a long pull from his water bottle. Nothing like physical labor to work up a thirst.

A burst of laughter from the kitchen pulled his attention to the ladies unpacking and organizing according to Ally's instructions. The entire move had gone without a hitch, and Zane had given all the credit to his bride-to-be and her exceptional organizational skills.

Hunter's gaze settled on Shannon, handing plates to Harper for her taller friend to stack in a cabinet. They'd spent this first Saturday morning of November moving furniture and dozens of boxes from both Ally and Zane's current residences. And a brand-new bedroom set had been delivered yesterday for the large suite the couple would share after the wedding a week from today.

So, apparently, folks still waited until after the *I do's* to share a bed, since Ally would live here until the big day, and Zane would stay with his mom and aunt, who had recently relocated to Arlington. Admirable, to say the least. Hunter had to admit his respect for Zane had ratcheted up a notch, that he could love a woman the way he loved Ally and be completely on board with waiting.

After another swallow of water, Hunter made his way out to the deck overlooking the pool, where the guys had gathered around a barbecue grill and a smoker. Like the ladies, the men had spent much of the day laughing while working. All in good fun without trying to one-up each other or use coarse humor to sound cool.

He'd never experienced anything like it, yet they'd included him in their antics all day. Just as they had at the basketball tournament and the night of Trunk-or-Treat. And after Brylie had gone home with one of the ConnectUP girls after church last Sunday when the ladies were out of town, Wyatt invited him over to join the guys for an afternoon of pizza and football. And without a drop of liquor in sight, he had the best time with a group of men he'd had ... well ... ever.

He spotted Brylie on the other side of the pool, bouncing baby Gracie on her hip, and walked over to join her.

"Isn't she the cutest thing ever?" she asked with a broad smile.

He tapped his sister on the nose. "You were the cutest thing ever when you were that small."

She giggled, and the baby gave her a toothless grin. "I can't wait to be an aunt."

"Whoa, there, Nelly. That's not even on the distant horizon."

Brylie turned her attention to the ladies coming through the sliding glass door. "Oh, I don't know. I think you should ask her out already. Can't get married and have babies until you go on a date."

"Have you been sniffing glue?"

"Ha. Ha. Just sayin'. Maybe you should make the effort."

"I'm taking away all your glue. And nail polish. Anything with fumes."

"Shannon would be an amazing sister."

"So, think of her as a sister. I give you permission."

"You know what I mean."

Yes, he did. But his assertion hadn't changed from that first night. Shannon was much too good for him. Full of Jesus and purity and goodness and all that stuff that would surely warn her away from a guy like him, with all of his baggage. All of his … sins.

Even if he was curious about her comment regarding her upbringing Wednesday night. He'd hoped she'd share more with him about that, but they hadn't spent any time alone since then.

What had she been searching for? Where had she gone searching for whatever it was?

As long as she always knows how important she is to you. More than work, more than anything. That's what Delaney's missing.

How could Brylie think anything was more important to him than she was? He'd cut hours away from the office, and his billables were down. Under the circumstances, it couldn't be helped, although he was still posting more than any other senior associate.

But the partners had noticed a significant amount of his work was being done from home. Working late into the wee hours after Brylie was asleep was the only way to ensure they could spend time together, whether over a meal or in front of a show, going over any homework she had questions about, or just talking.

He stayed late on Wednesdays now because she went home with Ellie after school and then to ConnectUP, so he didn't have to be home until nine to be there when Shannon dropped her off. And he tried to keep any Saturday work-from-home hours to mornings or late night, which was difficult if Alden or Gail were in the office on the weekend and needed something.

Brylie appeared open to compromising with him, though, and had even spent the Saturday afternoon following the sleepover reading a book in his office while he met with the other attorneys on one of the larger cases he was involved with. It had been an interesting five weeks since Brylie moved in, but they were making it work. They would be fine.

When his gaze moved across the pool, it snagged on Shannon's, and he returned her smile. Shannon. God knew they'd needed her and put her literally in his path. Thankfully, she hadn't let his less-than-charming self from their first meeting chase her away when she realized he was Brylie's brother.

Because they had indeed needed her. Needed her guidance and wisdom and joy and the caring that came so effortlessly to her.

Wait. Realization hit him like ice water in the face, and he looked away. *God knew?* Had he actually had a thought that included God? In a good way? In a *believing* way?

Brylie moved into his line of sight, her eyes narrowed. "You okay, Hunt? Need another bottle of water?"

"Um ... no. I'm fine. Just—"

Just ... what? He couldn't put his finger on it himself, so how could he possibly explain it to his sister?

Before Brylie could question him further, Harper came over and reached for her daughter. "You've been so great with her today, Bry. Thank you for all your help."

"It was fun. She's a great baby. Didn't cry once."

"Because she likes you."

Brylie's face beamed with the praise. "Let me know if I can help you again. Any time."

"I'll do that."

Harper walked away with Grace, and Hunter turned to his sister. "What time do you have to be at Ellie's for your sleepover?"

"Three. I'll go to church with her tomorrow, and Shannon can bring me home after. Unless you're coming?"

At the hopeful light in her eyes, he nodded. "I'll be there. I'll see if Shannon's free for lunch."

She clasped her hands at her chest and did a little jump. "Not a date. Lunch."

"Closest thing you've had to one lately."

True that. And he had to admit, if he wanted to date someone right now, he couldn't think of anybody he'd rather spend time with.

If only he were the right guy for her. One as pure and as good as she was.

He caught Brylie regarding him. "What?"

"You really okay?"

"I really am." When she seemed unconvinced, he reached out and tugged her into his arms. "Seriously, Peanut. Nothing for you to worry about."

"It's been a long time since you called me *Peanut*," she said in a voice muffled against his sweatshirt. She pulled back and smiled. "I like it. As long as you don't call me that in front of my friends."

"I'll do my best to remember."

Zane called everybody over for lunch, and after prayer, the group loaded up on brisket, sausage, potato salad, and coleslaw, with cookies and brownies for dessert. These folks threw a killer moving party. When he helped a friend from the office move into his house last year, they'd had cold pizza and warm beer waiting for them at the end, nothing at all like this feast.

With close to twenty people coming in two teams to merge two households into this one home, he hadn't crossed paths with Shannon since they'd arrived early that morning. Now that she'd finally settled in one spot, he unfolded a lawn chair next to hers in the grass.

"Hey, Shan."

The sun lit her unadorned face, or perhaps that was her own inner light. "Hey, there." Some strands of her hair had come out of her braid and floated in the breeze. "Still glad you volunteered your services today, knowing how hard we were going to make you work?"

"Oh, yeah. Better than any gym workout. And tons more fun."

"For sure."

He dug into his plate of brisket with both potato salad and coleslaw on the side, took a sip from his soda, and swiped a napkin across his mouth. He still couldn't put a finger on what had happened in his head. In his heart.

When had he begun to get in touch with God? That night, sitting on the floor behind the couch, trying to pray for his sister? The two Sundays he sat in church listening to every word of the pastor's message? The mornings he'd asked Brylie what she was reading in her quiet time?

Maybe he should talk to Shannon about it. But before he could ask if she had plans later, his phone vibrated with an incoming call. He pulled it from his back pocket and squinted at the screen in the sunlight. Not recognizing the number with the Houston area code, he pressed the icon to disconnect. It rang again and the same number popped up. Considering perhaps this was one of the Houston engineers he'd been vetting as an expert witness, he punched the green icon.

"Kavanaugh."

"Hunter. So glad you picked up."

An ice-cold current snaked over his skin, and his half-eaten meal turned to lead in his stomach. "I can't talk now. I'll get back to you, but do not call me again."

"Hun—"

He pressed the icon to disconnect, but it rang yet again a few seconds later. Had he not been clear? After rejecting the call, he silenced his phone and hoped nobody from work would need to get in touch with him.

"An old flame?"

His head snapped around to Shannon, whose grin faded

and eyes widened. "Oh, sorry. I was kidding, but that was serious, huh? Everything okay?"

Blood roared in his ears as he leaned toward her. "Do you have some time today we could talk?"

"I'll make the time. What's going on?"

Scanning the backyard, he found his sister sitting with the CU kids who'd come to help. He swallowed before meeting Shannon's gaze again. "That was my stepdad. He disappeared two years ago, and we haven't heard from him since."

Her jaw fell slack. "Oh, no. Do you think—?"

He shook his head. He didn't want to think about it. Because it could only be about one thing.

Brylie.

CHAPTER TWENTY-ONE

"Why don't you start at the beginning."

Up on the rooftop deck, Shannon took a seat on the padded rattan sofa next to Hunter and popped open her soda. They'd both already showered off their day of hard labor, and she'd finished a bit of homework while he dropped Brylie at Ellie's for the birthday sleepover. When he returned, she readily agreed when he suggested coming up here to watch the sunset and was grateful to find they had the entire space—and the view—to themselves.

She'd been afraid he would change his mind after asking if she had some time to talk. But she'd committed him to prayer over the last couple of hours, after that call from Brylie's dad had put a rage in Hunter's eyes Shannon had never seen before. Not even that morning she'd sent his phone to its doom.

He stared out over the city, a muscle in his jaw flexing on his handsome face.

"If you want to talk, I'm here," she said. "But if you'd rather sit and be quiet, I'm here for that too. Whatever you need."

His sigh came from a deep place. "I hadn't planned to tell you about all of this, until that call today."

"Why?"

"Because it's not pretty. I mean, all things considered, I'm not a bad guy. I don't drink that much, I've never done drugs. Maybe I'm not exactly what you'd call pure, but I don't sleep around. I don't even cuss. I've always believed people deserve to be treated respectfully. But then there's Mitch. And respect flies out the window with the sheer hatred I feel for that man."

"Hunter. I'm not here to judge. I've learned enough about you in the past several weeks to know you're not a bad guy. We all have parts of us we'd rather not have others see. But I hope you know you can trust me with whatever is weighing so heavily on you."

He nodded, but his gaze locked on hers for several seconds, as if searching for any reason to doubt her assertion. Hopefully, he could see he was absolutely safe with her.

"Today's been ... weird. First the God thing, then Mitch calling out of the blue. My head's all muddled up."

She tilted her head. "Wait. The God thing?"

He waved his hand in the air. "I was standing there watching Brylie and something about God popped into my head. And I realized that sort of thing's been happening lately. You have to understand, I haven't considered God in years, not since I was a kid. He hasn't been a part of my thinking, my speaking, not a part of my day-to-day at all. Because of Mitch."

"Okay." She paused to think for a second. "Let's start there, then. Why is Mitch the reason God hasn't been part of your life since you were a boy?"

He took a drink from the soda she'd handed him before coming up to the roof, then stared down at it in his hands for a long, silent moment. "I thought Mitch was the greatest thing when he came into our lives. My mom had me when she was seventeen. I never knew my father."

All the oxygen left Shannon's lungs, leaving her

lightheaded. Seventeen? Hunter had been born to a seventeen-year-old mother? And she'd kept him? She'd raised a little boy into this amazing man on her own?

"It was just her and me until Mitch came along when I was eleven." His voice pulled her back and reminded her to breathe. Thankfully, he hadn't noticed her momentary stupor. "She met him at church, and we clicked right away. He came to all my games and school events. Asked me for my blessing to marry Mom, included me as a groomsman. I was so excited to finally have a dad."

His voice hitched. "When he asked to adopt me, I couldn't wait to be a Kavanaugh. Brylie came along two years after they got married, and we were a whole family."

With another heavy sigh, he shook his head. "Then the drinking began. Or I guess I should say, began again. Mom told me some years later Mitch had struggled with alcohol addiction long before they'd met but had beaten it. Apparently not, because he spiraled quickly. By the time Brylie was two, he'd had three jobs in three different towns. And by then, I was done with God. If that was a so-called Christian man, I wanted nothing to do with it."

"Is this what you talked to Wyatt about?"

He nodded.

"And what did he say?"

"We didn't get that far before Bry was done with her session."

Sitting up straight with her hands clasped in front of her, she looked him in the eye. "So, what you're frustrated with is the hypocrisy of a Christian man letting past demons get the best of him. Am I understanding that correctly?"

"And taking his family down with him. The pain he caused is unforgivable. Two years ago, Mom called me. Mitch had left the week before. She had no idea where he was, but the rent was due, and she had no way to pay it because he'd cleaned out the bank account of what little they had.

"I went down there, found them in this rusted-out old trailer Mitch had moved them into only two months earlier — if I'd known that, I would've gone to get them right away — and moved them back to Gran's in Mount Pleasant. It took me a couple of months, but I finally talked Mom into filing for divorce and appointing me guardian of Brylie if anything should happen to her. I thought we were finally free of him."

"Until today."

"Until today."

"Has he called again?"

"Twice."

"And you —"

"No. I haven't answered. I will, but I need to get my thoughts together first. I mean …" He turned to face her. "I've listened, Shan. I honestly have. To the pastor the last two Sundays. To Brylie when I've asked her what she's reading in her Bible. But I still don't get why a good God would let someone like my mom — a loving, godly woman with a beautiful, young daughter to raise — be killed in an instant in a senseless car accident. And a no-good, selfish drunk like Mitch gets to live. Why? How is that good?"

Her heart hurt for him, because she understood his question. She'd voiced it herself. Wondering how a loving God could let good people suffer while others making horrible life choices seemingly got off easy.

"I know, Hunter. I know that's impossible to understand. This world is a broken, evil, dark place. It's not perfect. And we're not puppets being strung along by a dictator God. He's a loving Father who's given us free will to choose the lives we want to live. But with those choices come consequences, not only for ourselves but for others."

"Free will. To do whatever we want."

"Yes. Your mom, for instance, in her innocence, made a bad choice and got pregnant outside of marriage. But then she made a good choice to become a godly young mother, took her little boy to church, then married who she believed to be a good, Christian man. Mitch made a good choice in a wife, then he did not make good choices as a husband. The driver who drank himself into oblivion that night and got behind the wheel made a bad choice, and it killed your mom, someone who had no ties to him. Until that very instant.

"But do you believe that driver, or even Mitch, have lived unscathed by those choices? They've left victims in their wakes, no question. But they've brought disaster into their own lives. Things they may never recover from without the Lord's help."

He shook his head, his lips pressed together for a long moment. "I see that. But, in my book, the disaster should've only been theirs, not innocent people who had no part in those bad choices. That's where I get hung up, trying to understand how a good God allows that to happen. That our family was victimized by Mitch's drinking, and Mom was killed by another man with the same demons."

Nodding, she considered his quandary, praying for the right words. "Those are valid questions, Hunt. The way I look at it is God is good in that your mom is with Him now, in glory. He's good in that you and Brylie are together, and He's provided a support system you never even knew you had. He's good in that He's given you the freedom, the choice, to continue doubting Him, ignoring Him. Or you can choose to overcome and let Him heal those wounds inflicted by a flawed, damaged human being who's created in God's image, as you are.

"He's good in that He loves you so much, He paid the ultimate price for you yet still has given you the freedom to make your own decision about Him. Even if it breaks His heart."

Silence hung heavy in the air as traffic moved along the streets below, and the smell of pizza baking wafted in the breeze from Luigi's next door.

The sun sat low on the horizon when Hunter leaned forward and bowed his head. "I miss her."

Such anguish in those three whispered words.

Fighting back tears, she placed her can on the table, then put her arms around him as she had his sister exactly two weeks ago. He'd been so brave, so stoic, covering up his own pain all these weeks to take care of Brylie. To be strong and provide and be there as much as he could with all the demands of his job.

"I don't know how to stop."

"You don't have to stop missing her. You'll always miss her."

Pulling away, he sniffled and shook his head. "No. Being mad. I don't know how to stop being mad at God." His tear-filled eyes met hers. "How do I stop, Shan? Tell me."

Her throat tightened. Oh, how she wished she had the words.

CHAPTER TWENTY-TWO

This couldn't be a good idea.

Hunter followed Shannon, who followed Wyatt through the warm and welcoming foyer of the McCowans' white limestone home. When he'd asked her earlier how to stop being angry at God, she hadn't said anything. Simply pondered him, her blue eyes shimmering under the lights strung overhead that had come on once the sun had gone to the other side of the world. She still hadn't answered when she reached for her cell phone and called Harper.

So, here they were, walking into their friends' home at the dinner hour, which didn't feel like good form at all.

Harper looked up as she closed the oven door. "Oh, I'm so glad you're here." Her bright smile would have him believing she'd been expecting them all day. "I always have a pan of something or other in the freezer for this very reason, so I hope you like King's Ranch casserole. It'll give us a chance to talk while it heats up. I've already thrown together a salad, and then we'll eat."

Shannon shot him a grin over her shoulder. "Told you."

"Told him what?"

"He was worried about bothering y'all on short notice. But

I told him you could entertain royalty if they showed up on your doorstep."

Laughing, Harper set the timer on the oven. "I don't know about that, but it's never a problem having folks drop by. I usually have enough vittles in the freezer to feed an army of ConnectUP kids."

"Exactly," Wyatt said. "It's never a problem. And if it involves questions of a spiritual nature, we prefer not to wait." He gestured toward the family room. "Let's have a seat."

"Gracie sleeping?" Shannon asked on their way over.

Harper shook her head. "Wyatt dropped her off at Rhonda and Mason's. Figured it would keep us from being interrupted for an hour or two."

Wyatt chuckled. "And Mason says he needs the practice. Not sure how I feel about him practicing his daddy skills on my daughter, but as long as Rhonda sticks close, he should be fine."

Harper gave him a playful nudge with her shoulder. "Gracie adores Mason."

They took their seats on the leather sectional, Harper on the short side while Hunter sat between Shannon and Wyatt on the long.

Her hands clasped together in her lap, Harper stared at them for a moment before meeting his eyes again, her expression now more sober than moments before.

"Shannon told me a bit about what you're struggling with, Hunter, and as we've said before, you have our most sincere condolences. The loss of family is a deep loss you and Brylie will feel for the rest of your lives. I haven't lost a parent." She swallowed hard, and Wyatt reached over to cover her hands. "But I have lost a child."

Hunter's stomach knotted. "I-I didn't know that. I'm so sorry."

"I wasn't a believer in high school, or in the several years after, and made some very bad decisions. One of those was choosing to sleep with my boyfriend and getting pregnant as a result. We got married and had our baby girl, and although the marriage was the stuff of nightmares, she was the absolute joy of my life. Then she was diagnosed with cancer and passed away when she was four years old."

His thoughts raced, unable to equate such a tragedy with the joy-filled woman he'd recently come to know. How had she reconciled her daughter's death with a good God?

"I didn't know the Lord when I lost Megan, but my sister did. I told her many times I didn't understand how she could trust a God who could let a child suffer like mine did, then take her away."

Hunter's gaze remained fixed on Harper. Exactly his question. How to trust God when He allowed a child to suffer, then take her from her mother. How to trust God when He took Mom but left the drunk who killed her alive and able to walk away with barely a scratch.

"Eventually, she helped me see God didn't cause Megan's suffering, and He didn't take her away but delivered her from her pain. It took a while, but through faith-based counseling, a lot of crying out to God, and even more questioning of God, I was finally able to forgive Him, and give my life to Him."

A chill ran through his body and settled in his chest. "Forgive God?"

She nodded. "That sounds blasphemous, I know. God didn't do anything wrong. He *can't* do anything wrong. It's against His nature. But we forgive to allow ourselves to heal. Megan was still gone. The hurt was still there. The circumstance had not changed. But there was a peace where I could finally say, *Okay, God, I'm not mad at You any longer. I'm ready to trust and see how You can redeem this awful thing.*

"And I've seen God do exactly that. The way He's allowed me to minister to other parents who've lost little ones, the way I get to serve the teens we work with every day. Even getting to talk to you right now. I pray it will somehow answer some of the questions you have."

As he tried to wrap his mind around what she'd shared, she took a moment to study her hands again before looking up at him. "You know what I think of the most when I see how God redeemed my grief over the death of my daughter? Megan was the child of a messed-up relationship. I have no doubt the marriage would not have survived even if she had. But neither of us were believers. My ex was an alcoholic abuser who eventually became a drug addict. Now?"

Shaking her head, she exchanged a quick glance with her husband. "Brett's saved and working at a Christian halfway house for addicts being released from my parents' drug and alcohol recovery centers before transitioning back into society. He's been able to bring numerous addicts to the Lord. And my parents have also become staunch believers instead of holiday churchgoers, all because my sister showed me God's love and showered me with His grace through my life's biggest tragedy."

Leaning forward, she focused directly into Hunter's eyes, and the sheer love and comfort he saw there reminded him so much of Mom. "Can I ask you, do you believe your mother prayed for you?"

He nodded.

"Daily?"

"Yes." He cleared his throat when all that came out was a whisper. "Yes. She told me she did."

"For your safety, your job, your health."

"Probably."

"Do you believe she prayed for you to come back to the Lord?"

His lungs seized and throat burned. Flames crackled in the gas fireplace and the aroma of the baking casserole wafted in the air. Shannon sniffled beside him, and her hands slipped around his arm.

"Yes. I'm sure she did. I know she did."

Harper stood and sat on the coffee table in front of him, then grasped his hands in both of hers as Wyatt's hand came to rest on his shoulder.

"Hunter." The power with which she peered into his eyes had him fighting against the tears that threatened. "If she knew going to her home with Jesus would bring you back to Him, would that have been her choice? Would she have given her life to save yours?"

His breathing shallowed. He was going to lose it. Right here. With these people he hadn't even known mere weeks ago. These people who'd shown him more love and support and encouragement than any of the others he'd surrounded himself with over the past several years at the firm. Except for Jules, herself a believer.

He'd thought about God today, but that's not when it started.

Turning, his eyes sought the wet, baby-blue ones of the woman still holding onto his arm. "That night you came when I called …" His voice rasped against the knot in his throat. "When Brylie went to pieces, and I didn't know what to do. Listening to you pray … it was almost … reverent. I'd never experienced anything like that, but those moments with you praying the same words, over and over …" His breath hitched, and he could only continue in a whisper. "It felt holy."

He bowed his head as he lost the battle with the tears that coursed down his face.

Wyatt cleared his throat. "Knowing Shannon, she was praying scripture. And it *is* holy. From God's own spirit-breathed Word. She brought power into your home that night, Hunter. That's what you felt."

"*Have mercy on me, my God,*" came Shannon's quiet voice. "*Have mercy on me, for in You I take refuge. I will take refuge in the shadow of Your wings … for great is Your love, reaching to the heavens; Your faithfulness reaches to the skies.*"

Releasing a shaky breath, Hunter swept his hands over his face. He never cried. All of this was such new ground for him, but he couldn't deny there was a part of him inside coming alive.

Or maybe waking up.

He turned to Shannon. His memory of that night was as clear as if it had happened an hour ago. Shannon, holding Brylie on the couch, rocking her back and forth, eyes closed tight.

Have mercy on Brylie, Father. You are her refuge. Comfort and protect her in the shadow of Your wings. Shower her with Your love that reaches to the heavens and wrap her in Your faithfulness that reaches to the skies. Have mercy on Brylie, Father. You are her refuge …

And on she went until Brylie's sobs quieted and Shannon's prayer was a near whisper. Then he heard her.

Have mercy on Brylie, Father. Have mercy on Hunter. You are their refuge. Comfort and protect them in the shadow of Your wings. Shower them with Your love that reaches to the heavens and wrap them in Your faithfulness that reaches to the skies. Have mercy on Brylie, Father. Have mercy on Hunter. You are their refuge …

Until her solemn *Amen,* and all was still. When he finally stood from behind the couch, his sister was asleep in Shannon's arms. And he realized he too was at peace. He just hadn't had the words to describe it until that morning on the balcony with Brylie.

Like everything was suddenly okay even though nothing had changed.

The memory caused his breath to catch. "Where is that? In the Bible?"

"Psalm fifty-seven."

He studied her a moment before turning to Harper. "I want to have that kind of faith, but I'm not even sure where to start."

Wyatt put his arm around him and squeezed his shoulder. "Right here, my friend. If you're truly ready to give your life over to Christ, to live as a man following hard after God in his words, thoughts, work life, home life, in every facet of who Hunter Kavanaugh is, we can take care of that right here, right now."

Harper nodded. "God's all in with you. It's all about grace, what Christ did on the cross. You don't have to do anything to earn His love, His faithfulness, His salvation. He just wants *you*. But when a heart is truly given over to Christ, there will be a change in that heart. So, you just need to know if you're ready to fully surrender."

Hunter leaned forward with his hands clasped between his legs. Could he surrender his heart? His life? All of it? Give up the anger over losing Mom? Trust that God could take all of that and do something good with it?

Would she have given her life to save yours?

Yes, Mom would've given her life a dozen times over if she knew it would save his.

His pulse skipped. And there was the answer. Could he trust that God could take his mother's death and redeem it for something good? If he surrendered his life to Christ right now, in the next minute, Mom would be cheering at the top of her lungs in heaven, exactly as she had at his Little League games.

Taking a deep breath in, he sat up before releasing it. "I'm ready."

CHAPTER TWENTY-THREE

Shannon couldn't contain the joyful tears that spilled over the moment Hunter and Brylie started down the aisle toward the platform.

Harper smoothed her own tears away as Zane and Wyatt exchanged fist bumps. As if they'd scored a slam dunk.

In a way, that's exactly what they were witnessing, a slam dunk against the enemy as brother and sister stood hand-in-hand with a prayer team member. Hunter hadn't told Brylie about his decision until he met up with her in the church lobby when she arrived with Ellie and her family. And Shannon thought her heart might burst when they made their way to the front as soon as the worship team launched into their closing song.

Ally wrapped her arm around her and squeezed. "You did good, sister of mine."

Shannon swiped at her face and shook her head. "It was all God. I just happened to be at the right place at the right time. And Harper and Wyatt too."

"Many times, that's all He requires of us." Ally gave her another squeeze and let go.

Following the service, Shannon waited for the Kavanaughs

in the lobby while everyone else went home to pick up their contributions for their monthly potluck lunch, which today would be held at Rhonda and Mason's house.

When Brylie came out of the sanctuary and spotted her, she ran over and engulfed her in a hug. "We're getting baptized together. I'm so excited!"

"That's very exciting, Brylie-girl. I'm so glad for you." Her eyes met Hunter's as Brylie released her. "For both of you."

Reaching out, he pulled her into his arms. "Thank you." The huskiness of his voice sent prickles along her skin. "For everything." He pulled back and peered down at her. "I mean it. I'm truly grateful. We both are."

She nodded as tears once again threatened. "It's a privilege." Back at their building, they retreated to their separate units to grab their dishes for the potluck lunch.

Hunter grinned when she met them again outside their apartment carrying a casserole dish. "You made something?"

"I did." She returned his smile, somewhat proud of herself. "It's Ally's recipe for a potato casserole. Thankfully, it was easy to follow and pretty much foolproof."

"I can't wait to try it."

Brylie preceded them into the elevator, carrying a plastic grocery bag. "All we have to offer are store-bought cookies and some chips."

"Nothing wrong with either of those things. Trust me, this group eats anything."

At the Carlysles', while Brylie and Hunter were being hugged and congratulated, Shannon placed her casserole in the oven to heat and set the timer.

Harper placed her hand on her shoulder. "I'm still on a high after last night."

"Right? Me too. Could hardly sleep."

"Hunter asked Wyatt to baptize them. How cool is that?"

Fresh tears pooled in Shannon's eyes. She'd cried buckets since the night before, all happy tears, so she should be reaching her limit soon. "That's very cool. Do they know when?"

"Next baptism is scheduled in two weeks." Harper glanced at Hunter standing with Mason and Zane in the family room, then leaned close to Shannon, even though they were alone in the kitchen. "The two of you have grown close in a short amount of time."

"I guess we have. Because of Brylie, mostly."

"So, there's nothing …"

Shannon tilted her head. "Nothing …" Her eyes widened. "Oh, you mean like romantic or something?"

"You're both single, extremely attractive. He's charming as all get-out, and you, my friend, are a catch. Guess I was wondering if there was something there."

"Nothing like that. Hunter and I are friends. I'd never consider a relationship with a man who couldn't share my faith, so dating has never been on the radar."

Harper nodded. "That's what I assumed, knowing you like I do. But that's changed now, so how do you feel?"

Shannon looked around, wishing someone else—or a lot of someone elses—would make their way to the kitchen to end this uncomfortable conversation. How was it Harper could see so far into her soul? She'd always been able to do that, and Shannon had never hidden anything from this friend she loved like a sister.

Had Harper somehow picked up on her struggle to keep Hunter firmly in the friend zone? Not that he'd ever given her reason to suspect he wanted anything more. Still, her always vivid, way-too-romantic imagination would sometimes tease her with things that could never be, as long as Hunter continued down the road of unbelief.

But Harper was right. That had changed, literally overnight, removing the biggest obstacle keeping Shannon's heart from tumbling after her handsome and charming neighbor. The biggest, but certainly not the only one.

She cleared her throat, accepting she had no choice but to answer when no other bodies turned up in the kitchen to interrupt. At least Hunter had gone out back to throw a football around with the guys, so there was no chance he'd overhear.

"That's true. A lot has changed, but only for a matter of hours. I haven't considered him as dating material and *that* hasn't changed. I haven't been in a dating frame of mind for a long time."

Harper reached out to rub her arm. "I know. And I understand why. But as I've said before, only you can decide the right time to let go of all that pain from the past. You're so amazing and have so much to offer. Don't close yourself off to the possibilities.

"Yes, you would have to make yourself vulnerable again. But you could also find a wonderful gift that makes the risk well worth it. I'm not saying that's with Hunter, but you can still be there for him, like you've been all along. Don't let fear keep you away."

Shannon nodded. If she believed in such things, she'd almost suspect her friend had some sort of psychic power that allowed her to see things that had never been said.

"Let me know if you ever want to talk. About anything."

"I will. Thank you. For everything. Last night was … amazing."

"It was, wasn't it?"

Once all the food had been set out, Wyatt called everybody to attention for prayer, but first presented Hunter with a new study Bible. "Harper and I keep several of these on hand so when we introduce folks to the Lord, we can get them started on the road right away. We completely forgot in all the excitement last night to give it to you."

Hunter's smile spread across his face. "And the buzzer was going off for the casserole, so there was that."

Wyatt laughed and clapped him on the back. "Welcome

again, brother. We're beyond excited to have you in the family."

The others whooped and clapped before quieting for prayer. Afterward, the ladies led the way through the buffet line, everybody taking seats at either the kitchen or dining room tables.

Brylie took the chair next to Shannon and put her head on her shoulder. "I love you."

Shannon laid her cheek against the teen's silky hair. "I love you, too, Brylie-girl."

Sunday lunch passed with boisterous laughter and conversation, as it always did with this group she considered more family than her own.

After the men handled the clean-up, they settled around the television for football while the girls set out the desserts. Shannon's phone vibrated in her pocket, and she pulled it out to check the ID. Not recognizing the number, she disconnected and put it back. A few minutes later, it went off again.

"Same number as last time?" Harper asked.

"Yeah." With a shrug, she pressed the green phone icon. "Hello?"

"Yes, I'm trying to reach Shannon Trent?"

"This is Shannon Trent." Prickles danced along her skin when a distant siren sounded on the other end, blending with multiple voices, including one over an intercom system requesting a doctor report to the ER *stat*.

"I'm calling from the emergency room at Memorial Hospital. Please hold."

"Wha—" Staticky music replaced the chaotic noise.

"What's going on?" Ally asked.

"I don't know. It's Memorial Hospital. Emergency room. I'm on hold."

Ally, Yolanda, Harper, and Rhonda abandoned their tasks and gathered close. Hunter must have noticed, because after a moment, he joined them. Shannon's heart beat hard behind her sternum. Her parents were still out of the country, so if it was a family member, it would have to be Camden or Delaney. Or maybe one of her CU girls had asked them to call her?

Closing her eyes, she whispered a quick prayer that everybody was safe.

The canned music stopped. "Miss Trent?" A different female voice this time.

"Yes, ma'am."

"This is Officer Bonnie Kemp, Dallas PD. Delaney O'Connor was brought into the emergency room early this morning but was only recently identified. Are you able to come in?"

Delaney. "What happened?"

"We'd prefer to discuss that with you in person."

"Oh, no. Is she … I mean … she's—"

"She's alive, yes, ma'am. But sedated."

"Why'd it take so long to ID her?"

"I'd prefer to discuss this with you in person, if you could come down, please."

That couldn't be good. Had she been hurt in such a fashion that she no longer resembled her driver's license photo? Shannon's lunch threatened a revolt in her stomach.

"Oh—uh, of course. I'll come right away."

Ally put her arm around her. When had she started shaking?

"Come to the emergency department and ask for Officer Kemp."

"I will. Thank you."

Thank you? Was that the proper response for someone who'd told her nothing other than her sister was alive but unrecognizable?

Hunter took the phone from her tremulous hand and disconnected for her, his face etched with concern. "What happened?"

"It's Delaney. She was brought into the emergency room

early this morning, but they only just now ID'd her. They wouldn't tell me what happened, only that she's sedated, whatever that means."

"Means she's not in a coma," Ally, the nurse practitioner, explained. "That if not for sedation, she'd be conscious and able to speak on her own."

"I wonder why a police officer is telling me that instead of a nurse."

Ally and her best friend Yolanda, herself a nurse practitioner, exchanged a look.

"What?"

"Honey, I should warn you, that usually means there's a possibility of some criminal activity."

Shannon's jaw fell slack as the blood drained from her head. "You mean that she was the victim of a crime?"

"Don't assume anything until you get there and get the information you need. I can go with you if you'd like. I'm doing another part-time freelance gig at Memorial right now. Through Wednesday, anyhow, with the wedding being next weekend. My ID's in the car."

Hunter clasped her hand. "I can drive you, since we came together. If you want me to, Shan. After all you've done for us, please let me do this for you."

She glanced over her shoulder where his sister sat watching the game. "If it's bad, I really don't want Brylie there." And all the scenarios running through her head were very, very bad.

Harper wrapped her arm around Shannon's shoulders. "Don't worry about Bry. She can come home with us and stay as long as needed. We can even take her to grab homework. It's not a problem at all."

Hunter shook his head. "She got it all done before Ellie's sleepover last night."

"Okay, then. It's all good. You three go on."

While Harper, Rhonda, and Yolanda gathered Shannon

into a hug, Ally told Zane she was going to the hospital, and Hunter walked over to explain the situation to Brylie.

In the car, Shannon couldn't speak past the fear blocking her throat, and neither Hunter nor Ally tried to fill the silence.

How had their day of celebration turned into this?

143

CHAPTER TWENTY-FOUR

Not even a full day into his fledgling relationship with God, and Hunter prayed as best he knew how the entire twenty-minute drive to the hospital. That Delaney would recover from whatever had befallen her. That God would give Shannon the comfort, strength, and wisdom to get through whatever awaited her in the next few hours. Because so much of her heart belonged to her sister.

Shannon. The woman who gave and gave and gave and never asked for anything in return. He was determined to be here for her through this, as she'd been for them from the moment she entered their lives.

Still lifting silent prayers to the Lord, he followed Ally and Shannon to the front desk in the emergency department.

Shannon waited until she had the attention of the triage nurse. "I'm here to meet with Officer Kemp?"

"Regarding which patient?"

"Delaney O'Connor."

Hunter snapped his attention from the nurse to Shannon. *O'Connor?* How did Shannon's sister have a different last name? She was only twenty, so the chance she'd been married was pretty slim. Did they have different fathers, like he and Brylie?

A few minutes later, the female officer walked into the waiting area, hand braced on the gun strapped to her belt, dark hair pulled into a tight bun. After introducing herself as Officer Kemp, she escorted them through the swinging doors to a conference room where another nurse joined them.

"When can I see Delaney?" Shannon asked, her voice laced with fear.

"In a moment. I wanted to update you first." The officer peered at Ally's hospital ID badge, then at Hunter. "Are you family?"

"No, ma'am," he answered.

"Due to HIPAA regs regarding privacy, we can't discuss medical info with anyone other than those persons designated by the patient. And those being Shannon Trent and Camden O'Connor." She regarded Ally with steely dark eyes. "Are you here at the request of the family?"

"She is," Shannon answered.

"And that would include any legal representation?"

"Is that necessary?"

"I would recommend it."

Shannon looked up at him, and he nodded. She turned back to the officer. "That would be Mr. Kavanaugh here."

The officer narrowed her eyes at him. "You're an attorney?"

"Yes, ma'am. Hunter Kavanaugh, Senior Associate, Williamson, Sheffield, and Moore."

One eyebrow cocked. If she'd lived in the DFW Metroplex longer than five minutes, she knew of the large, prestigious, century-old law firm. "All right, then. Have a seat." She cleared her throat, and he took the chair next to Shannon while Ally sat across the table. "Miss O'Connor's been involved in an automobile accident and will be charged with driving under the influence."

The room tilted. A DUI? His hands clenched hard onto his thighs as blood pounded in his ears.

"Oh, no," Shannon said, her eyes wide. "Did she hurt anyone?"

"Only herself."

Hunter let out the breath trapped in his chest. At least she hadn't hurt or killed anyone. Someone's wife, husband, sister, brother ... mother. Still, she'd made the ignorant decision to drink, then drive. No excuse for that.

"And the bistro she destroyed when she drove into it at sixty miles an hour. She's lucky it was closed, and she's not injured worse than she is." The officer regarded him again. "There will certainly be a hefty personal property suit for that."

A simple nod was all he could muster.

Shannon cleared her throat. "You said you couldn't ID her when she came in. What does that mean?"

"The ID your sister had on her at the time of the accident identified her as Dee Connor, aged twenty-three. Address doesn't exist. License number doesn't exist."

"A fake ID."

That much he'd surmised. If only he'd been aware of that the night he encountered her while out with his friends. At a club he would never set foot in again. He would've dragged her out of there, for Shannon's sake if not her own.

"Correct. She'll be charged with that as well as for purchasing alcohol while underage. Additional charges are pending."

Hunter's gaze went to Shannon. While he didn't hold much sympathy for Delaney, his heart hurt for Shannon, who seemed to shrink in her chair as the officer rattled off more bad news. Delaney wasn't in a little bit of trouble. This was serious. Life-changing serious.

If her sister ended up doing jail time, which she deserved, he had no idea how Shannon would handle that, as she would probably blame herself for Delaney's failings.

And nothing could be more wrong.

"Plus, she was in somebody else's car, so we couldn't ID her from the registration. Car was registered to a …" Officer Kemp consulted a small notebook. "Dana Washburn."

Shannon cleared her throat. "One of her housemates."

"Yes. We couldn't reach Miss Washburn until this morning. Visiting her parents in Idaho. She was able to identify your sister by the photo we texted her and had your name and that of your brother but no contact info. Our cyber guys were able to get that from Delaney's phone."

"You've notified Camden?"

"Left a message. Miss Washburn also mentioned your parents are out of the country?"

"Correct. Camden and I can act on their behalf until they get here."

"Noted. By the way, Miss Washburn's car is a total loss, and she indicated Miss O'Connor did not have her permission to drive it. She's consulting with her parents as to whether to file vehicle theft charges or not."

And the hits kept coming. Hunter rapped his knuckle against the tabletop. "Has Miss O'Connor been placed under arrest?"

"She hasn't been coherent enough to understand her rights. Once she's regained full consciousness, she'll be placed under arrest."

Shannon swiped her hand across her cheeks. "Does she have a head injury?"

"I'll defer questions regarding her medical care to Jane here. She's the head nurse in the emergency department."

The dark-skinned woman in the navy blue scrubs cleared her throat. "Yes, let me start by saying Delaney is in stable condition, and her injuries are non-life-threatening, so that's some good news. I know this has been difficult today, so hopefully that helps."

The nurse's kind eyes were a bonus in her profession. She

must see horrendous injuries and loss of life due to drunk driving all the time in her line of work. Yet she hadn't passed judgment on Delaney, making her a better person than he. But maybe she hadn't lost somebody of her own.

"She did suffer a small skull fracture, but an initial CT showed no brain bleed, only a mild to moderate concussion. The choice to leave her sedated is due to the severe injury to her leg that will require surgery. As soon as we have your consent, we can start that process."

"Yes. Absolutely. But can I see her first?" Another tear slipped down Shannon's face, and Hunter's anger seethed. If only Delaney could see the pain her actions had caused her sister, much less the damages to her friend and an innocent business owner. But would she even care? Most drunks couldn't care less who they hurt.

"Yes, dear. But I can only take you. The others will need to remain in the waiting area."

He reached out and touched Shannon's arm. "Take your time. I'm not going anywhere."

The desolation in her eyes had him wishing he could wrap her up in his arms until this was all behind her. But he didn't have that place in her life. All he could offer was his support, his presence, as she had for him in these last weeks when he'd needed her so much.

"If you need to go, I understand."

Leaning forward, he took her hand in both of his. "Shannon. I'm not going anywhere. Okay?"

She nodded, but he didn't miss the flash of relief in her eyes. "Thank you."

They filed out of the conference room, the officer to the nurses' station, Shannon behind Nurse Jane, and he next to Ally back to the waiting room.

He released a heavy sigh as he sank into a chair in a far corner.

"Ditto." Ally took a seat next to him. "That's a lot to take in.

Shannon's been asking us to pray for Delaney, that somehow she'd turn things around. Maybe this is what it will take."

"Yeah." He swallowed the knot in his throat. "Maybe." He stared at a painting of cattle in a field of bluebonnets on the opposite wall and let his thoughts churn before he looked at her. "Can I be transparent for a second? Without you thinking I'm a horrible person?"

"You absolutely can."

"Is it awful I can't work up any sympathy for Delaney? That she chose to drink, then get behind the wheel of a car? That I'm thankful the only person she hurt was herself?" He turned back to the painting. "Oh, wow. I am a horrible person, aren't I?"

"You are not a horrible person. You're wounded. You have a very fresh loss of someone you love deeply at the hands of another who made the same choice Delaney did. If I were in your shoes, I can't say I wouldn't feel the same way."

"So, what do I do? To support Shannon when I'm kind of angry at her sister?"

"Well, I wouldn't tell her *that*."

He chuckled. "Heard."

"Best advice I have—and this is hard—but you need to pray for Delaney. She's broken, like we all are. Yes, you're angry with her now, and rightfully so. I get it. But if you can find some tiny piece of your heart where you can somehow say a two-second prayer for her, something as simple as *keep Delaney safe, Lord,* or even *help me not to be angry at Delaney,* that's a start. And He'll work in you to heal the place where that anger lives. Then someday you'll find you truly care what happens to her."

Hmm. He couldn't imagine that right now, but with God's help, perhaps he would be able to shake it. In time.

Because if he couldn't, it could cost him the closest friend he'd ever had.

CHAPTER TWENTY-FIVE

The sky had turned inky black three hours ago while Shannon sat in the surgical waiting room trying to finish one of the sandwiches Harper sent with Zane.

After her sister was wheeled up to the OR, she'd joined Hunter and Ally in the waiting room, where neither left her side until Dee was taken to a room after midnight. She tried to get Hunter to go home, but he assured her he'd already made arrangements with Emily for Harper to drop Bry over there to stay the night after picking up what she needed for school at the condo.

How grateful she was for this pseudo-family she'd found through CU, and the neighbor turned good friend. The only way through this would be to lean hard into the Lord, with the help of these sisters and brothers she could count on to hold her up.

But how was she going to get *Delaney* through this? When Delaney didn't believe? Didn't have the same foundation? The same hope?

"Mmmm."

The groan from the bed reached her where she stood, and

she hurried over. "Dee, honey. Don't move. You're going to be okay."

Delaney's eyes drifted shut again.

"That remains to be seen."

Shannon spun at the sound of the voice behind her. "Camden. Oh, it's so good to see you." Arms extended, she started toward him, but he put his hands out to stop her. Typical Cam. Not one prone to outward displays of affection. Had he never needed a hug? "You just got into town?"

"A few hours ago. Stopped at the office first."

Shannon's spirits fell. Of course. The apple didn't fall far from the tree.

He strode to the bed, stared hard at Delaney, once again sleeping, and stuck his hands on his hips. Camden was a handsome man. As tall as Hunter at six-foot-one, thick sandy-blond hair cut short, dressed in slacks and a long-sleeved dress shirt. He kept himself fit with thrice-weekly workouts and regular runs.

Now twenty-eight, he'd never been married. Didn't have children. Seemed like a lonely life to Shannon, only having his work to keep him company.

"She's really done it this time, hasn't she? Dragging our name through the mud. We'll have to get our public relations team on damage control first thing tomorrow."

Her jaw dropped. "Are you kidding me right now?"

He turned to face her. "Do I sound like I'm kidding?"

She pointed to Delaney, thankful she lay unaware of their brother's complete lack of compassion toward her. "Our sister could have died, and all you can think about is damage control?"

"She did this to herself, Shan. Not to mention her family. And she's going to be fine. The nurse said so."

"Physically, yes."

With a sigh, she grabbed his arm and dragged him out into the hall and down to a small alcove. "There are going to be charges, Cam. A lot of them. We need to stop worrying about the public relations team and get Dad's legal team on this. I assume a prosecutor will be assigned in the next few days, so we should try to get ahead of this."

He swept his hand through his hair. "This is a nightmare. I should've been an only child. Mom and Dad's lives would've been a lot easier."

A punch in the midsection would've been less painful. "Excuse me, *what*?"

"Sorry. I shouldn't have said that out loud."

"Oh, so you're not sorry you thought it, only that you said it."

"Okay, so I shouldn't have thought it. At least you got your act together. All this religious stuff is a little out there, but you haven't run off and done anything stupid again. Maybe this last mess will finally convince Dad to cut off his little princess. It sure worked with you."

She took a step back, her heart beating hard. Did he honestly have no idea how much a youthful indiscretion had cost her? A punishment far greater than the offense. One she still lived with every day.

Closing her mouth, she swallowed hard against the familiar ache. "I'm done here. I'm staying with Delaney. If you have nothing positive to contribute, then I suggest you leave."

She turned from her brother, her one-time childhood hero, and walked away. It had been seven years.

Would he never let it go?

Shannon stopped her pacing when the elevator doors opened, her breath leaving in a rush when Hunter stepped out and scanned the waiting area. His eyes met hers, and he moved toward her at a fast clip.

"What's happening? They decided to go in?"

Nodding, she was unable to hold back the tears any longer. He pulled her close. "I'm so sorry."

She took a moment to collect herself, unable to speak but taking in the strength of his arms around her. Monday had passed in a blur, mostly with Delaney in and out of sleep, complaining of pain until the next dose of medication took hold.

Hunter and Brylie brought pizza for dinner while Delaney once again slept. Enough to feed Zane, Ally, and Wyatt, who had come to check on Dee's progress and make sure Shannon had everything she needed. After her friends left, she stayed through the night, planning to go home sometime today to shower and change clothes.

Until Delaney's complaints upgraded from pain in her splinted leg to tightness in her chest.

Pulling back, she swiped a hand across her cheek. "They tried to dissolve the embolism with medication, but when she started coughing up blood, they decided to go in and remove it." Fresh tears fell. "I'm so scared."

"I know you are. Let's sit."

With his arm still around her, he walked her over to the chairs in the surgical floor waiting room and sat with her pulled close to his side.

"Where's Bry?" she asked.

"I didn't know how long I'd be here, so I dropped her off at home after her session with Gretchen. Mrs. B said she'd make sure she had dinner, and they both said to tell you they're praying."

"Thank you. I'm sorry to be taking up your evening. I know Ally or Harper would've come if I called. But Ally's getting married Saturday, and Harper needs to be home with the baby. They both already have enough on their plates."

Shannon had also phoned Camden but had to leave a message with his assistant. She'd just disconnected when Hunter called to check in. After she told him a clot had traveled to Dee's lungs, he said he'd be there as soon as he could.

"I'm glad you told me what was going on. I'm happy to be here for whatever you need." He gave her a squeeze, and it bolstered her to have someone else there.

No, not someone else. Hunter.

The thought should be disconcerting, if she didn't have so much on her mind already. For now, she simply wanted to lean into his strength and soak up that easy confidence he wore so well.

His fingers stroked her shoulder, the gentle pressure calming her humming nerves. "Are your parents coming?"

"I called but neither of them answered. It's the middle of the night in Paris. When I spoke with them Monday, Dee's status wasn't serious, other than her leg, so they decided to stay put. Still, I don't understand how they could turn off their phones when they have a daughter in the hospital."

But maybe now they'd come. After her dust-up with Cam Sunday night, Shannon had been the lone representative from her family keeping vigil. Unless Fiona, her parents' house manager, could be considered *family*. Their maternal grandparents had passed, her father's parents were in Ireland until the holidays, and aunts, uncles, and cousins on either side were distant at best. Mom and Dad hadn't been great at keeping their siblings close, unfortunately, as they'd built their fortune.

So, it was her CU family—and Hunter—sitting with her, praying with her, making sure she ate. When Zane and Ally showed up yesterday morning, Ally took her to the nurse's locker room where she was able to freshen up and change without having to leave the hospital. Later, Harper came by after her morning class with scones and a thermos of hot chocolate.

More folks had called or texted throughout the last two days—Yolanda and her husband Steve, Rhonda, Mason, all of her Fort Worth club leaders and several of the kids. Brylie called during her lunch hour, and so had her brother, who had also texted twice for updates before showing up last night with their pizza dinner. And now here he sat beside her once again.

The elevator dinged and a man stepped out. "That's Cam."

Hunter followed her line of sight. "Your brother?"

"Yes. I'll be right back." She met him in the hall before he reached the waiting room. "Camden. I'm glad you ca—"

"How bad is it?"

She pulled up in front of him, his furrowed brow, hands stuck on his hips, and pursed lips either evidence of concern or irritation. "Bad. The blood thinners didn't work, so they're having to do an embolectomy."

"How'd they let that happen? Weren't they monitoring her for blood clots? This could be a lawsuit in the making."

Her hopes deflated, and she shook her head. "Your concern for Delaney is touching."

"I *am* concerned for Delaney. I'm concerned that she gets the best care. And if they couldn't see she had clots forming, perhaps she should be transferred to a better facility."

"Maybe we should wait until she's actually out of surgery before we have her shipped somewhere else. You think?"

"Don't be a snot, Shannon. It doesn't become you."

She rubbed her forehead with her fingers before returning her gaze to him again. "Are you going to stay?"

"Can't. Business dinner with the Denton folks tonight. We have a two-hundred-million-dollar sale that's too close to cancel now."

"Right. A big sale. Got it."

"Text me with any updates. I can come later if needed."

"What about Mom and Dad? Do you think they'll come home now?"

His forehead creased even more, making him appear older than his years. "Why would they?"

"This is serious, Cam. And she's their *daughter*."

"And they're across the globe on a month-long trip they've been planning for over a year. They need this time away and shouldn't have to come back because of one of Delaney's self-imposed calamities. If things get bad, we'll let them know. No need for them to cancel their plans at this point."

Shannon let out a humorless chuckle. "Right. Because all families are as warm and fuzzy as ours. Go to your dinner, Cam. Enjoy. I'll be here for Delaney and let you know when she's out of surgery."

Turning, she walked to the chairs, where Hunter stood with a scowl on his face. Had he heard any of that? Heard her brother's indifference? Her reported snottiness? What must he think of them if he had?

He peered over her head as she approached. "He's not staying?"

"Business dinner." With a sigh, she crossed her arms over her middle and stared at the bank of windows on the opposite wall. "He's of the mind Delaney made her own mess, so she should have to live with the consequences. No one's ever accused Cam of being overly sensitive."

"Hmm."

When he didn't say anything more, Shannon looked up at him. "What? You don't agree, do you?"

"Uh … well …. this isn't really any of my business. But it seems to me it shouldn't matter whether he thinks she's wrong or right, he should be here for his sister. For both of you."

"Exactly. But like Dad, it's all about the company."

A nurse walked out of the OR and headed their direction.

"Ms. Trent?"

"Yes?" She straightened and dropped her arms as Hunter pulled her to his side.

"Delaney did very well. The clot was located and successfully removed. She'll be taken to the intensive care unit for monitoring and will remain on anti-coagulants for the next few days. It'll delay her release about a week, but she should recover completely if there are no other issues."

That was some good news, at least. As long as no other clots broke off from her leg injury to move up to her lungs. "When can I see her?"

"They're closing now, and she'll be taken upstairs. So, probably in another hour or so." The nurse focused on Hunter, still standing with his arm draped around Shannon. "Might be a good time to get your lady something to eat? I'm sure she'll be staying overnight again."

"Yes," he said before Shannon could correct her. "I'll make sure she eats something."

"Excellent. You can go on up to the ICU when you return."

The nurse left the way she'd come, and Hunter extended his hand toward the elevators. "Shall we, milady?"

She put her hand through the crook of his elbow and tilted her head at him. "Funny."

He shrugged. "Just following orders."

Yes, of course. No reason for her over-active imagination to wonder, even for a second, what it might be like to be Hunter's lady.

No reason at all.

CHAPTER TWENTY-SIX

"Thank you. I'll be right down."

After disconnecting with the firm's receptionist, Hunter took a deep breath and released it through pursed lips. He'd rather be in bed with the flu than here about to meet with the man he'd hoped to never lay eyes on again.

When he finally returned his stepfather's call on Monday, Mitch asked to meet right away. Thankfully, Hunter's busy schedule the past two days between work and time spent at the hospital with Shannon helped delay this dreaded reunion until today—Wednesday morning. That also gave him time to consult with an associate in the family law department. He wanted to know where he stood should Mitch make some kind of claim to Brylie.

The news hadn't been good, but not unexpected. Even though Mom had made him legal guardian should anything happen to her, the courts usually sided with a biological parent. That *this* particular parent had a history of alcohol abuse, a spotty work history, and abandoned the child in question could work in Hunter's favor, however. Especially considering he could provide for her better than Mitch ever had. But a lot would depend on what judge they might be assigned, should it come to that.

He would've talked to Shannon about it, but she had enough on her mind with Delaney's mess. She didn't need him piling his own on top of it.

With another heavy sigh, he braced his elbows on his desk, clasped his hands together, and rested his forehead against them with his eyes closed. *Hey, God. I know we're still getting acquainted and all that, but I'd sure be grateful if You could give me some peace about meeting with Mitch. Oh, and some of that wisdom You're so good at would be awesome too. I appreciate it.* "Amen."

He opened his eyes to see Julia standing in his doorway.

"Well, hang me up and call me a Picasso." She walked in wearing a big smile. "Was that Hunter Kavanaugh I just saw praying?"

He chuckled as he stood. "Yeah. God and I had a little meet and greet over the weekend. I've been meaning to tell you about that, but it's been kind of hectic around here."

She met him as he came around the desk and grabbed him in a hug. They may have started out early on as boss and employee, but somewhere along the way, their relationship had morphed into a close-knit friendship he treasured. "Oh, you have no idea how long I've been praying for you. No idea."

"Oh, maybe four years? Since the day you were foisted on me?"

"Okay, you do know. Well, anyway, I am so happy. Yes, please do tell me when you can. I want all the details." She leaned in. "Does this have anything to do with that adorable Shannon I'm still dying to meet?"

"How do you know she's adorable?"

"I could hear it in her voice. Is she not adorable? Is she hideous? Ugly as sin?"

"No. She's pretty adorable. And, yes, she's the one who helped me find my way. Right now, though, I have someone in the waiting room. But since you now know I'm a man who believes in the power of prayer, will you pray about this meeting, please? It's … my stepdad."

Her eyes rounded. "Oh, wow. You better believe I'll be praying. You think he's here about your sister?"

"He hasn't said. He may only be here to get the details about Mom. But I talked to Lee yesterday to get an idea of where I stand if it comes to anything."

"Good thinking. We're all in your corner. You know that."

"Thanks. That means the world."

Shrugging into his suit coat on the way out the door, he ordered his breathing. He had to admit he had his reasons for wanting to meet here. Since Brylie hadn't had a phone at the time her dad left, Mitch had no way of reaching her without going through Hunter. And he wasn't going to mention to Brylie her dad had been in touch until he confirmed Mitch's intentions.

And then there was the power. He'd been an attorney when he'd last seen Mitch, but Mitch had never been in his territory. He wanted Mitch to see him as the man he was, the man he'd made himself to be, without an iota of his stepfather's help. To see what he'd accomplished despite how difficult Mitch had made his life.

It might be pride, and God would probably have something to say about that. But he needed to deal with Mitch on his own turf. Because he'd lived on Mitch's and hadn't let it destroy him.

In the waiting room, he spotted his stepfather before the man saw him, and he stopped to take another breath. The last time he'd seen him, Mitch had been unkempt, cheeks sallow, eyes red, and skin splotched from his battle with the bottle. It was during that visit Hunter had once again begged his mother to leave her husband. But she said she couldn't, that she loved the man she'd married and thought she could help him find himself again.

Mitch moved them to Houston two weeks later and abandoned them a month after that.

The man standing at the window now stood tall, shoulders back, with a little more meat on his bones. Well-dressed with a good haircut. The hands at his sides didn't shake, and his dress pants fit well with a tucked-in dress shirt and sport coat, no tie. As if sensing Hunter's eyes on him, he turned.

Hunter approached but didn't offer his hand. "Mitch. We can speak in my office."

"Son. Good to see you."

"You can call me Hunter."

"Hunter. I'm sorry."

No more sorry than Hunter. At one time, they had indeed been father and son. Hunter was so proud to finally have someone he could call *Dad*, and whenever Mitch called him *Son*, he felt a completeness he never had before. But that had been short-lived.

As they passed through Julia's office, he let Mitch go in first through the inner door. Mitch took a seat in front of the desk while Hunter sat on the other.

The older man looked around. "Impressive, Son—Hunter. What kind of law do you specialize in?"

"Corporate law. Senior Associate. But I don't have time for catching up. What can I do for you?"

Mitch's face sobered. "I was devastated to hear about Sylvia. I didn't know until a couple of weeks ago, when I got out of rehab. I went to the house in Houston, and somebody else was living there."

"I'm surprised that old trailer was still standing. It was more rust than anything else."

Mitch's face reddened. "When were you there?"

"The day I moved them out of there. About a week after you left." He leaned forward with his hands on top of the desk. "If I'd known that's where you had them living, I'd have been there a lot sooner to get them out. I can't believe you thought that was suitable for your wife and little girl. And then you just *left* them there? What kind of man does that?"

Tears filled Mitch's eyes. "No kind of man. There was nothing left of me then. I'm not going to offer you any excuses because I have none. I chose to leave them there to live homeless under a bridge because I couldn't find my way out of a bottle."

"So, how are you not dead? Why are you here and Mom's—"

His words shocked even him, and he stood quickly to turn toward the window. He'd cried enough on Saturday, before God and his friends, laying out his grief and his pain and his sins, accepting the love and grace and peace so freely offered at the feet of Jesus.

But he would not cry here, in front of this man. This man he loathed with every fiber of his being.

He hung his head as shame engulfed him. Four nights ago, he'd accepted a love freely offered to him through the death of an innocent Man. And he couldn't offer an ounce of it to one broken by life?

Silence stretched between them.

"I'm sorry." He hated saying he was sorry. Had always considered it a weakness, preferring to own his actions and let the chips fall where they may. But maybe that had been more about his pride than true virtue.

He turned from the window. "That was uncalled for, and I apologize."

Mitch ran a handkerchief over his eyes and under his nose. "I deserve every bit of it. But there's nothing I can do about the past. I can't fix what I broke. I wanted to make amends. To Sylvia and Brylie. To you. But I couldn't find them. I thought maybe they'd moved to Mount Pleasant and tried to call Sylvie's mom. No listing for her either. Then I found her obit. I'm so sorry to hear about your gran, too, Hunt. You've lost too many people."

Taking his seat again, Hunter let out a sigh. "I'm just thankful Gran was gone before Mom died. That would've been very hard for her."

"How'd it happen? The accident?"

"Drunk driver broadsided her running a red light. Killed her instantly."

Mitch closed his eyes and let out a breath. "Oh, Sylvie. It should've been me."

Clutching the arms of his chair, Hunter pressed down the retort he wanted to shout. *Yes! It should've been you! It's not fair that I'm sitting this close to you, and I'll never see Mom again.*

Several seconds passed before Mitch opened his eyes and dabbed at them with his handkerchief again. "I can't imagine what you've been through."

"I miss her. Very much."

Mitch nodded. "I can't find Brylie. A neighbor of your gran's said she left with you?"

Hunter stared at him across the desk. "She's with me. Mom made me her legal guardian once the divorce was final."

Shock paled Mitch's face. "Divorce? Silvie divorced me?"

"In absentia. We hired an investigator to find you. Placed legal notices in newspapers. It was final a little over a year ago."

"And you have Brylie. Can I see her?"

"Why?"

"Because she's my daughter."

"Why weren't you concerned about that when you left her?"

"I told you. I was in a bad place then. I've come a long way in the past year-and-a-half. Found my way off the streets to a shelter sponsored by a church, started rehab, got a good job. My employer is a devout Christian who's a recovered alcoholic himself. Provides resources for recovering addicts to get into housing, start savings accounts, even reunite with their children."

"Reunite? Or take back?"

"In my book, they're one and the same."

Hunter's heart raced, his fingers and scalp tingled. "Certainly, you can see she's better off with me than she would be with you only, what? Months? Maybe a year into recovery?"

"I can't see anything yet." He waved his arm. "Except this impressive office I'm sure is the result of a lot of hours spent here. I work remotely, so I'm home. Every day." He glanced at Hunter's left hand. "I take it you aren't married, so no one to help you at home."

It took a concerted effort to control his tone. "I may not be married, but I have friends and an abundance of help. I'm home every evening, and Brylie and I spend a lot of time together."

"Listen, can we start with a visit? I'd really like to see her."

Hunter studied the man across from him. "Do you live here, in the Metroplex?"

"No. Still in Houston."

"So, you'd want to move her again? She's already been in two schools in less than three months."

"If need be, I could probably relocate up here so she could stay at her current school. And close to you. As I said, my job's remote. But my boss would want to make sure I could be held accountable."

"So, he doubts you, in other words."

"That's not what I said. Accountability is important for anybody in recovery."

"Hmm. So, where are you staying while you're here?"

"With one of his partners. Working while I'm here."

"Is this a telemarketing job or something?"

"No. We coordinate logistics for shipments of supplies to missions facilities all over the world. Medical supplies, school supplies, clothing, construction materials for buildings and infrastructure, even vehicles and animals. If they need it, we get it to them."

A job a judge might find credible. "How long are you here?"

"Open-ended. I'd like to spend some time with my daughter. Both of you, if possible."

"I need to think about it. We have a lot going on, and I don't want to upset her during the school week. I can talk to her about it this weekend. But I'm not going to force her to see you. It has to be her choice."

"She's thirteen. You can't leave it all up to her."

Hunter shook his head. "She's a very grown up fourteen and making good decisions for herself. I'll talk to her on Saturday and be in touch. That's all I can promise right now."

Because there was no way he would force his sister to see the man, regardless of the fact he was her father. The father who deserted her.

His stomach still churned every time he thought about that decrepit trailer Mitch had left them in. Very little food in the pantry, no gas in their twelve-year-old Buick, no money in the bank.

Hunter couldn't get there fast enough when Mom had finally accepted Mitch wasn't coming back and called for help. Help that was delayed, but, thankfully, not too late.

When he stood and walked around the desk, Mitch stepped in front of him. "Please. Hunter. Let's not make this ugly. I told you my boss has resources to help reunite us with our families. Some of those resources are lawyers. Maybe they don't have highfalutin' offices like this one, but I'm the biological parent. From what I hear, the weight of the law will probably rest heavily on my side, regardless of whatever document you have that your mother signed. Think about whether you want to put Brylie in the middle of that."

Mitch's cheap cologne wafted off him as Hunter stared him

down. Threats, veiled or not, only strengthened his resolve. He would not allow this man the satisfaction of having the upper hand.

After a long, silent moment, Mitch turned toward the door. "I'll see myself out."

CHAPTER TWENTY-SEVEN

"When was the last time you ate?"

Hunter waited for Shannon's answer on the other end of the silent line, but all he heard was rain splattering against her car.

"Yeah, that's what I thought. It's after nine o'clock, Shan. I'm not even going to ask about dinner, but did you at least eat lunch?"

"I think so?" She yawned. "I know I got something out of a vending machine at some point."

Figured. She fretted over Delaney but gave no thought to her own well-being. "Not good enough. I'll have a ham sandwich waiting for you when you walk in my door. With mustard."

"Oh, you don't have to do that." Her blinker tapped in the background and windshield wipers swished back and forth. "I'll eat something when I get home."

"Just press the number three when you get in the elevator. My door will be open."

"Really, Hun—"

He disconnected and walked over to the refrigerator to pull out what he'd need to make her a sandwich. She liked ham on wheat with lettuce, tomato, swiss cheese, and mustard. He hated mustard but started keeping it because whenever they made sandwiches here, she had to run up to her condo to grab a jar of Dijon.

Shaking his head, his hands worked automatically. He should've gone to the hospital to make sure she had something to eat. But this was the one night he could stay at the office late because Bry went home with Ellie after school, then to ConnectUP. The trial with Gail was coming up fast, and so much still needed to be done.

The junior partner had been beyond understanding of his situation, more so than Alden. Probably because she herself was the mother of two teenagers. So, when she asked if he could stay this evening, he couldn't skip out on her. When he'd called Shannon around 5:30, she assured him all was well at the hospital, and she'd finally be home to sleep in her own bed, since someone—a friend of the family, was all she said—was staying with Delaney to give her a break.

Guess that didn't include bringing dinner. And he'd had a feeling she would forget. The girl had a habit of taking care of everybody else while setting her own needs aside.

A key scraped in the deadbolt before the door opened and his sister walked in, her jacket slung through the straps of her backpack.

"Hey, Peanut."

"Hi, Big Nut."

"Leave the door unlocked, please. Shan's coming by."

"Oh, good. Missed her at club tonight." She dropped her backpack onto one barstool in front of the island and took a seat in the other. "I guess that's for her, since you're slathering mustard on it."

"Good guess."

"That must mean you didn't go by the hospital?"

"Got caught at work. That's why I asked Ellie's mom if she

wouldn't mind bringing you home. Super nice family. I think she would've agreed if we lived fifty miles away."

"They're the awesomest. So, you still haven't met Delaney?"

Oh, he'd met Delaney, all right. Twice now. Once in front of the building, the second the night she'd draped herself all over him, drunk and in the hopes he'd bring her home with him. Something he hadn't shared with her sister.

Twenty years old. Only one year out of her teens. It gave him the chills.

"Not officially, no. She was with Shannon the day we ran into each other by the fountain, but I didn't know they were sisters then." He hadn't known anything about either one of them then. Only that his new neighbor was awfully pretty, and he'd more than likely blown any shot at getting to know her better.

Brylie's eyes lit up with her laugh. "Oh, wow, she's going to be surprised when she does meet you and sees what good friends you and Shannon are now."

Unless Shannon forewarned her, she was certain to be very surprised.

"I assume you finished your homework?"

"Most of it. I still have a little reading to do. I'll say hi to Shannon, then leave you two *aloone*."

He threw her a look. "It's a sandwich. Not an engagement ring."

"Not ye-et."

"What kind of books have you been reading from that second-floor library?"

The door opened again, and Shannon walked in. "You hung up on me."

"Call dropped."

"Right."

He grinned at her. "Sandwich is waiting with chips on the side. Cocoa is heating on the stove."

"You do know how to charm a lady." She smiled as she and Brylie met halfway for a hug. "Hey, Brylie-girl. How was club tonight?"

Brylie threw her backpack on the floor so Shannon could take the barstool next to her. "Great, as always, but we missed you. Clay had us all gather in a big circle to pray for Delaney."

"That was nice."

"How is she today?"

"Better. Still a lot of pain but no more clots, thankfully. They hope to have her moved out of ICU and to a private room in the next couple of days. They want to start physical therapy on her leg, but they need to make sure her chest incision is healing and there are no more clots. So, hopefully by early next week."

Hunter busied himself with pouring hot chocolate into large mugs. Recalling the micro-mini skirt and low-cut blouse she'd worn that night at the bar, Delaney probably wouldn't take well to the scarring on her chest and leg she'd wear the rest of her life from her poor choice.

But as their brother had said, she needed to come to terms with the consequences of her actions. The price she'd pay might be the only thing that would keep her from repeating the same patterns of behavior.

"Now that you're both here, I have some news." Brylie's face lit up. "I got a solo in the Christmas show!"

Shannon grabbed her in a hug. "That's so great! Congrats."

"Yeah, Peanut. That's awesome."

"Not a whole song, but it's a whole verse. Super excited."

"The concert's already on my calendar." Hunter placed steaming cups of cocoa in front of the ladies and stood with his elbows planted on the opposite side of the island, sipping from his own. He studied the girl eating and nodding as his sister shared everything they'd talked about in their circle that night at CU.

Exhausted. That was the best word he could use to

describe her. Other than beautiful, as usual. Even without a speck of make-up, as she was now, Shannon was a natural beauty. Skin like cream, with eyes the color of the ocean he'd witnessed during a Caribbean vacation. Bright, clear, shimmering. Full lips usually adorned with nothing more than lip balm.

She'd pulled her waist-length, light-blonde hair into a haphazard ponytail halfway up the back of her head, as if it had started higher and slipped as the day dragged on. He loved that she felt comfortable being herself around him, with no embellishment necessary.

But the woman needed sleep. About two days' worth. Except she'd be at Dee's side again early tomorrow morning, poring over homework while Delaney slept.

"Mmm." She wiped her mouth with a napkin. "Best sandwich ever."

Her voice forced him to attention, and he straightened when he found those tired but still dazzling baby blues trained on him.

"Guess my culinary skills are improving."

Brylie chuckled. "Yeah. You're the Bobby Flay of sandwiches."

"Bobby who?"

Rolling her eyes as only a teenager can, she reached for her backpack and started for her room. "I'm going to finish up my reading for English. Get some sleep, Shan."

Shannon nodded. "Definitely my plan."

When Brylie closed her door, he took her place on the barstool she'd vacated. "She's right. You need to get some sleep."

"I do. But thank you for this. I honestly didn't realize how hungry I was. I didn't exactly skip lunch. I had a granola bar and energy drink to keep me awake to get my homework done while Delaney slept."

Exactly as he'd thought. "And dinner?"

"I missed dinner because I was talking with Dee's attorney."

He cocked his head. "Did Cam send one?"

She shook her head. "Dad arranged for Conrad Penson to handle her defense. He, Cam, and I met with Dad over video call."

Hunter about fell off his chair. "Conrad Penson. Most famous defense attorney in Dallas. Probably Texas."

She shrugged. "I don't know. I guess so."

"Shan. That's like sending Babe Ruth in to bat for a Little League team."

Her eyebrows rose and eyes brightened. "Then, that's good. Right?"

Good? Conrad Penson had defended, successfully, some of the highest profile defendants in the area. The kind that made national news. The oil baron suspected of having his fourth wife murdered. The tech billionaire accused of defrauding investors out of hundreds of millions of dollars.

"He believes he can get most of her charges dismissed. Cam settled with Dana to replace her car for well over what hers was worth if she agreed not to press vehicle theft charges. And Dad's people are meeting with the bistro owner Friday with plans to completely overhaul his restaurant. There'll be no lawsuits or charges stemming from either of those, so she's in the clear."

Hunter's head swam. What on earth was this family business? Okay, so he'd surmised her family was wealthy. But this went beyond wealthy. This was like Rockefeller wealthy. And he'd never heard of any Texas Trents with this much power.

Except her siblings' name was O'Connor.

A shiver ran up his spine. The name on all the paperwork he'd had to sign to take out a mortgage on his condo in this building was O'Connor. As in O'Connor Property Development, Inc. The largest and most powerful property development company in Texas. Or, more accurately, west of the Mississippi. Run by Harrison Channing O'Connor, a fixture on the Forbes List of Billionaires.

Dad's people are meeting with the bistro owner Friday with plans to completely overhaul his restaurant.

If Shannon was one of *those* O'Connors …

"There's no going around the DUI." She covered her mouth when she yawned. "But it'll probably be knocked down to a misdemeanor since nobody else was involved, no other injuries, and it was a first offense. Same with the underage drinking. And as part of a plea deal, if she'll disclose where she obtained her fake ID, that charge will be dropped altogether if an arrest is made against the party or parties disseminating fraudulent papers. So, she may get out of this with a fine and maybe some community service. Doubtful any jail time, which is a huge relief."

Nodding, Hunter tried to keep his anger in check. But what was it the Bible said about taming the tongue? "Huge relief. That Delaney can go right back to doing whatever she wants to do, with only a few scars to show for her little mistake."

Her eyes widened. "What?"

"First offense? Shannon, do you honestly believe this is the first time she's ever driven while under the influence? Of course it isn't. It's just the first time she's been caught. And she and everybody she passed is fortunate she ran into a closed restaurant instead of a car full of innocent people." His breath hitched. "Or a woman coming home from a late-night grocery run."

Brylie's bedroom door opened, her own eyes wide as she peered around the frame.

He stood and moved to stand between her and their friend, turning toward Shannon, who was now on her feet and staring at him with tears pooling in her rounded eyes, her jaw slack.

"Hunter, I'm sor—"

"No, I'm sorry. I shouldn't have said that. This is—it's too much. I've struggled with this all week." He looked over his shoulder at his sister. "It's okay, Bry."

She blinked. "Are you sure you're okay?"

"I'm sure. I'm sorry I raised my voice. Can you give us a minute? Please?"

Nodding, she went back into her room and closed the door.

He turned to Shannon. "I think maybe we're both too tired to talk about this right now. But please know I am sorry for what I said."

"I'm sorry you've been struggling with it, and I didn't know. But I can't be sorry my sister probably won't go to jail, Hunter. I can't bear to think of that."

"Better to serve a couple of months in county lockup now for a first offense than twenty-five to life hard time later if she kills someone as a repeat offender because she got off easy the first time."

Her head popped back, her expression stricken as if he'd backhanded her, before a lone tear made its way down her face. Hurting her tore him up. But how could she not see that her family using their power to make it all go away could very well be signing someone else's—perhaps even Delaney's— death certificate?

"Thank you for the sandwich." Her voice, quivering under the pain he'd caused, barely crossed the space between them. "Good night."

He said nothing as she pulled her jacket from the barstool and let herself out.

CHAPTER TWENTY-EIGHT

Shannon smiled when Zane took Ally in his arms at the pastor's blessing, sharing their first kiss as husband and wife. The guests in the chapel at their country wedding venue outside of Dallas erupted in applause as the couple walked up the aisle toward their new life together. Linking her arm through Keller's—Zane's former college roommate—Shannon took her place in the line of five bridesmaids and the groomsmen escorting them.

Scanning the guests, her gaze slid by a pair of blue-gray eyes before snapping back. Hunter held her focus until she'd passed their pew.

Keller leaned in. "Beautiful ceremony."

"Stunning." She resisted the urge to glance over her shoulder at the man who'd taken up a lot of space in her thoughts the past few days. "I'm so happy for them."

"Me too. Zane's a great guy, and he sure found himself an amazing girl. I've enjoyed getting to know Ally while I've been here this week."

"They're perfect together." They joined the others in a room off the foyer where they'd wait for the chapel to empty before photos.

"What about you? Anybody special in your life?"

Why a certain young lawyer came to mind, she didn't know. Hunter had never expressed an interest in her. Had always kept things firmly in the friend zone. And that was when things had been good between them.

Now … who knew if that was even the case anymore. Had they gone from neighbors to friends back to merely neighbors?

Keller chuckled. "From that expression, I take it there is, or you want there to be."

"Oh … uh, no. Actually, I'm not seeing anybody. What about you? Thinking of taking the plunge?"

He shrugged. "Could be. I've been dating someone from church the last few months, and she's pretty special. She couldn't get away this weekend to be here, though."

"I would've liked to meet her. I wish you all the best."

"And I for you. Whenever you find your someone."

Her someone. She'd always hoped there would be a someone. The *right* someone. But there were things she'd have to bring out into the light to have an honest relationship. Things she hadn't been willing to trust with anyone. So far.

After photographs, the wedding party entered the rustic barn to a festive country song, each couple two-stepping across the dance floor to the head table.

Laughing, Shannon took her seat between Keller and Harper. "I'm glad we practiced that last night. It's been a while since I've two-stepped."

Keller gave her a wink. "You did great. That was fun."

The bride and groom shared their first dance, then the wedding party followed them through the buffet line, filling their plates with fajitas and all the fixin's. From her place at the head table, Shannon scanned the rustic venue. Yards of ribbon and white lights hung from the beams, hundreds of flowers adorned tables dressed with cloths of pink, green, and white, and a wall of windows had been draped with white sheers left open to allow a view of the starlit sky.

Shannon couldn't help it when her eyes wandered to Hunter at a table with several ConnectUP leaders. With his attention focused elsewhere, she could linger for a moment. Matt, captain of the Grand Prairie club, asked Hunter a question, and his lips turned up in that charming way she'd only seen in her dreams the past few nights of fitful sleep. Goosebumps sprang up on her skin before she caught Brylie watching her from the next table full of CU kids. Hoping his sister hadn't noticed her staring, she smiled and waved.

She'd been glad when Ally told her she issued Hunter a late invitation, since they were now regulars among their friends. Because the truth was, she'd missed him the past few days following their ... what was it? Misunderstanding?

No, that wasn't it. They'd definitely understood each other. So, while not exactly an argument, it was most assuredly a disagreement. And one there was no going around.

When Best Man Steve stood and took the microphone, Shannon concentrated on his toast. She'd already missed all the wedding preparations this week, another failure on her part. So, she needed to be fully present tonight, especially considering last night she'd been pulled between the rehearsal, with dinner afterward, and a barrage of texts from Delaney, spending her first full evening alone and not liking it.

Thankfully, Fiona, a long-time member of her parents' household staff who had practically raised the three of them, insisted on keeping Delaney company this evening, as she had on Wednesday, leaving Shannon to enjoy the festivities.

After Ally's dance with her father and Zane's with his mother, the party picked up steam. At Keller's invitation, they joined several others from the wedding party on the floor. She needed this tonight. Time with her friends, celebrating Zane and Ally, laughing and dancing and not worrying about things she couldn't fix. Like her sister. Or Hunter's pain.

When a slower country ballad wafted through the speakers, a man walked up behind Keller.

"May I cut in?"

Her wedding escort stepped back and gestured toward her. "Sure."

"Thank you." Hunter's usual confident grin appeared a bit uncertain as his eyes met hers and he extended his hand. "Shall we?"

After a moment's hesitation, she placed her hand in his. "It would be my pleasure."

His eyes brightened as he brought his arm around her waist and held her hand to the side, her other slipping up to rest on his shoulder. "You look stunning tonight, Miss Shannon Trent. Pink is definitely your color."

"Thank you, Mr. Kavanaugh. Ally's favorite. Probably my second favorite, close behind yellow."

"Yes, you and your sunny yellow. Which suits you."

How she wished the easy banter they'd always shared didn't now feel so contrived, as if each were trying too hard to recapture what they'd had. Before.

Unable to maintain eye contact with all that still hovered between them, she let her gaze wander around the dance floor. She didn't like this outward politeness. Not with Hunter, who had grown into a very comfortable friend. They'd exchanged keys to each other's condos, she'd driven his car, they'd prepared meals together—even if they came semi-prepared already—watched movies together, shared cocoa and conversation into the late evenings.

He'd sat with his arm around her while Delaney had been in surgery. A gesture meant to comfort. Not romantic or possessive. An affection between friends.

But this was … awkward. Because their last moments together had been fraught with discord.

She looked back at him but landed her focus somewhere around his nose. "How are you?"

"I'm okay. The trial I'm working on is ramping up. Bry spent some time with me in the office today, but she brought her homework, headphones, and a book and didn't seem to mind when I told her there might be more weekends like this in the future."

"She's a trooper, and now that she's seen how hard you've worked to rearrange your life for her, she's willing to give a little too. You're a good team."

"Yeah." He swallowed hard, and his gaze drifted over her head, a deep furrow marring his brow.

"What is it?"

His attention returned to her, as if he'd been away for a second. "I had a meeting with Mitch this week."

Stopping in place, she put her hand to her chest. "Oh, my gravy. Hunter, I completely forgot. How did I—oh, I'm so sorry. I never even asked."

Others continued to move around them. "It's okay."

Unshed tears constricted her throat. "No. No, it isn't."

Taking her by the hand, he led her to an empty table in the corner and sat her down, then took the seat next to her. "Shannon. It's all right."

"No. I totally forgot about Mitch calling you last weekend. I'm the worst friend ever. First not helping Ally with any of her wedding preparations this week, then forgetting about Mitch. I never even asked you about it."

"You're not a terrible friend. I was here Thursday night to help, and they had a ton of people show up. So, I'm sure Ally would agree with me. And I didn't tell you about Mitch because you already had enough going on."

"You actually met with him? In person?"

"In my office. Wednesday."

Wednesday. The day everything unraveled between them. Had the stress of seeing his stepfather face-to-face combined with her news been too much? Had he been pushed too far?

"How did it go?"

Pausing, he shook his head.

"Oh, no." Her heart fell to her stomach. "He wants Brylie?"

"He does. But we're starting with a visit. Tomorrow after church. Lunch. Brylie's a little nervous."

"I'm sure she is."

"It's going to be an uphill fight if he takes me to court."

"Hunt, I'm so sorry. Really. And that I haven't been —"

"Shannon." He took her hand again. "It's okay. I'm only mentioning it now because Brylie might say something. So, I wanted you to be aware."

She nodded. "Okay. I'll be praying."

"That's all I ask." He studied her for a second as his fingers held hers in a tender grip. "How have you been the past few days?"

"I'm … good."

"Is Delaney making improvement?"

"A little. She's in a lot of pain. They're not sure yet if she'll regain full use of her leg."

He winced. "I'm sorry to hear that."

But was it enough for him? Or would it only appease him if her consequences included time behind bars?

His gaze raked the room before returning to her. "Listen. I'm not happy with the way we left things Wednesday night, and that's my fault, I know."

"But you haven't changed your mind."

He didn't answer, but he didn't have to. She could read it in the tight line of his mouth and the crease of his brow.

"I understand it, Hunter. I honestly do. And I'm truly sorry I didn't see past Delaney's issues to understand how it was affecting you. I hate that this is coming between us, but I don't know a way around it. You want her held accountable to a degree I can't bear to even contemplate. If God should see fit to punish her that way, He'll have to give me the strength to endure it, because right now, it takes me to my knees to think of Delaney in a place like that."

"It's not just the sentence, Shan. Can't you see that? Clearly, your family holds some significant power. And it's the way they're wielding it that has me wondering if Delaney will ever be held accountable for her actions. And it's only going to lead to more trouble down the road."

"You can't know that. Nobody can."

He released a sigh. "This isn't the time or place to get into this. Just know I'm praying for you. I care about you, and I've missed my friend the last few days. But you're right. I don't know a way around this. Just know I'm here for you if you need me. Always."

"Same. For you and Bry."

Except nothing seemed the same. How had this man come to hold such a large piece of her heart in so short a time? Her life? That she missed him as she would a friend of a dozen years?

As he stood, he leaned over and laid a kiss on her cheek before turning to walk away.

And all she wanted was to go after him, to close this distance before it could swallow what was left of them.

CHAPTER TWENTY-NINE

"Ou're totally quiet today."

Brylie's voice pulled Hunter from his thoughts as they made their way through Arlington traffic for her counseling appointment. "Sorry, Peanut. Just thinking."

"Work stuff? Or Dad stuff?" She dipped her head so he could see her out of the corner of his eye. "Or Shannon stuff?"

Chuckling, he shook his head. "All of it?"

"That's fair. I'll probably talk to Gretchen today about Dad. No offense, but I know you don't like him, so I don't want to dump all my stuff on you. It's just confusing in my head. And Sunday was ... weird."

He grimaced at the ugly truth of her statement. Guess he hadn't done an adequate job cloaking the waves of hostility coming off of him during their lunch on Sunday. Mitch sitting there, acting like he'd just returned from a long vacation instead of having abandoned his daughter in a roach-infested single-wide, had Hunter clenching his fists under the table.

"I'm working on it, Bry. God and I have had some long conversations about your dad. And you know I'm going to fight for you." Now stopped at a red light, he looked over at her. "Right?"

She studied him back. "Even though I get in the way of work and stuff?"

Reaching over the console, he grasped her small, thin hand. "You're my number one priority. But the reality of my life is I have to work. I'm sure all of your friends' dads have to work. I may not be your dad, but I provide for us, and my job is how I do it. But I've rearranged things as best I can to make sure I'm home as much as I can be."

"I know. And it's been great."

He let go of her hand when the light turned green. "Completely agree. I have to admit, this work-life balance stuff has some merit. Before you came to live with me, my life *was* my work. I wasn't concerned about balance."

He hadn't needed it. Or so he thought. His confidence came from work, his status came from work, his relationships came from work. But having Brylie made his life … full. Rich in a way his six-figure salary never had.

"Wait, so you really do like being home earlier and hanging with me? Even when I prattle on about my friends and school and stuff?"

"I love it, Bry. It's the highlight of my day, hearing about yours over dinner. About school and ConnectUP and all your friends."

And he had his own real friends now. Friends who cared about his life, who wanted to know how they could help or how they could pray. Friends to socialize with and friends he could count on. Who counted on him.

He enjoyed Sunday morning church, followed by lunch, laughing and talking over a meal with no alcohol or profanity or blustery, overblown stories imparted by young lawyers who'd had to deal with senior partners' lofty expectations all week. Holding hands around the table and praying, sharing news of their families or jobs or how ConnectUP had touched more kids' lives that week.

Her smile lit her face. "Cool. I like it too. It's what Mom and I would do, talk over dinner because Dad was never there. I think that's why Sunday was so strange. Not only have I not seen him in two years, but we hardly ever had dinner together."

Memories flooded his thoughts. Sitting at the table with Mom and Gran as a boy. Chattering on about his buddies and his sports and whatever mischief he'd happened to get into that day. Then Mom married Mitch, and the four of them would talk about their day over dinner.

Until Brylie joined them, sitting in her high chair between him and Mom. He'd loved this little girl from the day they came home from the hospital. Once she was on baby food, he fed her as often as Mom did, making faces at her to make her giggle.

Then Mitch became more and more scarce, rarely making it home for dinner with the family. Yet Mom never complained, never let on how much it hurt that her husband would rather drink with his buddies after work than come home to her and their kids. It had taken a lot of years for Hunter to appreciate how hard she'd worked to make life good for them, even when they had to pack up to move for another job Mitch would eventually lose.

Mom was gone from this earthly life, and it hurt in a deep place that always would. But she was forever with her heavenly Father. The same Father who had given him and Brylie a new family of friends right here on this rotating orb until they could be reunited.

All because of one tiny, blonde-haired, spunky lady with a heart full of love. Even for a grumpy attorney late for a meeting not watching where he was going. And a lonely teenage girl who'd just lost her life's compass.

His chest tightened. If only he could figure out how to

bridge the ever-widening gulf between him and the best friend he'd ever had.

Hunter's new Bible lay open on his lap as he sat across from Wyatt in his friend's office. Last week, Wyatt had offered to do discipleship with him during Brylie's sessions, and he was only too happy to learn from somebody he considered a spiritual giant.

"This one's been a whopper for me this week, for obvious reasons." He bent his head to read from Romans 12. *"Do not take revenge, my dear friends, but leave room for God's wrath, for it is written: 'It is mine to avenge; I will repay,' says the Lord. On the contrary: 'If your enemy is hungry, feed him; if he is thirsty, give him something to drink. In doing this, you will heap burning coals on his head.'"*

He looked back up at Wyatt. "I hope lightning doesn't strike me for saying this, but the only thing I like about that is the thought of Mitch with burning coals on his head."

Wyatt laughed out loud, to Hunter's relief. At least he hadn't offended his God-fearing friend. "Trust me. We've all been there. And I wish I could tell you there's an easy way through forgiveness. Unfortunately, that can be a painful road, but one well worth traveling."

"I don't know how to let him off the hook for everything he's done to us."

"Forgiveness doesn't mean you're giving that person a free pass. You're not saying what they did was right. You're telling them their debt to you is paid. As your debt has been paid by Christ.

"Many times, people will ask us to forgive them, and we have to decide if we're going to hold a grudge or let it go. Telling someone we forgive them can allow them to move forward, if they can forgive themselves, but it will also bring healing to *our*selves, to allow us to move forward."

Move forward. With Brylie living with Mitch? Hunter didn't know how he would handle that, but none of the scenarios in his mind included *forgiveness*.

"Other times," Wyatt continued, "we have to be willing to forgive someone who may never ask for it. They may not feel they've done anything wrong or may not even know they've done anything to hurt us. At that point, it's not about getting a confession out of them. It's about us. To move past whatever is keeping us from our own healing, which means you'll need to forgive Mitch to begin yours."

Wyatt should've just asked him to walk on thumbtacks barefoot, holding fifty-pound weights in both hands.

"If he takes me to court for Brylie, I don't know how I can sit across the aisle and forgive him for all the pain he's caused us. And is continuing to cause us."

"I understand. But the key may be to build a bridge between you and Mitch instead of a wall. Change your thinking. You're a lawyer, so you know if he's not your adversary, he's your ally. Come up with a solution, a game plan, one that works for all parties involved and makes Brylie the overall winner. And who knows? It may never get to court."

Make Mitch his ally. He'd never once considered that because from the second he heard Mitch's voice on the phone that afternoon, he'd been the enemy. But the one common denominator that tied them together was their love for Brylie.

Hunter had negotiated hundreds of settlement agreements worth millions of dollars. But if he could settle this one, it would be the biggest win of his life. And the most important one. Could he put aside his deeply rooted hatred for the man who'd caused his family so much pain to make him an *ally*? For himself? Probably not.

But for Brylie?

"I'll have to give that some thought."

"Good man. Now, at the risk of getting entirely too personal, my wife and I witnessed a little exchange between you and Shannon at the wedding on Saturday that appeared a bit … off. If I'm way out of bounds here, say the word, and we'll move on."

Hunter released a heavy sigh. "No, and, actually, I was hoping to talk to you about it."

Wyatt nodded. "I'm assuming by the timing it might have something to do with Delaney and your mother?"

Hunter chuckled. "Does your psychologist brain ever shut down?"

"Unfortunately, not often. And I can see how that situation might be hard for you."

"Yeah, but I was handling it okay at first. Really trying to be there for Shan." Pausing, he closed his Bible and set it on the table next to him. "She's never told me anything about her family, but I've picked up on some things. Like there's some kind of disconnect there."

He studied Wyatt's face for any hint he was on the right track, but his friend had his counselor mask firmly in place. "I've also deduced over the past week they're fairly influential."

Wyatt finally nodded. "You aren't wrong. I won't speak out of turn because all of that is Shannon's story to tell. I only know because, to become a leader at ConnectUP, we run a full background. She asked to meet with me beforehand and told me about her family. I know she's confided in Harper and Ally, but it's something she plays close to the vest."

"Understood. But that's where we've hit our speed bump, I guess you could call it. This family—and to be up front with you, I know who they are. They're determined to see Delaney isn't held accountable for her actions. So, yes, I was having a hard time with her decision to drink and drive. But to get off with a slap on the wrist? And Shannon's on board with that?" He shook his head. "We can't seem to get past that to get back to what we had."

"And what was that, exactly?"

Good question. What he'd had with Shannon was something he'd never experienced with a woman before. With *anyone* before. A friendship that blossomed practically overnight. With her, he could let down and be himself. Say what he wanted or not say anything at all. He could laugh. He could brood. He could think. He could joke.

It was comfortable. And it was torture. Being with this woman he could fall in love with if he let himself. Who deserved so much better than he could ever be for her.

"She's the best friend I've ever had in my life. I miss it. I miss *her*."

Missed their back-and-forth texts during the day. Sending gifs to make each other laugh. Seeing her at the end of the day, either over dinner or a late-evening cup of cocoa.

Dancing with her those precious few minutes Saturday night had been heaven on earth. He'd longed to wrap her close until there was no room for the awkwardness between them.

He gave his head a shake. "If I could only get past this … whatever this anger is inside of me whenever I think of Delaney getting off scot-free."

Leaning forward, Wyatt braced his elbows on his knees. "I'm going to say something, Hunter. And you may not like it. But I'm going to say it because I know you're man enough to take it and think about it and pray about it."

Hunter's gut clenched. "Yeah, no pressure there."

Wyatt grinned, but it quickly disappeared. "You're in the way."

"Pardon?"

"You're in the way. You need to let go and let the Lord work the way He sees fit. Because right now, the way you're feeling is feeding a root of bitterness that's growing into your soul. And that's getting in the way of the Spirit working in you. So, get out of the way, my friend. Because until you do, you won't stop feeling angry."

"And how do I do that? Specifically?"

Wyatt pointed to the book sitting on the table next to Hunter. "That's your first weapon. Use it. Every day. Memorize it. I'll give you some places to start. And prayer. You have to pray. Pray for Shannon. Pray for Delaney. I don't care how hard it is, you have to say her name and take her to the feet of Jesus. Every. Day."

"Yeah, Ally said the same thing, for me to pray for Delaney. And I have. Some. A little."

Precious little. Because every time he tried, the image of his mother would flash before him, lying in the morgue that awful night, her body broken, her beautiful face battered and nearly unrecognizable. Because a repeat offender who'd gotten off before got drunk … again … and got behind the wheel … again.

But this time, instead of only being pulled over and hit with some fines and a little community service, he smashed into the Toyota Camry Hunter bought for Mom when he moved them back to Mount Pleasant. No match against a Ford F-150 blowing through a red light at seventy miles an hour.

Is that what it would take for Delaney to understand the seriousness of her actions? When it was far too late?

He took a deep breath and let it out. "I've tried, anyway. Can't say I've been very successful."

"I get it, but keep at it. I think you'll find it gets easier each time. But here's the thing. You want Delaney to pay with, what? Jail time?"

"If that's what it would take to straighten her out."

"And I'm sure the thought of that is terrifying to Shannon."

"Which is why she's all for this high-priced attorney getting Delaney off."

"So, if the roles were reversed, and it was Brylie facing

time, would you not use everything at your disposal to help her escape a jail sentence? Then try to help her yourself to find her way?"

Hunter's heart slammed against his ribs. He'd stand between Brylie and a wall of fire if he needed to, using every resource he had.

Wyatt folded his hands in his lap. "That's what Shannon's doing. She's spending time with Delaney, showing her an abundance of love when 'most everybody else has abandoned her. Her own parents haven't come home from a *vacation* to be with their daughter in the hospital. Her brother's only been by a couple of times for a few minutes. Her housemates kicked her out, and most of her friends have written her off. And she's going to have to repeat all of her classes from this semester because she's not going to finish. The last thing Shannon wants is Delaney doing time, afraid it'll do more harm than good, because she's already lost everything."

Hunter's mind churned. "Shannon's told you all of this?"

"Harper's been by the hospital a few times to check on her, and she met Delaney. A very sad young lady. Described her as empty."

"Empty."

Heaviness, like a cinder block, settled in Hunter's chest. He hadn't pictured Delaney as empty, only the lovely girl with Shannon that first morning, dressed in hip, young clothing, her ponytail bobbing in blonde curls from high on her head.

Then that night at the club, when he'd had to take a second look to make sure she was the same girl. Hair down and hanging past her shoulders, red-painted lips, and bold, dark color on her eyes. Short skirt with sky-high heels showing off long legs. Very popular in the place, but then she was gorgeous and vivacious, if not a little tipsy.

No, he'd never considered the emotional cost of Delaney's actions on *Delaney*. Hadn't been satisfied knowing she more than likely wouldn't spend a day in jail for her choice.

Wyatt was right. He'd taken it upon himself to step where he didn't belong.

And he'd hurt someone who hadn't deserved it.

CHAPTER THIRTY

Shannon jerked awake at the knock on her door, her textbook falling off her chest onto the floor next to the sofa. What time was it? What *day* was it?

A quick glance at the clock on her way to the door told her it was 8:25. And still Friday night, since no sunlight bled through her closed blinds. So much for making up some of the homework she'd missed while at the hospital. The lack of sleep had clearly caught up with her.

At the door, she peered through the peephole, then pulled back with a hand to her midsection. *Hunter.* And here she was in her baggy gray sweats and puffy socks. Her I-won't-be-seeing-anybody-tonight, hang-out-at-home clothes.

They hadn't spent more than five minutes together following the wedding six days ago, and that at his door when she dropped Brylie off Wednesday night. He'd left her with a hug and what had appeared to be an earnest *I'm praying for you and your sister.*

She unlocked the deadbolt and opened the door. "Hey, there. What's up?"

"I bring chocolate." He held out a steaming red mug in one hand, a blue one held in the other. "With a drizzle of caramel."

Leaning toward him, she closed her eyes and inhaled, then stepped back and gestured with her arm. "You may enter, sir."

"Hope it's okay I stopped by without calling first." He turned to her after she closed the door. "I saw your car in the garage when I got home after dropping Brylie off. She said you weren't going to the CU girls' overnighter tonight, so I thought I'd take a chance."

"The overnighter rotates between leaders every month. I would normally go, but I needed the evening to get caught up on some things. And it's never a problem to drop by. Especially when you bring me hot cocoa with caramel." She ran her fingers through her snarled hair. "Sorry I'm such a mess. Guess I fell asleep."

He handed her the mug as she took her place again on the couch. "You're beautiful as ever."

"You had me at *chocolate*. No need to exaggerate."

Shaking his head, he took a seat next to her. "Not exaggerating."

Her first sip from the mug sent the warmth of chocolate tinted with the sweetness of caramel sliding down her throat. "This is beyond perfect."

"Guess I'm the Bobby Flay of hot chocolate."

"Guess you are." Tilting her head, she stared up at him. "Why are you here? Gifting me with hot cocoa when I've been the worst friend imaginable to you?"

His jaw dropped. "How do you figure?"

"I've been so caught up in all my own mess that I completely forgot about Mitch calling you. And all of this with Delaney being so difficult for you after what happened with your mother. I've never thought of myself as insensitive, but—"

"Stop." He sighed and placed his mug on a coaster. "You are the last person on this planet I would ever describe as insensitive. You shouldn't be worrying about what's going on with Mitch right now. And I would've never expected you to put the brakes on taking care of Delaney to take care of me because I couldn't separate my feelings about the man who killed my mother from your sister."

"I understand it, though. And I see your perspective that paying a harsh penalty now might keep her from a harsher one later."

She grabbed a coaster and placed her mug on the side table. "But, Hunt, I haven't changed my mind. I don't want Dee to go to jail. I would go crazy with her in there. I know we don't agree, and I don't know how we get past it. But I want to. I really do."

He reached for her hand, his eyes focused on where they joined for a long moment as a MercyMe CD played softly in the background and the aroma of warm chocolate floated in the air.

Finally, his gaze returned to hers. "You know how I'm certain God is real and my decision to follow Him was authentic?"

"How?"

"Because from the very day I felt the first inkling of the Spirit moving—that day standing in the Carpenters' backyard —I've been under attack. That was the day Mitch first called. We heard about Delaney's accident the next day. I met with Mitch that Wednesday and found out he wants Bry. Then the enemy got between you and me that night. He's doing everything he can to drive a wedge into this friendship. And I'm going to do my best not to let him use *me* to do that anymore."

Leaning in, she sandwiched his hand between both of hers. "But I've definitely played my part in that with being so focused on myself."

"On yourself? You've given up your entire life for nearly two weeks for your sister. I should've been here for *you* these last nine days instead of staying away. But I didn't know how to get past the things I said. Because, at the time, I meant them. And although I knew it hurt you, I didn't know how to change it. So, I figured it was better to keep my distance so I didn't say something else that would put that look on your face again. That leveled me, Shan. I didn't sleep at all."

"Yeah, I didn't get much sleep that night, either."

"And you were dead on your feet. I am so, so sorry. I wanted to take it back as soon as it left my mouth. Even if it was my opinion at the time, it was something I should've kept to myself."

"That's twice you've said *at the time*. What does that mean?"

"It means I've done a lot of soul-searching. And I've come to the conclusion it's not up to me to decide how God works in Delaney."

He moved his head from side to side. "Okay, so Wyatt kind of told me I needed to get out of the way. But he was absolutely right. I didn't realize that's what I was doing. That I was acting as judge, jury, and executioner, and I had no right. But what's worse is I realized every time I thought of Delaney, I saw Hugh Eddler."

"Who's Hugh Eddler?"

He swallowed hard. "The man who killed my mother."

Tears flooded her eyes. "Hunter," she said on a breath. Before she'd even thought about it, she leaned in and drew her arms around his neck. He wrapped his own around her waist, pulling her even closer. She offered all the comfort she could in her embrace, wanting him to know she understood his pain, that he could trust her with it, and she would help him carry it any way she could.

But when he pulled her in tighter, a longing she'd never experienced ignited inside her. As if she could climb farther into him and stay there and she would be safe and loved and never alone—

She pulled away and pressed back against the couch. Had he felt the same thing? That their connection had escalated to another level?

No, it had to be her fragile emotional state making her

more prone to inflated romantic ideas. This thing with Hunter had taken her by surprise. That's all it was. Their friendship happened quickly, and he and Brylie had worked their way so deeply into her heart, no wonder she felt a stronger bond to him than any other man in her life.

"How can I help you?" she asked, brushing her hand across her cheek.

"Help *me*? You've done enough for me. It's my turn to help *you*."

"But you have. Last week, when I first got the call about Delaney, you were great, even though you were struggling. Kept me together both times she was in surgery, fed me dinner three nights in a row."

"Then pushed you away instead of celebrating your good news."

"Forgiven. And please forgive me for not understanding right away how all of this was affecting you and for forgetting about Mitch calling you. I truly am sorry."

"Done. So, Miss Shannon Trent. Are we good? Do I have my friend back? Because I've really missed her."

"She's really missed you too. Yes. We're very, very good, Mr. Kavanaugh."

His grin almost tripled her pulse. She needed to get a grip. Or a good night's sleep.

"Now. At the risk of losing our newly reclaimed goodness, I need to ask. When were you going to tell me Harrison O'Connor is your father?"

CHAPTER THIRTY-ONE

"$\mathcal{I}$ had a feeling you'd put that together."

Shannon reached for her mug. If she was going to get into this with Hunter, she needed a chocolate fix.

"When I realized Delaney's last name was O'Connor, I wasn't sure what the story was, although it became obvious your family wasn't exactly middle class. I mean … *Conrad Penson?* I imagine there are only a few people he'd even pick up the phone for, much less represent their kid for a first-offense DUI.

"A quick internet search of Camden O'Connor told me he was VP of Development for O'Connor Property Development, Inc., son of CEO Harrison O'Connor, which would make you his daughter. Although, I can't figure out the Trent thing, unless it's your middle name."

Turning her attention to her cup, she ran her finger around the rim. The tomato soup she'd eaten earlier churned in her belly as her mind searched for the words to explain the horrid decisions she'd made as a younger version of herself.

She should've told him sooner but could never bring herself to ruin the time they spent together by going over history she preferred to leave well behind. It had been a dark time for her. A Shannon she'd left long in her past, and one she avoided dredging up.

Aside from a deep-dive, professional background check, it would be difficult for the average citizen to put it together. Delaney's social media accounts didn't use the name *O'Connor*, only her first and middle names. Shannon hadn't gone by her father's name since she was eighteen, and neither of them ever posted about their family or the business.

But she should've known Hunter would find Camden online.

He cleared his throat when the silence lingered. "From the first night I walked you up here, I wondered how you could afford this place while going to school and working part-time. But it's your dad's building, so I guess that tracks."

She grimaced. "I resisted for a long time. I've paid my own way the last few years, but with school, my internship last year that led to the part-time job I have now, then becoming captain of the Fort Worth club, it was getting harder to do that. My dad finally talked me into it, told me to take the condo until I started my career and had a steady paycheck, then I could either buy it or move out. Figured it was my pride keeping me from taking it, so I gave in."

"Sounds like a wise decision."

"I think so. I haven't had to worry about finances as much." Although, in reality, her trust still sat there untouched, and would remain so unless some disaster she couldn't pull herself out of by her own grit and determination came along. She prayed that day would never happen, and the money could be used for something important. Something outside of herself.

"You changed your name at some point?"

"You could say that." After another sip from her mug, she set it down and settled into the cushion with her arms crossed over her stomach. "I wasn't raised in a Christian home, and the business was always the center of my father's world. We kids were well aware of where we stood in the order of priorities.

"And Mom ... well, while Dad is all about the work, Mom is all about the status—wearing the right clothes, being seen with the right people. Her children had to go to the right schools, do all the right things, blah, blah, blah. Camden and Delaney fell in line with all of that. Me, not so much. I was the wild child. The one who wouldn't play along."

His eyes widened. "You're kidding me. Not Delaney?"

"Nope. We've definitely changed roles in that regard. But, like Delaney, I had to learn the hard way. Thankfully, though, I don't have any felonies to show for it." Maybe nothing criminal, but something no less life-altering. With ramifications that would remain forever.

At the other end of the sofa, Hunter kicked off his tennis shoes and settled in with his legs stretched out, crossed at the ankles on the coffee table. She loved the buttery softness of his leather couch, but her overstuffed, cream-colored fabric sofa was like sitting on a giant cotton ball, inviting its guests to snuggle into it for a long stay.

And this could definitely qualify, if he truly wanted to hear this story of who she used to be.

"I was a senior at a hoity-toity private school in Dallas, and I met this college guy at a concert I wasn't even supposed to be at. Nick Trent. We exchanged numbers, started dating. My parents took an instant dislike to him—which, of course, upped him in my estimation—and we eloped the day after I graduated."

If she could somehow come up with any semblance of humor, she'd laugh at the dropped-jaw expression of disbelief on his face.

He gave his head a slow shake. "If you hadn't told me, I'd never believe we're actually talking about *you*. It's like a completely different person."

"Thank the Lord. He's made me completely new."

"I'll say. And, obviously, the marriage didn't stick."

"Because he didn't marry me. He married my money. And when Dad cut me off, Nick was history. Forty-two days after the *I do's*, I came home from shopping with some friends to an empty condo. All the furniture—that I'd paid for—all the kitchen stuff—that I'd paid for—and all the money from our account—over a hundred thousand dollars—was gone. All the food, even my dog. Only my clothes were still in the closet.

"I was absolutely devastated. Actually stayed in that empty apartment for a week, sleeping on the floor, hoping he'd come back. Pathetic. By then, though, I wanted my dog back more than I wanted Nick."

His brow crinkled as his eyes searched hers. "And you kept his name?"

She shrugged, understanding his confusion at why she would keep a name she'd worn less than two months. "What difference did it make? I hated being an O'Connor. Hated the wealth and all it meant. Trent at least made me an authentic nobody, which I preferred over being a somebody only because I was born an O'Connor."

His countenance softened. "You're hardly a nobody. You're special to a lot of people for all the right reasons."

"Thank you for that. I know now my value is measured in the eyes of God, not by my lineage or social status. But back then? I was aimless. Had no purpose. I'd chosen Nick over going to college. I'd never worked a day in my life, had no skills, and I was too stubborn and angry to go home.

"I tried a few different jobs and was wretched at every one of them. Couch-surfed for a while until my so-called friends realized I had nothing to offer them. Funny how the people I thought were true friends were only true as long as I was like them. Once they realized I didn't have the backing of my family, or their money, they turned on me faster than a revolving door."

"Sad."

If only that was the worst of it. But what would he think if he knew all of it? What she'd compromised to survive. What she'd been forced to surrender to come home.

"I finally had to go back to my parents' because there was nowhere else to go. But I was broken. All of that fire inside of me had died. I had to make a deal with my father before he'd let me come home, but I agreed to his demands as long as I could keep the name *Trent*. Not because of any loyalty to Nick, but because of the anonymity it gave me."

She uncrossed her arms, throat constricting as she stared down at her hands in her lap. "I was going to end it."

Silence stretched for a long moment as he studied her with narrowed eyes. "End ... what?"

"I raided Mom's bathroom and found a bottle of Valium. Wrote all the notes I needed to, planned to do it that night. But before I did, I wanted to go walk in my favorite park one last time."

Tears welled along his lashes, but his focus never wavered.

A cold chill ran along her skin with the memory of the utter desolation she'd carried with her into that park. "I sat on a bench by the lake, watching the sun go down, and this old woman came and sat beside me. She smiled at me, then we watched the sunset together. *'Isn't God good?'* she asked me. *'To give us this beautiful show for free every single day? Isn't He so good?'"*

She swallowed against the emotion that threatened to choke her. "I'd never heard anybody talk about God like that. The private school I went to wasn't a Christian school, and we never went to church. I asked her what it was about God she thought was so good. Her eyes, they lit up as she talked, and we sat there until well after the sun went down.

"I walked her to her house, her arm through mine like we were old friends. Then I went home, put the pills away, tore up the notes I wrote, went back to the park at sunset the next day, and the next, and the next, and listened to this old woman talk about God.

A deep breath in helped her keep her composure. This story still hit that raw place deep inside. "Until one day I told her my story, that I wanted to know her God. I wanted to be made new and have the hope she had. I went to her church, was saved, baptized. I spent a lot of time with her ... Miss Nadine ... at her home, at her church, until she passed two years ago."

She grabbed a tissue from the box on the side table and swept it under her nose. "She saved my life that day, just sitting down on a bench next to a lonely, lost nineteen-year-old girl. And talking about God like the friend He was to her. I think that's why when I saw Brylie, I prayed for an opening to speak with her, because she looked so alone."

Hunter released a breath. "Wow. That's ... incredible. And look at the legacy she left behind through you, the people whose lives you've touched. Lives you've changed. Like Brylie. And me. We probably wouldn't be getting baptized this Sunday if not for you."

He sat up and leaned in to reach for her hand. And despite the sleeve of her sweatshirt, gooseflesh crawled up her arm when he clasped her fingers in his. "I'm so thankful God brought you into our lives. That Miss Nadine found you that day."

Nodding, she swallowed hard, but that lump in her throat remained. "Me too."

Their eyes held as his thumb stroked the tops of her fingers. She'd never had this with another man. Not this fast, not this strong.

She pulled her hand away and averted her eyes to reach for their mugs. "Let me heat these up in the microwave."

In the kitchen, she put the half-full cups in to heat and stood with her arms crossed and head bowed. It had been easier to push down her feelings for Hunter when he didn't share her faith. Now that he talked so freely about God, it was harder to keep her heart in check.

But there was something he still didn't know. About her. Her past. A choice she'd made from which she still carried scars.

A choice she could never expect him to understand.

CHAPTER THIRTY-TWO

Hunter pulled the car to a stop in front of an attractive brick home and peered out at the well-lit porch. "This is different."

And unexpected. This upper-middle-class neighborhood was a far cry from the other two they'd visited this night prior to Thanksgiving. The annual ConnectUP holiday meal delivery night, when leaders and parents carted club kids around to various homes to deliver meals to families who might otherwise go without.

He pressed the button below the steering wheel to pop the trunk as Brylie, Ellie, and Samantha climbed out of the back seat. "What's the story here?"

Shannon unbuckled her seatbelt. "This is Zach Brant's house. Sophomore at Bry's school. His mother passed last Friday from cancer."

His chest clenched. "Last Friday? Is that the funeral you went to yesterday?"

"It is. And they're the most amazing family. Zach's the oldest and has two younger sisters, one in junior high, the other in fifth grade. There's still some out-of-town family here, but they shouldn't have to be burdened with making a Thanksgiving meal."

"Agreed." He peered at the side mirror at the girls standing behind the car unloading the trunk. He'd have to keep an eye on Brylie to see how she handled this visit. Stick close if she needed him to.

Silence lingered for a moment before Shannon reached over to touch his hand. "If you're concerned about Brylie, you should know she specifically asked if we could have the route that included Zach's family."

With a chuckle, he shook his head. She could read him too well. With her insight and empathy, she was going to make an excellent counselor. "How do you always seem to know what I'm thinking?"

Her smile grabbed his heart. "I just knew you'd be concerned when you realized what the story was here. But when she found out Zach had two younger sisters, she wanted to make sure she saw them in case she had the opportunity to let them know she understood their loss."

"That's really something."

Mom hadn't had it easy with Mitch, yet she'd raised a spectacular daughter. Although she herself hadn't had much to speak of, she would often seek ways to help others in need. It appeared to have rubbed off on Brylie.

They joined the girls at the back, where he picked up a large wrapped, cooked turkey out of the trunk and shut it after everybody had their bags. This would be their last delivery of the evening, but no less deserved, no matter how immaculate the lawn or attractive the curb appeal.

Shannon walked alongside him. "When we told Zach we were going to bring a meal to his family, he insisted on helping with the other deliveries tonight."

"You're kidding. With his mom passing only last week?"

"That's the kind of kid he is."

"Wow."

After being welcomed into the home by a gray-haired gentleman, Hunter placed the turkey on the kitchen counter. When he turned, an older woman with red-rimmed eyes enveloped him in a hug.

"What a blessing this is," she said. "Zach has told us so much about this group he's with here, but we had no idea how truly special it is. Thank you so much."

"It's an honor. And you have our sincerest condolences for your loss."

"A mother should never outlive her child, but knowing my daughter's with her Lord is the only thing that makes it bearable."

A tragedy all the way around. A daughter leaving this earth ahead of her parents, a mother leaving three young children behind.

Now, as a believer himself, he understood the comfort the woman grasped at knowing her daughter was in glory. It gave him untold peace knowing Mom was with the Lord, and he'd be there with her someday.

When the woman moved over to help the girls empty their bags, Hunter let his gaze roam the kitchen and adjoining family room. Spotting a man watching from beside the fireplace with desolation written across his features, he walked over and held out his hand.

"Mr. Brant?"

"Tim," he answered, taking it in a firm shake.

"Tim. I'm Hunter. Shannon told me about your son. Said he's a stand-up young man. It says a lot that he's out right now delivering meals to other families."

The widowed father cleared his throat. "He's a good boy. And we appreciate this. Especially knowing there are probably other families more in need."

"Need comes in different forms. It's absolutely our pleasure to do this for you."

"We're grateful."

Hunter scanned the well-furnished, cozy home, with the smiling faces of a happy family captured for eternity in frames hung on the walls. "What is it you do, if I may ask?"

"I'm an attorney."

"Really? Where do you practice?"

"I'm in private practice here in Fort Worth. Opened up on my own about six years ago with one assistant and now have one associate and a support staff of five."

"Is that right? I'm at Williamson, Sheffield, and Moore. A little over four years now, since I graduated law school."

"Impressive. I started out on one of those hamster wheels myself. The Skylar firm downtown."

"I know it well."

Tim chuckled. "I'm sure you do, probably as opposing counsel. I worked there for several years, before I realized how much of my kids' lives I was missing. Decided to get my priorities straight and open my own practice. I'm thankful now the Lord put that on my heart when He did. I was able to be with my wife through everything this past year. And my kids. Would've been impossible if I'd stayed at the firm."

Hunter nodded, his thoughts swirling. Hamster wheel. Running like mad but getting nowhere. Is that what he was doing?

No, he had dreams. He worked a lot, no question, but he'd been promoted twice already, was the youngest senior associate by a couple of years, and was on his way to a partnership. He'd been commended and rewarded handsomely along this journey, so it wasn't all for naught. It couldn't be.

Tim studied him. "What division are you in at WSM?"

Hunter refocused on the man while the girls sat huddled on the sofa leafing through a book of photos with Zach's sisters, and Shannon visited with the other ladies in the kitchen. "Corporate."

"Setting up, mergers, acquisitions, torts?"

"All of that, yeah."

Tim pulled out his wallet. "Here." He handed Hunter a business card. "If you ever find yourself wanting to take your foot off the gas a little, give me a call. I'm looking to bring in a partner in the next few months. The Lord's blessed me with a good amount of work, so I need more hands. Like I said, I'm not interested in overtime anymore." He swallowed. "Especially now."

Hunter stared at the card for a moment, then back up at Tim as he slipped it into his pocket. "Okay. I appreciate it."

What was that pressure in his chest? He put his hand to his sternum, shifted his weight from one foot to the other, but the sensation wouldn't ease. As if prodding him to—

"Would you let me pray with you real quick?" The sudden request surprised him more than the man he'd just met. But calm replaced the disquiet of a moment before.

"I'd like that. Please."

Clearing his throat, he put his hand on Tim's shoulder and bowed his head. "Father, I pray for my friend here, and his family, that You'll bring them peace this holiday season and the comfort they need during this time of loss. A loss You know I understand. Bless them and keep them in the shadow of Your wings. Amen."

He gave the grieving father a squeeze on the shoulder. "Enjoy your day with your kids tomorrow, and know you have many people praying for you."

"You said you understand my loss?"

"I lost my mother suddenly in late September."

"And you're here doing this for us? Thank you, man. Thank you."

"It's my privilege."

Shannon and the three girls waited outside when he exited the front door. The teens walked ahead of them to his car, but Shannon took his arm in both of her hands, walking by his side.

"Hunter," she said quietly. "That was amazing, what you did back there."

"I don't even know where that came from."

They stopped at the sidewalk as the girls piled into the vehicle. "It was the Spirit prompting you. And you listened. That's all He asks us to do. Listen and act. And you did. That man is changed tonight because of it."

"It's because of all of this. This is an amazing ministry y'all have here. I'm glad you told me about it, even if I wasn't so crazy about it at the time."

"You were a different person then."

"You guys on a date?" came the chorus of three voices from the back seat, followed by an eruption of laughter.

Shannon grinned and rolled her eyes.

He held the door open for her and peered inside at the girls. "If we were, we sure wouldn't have brought you three hooligans along."

Giggles filled the car, and when he looked at Shannon, she wore the most endearing blush he'd ever seen.

Later, with two girls dropped off at home and Brylie hunkered down with a novel in her new bed, Hunter regarded Shannon seated on his couch, staring into the gas fireplace and sipping her favorite hot beverage.

Even after a morning of classes, an afternoon spent at the office, and an evening of Thanksgiving meal deliveries, she was stunning. Her cheeks still pink from the chill, her blonde locks in a charming disarray cascading over her shoulders.

Before he could pull his eyes from her, she turned and caught him staring. "What?"

"Nothing. Um … so, what are your plans for tomorrow? Since your folks are still out of town?" Clumsy save, but he couldn't come right out and tell her he was pretty sure he was falling for her. She'd probably flee the premises and block his number on her phone.

"Cam's going to some big wingding at one of the company

vice president's homes, and Fiona's going to her sister's for the day. She's dropping Dee over here in the morning—since Dee can't get into my Mini—and come get her tomorrow night on her way back to the estate."

"Is Dee doing okay at your parents' house?"

She hitched a shoulder. "She doesn't really have much of a choice, but Fiona's taking very good care of her. She was our nanny growing up, then became the house manager once we no longer needed one. I was going to bring Delaney to my place when she was released on Monday, but Fiona insisted she could cover her better at the house and drive her to PT three times a week."

She stared down into her cup with a pensive crease in her forehead.

"What is it?"

She shook her head before looking over at him. "I think she was afraid if left alone, Dee might … do something. She's been so despondent. Mom and Dad have called a few times but didn't come home. Cam's more concerned about the family name than our little sister. And her friends … there are only a couple who've been in touch. When this happened, they scattered."

"Revolving door friends?"

"Exactly. Dee was always so full of life, but … she's like a shell of who she used to be."

Empty. Wasn't that the word Wyatt said his wife used to describe Delaney? "I'm so sorry, Shan."

She gave her head a quick shake. "Both Harper and Ally invited us to spend the day with them and their families tomorrow, but Delaney said she didn't want to spend an entire day with my *'judgy church friends.'* As if they're anything like that."

"They certainly treated me like a friend from the get-go. I never once felt they judged me."

"That's just who they are. I didn't want to force the issue, so she and I will have a sister day of sappy Christmas movies and eat Thanksgiving pizza. But Harper said y'all are going to their place tomorrow?"

"That was the plan. Then Mitch called. Wanted to spend the holiday with us. I called Wyatt to give him our regrets, but he insisted we bring him. Said his dad would be great company for Mitch. Could be interesting."

"No, he's absolutely right. Mr. McCowan is a hoot, and their family Thanksgiving dinners are a blast. I spent last year over there because Mom, Dad, Cam, and Delaney were on a cruise. I couldn't go because of school—Delaney had the week off—but it was probably my favorite Thanksgiving to date. Mitch should feel very welcome. And they have zero alcohol."

"Good to know. I wasn't sure about spending the entire day with him."

"How are things going?"

Shrugging, he released a sigh. "I'm trying to keep the past in the past and get to know the man he is now. But it's hard. There's so much damage there he left behind. But I get what Wyatt said. If I make him my adversary, it could get ugly, and Brylie could end up being the one hurt. I can't imagine her life if she should have to go live with him."

A shudder wracked her body. "That would keep me awake at night."

"It does. Trust me. But when those thoughts take over, I take out my Bible, go over the verses Wyatt gave me, and pray like crazy. I'm working on a settlement agreement I hope Mitch will go for, but I need the right timing to present it to him. He hasn't said anything yet about filing for custody, so I'm not going to rock the boat."

"Good thinking." She checked her watch. "I should go. It's been a long day. But thank you so much for helping us organize everything last night and going with us tonight. I know you usually work late on Wednesdays, but you were a huge help."

"I enjoyed it. Let me know if there are future events I might be able to help with."

Her eyes lit up with her smile. "That would be great. You'd be welcome."

"Count me in."

They stared at each other for a beat before she gathered her jacket from the back of the sofa. "Better go. Enjoy your day tomorrow."

"Yeah, you too." He followed her to the door, opened it, and stood with his arm braced above her head. "Oh, and hey."

"Hmm?" She turned and trained those azure eyes on him, and for a moment, he toyed with the idea of kissing her.

"Umm …" Yeah, not a good idea. He really didn't want her to block his number. "Oh, I'm taking Brylie to Holiday at the Arboretum on Saturday and thought you might want to come along. We went a couple of years ago, and it's pretty fantastic."

"I'd love to. I haven't been in a few years, so it sounds like fun."

"Great. I'll catch up with you sometime tomorrow to see how everything went with Delaney. And be sure to let me know if you need anything."

"I appreciate that. I hope all goes well with Mitch, and I'll be by Friday morning to pick up Bry for Black Friday shopping."

"It was nice of you to ask her along with you and your friends. And while you ladies are doing your thing, I'll be at the Carpenters' watching football with the guys."

"Have fun."

Once she'd disappeared into the stairwell with a wave over her shoulder, he locked up and returned to the couch, collapsing onto it to stare at the ceiling.

This was bad. Really, really bad. He couldn't remember ever feeling this way. And it was driving him crazy.

Because, although his heart urged him to go for it, his head didn't know if he could be enough for her. A man like Wyatt or Zane, giants in the faith, working in ministry, and bringing others like him into a relationship with the Lord—husbands who were strong spiritual leaders …

Shannon deserved no less.

CHAPTER THIRTY-THREE

"I think I'm done with cheesy Christmas movies for the day." Delaney, spread out on the sofa with her legs under a fluffy blanket, stretched her arms over her head before letting them fall again. "Maybe the year."

"Already?" Shannon leaned forward to grab the remote from the coffee table and muted the television. "You used to love these movies."

"Yeah, well, times have changed, haven't they?"

Shannon's heart sank. Five o'clock on Thanksgiving Day, and all they had to show for it was three movies watched, half a frozen pizza consumed with two sodas, and a bag of microwave popcorn. Rain had drizzled outside off and on throughout the day, doing nothing for Delaney's disposition, no matter how hard Shannon tried to cheer her up.

When a knock sounded at the door, Delaney glared over her shoulder. "I thought you said you weren't expecting anybody."

"I'm not." Shannon stood and let her throw blanket fall to the floor. "Could be Mrs. B. She's super sweet, and it wouldn't surprise me if she isn't bringing us a pie or something."

She peeked through the peephole, her spirits lifting as she

unlocked and opened the door. "Ally! Zane! What are you doing here?"

Zane grinned at her, holding a slow cooker while his wife carried a plate covered in aluminum foil with a bag hanging from her arm.

Ally walked in ahead of her husband. "We come bearing Thanksgiving leftovers. Figured you probably weren't cooking."

"You figured right." She closed the door and turned. "This is my sister, Delaney. Dee, these are my good friends, Ally and Zane Carpenter."

Delaney lifted her hand in a wave. "I'd get up, but …"

Zane laughed. "Not a problem. Let us serve you. Just tell us what you like."

"What do you have?"

Ally made her way to the kitchen she knew as well as Shannon did, since she'd been there so often. That explained how they'd surprised them, because they were registered with the concierge. "Turkey, cornbread dressing, mashed potatoes and gravy, green bean casserole, of course, and rolls."

At the island, Zane plugged in the slow cooker. "And apple cider."

Dee's eyes lit up for the briefest of moments, and Shannon held onto it like a drowning man to a life preserver.

"I'll start with some apple cider, please. It smells amazing."

"Comin' right up."

"Shan, help me move to your chair so your friends can sit. I can put my leg on the ottoman."

Shannon walked over to the couch and put her arms out like the therapist at the hospital had shown her so Delaney could pull herself up to a stand, which took some doing considering her baby sister towered over her once on her feet. She handed her the crutches Delaney despised—because, honestly, who didn't?—then helped her down into the chair. "Comfy?"

"Dandy."

Zane walked over with a cup and saucer and set it on the table beside the chair. "Here you go. Ally's warming up the food, then it'll be good to go. Mind if we stay for a bit?"

Shannon wanted to grab him in a bear hug but refrained. It lifted her soul to see them, and that they'd been so thoughtful had her on the verge of tears. "Please do. If you don't have company still at home, that is."

"Mom and Aunt Gina already left, and Ally's Dad and Nora are relaxing before they head home to Guatemala tomorrow. Since Michael and Paige were here for the wedding a couple of weeks ago, they're with her parents for the holiday."

Delaney cocked her head. "Whose wedding?"

"Ours."

Dee turned to Shannon. "This was the one you were in?"

Shannon nodded, and Delaney looked back at Zane. "Congrats, best wishes, and all that."

"Thanks, and all that."

She returned his grin, the first smile Shannon had seen all day.

Another knock sounded at the door.

"This place is a regular Grand Central Station all of a sudden," Delaney muttered.

After peeking through the peephole again, Shannon stepped back. "Oh, my gravy. You guys are not going to believe this."

She opened the door to a rousing chorus of "Happy Thanksgiving!"

"Hey, y'all! Come in."

She held the door for Wyatt, who gripped a baby carrier in one hand with a salad bowl clutched to his other side, and Harper, carrying a large platter of what looked to be both turkey and ham. She received a side hug from Brylie, because she had Gracie on her hip, followed by Wyatt's brother Reed and sister-in-law Jenny, each carrying a casserole dish. Rhonda, whose baby bump was growing by the day, preceded her husband Mason, both carrying even more bags. Last came Hunter, bearing two pies.

Leaning in, he kissed her cheek. "Happy Thanksgiving, Shannon."

"Happy Thanksgiving," she answered as she shut the door. "I can't believe y'all did this."

"We were sitting around watching football, and Harper and Jenny started talking about bringing the leftovers over here. We guys wanted to come, so Reed and Jenny left their kids at the house with their grandparents, and here we are."

The television sprang to life, and the white noise of thousands of screaming fans filled the room while the announcers compared the quarterbacks' stats thus far in the game.

"And Mitch?"

"Seemed to have a good time. He left around four to join his co-worker and his family for the evening."

"I'm glad it went well." She scanned her suddenly bustling abode from where she stood by the door and found Zane introducing a wide-eyed Delaney to everybody while the ladies made their way around the kitchen, setting out paper plates, plastic utensils, and cups. And enough food to feed an army.

Rhonda walked over to them and reached for the pies Hunter still held. "I see you didn't quite make it to the kitchen before you got distracted."

His eyes widened as she took them. "Oh, uh, sorry about that."

"No harm. You two talk."

Rhonda left with a wink at Shannon, and her face heated. A glance at Hunter reminded her she stood there in baggy yellow sweats, without a speck of makeup, and her hair stuck up in a messy bun.

She gave her bun a nudge with her hand. "I clearly am not company-ready."

"You're adorable."

"Liar."

"Am not. I'm a man of God now. I have to speak the truth." He shrugged. "Not that I was a liar before, but there's the whole accountability thing now I didn't have before."

"You mean the Holy Spirit."

"Exactly."

She giggled. "Well, you're very kind." Her gaze roamed around her living area and kitchen again. The guys were either on the sofa in front of the game or at the table, while the ladies gathered in the kitchen or sat at the breakfast bar, laughing and talking. "At least these people are my family and don't care if I'm in my ratty sweats."

"They're all pretty great." He leaned in. "Is Delaney looking over here?"

"Uh …" She peeked around him. "No. She's watching the baby."

He slowly turned his head to peer over his shoulder. Brylie sat on the arm of the chair, with Gracie on her lap facing Delaney, the two girls playing with the red-haired cutie. After a moment, he turned back to Shannon.

"She hardly looks much older than Bry. Not how I remember her. How I was picturing her. When I was being so hard on her, hard on you —"

"Hunter." She put her hand on his arm. "It's okay."

"No. It's really not. You said she didn't want to be around your *judgy* friends, but the only one in this room who judged her was me. I was seeing her as I had that night at the club. And that wasn't right."

"But it says a lot about you that, even before seeing her like this, you left it in God's hands."

Her eyes moved to Delaney and back again. "And you weren't wrong. She does need to be held accountable. When

Mom and Dad get home, I'm going to talk with them and insist she pay all her fines from her own funds. And I've already started researching places where she could do some community service. I'll give those suggestions to Mr. Penson. I don't want her in jail, but she needs to take responsibility for her decision to drink and drive."

"Does she know you know I saw her at the club that night?"

"She does. Didn't say much other than what you told me. That she saw you and you spoke for a minute."

He nodded, but his gaze drifted over her head.

"Hey, everybody!" Harper called from the kitchen before Shannon could ask if there was more she should know about that night, because she got the distinct impression she was missing part of the story. "Let's pray, then anybody who isn't too full from their first meal can help themselves to leftovers. But Shannon and Delaney go first. Honey, will you lead us, please?"

Wyatt nodded. "Glad to."

The group stood and gathered in a large circle to join hands. Brylie placed Gracie in her car seat so she could hold Delaney's hand while she stayed seated in the chair, and Mason took her other. Standing between Hunter and Jenny, Shannon bowed her head, tears gathering, then splashing onto the wood floor as Wyatt prayed.

She loved these people with her whole heart, and today, they'd wound themselves even more deeply into her soul with this amazing gesture to minister to her and her sister, broken in so many ways. When Wyatt said his *amen*, Hunter pulled her into a tender embrace.

"You're okay, Shan," he said near her ear. "You're all right."

"I'm so much better than all right." She pulled away and swiped at her face. "This is probably the best Thanksgiving I've ever had. Thank you, all of you."

She squeezed Hunter's hand as she walked by to help her sister, but Mason beat her to it.

"There you go," he said, handing Delaney her crutches before turning to Shannon. "You go on ahead of us, and I'll help your sister so you're not juggling two plates."

"Thanks, Mason."

Once everybody had their plates, they settled around the condo, Shannon sitting next to Delaney in a dining chair Reed brought over for her. Her sister watched the goings-on around the room as she ate—the different conversations taking place all at once, bursts of laughter punctuating the air.

She'd been included in a friendly, subtle way, nobody asking her a lot of questions, not putting her on the spot. Just letting her be part of their family for the day. And Shannon prayed she could see them for who they truly were. Not judgmental or self-righteous, but loving and kind and genuine.

Hunter walked around Shannon's chair and stood in front of them. "If you ladies are done, I can take your plates."

Shannon turned from Hunter to her sister, who stared up at him with crimson coloring her cheeks. "Did you get enough to eat, Dee?"

Delaney pulled her eyes from Hunter to Shannon and back again. "Uh, yeah. Yes. Thank you." She handed him her plate, and he took Shannon's as well.

"Can I get either of you a piece of pie, apple cider, hot chocolate?"

Shannon smiled. "You know my answer to that."

"One hot chocolate with a spritz of caramel. Got it." He grinned at Dee. "What about you? Do you love hot chocolate as much as your sister?"

"Not quite as much, but I'll take a slice of pumpkin pie, if you're offering."

"I am and comin' right up."

With another glance at Shannon, he walked away with

their plates, Shannon's eyes following him to the kitchen before she caught Dee staring at her. "What?"

"Help me to the bathroom?"

"Sure."

Once Dee was on her feet and had her crutches, they went down the hall to the master bedroom.

Shannon sat on the end of the bed. "I'll wait here. Let me know if you need any help."

"Actually, I wanted to get you alone to find out what's going on with you and Mr. Hot Neighbor."

Heat crept up her neck. "What do you mean?"

"Oh, honey. There's chemistry bouncing all over the place between you two. All that quiet talking when he first got here?" Delaney joined her on the bed, her splinted leg in front of her. "When you told me you and the guy we ran into that morning had become friends, I thought it odd because you don't usually hang with bad boys."

Her eyes widened. "He's not bad."

"Oh, I know that now. But you told me yourself he mentioned he saw me at that bar. Totally not your scene, trust me. And the women coming on to him … whoo-ee. The man didn't lack for company that night, that's for sure."

Her skin crawling at the thought, Shannon looked away. She could only imagine. A man with Hunter's looks, the way he carried himself … so confident, but without conceit. Any woman would notice him the second he walked into a room.

But there was so much more to him now, more in his heart, his soul. If only Delaney had the eyes to see *that* man.

"If he'd wanted any, that is."

Shannon snapped her attention to her sister. "Wanted any?"

"When I saw him with his friends, I kept thinking, I know that guy from somewhere. And so many girls came up to him. He was polite but definitely not interested and only danced with a couple of girls because his friends goaded him into it.

Then it dawned on me who he was, so I went up, asked if he remembered me. Again, super polite, said he did, we had a laugh about the phone thing, but he turned down my invitation to dance."

She stared down at her hands. "It's cool he's being so nice to me today. Considering." Bringing her gaze back to Shannon, she gave her a sad smile. "I made quite the fool of myself with him that night. When he walked in today, I wanted to crawl into a hole."

So, there was more neither of them had shared. But why? To protect Delaney? Protect them both?

That couldn't be it. If something had happened between Hunter and Delaney, he would have said something. She was sure of it. Especially after the accident, when Delaney's poor decision troubled him so much. No, if anything, he was probably protecting *her* from something Delaney might have done. That made the most sense.

And captured a little more of her heart.

"But then he came over, introduced himself, since we'd never formally exchanged names, and now he's bringing me pie? He could've made this really uncomfortable for me, but he didn't. That's a good guy."

If Delaney only knew the whole of it. How much he'd had to overcome to even be in the same room with her, much less showing her so much respect. So much care.

"He's a keeper, Shan. Don't let him go."

Shannon gaped at her sister. "Yes, he's a very good guy, but he's not mine to keep. We're friends."

"Friends. Yeah, we'll see how that goes. Because the way he watches you, and the way you watch him … that ain't just friends."

Shannon looked away. Had she been that obvious? Had everybody noticed? Yes, she struggled with her feelings for Hunter. Especially now that he was *a man of God*, as he'd put it. Could he possibly have feelings for her, as well?

Did it matter? Because as much as she'd love to build something with someone, something like what Wyatt and Harper had, what Zane and Ally had, some wounds cut too deep. Wounds he couldn't possibly understand.

Shannon stood. "Don't know what else to tell you. Are you ready to go back out?"

"Yes." She stood with Shannon's help and stuck her crutches under her arms. "Your posse is pretty cool, by the way."

With a smile, Shannon followed her sister out to the living room, stopping when Delaney halted at the end of the hall and glanced over her shoulder.

"If you weren't in love with him before, you will be now."

Peering around her sister, her heart tumbled all over itself at the sight of Hunter standing behind the couch watching the game, holding Gracie against his chest while she slept, gently rocking side to side. He'd told her once he used to carry baby Brylie all over the place, even as a teenage boy.

She took her eyes off the scene long enough to notice her hot chocolate and Delaney's pie waiting for them on the coffee table before looking back up and catching his eye.

Tiny pinpricks ran the length of her spine. Delaney was right. He was a keeper. And some woman, someday, would be very, very blessed to call him hers.

CHAPTER THIRTY-FOUR

Was there such a thing as an accidental date? If so, then this probably qualified.

Hunter walked next to Shannon on this chilly winter Saturday evening through the entrance of the Dallas Arboretum, decked out in all its holiday glory. He hadn't even known Brylie had been invited to go with several of the CU kids to the holiday thing at Six Flags until Emily called yesterday volunteering to take and pick up the girls. When he asked his sister about it, she said she felt bad canceling on him at the last minute.

"If you'd rather go with your friends, that's totally fine. If I were you, I know I'd rather do Six Flags with my crew than an arboretum with my brother."

She grinned. *"My crew?"*

"See? I'm old and not cool at all. You'll have a much better time hanging with the kids."

"You're sure?"

"Completely."

Having Bry along tonight as originally planned would've been great, no doubt. But he had to admit the prospect of an entire evening alone with Shannon held some appeal. They took their time meandering along the path through the gardens, standing a few minutes at each of the glassed-in gazebos representing "The Twelve Days of Christmas."

Grinning, he had to admit she was as much fun to watch as the scene around them. How could somebody be so full of light that she practically glowed with it? They would see something she thought was spectacular, walk a bit, and something else would delight her even more.

After they'd passed the six geese a-laying gazebo, she slipped her hand around his arm as they stood in front of seven swans a-swimming.

She exhaled an *oh* on a white cloud. "This one is my favorite. Isn't it stunning?"

"Very." He chuckled at the swans "swimming" on a pond, moving in a circle around a frozen fountain. "Love those tiny crowns on their heads."

"Let's get a selfie."

They turned their backs to the gazebo and smiled, cheek to cheek, at the phone she held in her hand. As they strolled along the path from gazebo to gazebo, they took several more selfies and split two hot apple ciders and one warm pretzel between them.

The rest of their walk flew by too quickly, and when they made it around to the Christmas Market, he was sorry their accidental date—which seemed more like the real thing with each passing minute—was near its end. Being here tonight, enjoying the sights and sounds of the season with Shannon, had filled him up inside. In a way he'd never experienced with anyone else.

Her gaze moved from one side to the other as they meandered through the quaint marketplace. "I'd forgotten how beautiful this Bavarian theme is. So charming."

"Is there anything you'd like to see?"

Her laugh caused a ripple of warmth through his chest.

"That's akin to asking the sun if it likes to shine. But I don't want to put you through the agony of shopping."

"It would seem a shame to come out here and not let you do some shopping at the Christmas Market."

Her mouth scrunched to one side. "Well … okay. I'd love to get their commemorative ornament and maybe some baked goods."

"Lead on, Miss Trent."

He stuck his gloved hands in his coat pockets as they moved from vendor to vendor. Until he took her bags of purchases to carry while they strolled down the other side.

So far, she'd bought colorful gingerbread cookies for Brylie and her friends, a loaf of Bulgarian bread for Mrs. B, and two of this year's commemorative ornaments—one for each of them. *"My treat,"* she'd insisted when he offered to pay for his own. *"To thank you for bringing me here tonight."*

He should've insisted on paying for them both as *his* thank you to her for coming with him. He'd been here before, but seeing it tonight, through Shannon's eyes and with her special brand of quirky delight, it was like experiencing it all for the first time.

In front of another German-themed booth, she held up a knitted hat with a bright yellow sunflower on the side. "This is perfect for Dee. Sunflowers are her favorite."

He studied the selection of hats and zeroed in on a purple one. "That one there, with the butterfly. You think Bry would like that?"

Her eyes brightened. "Definitely. She loves purple and butterflies."

After they made their purchases, he took the bag from the vendor with a *thank you and Merry Christmas* and moved on to the next.

"I think that's all I see here, but would you mind if we walked through the gift shop before we leave? I won't take long, I promise. They usually have garden things in there, and

I'd love to get something for Ally. She plans to start her garden this spring."

"I don't mind at all." Especially if it meant more time spent with his charming pseudo-date.

As they passed the gazebo with tables and chairs placed around it for patrons to enjoy a hot beverage or bite to eat, a band struck up a modern version of "Joy to the World."

Shannon halted in place and grabbed his sleeve. "Oh, can we listen? Just for a few minutes?"

"Sure thing."

With her hand nestled in the crook of his elbow, she tugged him toward the source of the music. Not that he needed coaxing. He'd follow her anywhere with her face lit up like that.

With all the seats taken, they stood to the side to watch the band. Shannon's bright smile beamed up at him over her shoulder, her cheeks pink from the cold under her red beanie. "Brylie would've loved all of this tonight. I'm sorry she missed it."

"I brought her and Mom two years ago. She loved it then, but hanging out with your brother to look at lights doesn't really compare to Six Flags with your besties."

"I'm sure she's having fun at the Six Flags thing, but I feel bad you got stuck with me all evening when I know you wanted to spend time with Bry."

"I don't feel stuck with you. I rather enjoy your company."

Her smile brought out his as the band of two brothers and their sister on lead vocals launched into a percussion-heavy version of "Little Drummer Boy." Shannon apparently knew every word, singing along with the crowd with her effortless, joyful exuberance.

As the sibling band started in on their next tune, she peered up at him again. "This cold snap makes it feel more like Christmas, doesn't it?"

"That it does."

And offered the perfect excuse to snuggle, if this were, in fact, a real date and not an accidental one.

They watched the band for a while, Shannon in front of him with her gloved hands folded at her chest, rocking side to side and singing along with the holiday tunes. When a shiver wracked her body and she crossed her arms, he set their bags on the ground and reached out to run his gloved hands up and down her jacket sleeves.

He bent his head near her ear. "Speaking of cold, maybe we should head to the gift shop where it's warm."

"Yeah."

Instead of moving, however, she leaned back against him. His pulse jumped, and it was a natural inclination to draw his arms around her, covering hers still crossed in front of her.

She fit just right there, pressed close, her shoulders to his chest. The light floral scent of her perfume tempted him to drop his face to her neck for more. A temptation he held in check, since their relationship remained entrenched in the friend zone.

Until this moment, that is. Standing here holding her had to be a notch up from *friends*. In his estimation, at least.

Content to keep her right where she was, he rested his chin on top of her knit beanie, over-the-top happy when she didn't move to put distance between them.

What was happening? She'd never given him any hint she had feelings for him.

But this … this felt almost … intimate.

She straightened and turned, breaking their contact. "Uh, right. Yes. We should probably … walk."

"Sure." Walking was fine, but he already missed having her in his arms.

As she moved ahead, he picked up their bags and chuckled to himself. It appeared Miss Shannon Trent was a little conflicted about her feelings, which was fine. He'd be happy to give her time to figure it out if it fell his way. Maybe he didn't think he was good enough for her, but if she did, he'd do everything in his power to prove her right.

Inside the much warmer gift shop, they meandered around the displays. At a jewelry carousel, she held up a pair of small gold butterflies. "These earrings would be perfect for Brylie. Don't you think? You should get them for her for Christmas. They'll match the hat you bought her."

He looked at the earrings, then at her. He'd been wondering about Christmas, clueless about what to buy a teenage girl. Mom had always let him know what was on Brylie's wish list or whatever new thing she was into.

This year, he was on his own. Their first without Mom. They'd made it through Thanksgiving without her, surrounded by friends and fun and laughter and gratitude. He only hoped to make Christmas as special.

But staring at Shannon now, maybe he wasn't as alone as he'd thought. "Great idea. Maybe we can go Christmas shopping sometime, so you can help me with what to get her. I'm a little out of my element."

"I'd love to help you pick out her presents." She nudged him with her shoulder. "I happen to know she got a good start on yours while we were Black Friday shopping yesterday."

"I hope she didn't go overboard. Only thing I want this Christmas is a happy Brylie."

"I think you'll get your wish."

The way she smiled at him had him thinking maybe that wasn't the *only* thing he wanted this Christmas.

He made the purchase and waited while she bought a journal with a floral cover—*"for Harper"*—a necklace—*"for Yolanda"*—and a hand-painted pot with seedlings—*"for Ally."*

After he took the pot and a bag from the saleslady, Shannon rested her hand in the crook of his elbow again. "You've been such a good sport about all of this shopping. Thank you."

"Not a problem." A completely true statement, and he

wasn't ready to see their evening come to an end quite yet. "I'm thinking pie and hot chocolate on the way home would be a great way to warm up."

"I concur with that assessment, Mr. Kavanaugh."

Later, at his favorite open-all-night diner near downtown Fort Worth, they perused the list of available pies.

"What kind do you like?" she asked.

"Hmm. I'm pretty much an equal opportunity pie consumer."

Her giggle caused a tingle up the back of his neck. He loved her little girl giggle as much as her all-in laughter and always experienced a measure of pride when he could trigger either one, or anything in between.

She regarded him over her menu. "Did your mother bake?"

"She did. Some of my earliest memories are Mom and me punching out sugar cookies for Christmas, then decorating them." His heart caught. "Hers were beautiful, mine were a mess. But I thought they were the awesomest creations ever because she made such a big deal about them."

Her eyes shimmered. "What a wonderful memory."

"Yeah. I kind of lost interest in decorating cookies around ten or so. But once Bry was old enough to stand on the stool next to Mom to smear frosting and sprinkles all over poor, unsuspecting angels and Christmas trees, I would join in. Even when I came home from college. And I have to say, the cookies I decorated at nineteen didn't look much different from the ones I did at four."

Her laughter this time was the full-blown kind, and his reaction matched it. He loved how her entire face shone when she laughed.

They placed their orders with the waitress, and he folded his hands on the table. "What about you? Any bakers in your family?"

"Only if you consider our cook *family*, which we kids did, for sure. Chef Deb. She's amazing. The things she does for the holidays would blow your mind. Cookies and pastries and those croquem-whatevers with cream puffs stuck together with caramel, and her prize-winning *Bûche de Noël*."

"Bush what?"

"A yule log. Like a glorified Swiss roll, but it looks like a log. Once you've had one of hers, you'll dream about it. It's that good."

"That's some high praise."

Their pie arrived along with steaming cups of hot cocoa. She took a sip and shook her head. "Not nearly as good as yours, Bobby Flay of Hot Chocolate."

He chuckled. "Then I shall be happy to keep you supplied in cocoa whenever you want."

She tilted her head. "Wanna go with me after church tomorrow to pick out my tree? Then you and Bry can help me decorate it. Dee and I usually do it together, but she didn't want to come over to sit and watch me do all the work. Plus, I need someone tall."

"You do a real tree?"

"I do. I love the smell of a real tree."

"Tomorrow works for me. We can go pick out your tree after lunch with everybody, then do both our trees. Good for you?"

"Perfect."

"This will actually be the first time I've put up a tree since I left home for college."

Her jaw dropped. "Seriously?"

"Never took the time, and I rarely had anybody over, so who would see it?"

"You would. And it would make you feel all Christmas-y every time you passed it."

"Hmm. Guess I've been missing out."

"So, you have a tree? Ornaments?"

He nodded. "We bought a tree this morning—a fake one— and a boatload of ornaments Bry said we absolutely needed.

We also have the ornaments Mom collected over the years. I think we have enough for three trees."

Laughing, she cut off the tip of her pie with her fork. "If you're sure Bry doesn't mind me crashing your tree trimming, I'd be happy to help."

"I've no doubt she'll be fine with that."

They lingered over their pie—hers coconut cream, his chocolate silk—splitting each in two and sharing.

Hunter's phone pinged with an incoming text. "Bry's home and is going to bed." He put his phone down and looked across the table at his pretty date, whether or not she realized she was his date. "Guess we should head back."

She glanced at her watch and sat straight up. "Eleven-fifteen already? I had no idea."

"Time flies when you're having fun." He stood and helped Shannon into her coat. "And this certainly was fun."

She turned to face him as she zipped up her jacket. "It was. Thank you so much for this evening."

"My pleasure."

In the elevator up to her condo a few minutes later, he couldn't help wondering what the protocol was for an accidental date. An accidental kiss?

No, probably not appropriate. He'd have to settle for a very intentional hug and pray there might be occasion for something more in the future.

Carrying their bags in one hand, he grinned down at her as the doors slid open and they stepped out into the hall. "Well, Miss Shannon Trent, I can honestly say this is the best accidental date I've ever been on."

Her eyes widened for a brief moment. Maybe he'd been the only one to think of the evening as somewhat date-adjacent.

"Oh? Been on a lot of accidental dates, have you, Mr. Kavanaugh?"

Laughing, he stopped at her door and turned toward her. "Okay. How about this? I can honestly say this is the best date

I have ever been on. Thank you for spending the evening with me. Even if you didn't know it was going to be a date."

Her smile waned, then she bit her lip. When her gaze lowered to his mouth, the air around them fairly crackled with electricity. But before he'd decided his next move, she stepped into the space between them, took the front of his coat in her hands and—

He hadn't even closed his eyes before her lips were on his. But it took only a second to recover, to mold his mouth to hers and pull her more tightly against him with his free hand.

This kiss … so much better than he'd dreamed. Urgent, yet tender at the same time. He angled his head to—

She jumped back, her face reddening and eyes wide. "Oh, wow, I can't believe I did that. I am so sorry."

"I'm not sorry."

"Umm. Well, all right, then." She took her bags from him. "Good night. Thank you. For a wonderful … evening." She turned to put her key in the deadbolt.

"See you in the morning?"

"Morning?"

"Church? Then trees?"

"Oh, uh, hmm, sure. Yes." She opened the door, stepped inside, and turned back to him. "See you then."

He put his hand out to stop the door. "Shannon. We good?"

She gave him a jerky nod. "Sure. All good. Thanks again."

After another moment, he dropped his hand and let her shut the door.

Maybe an accidental kiss was a thing, after all.

CHAPTER THIRTY-FIVE

"What were you thinking?" Shannon berated the girl in the mirror Sunday morning. "Kissing the man like that. Sure, he kissed you back, but I'm not sure you gave him a choice."

Her eyes widened as her stomach rolled. "What if I didn't give him a choice? What if I totally messed things up? Oh, gravy, I totally messed things up. He's probably still in the friend zone and there I went and pushed him into the romance zone and he probably doesn't even feel that way about me."

Another groan escaped—one of hundreds she had to have expelled throughout her sleepless night. "I kissed Hunter Kavanaugh."

Not that she hadn't thought about it a couple of times. Or a dozen. Or way more than that.

Especially last night when, as the evening progressed, it felt more and more like a date. At least, the closest thing to one she'd experienced in a while. And when he rubbed her arms to warm her up, she couldn't stop herself from settling back against him, content to stay there when his arms came around her. It had been so comfortable, so … safe. Even now, her skin warmed with the memory.

Walking arm in arm through the garden, talking with the ease they'd always had. Sharing each other's pie. It was all very date-like. Even if it was, as he'd put it, an accidental one.

But to actually *kiss* the man? Without letting him make the first move?

And, of course, it was as good a kiss as she'd imagined. Even better, actually. Best she could ever remember.

Accepting nothing could be done about the duffel-sized bags under her eyes, no matter how many layers of concealer she applied, she turned from the mirror to grab her bag and jacket from the walk-in closet. She couldn't beg off from going to church, no matter how mortifying the thought of seeing him this morning might be.

After locking her door, she started for the stairs, still unsure what she would say when she saw him. *"Hey, Hunter, I'm sorry about last night."* With her elbow, she nudged the door open to the stairwell. "No, no, I already said that. *Oh, hey, Hunter, forgive me for putting you on the spot last night."* She shook her head as she rounded the landing at the fourth floor. "On the spot? Really? *Um, hey, sorry about that little kiss I planted on you last night. Don't know what got into me."* She let out her five-hundredth groan. "No, that's just dumb. And that was no little kiss."

Sighing, she stepped out into the hall and started toward the door marked *3-0-4*. This shouldn't be so hard. *"So, um, Hunter, I'm sorry if I crossed a line last —"*

The door opened as she stepped up to it, and she jumped when the man who'd kept her up most of the night appeared in the flesh in front of her.

His face brightened. "Oh. Hey. Sorry about that." He held up the bag in his hand. "Taking the trash to the chute. Go on in. I'm all set, but Bry's not quite ready yet."

She blinked for a second to get her bearings. "Um, okay."

After a quick kiss to her forehead, he turned to walk down the hall to the garbage chute. Had she imagined that scene at her door last night? Had she dreamed it? Because he didn't act like anything was amiss at all. Still looked all handsome and put together like he always did. And she'd tumbled around in bed all night over it.

In the kitchen, she stood holding her Bible to her chest with her red pea coat draped over her arms. The gift from Delaney last Christmas was the perfect complement to the black slacks, red, black, and white print blouse, and black boots she'd chosen that morning. She started again when he came in the door behind her.

"Bry," he called out. "Shannon's here."

"Five minutes," the teen called back.

He gave her one of his easy grins. "Exactly what she said five minutes ago."

"Actually, that's fine. I was hoping I could talk to you real quick. Privately?"

"More privately than alone in my kitchen?"

"In the hall, maybe?"

His smile dimmed. "Sure."

He picked up his Bible, car fob, and the navy sports coat draped over a barstool. Since that first Sunday he'd worn a suit to church, he'd dressed more casually, this morning in light blue jeans, long-sleeved white shirt, and his Chukka boots. He had a natural sense of style, never like he was trying too hard.

"Bry, we'll be out in the hall." He followed her out, let the door close behind him, then stood in front of her. "You're gonna say it, aren't you?"

"Say what?"

"You're sorry you kissed me, it shouldn't have happened, blah, blah, blah."

"Uh, well, I feel my actions may have blurred the line a little. I think I got caught up in the evening, being with someone I really enjoy being with, how easy we find it to talk or even not to talk. Spending all that time alone together instead of with Brylie or other people."

"I agree. We have something good going here."

"Yeah, but I don't want to mess that up. We're good as friends. And I think that's where this should stay."

"Friends." He narrowed his eyes and cocked his head. "But are we, though? Just friends? I mean, you kissed me. I'm not used to friends kissing me."

Her face heated. "Um, well, yeah. But that was —"

"An awesome kiss."

"A mistake," she said at the same time, widening her eyes a second later. "An awesome kiss? Really?"

"A mistake? Really?"

"You don't think so?"

"I don't. Here I thought I might get another one today, only with me in the driver's seat this time. And you tell me we're good as friends and should stay that way. Kind of confused here, Shan."

She exhaled a heavy sigh. He wanted to kiss her again. So, of course, her gaze drifted to his mouth. Where it lingered. Too long.

A much too satisfied grin spread on his face. "You want to kiss me again too."

Her eyes snapped to his. "Hunter."

"Shannon."

"Okay. It was a good kiss."

"Good?"

"Great."

"Now we're getting somewhere."

"But I think it's too soon."

"Too soon for what? We've known each other almost two months. I've kissed women I've known less time than that."

She scowled at him. If he wanted another kiss, that definitely wasn't the way to go about it, regardless of how good he smelled right now.

He put a hand out. "Wait. I just mean ... this one *meant*

something to me. I like thinking we're forging a new path. One I'd like to go down a bit to see where it takes us."

Oh, how she'd love to be on that path. With Hunter. But there were things in the way yet. Things that could change their relationship forever. And not in the way he apparently hoped.

With her resolve bolstered, she pulled her shoulders back. "I care about you, Hunter. I really do. And I like being your friend. A friend who wants to help you discover your faith. I'll be here for you, but I think we need to not be physical. You shouldn't have any distractions from developing your relationship with Jesus before anything else."

"I can't have you both?"

"I don't want to get in the way. I know from experience how important it is to focus on God when you're first getting to know Him. I think that's where your energies need to be right now."

"I don't know how we back this train up, but let's talk when we—"

The door opened and Brylie stepped out. "Sorry. I'm ready now." After locking the deadbolt, she turned and stopped. "Oh, wow, you guys look way too serious. What'd I miss? Or should I go back inside and let you finish whatever this is?"

Hunter pulled his attention from Shannon to his sister. "Nope. We were talking while waiting for you, slow poke. Hope we don't miss the opening song."

Brylie rolled her eyes before she stepped in front of them toward the elevator. "We're not late. You just like to be early to everything."

Walking behind the teenager, Shannon caught Hunter's eye.

Later, he mouthed, and she nodded.

Except *later* wouldn't change anything. He might be persuasive in court or across a conference table, but she needed to stick to her guns here. All she wanted was to restore their friendship to pre-kiss status.

Because she wasn't ready to lose him for good.

239

CHAPTER THIRTY-SIX

e can go as slow with this as you need to, but I don't know how to not feel what I feel.

Hunter sat at his desk Friday afternoon, the previous Sunday replaying in his head. After they'd finished with their trees, he and Shannon decided to take their conversation Christmas shopping while Brylie did homework with Ellie and Samantha via video call from the condo. As they walked from store to store, he'd been transparent with her, let her know where he stood, and encouraged her not to close the door on what could be before they could even explore it.

Because now, aware she had feelings for him, he was determined to give it a chance. If only she would jump on board.

At least she'd agreed to their first *intentional* date. Tonight. He'd made reservations at a renowned downtown Fort Worth restaurant for seven o'clock, which should give him plenty of time to pick up some flowers and get home to change into slacks and a nice sweater.

Thankfully, she hadn't come up with an excuse not to go through with it, as he'd been afraid might happen when he issued his invitation Tuesday evening. After a moment's hesitation—during which he held his breath and prayed she'd follow through with her promise to at least give them a go—she accepted, and he whistled all the way down to his condo.

Until he lay in bed later and let his thoughts loose. Because he couldn't shake the suspicion something else lay under the surface of her reticence to explore a romantic relationship. With him or anybody else.

It wasn't necessarily something she said, but more in the way she didn't. As if allowing him to get only so close before putting out her arm to hold him back.

Rhetorically speaking, anyway. Because Shannon had no issues with showing affection. With everybody. Even this week, when he left her for the night after spending some time together after work, no matter what time that might be, she hugged him as usual at the door.

Unfortunately, no kiss, as he'd hoped before she dropped her *we're good as friends* bombshell. But if he remained patient and let her set the pace, perhaps there could be in the future. Hopefully, the near future.

Because he couldn't get that surprise kiss at her door out of his head.

He grinned at the memory. The way she'd studied him for several heartbeats, from his eyes to his mouth, before tugging him in for the best kiss he'd ever experienced. Maybe tonight, she'd let him take the reins and—

"Hunter."

His attention snapped to the door. "Hey, Jules." The pensive expression on his assistant's face sounded alarm bells in his head. "What's wrong?"

"There's a process server here."

"Okay." Nothing new about that. They used process servers every day to serve documents on defendants or witnesses.

"Asking for you."

"Asking for—" *Oh.* For him. Personally.

A sense of foreboding seized him as he came around the desk and followed her out to her office, where a young man in jeans and a hoodie stood with a backpack slung over one shoulder.

The man looked up from a clipboard he held with a manila envelope under it. "William Hunter Kavanaugh?"

The use of his proper name was a shock at first, until he reminded himself he was now the other party on the other end of whatever legal proceeding this was about. Nothing good had ever followed the use of his full name from as early as he could remember. If Mom or Gran ever used it, he knew he was in trouble.

Much like he felt right now, only this was on a much more serious level.

"I'm Hunter Kavanaugh."

The man handed over the envelope. "Mr. Kavanaugh, I'm J.T. Osgood. I'm to inform you you've been served with a Petition for Custody from one Mitchell R. Kavanaugh."

Hunter's stomach twisted as a current of apprehension raced down his spine.

Mitch. Filed suit. To get Brylie.

Being smacked upside the head with a two-by-four would have been less jarring.

The process server left as Hunter pulled the document out of the envelope and sat down heavily in one of the chairs in front of Julia's desk. She took her own on the other side.

"Hunter. I'm so sorry. Obviously, you didn't see this coming."

He swallowed against the acid taste of fear in his mouth and shook his head. "I should've. But I'd hoped he'd respect me enough to at least have a discussion before filing."

"He hasn't seen your settlement proposal?"

"No. I guess I thought maybe … I don't know." He sighed and returned the document to the envelope. "I'd hoped he would see Brylie's better off with me and not make us go through this. Make *her* go through this."

"I'll do whatever I can. An affidavit. Sworn statement. Letter to the judge. Even testify, if it comes to that. You have a huge roster of people who would go to bat for you."

Great to hear, but would it be enough?

"Thanks, Jules." The knot in his throat allowed only a broken whisper.

She came around the desk and sat in the other chair, leaning forward with her hands clasped on her lap. "Tonight's the big date, right? Are you going to tell Shannon?"

Right. The big date. The one he'd been so excited about. The one that may very well define their future relationship.

He couldn't bring this heaviness of spirit with him as a third party tonight. He'd have to put on a brave face and hope Shannon wouldn't be able to read him as well as she usually did.

"Maybe not tonight. But I'll definitely have to tell her. And Brylie, I guess, at some point."

The phone on Julia's desk rang, and she picked it up. "Julia Wolfe. Hunter Kavanaugh's office."

The furrow grew deeper in her forehead as she listened to the caller.

"Yes, sir. I'll send him up. Thank you."

She hung up the phone and brought her apprehensive gaze back to him. "Alden wants to see you."

Another twist in his gut. "*Now?*"

"Now." She checked her watch. "What could he need at five-fifteen on Friday?"

"Nothing good."

CHAPTER THIRTY-SEVEN

Whoever said pacing settled one's nerves had clearly never tried it.

Bringing herself to a stop in front of the window, Shannon peered out at the Fort Worth cityscape. The sun had set nearly an hour ago, and the city had lit up in all its urban glory. She watched the headlights of cars coming into downtown for an evening of fun and taillights of those leaving after a hard day's work. Not that she could tell from up here which car was Hunter's, but it gave her something to do other than sit and get tangled up with nerves.

It wasn't his fault, after all, that his boss had called him into a meeting after five o'clock, according to the phone call from Julia, and he was still stuck in it at 6:15. Shannon didn't even know what he'd planned, but it appeared their first official date might be over before it began.

Their talk Sunday afternoon had been eye-opening. She'd had no idea Hunter had been wrestling with his feelings for her even before that magical evening at the arboretum. She never imagined she would be enough to keep his interest, but his earnest transparency had won her over, and she'd agreed to be open-minded about exploring a relationship beyond their current friendship.

If only she didn't now wonder how many other evenings she might get a call from his assistant informing her he'd be late at the office. Could she live with that? With once again being overshadowed by the almighty dollar?

Her cell chimed with an incoming call, and she walked over to pick it up. "Hey, Hunter."

"Shannon. I am so sorry. I'm on my way down to my office and should be at your place in about twenty minutes. But we won't make our reservation, unfortunately."

The exhaustion in his voice pulled at her heartstrings. Or maybe stress? Either way, he probably needed sleep more than anything else. "It's all right. You want to call it and do something another time?"

"No, I'd really like to see you tonight. I'm just sorry I messed up our first official date."

"You didn't." Her thoughts spun as she scanned her apartment, spotless as a result of nervous energy between returning home from class and getting ready for their date. "In fact, why don't we do dinner here? I went over to Ally's last night to learn how to make lasagna, and I brought home an entire pan of it. I can stick it in the oven, toss a salad …"

"You mean a home-cooked meal by Shannon Trent herself? How could I turn that down?" An elevator dinged on his end. "How about I stop by the bakery on the corner and pick up a cheesecake for dessert? Will that help salvage this date night?"

"Cheesecake covers a multitude of sins. I'll see you in, what? Thirty, forty minutes?"

"Sooner if I can do it."

Exactly twenty-eight minutes later, he showed up at her door with not only a luscious-looking New York-style cheesecake in one hand but a bouquet of roses in her favorite color in the other.

His jaw dropped. "Oh, wow. It's too bad we're wasting that dress on an evening in when I should be showing you off."

Her cheeks warmed at the compliment. When she'd dressed for their date, she hoped the filmy, floral dress with the V-neck, cinched at the waist with a belt, and worn with high-heeled, knee-high boots would be stylish enough for wherever he was taking her.

She'd never been one to wear the usual *little black dress*, although she had one somewhere in the back of her guest room closet. Kept only for those occasions when her parents insisted she attend an event and look the part of a proper O'Connor.

"You're very kind. And thank you for the beautiful flowers."

Once inside, he moved toward the kitchen, gazing around the softly lit apartment. She hoped the table set for two with her beloved vintage china and two tapered candles in the middle wasn't too much for a *first* date.

"This might be even better than what I had planned to begin with."

Relieved, she smiled as she pulled a vase from a cabinet and put it under the tap. "You might want to reserve judgment until after you've tried my lasagna."

"If it tastes as good as it smells, it'll be amazing."

The CD player moved to the next song on the Christmas album she'd put on minutes before his arrival. "I'm grateful Al and Harper keep me supplied with meals, but I figured it was time I learned to cook. Ally said she'd love to teach me, so last night was our first lesson. I never knew cooking could be so much fun."

She put her yellow roses in the vase and placed them on the table between the candles. "Perfect."

Hunter slipped off his suit coat and draped it over a barstool. "I feel more relaxed already."

"Sit there and I'll finish this up." She turned her attention to the salad she'd been preparing before he knocked on her door. "No offense, but you look like you could use about twenty hours of sleep."

"None taken. I probably could." With his elbows propped on the counter, he scrubbed his hands over his face. "Long week. And I have to go back in the morning. So, I'm glad Bry's with Ellie tonight and tomorrow."

She added chopped cucumber to the bowl of greens and tomatoes. "Want to talk about it? The lasagna has to cook about ten more minutes, then sit for ten."

He shook his head, his eyes cast down to the counter. "Not over dinner."

That didn't sound good. She pulled her attention from him to finish up the salad and served up two bowls to take to the table. "We can start with this while the lasagna sits."

He took a seat at the table while she pulled the pan from the oven and set it on the stovetop. When she joined him, he reached for her hand.

Clasping her fingers, he bowed his head. "Father, we thank You for this quiet evening to be together, to unwind after a busy week. Thank You for this food, and I'm so grateful for Shannon who took the time to prepare it. And I also pray for Delaney, that she'll continue to heal and ultimately find her way to You. In Your name we pray, Amen."

"Amen." Her fingers slipped from his, and she picked up her fork. "Thank you for praying for Dee. She's been asking me questions about my faith when I go over there or whenever we talk on the phone. I think everybody showing her so much love on Thanksgiving touched her heart."

"You and your friends are good at that. At living your witness and not just voicing it."

Nothing could have pleased her more to hear. "You were a part of that day too. Not to mention what you did for Zach's dad. Zach even said something to his circle leader about the guy who prayed with his dad. That it meant a lot to him, even though Zach didn't know who you were."

"That's nice, but I was simply giving in to what I thought was a prompting, I guess you could say. I'm still getting used to all this."

"Aren't we all? God is a very big God, and there are always new things to learn."

She cleared off their salad bowls, dished up squares of lasagna, and returned to the table. "I'm wondering if we should pray again."

He chuckled. "I think we're good. It looks delicious." He took a bite, chewed, stopped, chewed some more, swallowed, and looked up at her. "Shannon. This is really good. I mean it."

"Honest? It is?"

"It is. Try it."

She did and squealed in delight. "It *is* good. Of course, I was standing right next to Ally copying everything she did. The true test will be the first time I do it on my own."

"I'll be happy to be your taste tester."

"You're hired."

The rest of the meal passed in comfortable conversation, although she couldn't get past the vibe something wasn't right. His eyes reflected a weariness, almost a sadness, his usual charming smile couldn't quite cut through.

An hour after they sat down, she folded her cloth napkin and placed it next to her dessert plate. "That cheesecake was wonderful, but I'm stuffed."

"I'll leave it for you if you let me take half the lasagna."

"Half the cheesecake for half the lasagna."

"Deal."

He rose and took their plates over to the sink. She blew out the candles and walked over to join him, working side by side to wash and dry their dinnerware.

Holding up a plate, he regarded it for a moment. "This china is so unique. I've never seen anything like it."

"It was my great-grandmother's. Made in Ireland and passed down to her eldest child—my grandpa O'Connor—

then passed down to his—my father. I've loved it since I was a little girl, and because Mother hardly ever used it, I asked if I could have it. Cam said he didn't care, so instead of passing it to him, she gave it to me."

"It's stunning. And in such great condition for being so old."

"Irish Belleek China has a rich history, starting with its inception in the mid-1800s. Most people, I guess, would keep collector's items such as this set locked away. But I'm of the mind it was created to be enjoyed by folks who valued gathering around a table, so I use it whenever I have a special occasion."

He threw her a grin as he put their leftovers into plastic containers. "I'm honored to be considered a special occasion."

Warmth tingled on her cheeks. "But of course. Plus, I thought nice plates might make my lasagna taste better."

"It wasn't the plates."

Her heart swelled with his compliment. "Thank you, kind sir."

After placing the leftovers in the refrigerator, he walked up behind her as she wiped down the quartz countertop, put his hand at her waist, and bent to kiss her cheek. "Thank *you*. That meal was delicious."

A smile crept across her face. "You're welcome."

She folded the towel, then he took her hand and led her to the sofa, where he gestured for her to sit before taking the seat next to her.

Leaning forward, she unzipped one of her boots. "We need to get comfortable. I'm getting rid of these, and why don't you toss that tie?"

"Excellent idea."

His hands worked to loosen the knot while she kicked off her boots. She tucked her feet up under the skirt of her dress, turning toward him with her elbow perched on the back of the sofa.

After dropping the tie onto the coffee table, he loosened the top button of his shirt along with the cuffs. "Much better."

His eyes moved to her other hand, lying in her lap, and he reached for it, his fingers playing with hers while flames crackled in the fireplace. As soft Christmas music played in the background, the tumult of emotions in his beautiful slate-blue eyes caused her pulse to quicken.

"If you want to talk about it, I'm happy to listen."

His focus shifted to her face. "I got served today. Mitch is suing me for custody."

Her breath caught in her chest. "Oh, no. I'd hoped it wouldn't come to that."

The bleakness in the set of his features tore at her heart. "I can't lose her. I can't."

"We'll fight." The moisture collecting along his lashes brought tears to her eyes. "You have all of us to speak for you. And won't they let Brylie have a say?"

He shrugged. "They might. But I hate to put that on her, asking her to choose. Plus, courts historically lean toward the biological parent."

"Even if that parent was drinking through most of her childhood and abandoned her?"

"My hope is we'll get a judge who'll take that all into consideration. Problem here is my job and the hours I put in."

"But you've changed that."

"And it hasn't gone unnoticed."

"What does that mean?"

"That meeting I got called into tonight? It was about my future with the firm."

"You're kidding. You're still working well over forty hours a week."

"Closer to sixty with the work I do from home. But you have to understand, before I had Brylie, work was it for me, and I was good with that. I wanted to be named partner by the time I was thirty and was well on my way. Made myself indispensable. I wanted to be *the guy,* the one they could depend on if they needed something done. I didn't care how many hours I had to work. How late or how many weekends."

"That's not a life, though."

"I can see that now. Now that I have Brylie and you and church and all our friends. But I still have goals. I still want to be a respected attorney. And I still want to be a partner at the most prestigious law firm in Fort Worth. Is that wrong?"

"Not if you're doing it for the right reasons."

"Being a provider. Being a success. Being somebody. Those are wrong?"

"But you are somebody, even without all the money or the title or the big office. God made you somebody simply the way you are. You can be a success hanging a shingle outside a storefront and helping people through legal things they don't understand.

"And a provider? All Brylie needs is you. She doesn't need stuff. Designer stuff, top-of-the-line stuff, more stuff. If you're sitting at the table with her at dinner, sitting in the audience at her performances, doing things with her on the weekends, that's how you provide for her."

The tempest in his eyes pulled at her, and she sandwiched his hand between both of hers. "Don't measure yourself by the world's definition of success. God's measure of a man is completely opposite of that. It's about the heart. The priorities. The way he loves his family and the integrity with which he lives his life. You're so much more than the hours you give to Williamson, Sheffield, and Moore."

"They apparently feel differently."

That didn't sound good. "Did they threaten to fire you?"

"No. They have no grounds. I'm still one of their top performers with my billables. But they're down quite a bit, so they thought it worth a conversation to see if I was going to be able to bring them back up."

He released a heavy sigh. "But I don't know how I can.

Even sixty hours a week won't look good in court if Mitch can show he works from home and his hours are flexible. I have this trial with Gail coming up that requires a lot of my time. I don't have any more I can throw in on top of that."

"How'd they take that?"

"Alden wasn't happy. I'm assigned to cases with him and another senior partner. Or was. I've been pulled off, which means no partnership. At least for the foreseeable future."

He stared at the fire. "Five years of non-stop work, sixteen months within reach of the finish, and it's all in pieces at my feet."

How she wished she had the words to help him. She understood the loss of a dream. The planning, the hoping, the worry, the anticipation. Then the agony of grief when that dream was lost.

Maybe there weren't any words she could find to help him, but perhaps that's not what he needed. She studied him for a moment, this man who'd planted himself in her heart, whether she'd been ready for him or not, and wished she could answer all his questions. Ease the pain of his disappointment. Take away the fear of losing his sister.

But all she could do was be present.

Lifting his hand with her own, she scooted closer, leaning into his side and letting his arm drape around her as she wrapped hers over his stomach. He covered her arm with his and laid his cheek to the top of her head.

And they sat there. Huddled together in the dim light of evening. The crackling of the fireplace accompanied the quiet music imparting the hope sent with the birth of a baby who would be the Savior of all mankind.

If only they could stay there until all was right with their world again.

CHAPTER THIRTY-EIGHT

"Excuse me, is this seat taken?"

Shannon pulled her attention from her cell phone to a woman standing in the aisle. "Yes, ma'am. So sorry."

"No problem. It's just me, so I shouldn't have trouble finding another. Enjoy the show."

"You too."

Shannon checked her phone. Again. For at least the tenth time since arriving at the high school fine arts center. Still nothing from Hunter. Peering over her shoulder, she craned her neck to see over the folks filling the rows behind her, but still no Hunter coming down the aisle toward them.

Harper patted her leg when she faced forward again. "I'm sure he wouldn't miss it. He knows how important this is to Brylie."

Shannon nodded, but the pit in her stomach deepened. Their friends occupied the entire row, and kids from the Fort Worth club took up more seats in front and behind them. But the one person Brylie most needed to be there still hadn't made an appearance, with only two minutes until showtime.

"He's worked late every night this week, but he absolutely promised he could get away tonight."

After their dinner last Friday, he'd gone into the office Saturday morning, then they picked up Brylie at Ellie's for a late afternoon and evening of Christmas shopping with dinner out. Sunday had been church, lunch with their friends, and an afternoon of homework for her and Brylie and deposition summaries for him. They'd finished their weekend with a Christmas movie at her apartment.

During the week, his work hours limited their time together, but he made it a point to at least come up to talk to her for a bit if she wasn't at his place with Brylie when he got home.

Harper leaned in. "Have you met Mitch?"

"Not yet."

"He's about six rows behind us."

Great. So, Mitch had shown and was no doubt aware Hunter was nowhere in sight.

Her pulse hitched when her screen lit up with an incoming text, her spirits sagging when she checked the ID. Delaney. She closed her eyes against the disappointment that sat in her chest like cement. With a sigh, she sent a quick reply, turned the volume off per the instructions in the printed program, and stuck her phone in her purse. Her last text had given him their row number, and she'd saved the end seat for him. Bry's solo wasn't until the sixth song in. Certainly he'd be there by then.

He had to be. This was Brylie's big moment, and he couldn't miss it. Not like Shannon's father had missed every one of her volleyball and soccer games, her National Honor Society induction, awards ceremonies, and most of her birthdays.

But when Brylie walked to the microphone, the seat next to Shannon remained empty. Irritation mixed with worry. Had he lost track of time, or had he been in an accident?

A sense of *déjà vu* crawled up the back of her neck. How many times had she wrestled with the same conflicted thoughts when her father failed to make it to an event? Wondering if he was hurt or sick instead of simply indifferent. Unsure which was worse.

Throwing off the black cloud of her memories, she clapped and whooped with the rest of their friends after Brylie's song. She prayed Hunter was safe, wherever he might be.

And that Brylie wouldn't forever remember this night as the first time her brother broke her heart.

Hunter jogged toward the auditorium, flowers in hand. He couldn't wait to see Brylie, to tell her—

A petite blonde burst through the doors and all but charged in his direction.

"Shannon—"

"You missed it. Her show she was so excited about."

His mouth fell slack when she halted in front of him. "No, I—"

"And her solo, which she rocked, by the way, and you missed it."

"Shan, listen—"

"But you know who *didn't* miss it? Mitch." Pulling back, she sucked in a breath, her eyes wide as she covered her mouth.

With a heavy sigh, he stared down at the tiny dynamo who made him crazy. Usually, in all the best ways. Tonight, not so much. "Are you done? Because if you need to get more off your chest, I don't want to slow your roll."

Pink blossomed on her cheeks, and she dropped her hand as people exited the building behind her. "I'm sorry. I shouldn't have said that. About Mitch. It was snarky and undeserved."

It was, but he'd ignore it. He took her hand and, once out of the way of foot traffic, turned her to face him. "I was late, yes, but I didn't miss her solo. I didn't want to be a distraction walking in after the show started, so I sat in the back. I texted you when I got here."

"Oh. Uh … my phone's in my purse. They asked us to turn them off or silence them."

"Well, I did see her. I can even show you the video I took on my phone. And you're right. She absolutely rocked it. I knew she could sing, but that … wow."

Her brow creased. "Then why did I just find you coming in?"

He held up the flowers in his hand. "In my hurry to get inside earlier, I forgot these in the car. During the encore, I ran out to get them."

Shaking her head, she took a step closer, her eyes fixed on his. "Hunter, I am so sorry. I thought you were just getting here, and the flowers were some kind of lame apology."

"Yeah, how did you get out of the theater so fast?"

"I ducked out during the thank yous to beat the crowd so I could stake out the spot I told her I'd be after the show. She's probably looking for me."

"Okay, but before we go find her, I think we need to set a time later to talk about what just happened."

"No, it was my fault. I went off half-cocked without all the information. I was worried something had happened to you, but when I saw you through the doors, walking up safe and sound, I guess it turned to anger when I should've been relieved."

He should be annoyed at her outburst, but how could he be when she'd been concerned for him? "I'm sorry you were worried."

"I'm just happy you're okay. And about the Mitch comment, I feel terrible. I'm scared of anything he can use for ammunition, so when Harper told me he was here, and I thought you hadn't shown, I guess I let my emotions run away with my mouth."

"I understand. I don't want to give him anything, either.

But I think there's more to this than simply me being late for Bry's show."

When her focus darted away, he sensed he'd hit a sore spot. He didn't want to hurt her, but if something stood in the way of them moving ahead with whatever this was between them, they needed to get it out into the open and deal with it.

He took her hand again and waited for her to look at him. "Listen, Ellie and Samantha are sleeping over tonight, so I can come up to your place and we can talk. All right? It'll give me a good excuse to escape all the giggles."

Her nod was barely perceptible. "All right."

He took a step closer and lifted her chin with the knuckle of his index finger. "Hey. For the record, I love how fiercely you stick up for the people you care about." He stared down into pools of blue, reflecting the glow of the lights attached to the building. "One of a million things I love about you."

Without giving her a chance to protest, he leaned in until his lips met hers, unhurried, until she moved closer and took the sides of his coat in her fists. Her soft floral fragrance mixed with the scent of an earlier rain as his hand moved from her chin to cup her cheek.

They hadn't kissed since that night in front of her door, when she'd taken him by such sweet surprise, and this wasn't how he'd planned the follow-up to go. But as the kiss lingered, he didn't have any regrets.

In deference to their location, he pulled back and grinned down at her. "We should argue more often. I like make-up kissing."

"I like the kissing part. Not the arguing part. Especially when I'm wrong."

"Okay." He took her hand on their way to the entrance. "Next time, *I'll* be wrong."

CHAPTER THIRTY-NINE

*H*unter led Shannon inside the auditorium lobby against the flow of exiting traffic and threaded their way to the designated spot Shannon told Brylie she'd be. When they spotted her, he waved, and her face lit up. Surprised at the heavier-than-usual makeup she wore for the performance, he was taken aback at how much older she looked.

Lord, help me, because I'm not ready for my baby sister to be so grown up.

As they pushed through the last of the crowd between them, she launched herself into his arms.

"Hunt, that was so much fun!"

He had to let go of Shannon's hand to catch her but held on tight as he spun her around in a circle. "You were awesome, Peanut. I'm so proud of you."

She clutched him hard around the neck, and he didn't even care that the flowers he'd asked Julia to purchase earlier in the day scrunched against her back.

With her arms still wound around him, she looked him in the eye. "You think so? Really?"

"Absolutely. You're a rock star."

She hugged him again, her feet still dangling inches off the ground. "You guys were holding hands," she whispered in his ear. "Does that mean …?"

"I think it means we were holding hands," he whispered back.

She let him go as he lowered her to the ground. "We'll talk later."

"I'm sure we will." He held out the flowers. "For you. A little smushed, but no less deserved."

Her mouth dropped open and eyes brightened as she took them. "Oh, wow, thank you!"

Shannon moved in for a hug. "Oh, Brylie-girl, I'm so incredibly proud of you. I didn't even think to get a video, but your brother did."

"Oh, that's okay. They did a professional video, and we'll all get a copy." She looked at Hunter. "But thank you for doing that."

He wrapped his arm around her. "Of course. I wanted to show everybody at work tomorrow."

She rolled her eyes, but her grin belied her annoyance. "Like a dad, huh?"

His heart puddled in his chest. "Exactly like a proud dad."

The McCowans, Carpenters, and the rest of the gang caught up to them, and Brylie blushed with all the hugs and compliments.

Harper waved her hands to gather them together. "Okay, pictures, everybody. Hunter and Bry, let's get you. Then Shannon, you hop in there."

As Harper continued taking pictures of Brylie with all of her guests and friends, Hunter's spirit filled to overflowing with all the love this group had shown them and how special they'd made his sister feel. He laughed as she made faces at the camera with Zane and Ally, then offered to take one of her with Harper and Wyatt.

When he returned the phone to Harper, a man cleared his throat behind him.

"I can take one of the whole group," Mitch said. "If you want."

Harper nodded. "Sure, Mr. Kavanaugh. That would be nice. But, first, let me get one of you with your daughter."

Mitch turned to Brylie. "Is that okay with you, darlin'?"

She nodded, then looked over at Hunter. Mitch followed suit. "Okay with you, So—Hunter?"

Hunter regarded his stepfather for a moment before reaching out his hand. "Of course. Please."

Mitch shook his hand, then moved over to stand next to Brylie.

Small, soft fingers slipped into Hunter's palm, and he looked down to find Shannon beside him, her eyes filled with a warm softness as she gazed up at him. A man would move mountains for a woman to look at him like that, and all he'd done was shake his stepfather's hand.

After Mitch's photo with Bry, Harper settled her amid everyone who had come to support her, with Hunter between Brylie and Shannon. He put his arms around them and smiled as Mitch focused on the small screen.

"There you go." Mitch handed the phone to Harper. "I got several in case anybody blinked."

"Thank you so much, Mr. Kavanaugh. Do you have a cell phone with you?"

Mitch reached in and pulled it from his coat pocket.

"Oh, good. Let me AirDrop these pics of you and Bry."

"Thank you kindly."

Once the photos transferred to Mitch's device, Hunter took Shannon by the hand and walked up to his stepfather. "I'm glad you could make it tonight."

"I appreciate the invitation."

"Of course." He pulled his attention to Shannon beside

him, then back to Mitch. "This is Shannon Trent, my friend and neighbor. Shan, this is Mitch, Brylie's... my stepfather."

"Miss Trent. Very nice to meet you."

"I'm so happy to meet you too. And call me Shannon."

"Miss Shannon. I've heard a lot about you from my daughter. And from this guy." He glanced at their joined hands. "I'm thinking *friend* is an understatement."

Hunter chuckled at Shannon's blush. "It's a rather new thing, but yes. In fact, she's who led me back to the Lord."

Shannon squeezed his hand. "You were already a good man."

"But not a godly one. There's a difference."

Mitch nodded, his expression somber. "There surely is."

Brylie came over and wrapped her free hand around Hunter's arm, still holding her flowers in the other.

He grinned down at her. "Ready to go?"

"I need to find Ellie and Sam, then we can hit it." She looked up at her dad. "Thank you for coming tonight."

Mitch's eyes softened. "You were fantastic. I was bursting with pride."

"Thank you."

"Well ... guess I'll be going. See you later."

Hunter followed him with his eyes as he walked away and, for a moment, saw the man he'd loved as a boy. The man he'd looked up to, wanted to be like. The man he'd called *Dad*. A man now alone in life because of the choices he'd made.

After Mitch walked outside, Hunter excused himself from the two ladies, jogged to the door, and pushed it open. "Mitch. Hold up."

His stepfather turned on the sidewalk to the parking lot and waited for Hunter to catch up. "I can't talk about the case with you."

Hunter chuckled. "Trust me. I'm aware. I was just going to invite you to meet us for dinner after church on Sunday. If you're available. I can see if Shannon can come too."

"She's special?"

"I'm pretty nuts about her, yes, sir."

Nodding, Mitch regarded him with narrowed eyes. "When you find a good one, don't mess it up. Like I did."

"Yes, sir."

Mitch stared at him for a long moment. "All this niceness. Inviting me to dinner. Does this have anything to do with that settlement agreement your attorney sent mine?"

"No, sir, not at all. I just wanted to apologize. I'm still learning how to handle things in a way the Lord would want me to. And I shouldn't have said what I said to you, about why Mom and not … well—"

"Why Sylvie and not me. Why she had to die and I'm still here."

"Yes. I'm not proud of myself for that. I hope you can …" He swallowed hard against the pride trying to rear its ugly head. "I hope you can forgive me."

Mitch studied him for another several seconds, but Hunter refused to look away. There was still a lot of pain between them, a lot of things he'd like his stepfather to answer for. But since the day Wyatt told him he would need to forgive Mitch for his own healing, he'd done his best to wrap his head around the concept.

Standing here now, having asked the man he couldn't imagine ever forgiving to forgive him instead, he finally understood what Wyatt had tried to explain. Forgiving allowed peace to take the place of bitterness. Allowed love to replace hate. How could he ask Mitch to forgive him if he refused to forgive Mitch?

"It's a fair question, why her and not me. One I've asked myself many times. And there's no good answer. All I can do is try to be the best man I can be for the rest of my life. To honor your mother. And make my dau—" His voice caught. "Make my kids proud."

Tears stung Hunter's eyes at the show of emotion from this

man he'd once considered larger than life. This man who still claimed him as his own.

"I understand why you don't want to be my son. But to me, you always will be."

Hunter swallowed hard, but the thickness in his throat refused to budge. "Mitch … Dad." A tear trickled down his cheek, and he swiped it away. "I've been so angry. At you. At God. But I let Him back into my life. Now I think He's telling me I need to invite you back. It's just … it might take some time. You know?"

"I do know. I let you down. I wasn't the man … the father … you needed me to be. I don't deserve your forgiveness, but you asking *me* to forgive *you?*" He shook his head. "You're a better man than I. And if, with the help of the Lord, you can ever find your way to forgive me, I believe you'll have freedom from your anger, Son. And, hopefully, with that, I can begin to forgive myself."

Hunter's heart hammered in his chest as he considered Mitch's words. His stepfather had come so far from the broken-down drunk he'd written off years before. And if his road to self-forgiveness sat tethered to any Hunter saw fit to offer, who was he to stand in the way?

He cleared his throat. "I do forgive you. You've paid a steep price for your decisions, but you've done the hard work to turn things around. I'm …" He swallowed hard. "I'm proud of you, Dad. Mom would be too."

Tears filled Mitch's eyes as he waited for several people to pass on the sidewalk behind them. "I'm proud of you, too, Son. And I'm so sorry I wasn't there to protect your mom. She should've never been there that night after working all day. That's on me."

Hunter shook his head. "I don't blame you. Don't blame yourself. A man chose to drink then get behind the wheel of a lethal weapon. That's where the blame should lie. Let's leave the past behind us and move forward from here. Whatever happens."

Nodding, Mitch regarded him for a long moment. "Listen, about that agreement. You think we really need these lawyers refereeing for us? Can we maybe sit down and talk it through? Man to man? For Brylie's sake?"

Hunter's pulse quickened. "We absolutely can. Join us for dinner on Sunday. Then you and I can meet, when? Breakfast on Monday? Lunch?"

"Breakfast sounds good. Text me where and I'll meet you, if you need somewhere close to your office."

"I'll do that."

Mitch reached out, and Hunter shook his hand again. "I love you, Son. You don't have to say it back. But I want you to know that's never changed."

Unable to speak past the emotion blocking his throat, Hunter nodded, then watched Mitch as he made his way to his car.

Tonight, surrounded by these friends he considered family, showering his sister with love and attention, it reminded him how very much he had to be grateful for. And in comparison, how alone Mitch truly was. How he'd forfeited everything in his life for the bottle.

But he'd come back from the brink and was making the effort to reclaim some of what he'd lost.

Including the son he'd always considered his own.

CHAPTER FORTY

I think there's more to this than simply me being late for Bry's show.

Shannon stood in front of her glittering Christmas tree with her cup of caramel-laced cocoa, the scent mingling with fresh pine. The tree's twinkling lights reminded her of the day she, Hunter, and Brylie had put it up, with that kiss she'd planted on him the night before hovering between them until they talked it out while Christmas shopping that evening. Such a shock to discover he'd been keeping his feelings for her in check for a while. Probably as long as she'd been wrestling with hers for him.

She had to admit, she enjoyed being on this road with Hunter, even if his words after the concert had hit a little too hard. *I think there's more to this …* Because hadn't she sat there in that auditorium letting her memories run amok with her emotions? Just as they had when she first met him and he'd missed dinner for a business call?

Now, here he sat yet again on her sofa, waiting for her to let him into the place she'd hidden her deepest regret. The disgrace that could change the course of their relationship.

She turned and settled next to him on the couch, one leg

tucked up under her. Would this be the last time they'd be here? Like this? Settling in for an evening of conversation or movie-watching and popcorn-sharing?

Or could she dare hope he'd be able to see past a circumstance that hit too close to home?

Father, You know what the future holds. Give me the words to say what I need to say and the grace to accept whatever is best for Hunter.

Her gaze settled on his face, so handsome, with those slate-blue eyes she saw in her dreams. "The girls are all settled?"

He nodded. "Furniture moved to make room for sleeping bags in front of the fireplace for maximum movie-viewing enjoyment. And a lot of giggling."

"I love those girls."

"I'm grateful for the way they've taken Brylie in, like they've been friends forever."

"They really are kindred spirits."

"You should've heard the grilling I got on the way home, though. Bry wanted to know why we were holding hands, how long had this been going on, were we a thing, and did I think you were the one."

"What did you say?"

"Hmm. Let's see. Because we liked each other, about a week, define *a thing*, and hopefully."

She cocked her head. "Hopefully?"

The silence stretched for a moment before he set his cup down on the coffee table. "Shan, this is new for me, the way I feel about you. And I'm done dating just for fun. So, yeah, I can't help hoping you're the one God has for me. That maybe that's why He's put us here.

"But I keep feeling there's something holding you back. And if it's because you don't feel the same, I can accept that and we'll be friends and that'll be the end of it."

"That's not it."

"Relieved to hear that. So, if there's something we need to talk about, let's get it out there and work it through. Together."

She sipped from her mug, then set it down next to his. "You said this is new to you. It's new to me too. I've been focused on my walk with the Lord, finding my calling, going to school to become a counselor, and just being who He wants me to be. On my own."

"Do you feel like I'm pushing you into something you're not ready for?"

She took a moment to think about that, then shook her head. "I want to be ready. I mean, I *am* ready. But if we're going to explore what's happening here, there's something of my past you need to know. Something that might make a difference in how you want this to go."

A crease appeared between his brows. "I can't imagine there could be anything that would change how I feel about you, but I'm open to hearing it if you think it'll help us move forward."

Her heart hammered against her sternum. "I do. Just give me time to get this out, okay?"

"I'll do whatever you need."

She took a deep breath and let it out. "I told you about Nick, that we eloped the day after I graduated, and he left when my dad cut me off. If only that's all it would've been, I might've gotten over it a lot quicker. Bounced back instead of spiraling into a pit of despair I couldn't see my way out of."

Unable to sit still, she stood and walked over to the fireplace, her hands clasped at her chest when she turned back to him. "I was so lost those first few weeks, it didn't dawn on me my body wasn't doing what it was supposed to do. And when I finally took a pregnancy test, well ..."

His jaw fell slack. "You were pregnant?"

Nodding, she let out a shaky breath. "And I couldn't even afford to go to a doctor. The job I had at the time was delivering meals from restaurants. And my friends had finally realized I wasn't going to get back into my dad's good graces any time soon, so finding places to stay was getting harder.

"Once I knew about the baby, though, I swallowed my pride, went home, and begged for forgiveness. Anything so I could get proper medical care, have a healthy child, and be the parent I always wished I'd had."

"What happened?"

When she wasn't sure her shaking knees would continue to support her, she sat in the chair and braced her elbows on her thighs. "I went home, sat down with Mom and Dad, told them I was sorry for what I'd done, and I was ready to grow up and be responsible."

She took a deep breath. "Then I told them about the baby. And my dad came unglued. Told me I was welcome to come home, but I could not bring an illegitimate child with me, although the word he used was a lot uglier. Told me I had to get rid of it, or I had to leave."

His eyes hardened. "He asked you to abort your baby?"

"That's what he wanted, yes. But I refused. Thing is, my baby wasn't illegitimate. He was conceived in marriage. Maybe Nick and I didn't exactly wait, but I wasn't pregnant when we got married."

"He? You had a boy?"

Tears she could no longer hold back slid down her face. "Eight pounds, nine ounces, twenty inches long. Born healthy at 2:12 p.m. on March fourteenth and placed in his mother's arms ten minutes later."

"He was adopted."

"I never even got to hold him. And I have no idea what his name is or where his family lives. Could be here in the area, could be on the other side of the world." She brushed her fingers across her cheeks. "That was the compromise I made with my father, that if he let me carry to term, I would agree to a closed adoption. The family lawyer took care of all the details."

And now a piece of her lived outside her body, somewhere else in the world, in the arms and heartbeat of another mother.

"I know that's hard for you to understand because your mom kept you, and it sounds like I gave my baby away to keep my status. But I honestly believed I had no choice.

"I tried to find other options. Cam was at Harvard, and he wouldn't have helped me, anyway, because he was so angry with me for eloping in the first place. All of my friends were in college or traveling the world. My grandparents on my mother's side were both gone, and my paternal grandparents live most of the time in Ireland. I'd already tried making it on my own and failed in epic proportions."

She shook her head. "I even tracked down Nick, hoping he might help me if he knew he had a child on the way. But if he wanted no part of me without my money, he certainly didn't want to be saddled with child support. All he would agree to was signing off his parental rights. I had nowhere else to go, but I absolutely was not going to abort my child."

He didn't say anything as he studied her, his expression unreadable. Except for the sadness in his eyes, for a baby given away so she could keep her parents' approval and wealth. How utterly selfish she must seem to him.

When he stood and gazed at the floor, she told herself to wait for him to leave before falling apart. Instead of moving toward the door, however, he walked over to the chair, sat on the ottoman in front of her, and leaned in to clasp her tightly clutched hands between both of his.

"I am so sorry you had to make that decision so young. Yes, your circumstance was similar to my mother's, a pregnant teenager without a husband, yet not the same. I never knew my father. He was a soldier a couple of years older than my mom. She went to stay the summer before her senior year with a friend who had moved to Killeen, and my dad was stationed at what was then Fort Hood.

"Mom said it was love at first sight, that things got a little intense the night before he left for his first deployment and they went too far. But he kept in touch with her, and they truly cared about each other. She hadn't had the chance to tell him about me when he was killed by an IED three weeks into his tour."

"Oh, how awful."

"Mom was devastated but said it made her even more determined to keep me. But the difference for her was my grandparents gave her enormous support. She was able to get her GED, and Gran watched me so Mom could work and not have to pay for childcare. Unfortunately, my grandfather died from cancer when I was two, so I didn't have a man in my life until Mitch several years later.

"But, you see, that's why my mother kept me. Because she had help. I would never judge you for giving your boy a chance at life. You could have been done with it a lot earlier, but you refused to do what your father asked, even with everything he was holding over your head. I think that's brave."

Tears continued to flow down her face—tears of relief that Hunter had stayed, tears of regret for the child she'd never see. "I wanted to keep him. So much. I was completely empty after they took him. The pain was unbearable, so I tried to lose myself in parties and drinking myself numb. Even at home when there wasn't somewhere else to go to get plastered. My parents keep a very well-stocked bar, so it was easy to get liquor any time I wanted it.

"But whenever I was sober, it would be there. The pain. The memory of watching them take him out of the room while I screamed for them to bring him back. I finally lost all will to live, and that's when God brought me Miss Nadine."

"Shannon." A lone teardrop trickled down his face. "Sweetheart, I'll be forever grateful God put Miss Nadine on that bench with you. You've touched so many lives by not letting the enemy win. I'm one of them."

Bowing her head, she gave in to the sobs torn from the deepest part of her. Hunter let go of her hands and stood, and a moment later she found herself cradled in his arms. Her own wound around his neck as he settled on the sofa with her in his lap. Her face burrowed into the crook of his shoulder, body shaking with the outpouring of her grief.

"Be with Shannon, Father. Be her rock and her fortress. Be her comfort and her healer. Wrap her in Your peace and cover her with Your love. Be with Shannon, Father. Be her rock …"

His prayer, repeated in a broken rasp, penetrated to her soul. Peace slipped in to replace the turmoil she'd lived with but had hidden far beneath all the good she'd tried to pile on top of it. Good thoughts, good words, good intentions, good ministry, good, good, good. As if she could atone for giving her child away to keep her name.

A name she still hadn't taken back. A name by which she'd never wanted to be measured.

Her tears abated, and his voice grew silent. Still, she stayed there, letting him hold her, taking comfort in the strength of his arms encircling her, the lingering scent of his sandalwood aftershave, the softness of his hair against her cheek.

When she finally pulled back, he reached up and cupped her face, brushing her cheek with his thumb. "I think you've judged yourself so harshly all these years, you think others will as well. Don't keep carrying that shame. Didn't Pastor Jason say in church last week that continuing to carry shame was akin to telling Jesus His blood wasn't enough to cover it?"

Startled, she stared into his glistening eyes. She'd heard the same message on Sunday, but it hadn't penetrated past the guilt she still carried. As if it were her own personal cross to bear.

But he was right. Jesus was the only One capable … worthy … to cover any shame. Cover all guilt.

He swept a lock of hair off her face. "I'm not trying to convict you. That's not my job. Just listen to the Spirit like you always do. He'll show you how to let it go. And how you can use it to help others. Like your CU girls or in your counseling career. If you're sitting in front of a scared, pregnant, teenage girl, you're going to know exactly what's going on in her head. In her heart. *That's* how God redeems bad for good. Like Harper told me that night. Right?"

"Right." Her voice barely crept past the lump in her throat.

Ally and Harper both cried with her when she told them her story. But she'd continued living with this haunting burden every day. Not wanting to share it, hoping nobody would discover what she'd been willing to sacrifice to win her father's acceptance.

But with Hunter's gentle care and exhortation to forgive herself, to accept Christ's redemption, her soul felt lighter, her spirit fuller. As if she could finally move past this barrier and allow someone to love her without fear they would find her undeserving.

To allow her to minister to another faced with the same decisions.

Her pulse raced. She'd never once considered using her experience for ministry. As much as she loved the Lord, as much as she treasured ConnectUP and the kids she served with such joy, she still had never thought to share her own pain, owning the decision she made and letting the Lord use it. Had she missed anyone along the way who might've been served if she'd been willing to be transparent?

Oh, Lord, don't let it be so. Please forgive me if I overlooked some precious girl out of my own selfish need to keep this part of myself hidden. Thank You for Hunter, who had the courage to speak truth to my heart.

With the fingers of one hand, she traced his face. From his temple to his jaw, over his late evening stubble, finally placing her palm against his neck. "You really are a good man, Hunter Kavanaugh. A good, *godly* man."

"Shannon." He swallowed as moisture pooled in his eyes. "I told you earlier tonight there are a million things I love about you. Did you understand what I was saying? It's not just *things*. It's you. I don't know how else to say it except to say I'm falling in love with you. And I have been, I think, from the moment I saw you standing in my kitchen, the girl by the fountain I couldn't get out of my head."

She slipped off his lap to his side, snuggled into him, and laid her head on his shoulder. Curling her legs up on the sofa, she reveled in his warmth so near, this newfound freedom to explore what might lie ahead for them. Now that she no longer measured herself by her failing but by how God had made her new.

"Hunter," she whispered.

"Yeah?"

"There are a million things I love about you too."

CHAPTER FORTY-ONE

$\mathcal{H}$unter leaned over the steering wheel, his eyes trained on the couple exiting the back seat of a black Lincoln Town Car in the circular drive of the massive estate the O'Connors called home.

"Is that Senator Cookson?"

Shannon nodded from beside him in the BMW. "And his wife, my dad's Vice President of Operations. The very definition of a power couple."

He shook his head. "This is going to be an interesting evening."

"It usually is," she said with a sigh.

He glanced at her as the Town Car pulled away. "You don't enjoy your family's Christmas Ball?"

"Sometimes." She smiled over at him as he drove up to the valet. "So far, this year might be my favorite."

"Because of your charming and handsome escort?"

"But of course."

After taking the claim ticket from the valet, he walked around to meet Shannon on the other side of the car and offered her his arm. "I know I've already said it, but you look stunning, Miss Trent."

Her cheeks turned rosy in that charming way he loved when she blushed. "Thank you, Mr. Kavanaugh."

At the steps leading up to the double front door, he paused while she gathered the full skirt of her gown with her other hand. From the moment she'd opened her door to him, he could barely catch his breath. Because in that red dress with the velvet top and satin skirt, she was a knock-out.

She'd pulled her abundant hair up into a blingy clip while several strands hung in soft curls between her shoulder blades, left bare by the deep *V* of the dress. She wore more makeup than usual, perfect for a formal event. Even the red-painted lips.

He leaned in as they walked up the half-dozen stone steps. "Guess we'll see later if that lipstick is my color."

There went that blush again when she grinned.

He'd still put in a lot of hours at the office the past couple of weeks, but knowing he would have the evening not only with Bry but with Shannon had him itching to get home. Although limited by his work or her CU commitments, the time spent with her was always his favorite part of the day.

He hadn't considered himself part of a couple in a while, but this was different. Probably because he'd never had somebody he couldn't wait to see. Somebody who exchanged messages with him throughout the day, memes to make him laugh, scripture verses to ground him, sweet messages to remind him she cared. Knowing he had a person, and she had him.

They reached the landing and waited to enter behind several other guests. "Are you nervous?" she asked in a quiet voice.

"Should I be?"

"*I'm* nervous. My dad can be a little much."

"I can handle dads. Even billionaire dads."

Even a billionaire dad who forced his daughter to give up her child when the family had every resource in the world available to help her raise him. Maybe if he respected Harrison O'Connor one iota, he'd be nervous about impressing the man.

As it stood, all he hoped to achieve was to hold his tongue, be courteous, and have a nice evening with his gorgeous date. Didn't matter to him if Shannon's father found him lacking. If she thought him worthy to be her escort to her family's annual Christmas extravaganza, nothing else mattered.

Her hand squeezed his arm. "I was less nervous at your firm's Christmas dinner last weekend. Even meeting all those partners. An imposing bunch, for sure."

"Didn't appear they intimidated you at all. You handled them all with grace and poise." But, then, being raised in this vast estate by one of the most powerful men in Texas, she probably had plenty of experience dealing with imposing businessmen. And women.

"Having you at the firm dinner made it the most fun I've ever had at one. I knew you and Julia would hit it off."

Like firecrackers. The two ladies talked and laughed throughout the evening, often at yet another story Jules shared about him from the early days, when she had to school him in office policies *and* politics. It didn't escape him that she was as responsible for his success as anything he'd done in the last four-and-a-half years.

"She told me she runs your office but lets you think you're in charge."

"A truer statement never spoken. She absolutely runs me."

Over his shoulder, he scanned the other guests waiting behind them on the steps, including a local talk show host, an assistant coach from the Dallas Cowboys, and none other than Conrad Penson, defense attorney extraordinaire.

Her eyes widened. "Oh, I forgot to tell you she and I are having lunch Monday, since it's a day off and you're working, anyway."

"Should've seen that coming." And at least Julia and Shannon could do something fun the day after Christmas while he worked with Gail at the office on what was actually a holiday.

Hunter let his gaze roam over the front of the estate, from the well-lit grounds to the spectacular French architecture. He couldn't count anybody he knew who had a home big enough to host the cream of Dallas/Fort Worth society for a *ball*. And to think Shannon had been raised in this vast house—if it could be called a house.

Finally at the door, they entered a two-story tall foyer. White marble shone beneath their feet, and pillars stood like sentries at four points, beyond which lay the living area that tonight would be the ballroom. Two curved staircases with intricate wrought iron railings flanked the foyer, ending above at a large open landing.

A young woman in black slacks, white blouse, and red vest with bow tie walked up to them. "May I check your coats, sir?"

"Yes, please." He handed off his overcoat and Shannon's white evening wrap and took the ticket she offered in exchange.

The senator and his wife stepped up to greet their hosts.

Shannon leaned close. "You do look amazing, Mr. Kavanaugh. I'm going to be the envy of every unattached female here tonight. Maybe even a few attached ones."

"I only care about one female, Miss Trent, and she's already attached to me." He put his mouth near her ear. "Don't be nervous. We've got this."

When the other couple stepped away, Shannon's father took her hand and kissed her cheek. "Who do we have here, Shannon Elizabeth?"

Before Shannon could answer, Mrs. O'Connor, dressed in a silver gown reflecting the light from the chandelier above, put her hand on her husband's arm. "This is Mr. Kavanaugh, dear. The young man Shannon asked me to add to our table."

"Hunter Kavanaugh," Shannon said. "Hunter, this is my father, Harrison O'Connor. And my mother, Regina."

"A pleasure to meet you both. Thank you for having me this evening."

Shannon's mother stepped in to allow him to place a light kiss on her cheek. It was easy to see why the O'Connor sisters were so beautiful. Their mother was lovely, her still-blonde hair swept up in a stylish updo, her figure lithe, and complexion creamy like Shannon's.

"Hunter Kavanaugh." Mr. O'Connor, standing the same height as Hunter and boasting a fit physique, regarded him with narrowed blue eyes as he took his hand in a firm grip. "And what is it you do, young man?"

"Senior associate at Williamson, Sheffield, and Moore."

One eyebrow rose toward Mr. O'Connor's still ample salt and pepper hairline. "Is that right? Well, welcome. I'm sure we'll have an opportunity to get acquainted later."

"I look forward to it." About as much as he would a root canal. But the man was Shannon's father, and for that alone, he deserved the proper respect.

With a nod toward Mrs. O'Connor, he took Shannon's hand and moved toward the ballroom. A bar sat at one side, and several bistro tables situated around the room allowed guests a place to visit and enjoy cocktails and *hors d'oeuvres*.

A string ensemble set up in a corner, next to the largest fireplace Hunter had ever laid eyes on, played Christmas music, adding to the ambiance created by the elegant holiday decor.

He peered down at Shannon as they walked hand-in-hand through the room. "You can breathe now. He didn't throw me out."

"No, but you can bet come Monday, he'll have Legal running a background check on you."

"Not worried. He'll find what he'll find because I am who I am. I can't help where I come from, but I'm not ashamed of it."

She pulled him to a stop. "I'm in no way embarrassed about who you are or what you come from. I wish so much I could have known your mother, because she raised two spectacular people, even with all she went through."

The now familiar grief squeezed his chest. "She would've loved you." No doubt as much as he did.

They continued through the room, and his attention was drawn to a Rockefeller tree wannabe in front of a wall of two-story windows with a view of the veranda and pool beyond. "I have never seen a tree so tall in somebody's home before. What is it? Fifteen? Twenty feet?"

"Usually runs around twenty, give or take a foot or two."

"Is it real?"

"Every needle."

"Where do you even get a tree that big?"

"The grounds manager orders it from somewhere in Arkansas. As a kid, I used to love to watch the guys bring it in and set it up. Then Mom's interior designer brings in her crew to decorate it. They cover the entire floor with tarps, build a scaffolding around the tree, and a one-man portable crane-slash-forklift thing, like they use at big box stores, lifts crates of ornaments to the decorators. That, along with outfitting the rest of the house, is a major undertaking that takes about ten decorators over three days. It's chaos around here the week of Thanksgiving, which is why my family usually travels for the holiday and leaves Fiona in charge."

"I can't imagine." He gave his head a shake. "I could use something to drink. Can I get you anything?"

"A ginger ale, I think, would be great for my butterflies right now. I've been coming to this event since I was sixteen, and it always puts a knot in my stomach."

"Did Nick ever make it to one?"

"One. About a month after we met. He didn't last long. Drank too much and my dad actually did throw him out."

"Well, Miss Trent, I promise a much less dramatic outcome tonight. I'll be right back with your ginger ale, milady."

He left her at one of the bistro tables and walked over to the bar, waiting behind several others to place their order.

A man in a black tuxedo with a red and green plaid tie strode toward the bar, his unsmiling gaze skimming past Hunter before coming back.

Camden O'Connor. Super.

Instead of going to the rear of the line, he stopped next to Hunter. Doubtful anybody would dare confront an O'Connor about cutting in line at their own event, although it still smacked of presumptuousness on his part.

Cam regarded him with narrowed eyes. "I remember you."

"Pardon me?"

"From the hospital. With Shannon."

"Oh, right." He held out his hand. "Hunter Kavanaugh."

Shannon's brother took Hunter's hand in a firm grip, not unlike his father's minutes before. "Camden O'Connor. I saw you'll be seated with us at the family table."

"An honor."

"May I ask what your relationship is? You and my sister?"

Taken aback, Hunter glanced over to Shannon, engaged in conversation with two other women, then back to her brother. "We're dating."

"Exclusive?"

"Yes." Not that it was any business of Camden's.

They stepped up to the bar, and Camden held up two fingers. "Champagne."

The bartender nodded and turned his attention to Hunter. "For you, sir?"

"One ginger ale, one cola, please."

Camden chuckled. "A teetotaler like my sister, I see."

Growing up with an alcoholic could have that effect, but that wasn't something he felt inclined to share with this man. "I don't like to imbibe on an empty stomach."

Cam took two flutes of champagne from the young man behind the bar but didn't leave.

"Thank you," Hunter said when he accepted the two crystal tumblers with tiny straws offered to him. As he moved away, Cam came with him.

"Shannon drank like a fish until she got messed up with all her Jesus business. I guess some good came out of that, though, since she seemed to finally grow up. At least she didn't drink, then plow a car into a building. Dee should thank her lucky stars all she broke was her leg."

Her leg and her spirit, but Cam apparently didn't care so much about Delaney's emotional health as long she didn't continue to embarrass the family.

"Now that I think about it, though, Shan didn't hit the hard stuff until after the baby. I didn't see her drink anything while she was pregnant." He clicked his tongue. "Oh, there I go. Spouting off about family skeletons, and you probably didn't even know that, did you? Sorry if I dropped a bomb on you."

Heat bristled at the base of Hunter's skull, and he fought the urge to throw the drinks in his hand in Cam's face. If he were a gambling man, he'd bet a year's salary Cam had dropped *this* bomb with clear intent. Too bad for him it was a dud.

"I'm well aware of what Shannon went through." Hunter's eyes bored into Cam's. "Everything. And I, for one, am beyond grateful she found her faith when she did, or she probably wouldn't be with us now."

From the way Camden's face blanched before he covered, Hunter's *bomb* had hit its target dead on. Clearly, Shannon's brother had no idea how close they'd come to not having her with them at all.

Camden cleared his throat. "I have a date I need to get back to. Nice meeting you, Kavanaugh."

"Pleasure was mine." A stretch of the truth, although no more than Cam's.

Camden took a few steps, then turned and strode back. "Nick Trent was a piece of trash who only saw dollar signs and an easy life when he looked at my sister. If that's what you're after, you can either walk now or be shown the door later. Your choice."

Before Hunter could respond, Camden stalked off, leaving him stunned. How had someone as spectacular as Shannon come from this family?

He counted to ten in his head before turning to join his beautiful date where he'd left her. To his surprise, Delaney stood with her, braced with her crutches under her arms. A stark contrast to the vivid blue sequined dress that fell straight to the floor with a thigh-high slit on one side, revealing her bulky splint.

"You look beautiful, Dee." He kissed her cheek. "Great to see you again."

Her smile lit her face. With her more subdued makeup and hair down around her shoulders, she appeared more her age. More … innocent.

"Thank you. You look pretty great yourself." She gave Shannon a nudge with her elbow. "That's no rented tux, is it?"

Shannon rolled her eyes. "Behave, Dee."

He looked back and forth between the sisters. "Sounds like there's a story there."

"Oh, she's being snarky."

With a laugh, Delaney shook her head. "Did she tell you about the ball her jerk ex came to?"

He glanced at Shannon. "Only that your dad threw him out."

"That was the best part of the whole night. I was only twelve, but Mom told me I could come. I was bored out of my mind until all the drama around Nick. He showed up in this rented tux, really tacky, like something out of a 70's prom. Ruffled shirt, bow tie, even a cummerbund. Thought he was all that, and poor Shannon was mortified."

Shannon took another sip and nodded. "True story."

"Then he got plastered, Dad took him out the back by his

collar, and had our driver take him home. Never set foot here again."

"I knew the second Dad sized him up in that awful tux, the night would not go well." Grinning, Shannon reached over and ran her fingers under Hunter's lapel. "Won't have to worry about that tonight, though. You do rock a vest and pocket square, I must say. My handsome man."

Her compliment warmed him better than the heat from the enormous fireplace, and he wondered if they could see his chest puffing out with pride at being Miss Shannon Trent's *man*.

"Oh, my, my, my." Delaney waved her hand up and down between their faces. "You two are so gone on each other. Should I leave?"

Somehow, he pulled his focus from Shannon's luminous face. "Of course not."

"Good. Because I'm dying to know what Camden said to you."

"Cam? Oh, uh. Just welcoming me." To walk right out the door.

CHAPTER FORTY-TWO

$\mathscr{W}$ith her handsome date holding her close on the dance floor, Shannon had so far enjoyed this event more than any before it.

Their five-star, catered dinner had passed relatively drama-free out in the large, heated tent erected on the grounds. Professional designers had spent the last two days transforming it into a Christmas wonderland with thousands of twinkling lights, miles of ribbon and garland, two dozen eight-foot tall, decorated Christmas trees, and lighted stars hanging from above.

If only she could shed the feeling something was brewing between Hunter and Cam.

Closing her eyes, she nuzzled her nose against Hunter's neck, pushing all thoughts of her brother out of her mind to revel in the moment.

He swallowed. "You keep doing that and we're going to have to find somewhere I can give you a proper kiss. Without all these eyes on us."

Giggling, she peered up at him. "Sorry. You smell amazing. Don't ever change your aftershave. I love it."

"Note to self. Order lifetime supply of aftershave to keep

Shannon happy."

"Excellent plan." She studied his face, his eyes fixed on hers. If she were to be so blessed, she could imagine spending a lifetime with this man. Making a home with him, having a family with him, growing old with him.

"What are you thinking?"

Jolted out of her reverie, she scrambled for something to say, not sure this would be the right time to reveal her romantic imaginings to the man at the center of them. "Are you going to tell me what Cam really said to you?"

His sigh was barely perceptible. "He's just being protective of his little sister."

"You mean the family name. They still haven't forgiven me for the Nick fiasco, even though it's been years, and I'm a completely different person."

"Don't worry about it. I'm here for you, not your family. Would I like to have their approval? Sure. Is it likely? Considering my name doesn't come with a pedigree, probably not. But if you're okay with that, I'm all good."

He gave her a chaste kiss that had her longing for the *proper* one he'd teased her about. Maybe later, when they weren't in a room full of the Texas upper crust.

"Did I tell you Delaney's coming to the Christmas Eve service with us tomorrow night?"

"You didn't, but that's great. Do we need to come get her?"

"If that's okay. She'll be able to get in and out of your car easier than my Mini."

"Of course that's okay. Are we still planning to do gifts after, since you'll be here with your family Christmas Day?"

"Sure. I have one I haven't brought here yet that she can open."

"How will you get out here Christmas morning if she's not able to get into your car?"

"They can send one for us."

"Or you can take mine. We're not going anywhere."

She cocked her head to the side. "Would you and Bry like to come here on Christmas Day? If Cam hasn't scared you away?"

"Shan. Do I look like I scare easily?"

"Is that a yes, you'll come?"

"Yes. If two more on Christmas Day isn't a problem, we'd love to. But we can come later, after you've had your family gift time. You take my car with Delaney, and Bry and I will come in yours. Assuming I can fit behind the wheel."

She put her head back and laughed. "You'll fit, but I'll still look forward to seeing that. I'll let Mother know tonight you're coming on Sunday. She'll be delighted."

"Great. We're doing gifts with Mitch in the morning, then we'll come out when he heads back to Houston. That'll give your dad that chance to grill me."

She laughed again, pulling away to applaud after the music died away. "I have no doubt you'll have the proper answers." She picked up her skirt. "My feet are killing me in these shoes. Care to sit for a while?"

"Works for me. I don't know how you've lasted this long on those sky-high things."

She peered down at her silver, rhinestone-studded stilettos and up at him again. "This is how I achieve five-foot-six status."

"Seems a steep price to pay for extra inches."

"Says the man who stands at a perfect six-foot-one." She laughed and took his hand. "Come on. I have the perfect spot."

Weaving through the guests still on the floor, she led him to a hallway at the side, through a large dining area to a back staircase that took them to the second floor. He followed her down another hall and onto a glass-enclosed balcony overlooking the front of the estate.

He gazed out over the winding private drive lined with luxury cars and limousines. Dozens of majestic oaks covered in white lights stood resplendent throughout the lush grounds. "This is gorgeous."

"This was always my favorite place to be during Christmas when I was a kid." She pulled two sodas from a mini-fridge and handed him one. "I'd bring my blankets and stuffed lion and sleep out here. When the weather's nice, these windows slide all the way to the side to open up the balcony. When I couldn't actually be outside, this was my alternative."

He twisted the top off his soda and took a long swallow. After another scan of the sparkling landscape, they sank down into an overstuffed couch that faced another identical to it.

She kicked off her offensively high-heeled shoes, pulled her legs up under her gown, and settled beneath his arm when he drew her close. "When you're here for Christmas, I'll give you a tour of the grounds. We have twenty acres of land with a running creek, ponds, walking paths, stables. Very serene. Really the only thing I miss about living on the estate."

"I have to say, I never saw myself with a modern-day American princess. Yet here I am."

"Oh, please. That might describe Delaney, but not me." She took a swallow of her soda and set it down on the glass-topped table. "Mom gave up on me early on. I'm short, but I was athletic. Preferred sports over dance or piano lessons, and I loved being outside. Mom didn't know what to do with me, so she put all her energies into Dee. She didn't start sowing her wild oats until college."

His soda joined hers on the table, then his fingers intertwined with hers on his leg. "Guess Delaney got tired of playing the game too."

"Yeah, I'm hoping this interest in spiritual things will lead to something. I've been asking her for years to come to church with me."

She put her head against his shoulder and let the silence surround them as lights blinked in the trees beyond. "I had an interesting conversation with Wyatt at work today."

"About?"

"How God might use my story to help other girls." She sat up to face him. "What you said, about God redeeming bad for good, hit me in the heart. I'd always tried so hard to keep that part of me secret. Buried. Because I was ashamed of the decision I made, to give up my baby to win back the approval of my father."

"That shame isn't yours, sweetheart. Although you bore the pain of it."

"I think I finally realize that now. And Wyatt agreed with you, that God could use all of that pain for good. So, we came up with a ministry plan we're going to run by the board of Becker Ministries, the organization that oversees funding for CU."

"What's the plan?"

"I have a trust. A sizable one. Once I was a believer, I wanted to be measured by who I was in Christ, not by who my family was or their wealth, so I didn't use it to live on. That trust money is just sitting there. Gaining interest and growing each year when my dad makes another contribution to it, which he'll do until I'm thirty.

"I donated some to CU when I first started with the ministry, but today I made a pitch to Wyatt that I'd like to use my trust to build a crisis pregnancy arm of ConnectUP, like Zane and Al did with missions. ConnectUP will be the parent organization, but any girl of high school age who finds herself in that situation can make use of its resources for guidance, financial help, legal help, medical, psychological. The whole gamut."

"That's amazing."

"If it's approved, I'm going to run it in conjunction with the position at Wyatt's practice he's offered me. I'll focus on crisis pregnancy, life after putting a child up for adoption, or post-abortion, and I'll be in charge of contracting with adolescent psychologists in other cities where we have clubs. We'll also provide parenting classes for any girls, teen dads, or couples who choose to keep their child."

His smile spread wide across his face. "Shan, that's fantastic. You have my complete support. Just tell me what you need—money, time, legal advice, whatever—and it's yours."

"That means everything to me." Sinking against him, her eyes stared into his in the dim light from the hallway. "You said something about getting away somewhere to give me a proper kiss?"

He pulled her closer still, his face but a breath from hers. "So I did."

When he closed the distance, her arms went around him, his now familiar kiss tender and unassuming, and the warmth of his embrace chasing away the chill of the room. Her heart raced when his hand cupped her face, and she lost all track of time until he pulled back and touched his forehead to hers.

"Was that proper enough, Miss Trent?"

"And then some, Mr. Kavanaugh."

After another breath-stealing kiss, he settled her once again under his arm. She fingered a button on his vest as silence surrounded them, punctuated only by distant strains of music from the ballroom.

A shadow from the doorway spread over them. "Shannon."

She started at the sound of her brother's voice behind them and turned out of Hunter's arms to face him. "What on earth, Cam?"

"Can I speak with you a moment?"

"Now?"

"Do I need to make an appointment?"

"That's preferable to *now*."

Hunter squeezed her hand. "It's okay. I'll wait here."

With a sigh, she rose and glared at her brother as she walked barefoot to meet him at the door. "Five minutes."

He turned and stalked down the hall. "In here."

She followed him to a guest bedroom, where he flipped on the light and shut the door before whirling on her.

"Didn't you learn the first time, Shan? What is it with you and these low-class guys who see nothing but money when they look at you?"

Heat suffused her face. "*This* is what was so important you had to talk to me *now?*"

"Better now than before you make another colossal mistake."

"You have no idea what you're talking about. And what *guys?* I met Nick when I was seventeen years old. Hunter's the first man I've let get close to me since, and he's a good guy. A godly man. He doesn't care about my money or my name."

"I'm just watching out for you."

"No, you're not. You're only worried about how I might embarrass the family. But you know what *I'm* embarrassed about? That my family can't look at a man like Hunter and see his breadth of integrity instead of wondering about his lineage."

She shook her head. "What happened, Cam? We used to genuinely like each other. Yes, I made a huge mistake. And I will always live with this aching void inside of me because of one stupid decision that cost me much more than it should have. Why did it have to cost me you too?"

When he said nothing, she turned, opened the door, and left him there. It had been years since her brother had regarded her with anything but disdain. The brother she'd idolized and followed everywhere when they were kids. The brother who'd take her teenage self out to dinner when he'd come home from college in Boston, just to catch up.

Until Nick Trent. And that appeared to be the one sin for which he would never forgive her.

CHAPTER FORTY-THREE

*B*rylie leaned toward Hunter. "Why do we all have so many plates and stuff?"

He chuckled at her wide eyes and whispered question as they took their seats at the long blue and silver decorated French Provincial table in the O'Connors' ultra-formal dining room.

He turned his head to speak close to her ear. "It's a five-course dinner. You'll use all of that, except the wine glasses. Water for you. And coffee with dessert, if you want it."

She nodded and straightened, her eyes still wandering around the elegant place setting in front of her—a salad plate situated atop a dinner plate that sat upon a silver charger, three forks, three spoons, a knife, a bread plate with its own knife for butter, three glasses, and a cup and saucer. He and Brylie hardly used that much dinnerware in a week, much less at one meal.

Delaney, on Brylie's other side, put her hand on his sister's shoulder. "Do what I do, Bry. You've got this."

Hunter took Shannon's hand under the table and threw her a wink. Brylie had been in a state of wonder from the moment they drove through the manned gate at the estate and up the quarter-mile meandering drive to the mansion.

"Shannon grew up here? It's like a fairy tale."

He couldn't disagree. Two nights ago, seeing this place lit up for the Christmas ball and dancing the night away with Shannon had indeed seemed like something out of a fairy tale.

Shannon smiled over at him. "I'm so happy you're here."

"Thank you for the invitation."

His eyes drifted to the necklace resting against her blue sweater dress, the pendant of one gold heart and another surrounded by diamonds overlapping each other. Designed by a well-regarded Fort Worth jeweler, the piece had cost him more than any he'd ever purchased. But the expression on her face when she opened her gift last night had been worth every penny.

And he'd already transferred everything from his old briefcase into the new one she gave him. The satchel-type case in burgundy leather, with a gold clasp and *HK* embossed on the flap, was a welcome improvement on the one he'd bought for himself fresh out of law school. He didn't even want to think about how much her thoughtful gift had cost. But he'd thanked her with a kiss—or three—up on the roof deck later, enjoying some alone time under the stars while their sisters watched a movie in Shannon's apartment.

His attention moved to a side door when two servers emerged with silver trays of *hors d'oeuvres* for the first course, followed by the meticulously plated one-bite appetizer course. Without words, Delaney demonstrated for Brylie which plate and utensil to use.

He'd have to remember to thank her later. At least he'd been at dinner parties in some of the partners' homes over the past few years, so had learned a bit about formal dining etiquette. Still, he'd never seen anything as opulent as this home and didn't know if he'd ever grow accustomed to it if he were to have a place in Shannon's future.

When she told him what Cam said to her Friday night, it galled him her brother equated him with her money-grubbing ex-husband. He had no interest in profiting from his relationship with her, and if anything came of them down the road, he'd happily sign anything the O'Connors put in front of him to prove it.

After the appetizer course came the salad course, then the main course an hour into the meal. Halfway through the salmon entrée, Mr. O'Connor peered at him from the head of the table, and Hunter suddenly had empathy for the poor fish. Looked like he was up next on the grill.

"You're an attorney, you said?"

"Yes, sir."

"Where'd you go to school?"

"UT Law."

The older man nodded. "Decent school."

One of the best in the country, it ranked a little higher than *decent*. "Yes, sir."

"Junior associate?"

"Senior, as of a year ago."

"Oh, right. At Williamson, Sheffield, and Moore. Impressive, especially at your age."

Finally. At least something met with approval. "I'm fortunate to be there."

Camden's eyebrows drew together as he stared at him across the table, his gaze drifting to Shannon and back again. "You're both in our Medallion Building, right?"

"Right."

"And when did you two meet?"

Hunter swiped his cloth napkin across his mouth. "Funny story, that. We actually bumped into each other, literally, in late September, but didn't formally meet until a couple of weeks later." He looked at Shannon next to him. "So, I would say early October."

"Right." She turned from him to her brother. "When I was

moving in, I ran into him with a box and knocked his phone into the fountain out front."

Delaney laughed. "It was hilarious watching Shannon wade in that fountain to get his phone."

"Only because I was in jeans, and he was in a very nice suit on his way to a meeting. No way was I making him fetch his phone out of the water."

Mrs. O'Connor put a hand to her chest. "Oh, my. Did you reimburse him, honey? For his phone?"

"I tried, but he wouldn't let me."

Hunter shook his head. "There was no need. I had a new one by the end of business that day, and it was more my fault than hers."

"Except I should've left one of those boxes in the car."

Camden continued to study him with a furrow in his brow, but if he had other questions, he didn't voice them, and the conversation moved to other topics.

Once their dinner dishes had been cleared and coffee poured, the chef herself presented their dessert. An elaborate piece resembling a log as it might rest on the forest floor, with beautiful poinsettias fashioned from icing. One would be hard-pressed to tell the real thing from the culinary one.

Shannon leaned in, their shoulders meeting. "*Bûche de Noël.* Beautiful, isn't it?"

"Too pretty to cut into."

"Except then you miss the best part. I told you, once you've tried it, you'll dream about this cake."

Two bites in, Hunter had to admit Shannon hadn't oversold the *glorified Swiss roll,* as she'd defined it. Most certainly the stuff of dreams.

Camden, who had remained relatively silent throughout the meal, made a hasty exit after dessert. *I need to check something* was his excuse when his mother asked him where he was going in such a hurry.

Apparently, business couldn't wait, even on Christmas.

His judgment left him chagrined. Hadn't he done the same the first night Shannon had dinner with them, left them to eat while he took a business call? It might not have been a holiday, but it still shamed him to remember.

Thankfully, Shannon hadn't let his less-than-polite self chase her away, and his life was forever changed because of it.

CHAPTER FORTY-FOUR

$\mathcal{B}$rylie stood in front of the living room tree, her gaze traveling up and down again. "Wow. That's a big tree. How do you decorate it when it's so tall?"

Shannon grinned at the teen's awestruck expression. "Designers do it."

The girl's forehead scrunched. "You don't even get to decorate your family tree?"

"Not this one. But there's a common area upstairs where our three suites are, and they'd bring in a much shorter tree for us to decorate when we were kids. That was our tree."

Brylie turned back to the twinkling behemoth. "I'd love to watch them put this one up next year."

"It's a date."

Her hand traveled to her necklace, fingering the lovely diamond and gold pendant Hunter had surprised her with last night. Two hearts connected with no way to come undone. How blessed she'd be if that proved true.

Because, whether or not she'd been ready for it, she'd fallen headlong in love with Hunter Kavanaugh.

"Would you like to see the grounds?"

He nodded. "Absolutely. It was beautiful all lit up Friday

night, but from what I saw driving in today, it's breathtaking even in the daylight."

They took their time walking along the stone path behind the house, past the pool, outdoor kitchen, and gazebo, to the stable where they kept their five horses.

"How'd it go with Mitch this morning?" she asked as they strolled toward the house. "Now that the custody suit's been settled?"

Brylie's face brightened. "Really good. He brought cinnamon rolls he made himself. To remember Mom, he said. She used to make them every Christmas morning."

"What a nice way to honor her."

Hunter gave her hand a squeeze. "Like your cookies yesterday. I know we got a little choked up when you surprised us with that, but it was really fun."

Brylie nodded. "Totally. I hope we can do that every year."

Warmth suffused Shannon's face as she looked up at Hunter. "That memory you shared with me over pie on our accidental date touched my heart. So, I asked Ally for a good sugar cookie recipe that would be easy enough for me to follow. I thought they turned out pretty good."

"They were great," he said. "Exactly like Mom's."

"I'm so glad." She led them through the house. "Did your dad like his tie you got him?"

"He said he did," Brylie answered. "And would wear it to church next week. He gave me a gift card to go shopping, which is cool. I was happy with that. Hunter got one, too, to his favorite store."

Hunter regarded his sister with a crease in his brow. "Yeah, how'd he know that?"

"He asked me where you liked to get your clothes, and I remember going there with you once."

They stopped again in front of the tree. "He didn't need to give me anything. Signing the custody settlement last week was the best Christmas gift I could have asked for. He'll be moving here in January, and I'll cover half his rent, as stated in the agreement."

Shannon's mouth fell open. "I didn't know you'd offered to do that."

"I didn't want the high cost of rentals close by to deter him from accepting. He should be able to find something, maybe even within walking distance of us, so we can see him more often."

"I'm beyond happy things have worked out so well. That you can welcome him into your life is a gift in itself. For all of you."

Moisture filled his eyes. "When Mom died, I considered myself an orphan because, as far as I was concerned, Mitch was as good as dead. But now … having him back, whole and sober and getting right with God … Well, it's nice to call him Dad again. I went from not wanting him anywhere near my life to looking forward to spending time with him."

Brylie swept a tear off her face. "You should've seen him, Shannon. My dad, I mean. When Hunter gave him season tickets to the Rangers and told him he bought two sets so they could go together, he got really emotional."

Shannon looked up at Hunter. "A lot of healing's been done there, between you all."

"Can't argue with that." He cleared his throat. "How did Delaney like the Christmas Eve service?"

"She loved it. She'd never been in church before and was surprised at how cool it was, with the music and the lights and how friendly everybody was. She wants to come with me next Sunday. Maybe eventually, I'll get them all there."

"Keep doing what you're doing, and we'll keep praying for them. Especially Dee, since she's asking questions."

Shannon took them through the rest of the house, sharing stories from her childhood. The happy ones. Before rebelliousness had set in as a desperate attempt to garner the attention she'd craved.

Shaking off the regrets of the past, Shannon laughed several times as Brylie gaped at something else she'd taken for granted, growing up in this gilded cage. She'd never looked at this place through another's eyes before today, seeing it through Brylie's.

When they returned to the living room, they met Delaney heading their way through the living area as fast as her crutches could carry her.

"I don't know what's going on," she said. "But Camden's looking for you both. And he is not happy."

Shannon heaved a sigh. "What is it this time?"

"I don't know. But I thought I'd warn you."

With a shake of her head, she turned to Hunter. "Would you rather make a break for it instead of sticking around? I can see what's going on and let you know later if it's important."

"No, it's fine. If he's looking for us both, let's see what he wants together."

"All right. Let's go get it over with." She turned to her sister. "Dee, can you take Bry up to the screening room for a movie? We'll join you after we find out what's up with Cam."

Brylie's uncertain gaze moved from Shannon to Hunter and back again. "Everything's okay?"

"It's fine. He can be a bit intense when he has something on his mind."

An understatement, but she didn't want to give Brylie anything to worry about.

Both their sisters made their way to the elevator—camouflaged as what most folks would assume was a coat closet—that would take them upstairs. And not a moment too soon.

Camden rounded the corner from the dining room and marched toward them with a document in his hand. "I think I finally figured it out."

"What are you talking about?"

Camden tipped his head. "Him. I thought the name of that law firm sounded familiar."

"What about it?" Hunter asked.

"You said you bumped into my sister in late September, then met again in early October? A month before O'Connor Properties is served with a lawsuit from none other than Williamson, Sheffield, and Moore."

A chill ran up her spine. "We ran into each other totally by accident."

"You sure about that? Maybe this has all been a way to get close to us."

Hunter's chuckle was without humor. "This is crazy. We have over a hundred lawyers. I can't possibly know every suit filed by my firm."

Camden's eyes narrowed. "We're just supposed to take your word you're not involved with this questionable lawsuit?"

"I can't speak to its strengths or weaknesses, but, yes, you can take my word I know nothing about it. If it were questionable, though, I doubt my firm would pursue it. We're not in the business of taking on cases we know have no merit."

"Then you might want to talk with Richard Norkowski, because there are some things here that don't add up. Such as how nobody saw or heard the plaintiff fall from the second floor. If he now has life-altering injuries, how'd he get up and walk away?

"And when the work order came through to fix the balcony railing this guy claims gave way, it was a simple repair to replace the screws. No damage to the railing, no debris from drywall or masonry as if the screws had ripped from the wall. More like they'd been manually removed. To our maintenance supervisor's credit, he had every single railing checked, and not one of them had a loose screw. Why just this one?"

"Again, I have no knowledge of—"

"Usually our legal department will settle personal injury

suits out of court, especially when someone claims they can barely walk and can't ever work again. But one of our attorneys brought this one specifically to me. Said at his last place of employment for an international hotel chain, a suit came in that was practically identical to this one, and it settled for a low six figures. Different plaintiff, same complaint, same law firm."

Hunter's brow furrowed. "Mine?"

"Yours. And while I'd like to believe this innocent act is legit, this all seems a little too coincidental for my liking."

Hunter put his hand out. "Okay, look. I honestly know nothing about this. But I can't talk to you about it, either, because I'm employed by the firm representing the plaintiff."

"Well, first thing Tuesday, when they're back in the office, I'm advising our legal team to file for a dismissal because your firm has a conflict of interest. Namely, you and your involvement with my sister."

Her heart in her throat, Shannon's gaze roamed from one man to the other, her head swimming. But she couldn't wrap her brain around Cam's suspicions their meeting was somehow attached to this lawsuit. It made no sense.

"Do what you have to do," Hunter said. "But I doubt it will be granted because my firm can prove I'm nowhere near this case. I've never even worked with Mr. Norkowski."

"Guess we'll see, won't we?"

He turned on his heel and walked away, leaving Hunter staring after him for a moment before he turned to her.

"You okay?"

Her eyes moved to him, but she couldn't find any words.

"Shannon, you can't believe for a second I conspired to meet you for a lawsuit. That's ridiculous."

Swallowing, she shook her head. "No. I don't believe that. I'm the one who approached Brylie. But it all sounds a little weird, doesn't it? That your firm would sue another large company for the same thing?"

"It could. But personal injury suits can be similar in nature."

"Six figures is a lot of money."

"It is for most people. To corporations like O'Connor Properties or a large hotel chain, it's a drop in the bucket when they could end up paying into the millions if a jury goes against them."

"So, this guy could end up with over a hundred thousand dollars simply because our company wouldn't want to take it to court?"

"It's possible. Depends on how far Cam wants to push it. I find it hard to believe my firm would file a personal injury case without merit. So, I'd be surprised if they would take a low-ball settlement if the guy is permanently disabled."

"If that's what happened."

"Right." He looked away, staring in the same direction Cam had left. "If that's what happened."

CHAPTER FORTY-FIVE

"What is it?" The hair on the back of Hunter's neck bristled at the pensive expression on Julia's face.

Her arms laden with file folders, she closed his door and took a seat in front of the desk. "You know we could lose our jobs for this."

"You found something."

"I found a lot. Hunter." She swallowed. "This could be coincidence. Or it could be bad. Very bad."

"If you want out, I totally get it. But I have to know, Jules. Not just for Shannon. But if there's something going on under our noses, something not right, we need to know."

Her eyes widened. "I never thought of myself as a character in a legal thriller."

He chuckled. "I doubt a couple of low-dollar personal injury suits would be considered the stuff of legal thrillers."

"A couple?" She dropped the stack on his desk. "That's six right there. And that's all I could pull without arousing suspicion."

His smile disappeared. "Six? You're sure?"

"All neck and spine injuries allegedly incurred by faulty

decks or balconies, all at major commercial properties, all with the same doctors, all with six-figure out-of-court settlements."

"All Rick's?"

"Every one. There are more I found in the system, but like I said, I couldn't pull them all without somebody noticing. I pulled these while the file clerks were at lunch."

Sitting up, he grabbed the file on top. "Okay, you're out. I don't want you mixed up in this. If anything comes down, it comes down on me. Understand?"

She shook her head. "That's not how I work. We're a team. We've always been a team. If we go out, we go out together. Besides, if you were no longer here, I'd go with you, anyway. How on earth would you make it without me?"

He couldn't help laughing, even with the enormity of the situation sitting on top of them. "You have me there. If I end up hanging my own shingle, having you at the helm would definitely be a plus."

"Then there you go. You're in, I'm in. What do we do next?"

"Divide and conquer. I'll take these home tonight and go through them. I want to get an idea of who these plaintiffs are, who these medical professionals are, and if there truly is something to be concerned about here. I already have a bead on the whereabouts of the plaintiff against the O'Connors, so I thought I might check him out. From a distance. See if he's as injured as he claims."

"And I'll do some digging online."

"Sounds good." He sat back in his chair and let out a breath. "I really hope there's nothing here."

She eyed him across the desk. "But your gut's telling you something different."

"I don't know, Jules. Rick's a partner. Nobody's looking over his shoulder. It would be easy for him to manufacture claims, hire folks who are down and out to pose as plaintiffs for a low four-figure pay-out, pay off a couple of doctors, get a six-figure settlement. The firm gets a third of that, but he pockets the rest, plus his percentage of the firm's one-third, and nobody's the wiser."

"Until it hits the wrong desk at the legal office for OPD and they take it to the Vice President. Who just so happens to be your girlfriend's brother who now thinks you're in on it."

He rolled his eyes. "Cam would believe anything if it meant getting me out of the picture. I guess he doesn't think someone could love Shannon for who she is and not for her name. Shows how short-sighted he is."

A grin spread across her face. "Love?"

"Say what?"

"You said *love*. That he doesn't believe someone could *love* Shannon for who she is. Is that you?"

His gaze fixed on her across the desk, he let his thoughts meander through the past couple of months. He'd been on a roller coaster since the death of his mother and his sister coming to live with him. Changes in his work life, his home life. Meeting Shannon, becoming fast friends. Someone he depended on and respected. Coming to know the Lord and forging new friendships with an amazing group of people.

And falling in love. Yes, he was definitely in love with Shannon. Maybe it had all happened in a short span of time, but there was no denying what had happened in his heart. His soul. He was hers if she wanted him. For as long as that may be.

"That's me."

"To be honest, that's not exactly news. I could see it the night of the Christmas dinner. What the two of you have, even though it's new, is really special. Hold onto it."

"That's my plan."

Her expression sobered. "If you're right about this, how deep do you think it goes?"

"You mean, as far as the partners are concerned?" He

shrugged. "Who knows at this point? You didn't find suits like this with any of the other partners, did you?"

She shook her head. "I didn't find anything with anybody else that had such similar claims. These stood out not only because the claims were the same, but the doctors are all the same. And every one is against a major corporation with deep pockets. As in, Mariana Trench deep."

"Like O'Connor Property Development."

"Exactly."

He folded his hands on the desk. "Do you think anybody's aware we've been nosing around? They can't track what you're doing online, can they?"

"Not that I'm aware of. There are cameras in the office, though. Including the file room. If anybody were to look closely, they'll see I'm in there pulling closed files that aren't ours. But what I don't get is why he would keep these files here if they're bogus."

"Because he had to have accounting take out the firm's one-third contingency fee since that's how we're paid for personal injury cases. That's the only way to make it appear legit."

Her face paled. "So, if you're right, and these are fraudulent claims Rick's spearheading, it's not only him on the line but the firm? There would be sanctions for that, wouldn't there? Hunter, this firm has been here over a hundred years."

"I know. Let's not get ahead of ourselves. If there are only these cases—"

"Maybe a few more that I saw. No more than perhaps three."

"Okay. Maybe six to nine cases, the firm could probably find their way to simply paying back the settlements. It'll be a kick in the teeth, and there might be some punitive sanctions from the bar. But if Rick's the only one involved, he'd probably be the only one to lose his license to practice. And he'd be hit with some criminal charges, as well."

"With only those six cases there, settlements total a smidge north of a million dollars. Can the firm afford that?"

"I would imagine they could bear it. If they fire Rick, which they would have to do if he's disbarred, they'd have to buy out his share, though, as an equity partner. Unless they require him to forfeit it, since this would be considered a criminal act. But with his income being well over a million, at least they'd have that to use to pay back settlements if they don't replace him right away. Plus, they would probably sue him in return to recoup any settlements they have to pay out."

"This could get messy."

"It could get very messy. And with us right in the middle of it."

CHAPTER FORTY-SIX

Shannon peered into the doorway of her sister's suite. "Knock, knock."

Delaney looked up from the book in her lap, her face lighting up. "Hey! I didn't know you were coming out today."

Shannon walked into the sitting room and dropped onto one of the chairs opposite the couch where Delaney sat with her legs stretched out in front of her. "Yeah, kind of a spur-of-the-moment decision. Thought I'd come see how you're doing."

"Better now that my dictator of a physical therapist is gone. I swear he gets some sort of sick pleasure out of torturing me."

"At least he comes to you now instead of you having to go into Dallas three times a week."

"Maybe that's why he punishes me, because Dad insisted on that arrangement. Takes more out of his day to come all the way out here for poor little me."

Shannon chuckled. "Is your leg getting stronger?"

Delaney tossed her head side to side. "Yeah. But still."

"Still, nothing. You knew PT would be painful, but if it's working, that's what matters, right?" She grinned at her little sister. "Or is it because your therapist is drop-dead gorgeous but hasn't asked you out yet?"

Delaney's pert little nose went up. "Of course not." After a moment, she sighed, her shoulders slumping. "Okay, so he's hot. And not only has he not asked me out, he's shown zero interest in me at all."

"Maybe he has a girlfriend."

"He doesn't. I asked."

"Why does that not surprise me?" She sat forward. "Dee, it's probably best to concentrate on healing right now and not worry about having a guy. You're fine without one."

"If you say so."

"I do. And I'm older and wiser, so you should listen."

"Easy for you to say. You have an amazing guy who absolutely adores you."

Shannon's grin faded as her gaze moved to the window behind her sister.

"Everything okay, Shan?"

Shannon brought her focus back to Delaney. "Fine. I think."

"Boy, that was convincing." She closed her book and put it on the table. "Finally. My turn to be the listener. Tell me what's going on."

If Shannon only knew. Being here at the estate this Thursday night hadn't been her plan. But suddenly at loose ends, and with her imagination running in all directions, spending the evening alone was the last thing she wanted. Or needed.

"Is it Hunter?"

"I don't know. Yes?"

"You don't sound too sure."

She paused for a moment to gather her thoughts. "I think something's going on at work. Maybe something with this lawsuit against OPD. Ever since Camden brought it up on Sunday, Hunter's been ... distant. Preoccupied. Working late.

"Mrs. B brought Bry for her counseling session on Tuesday because he got caught at the office, so I brought her home. We ate dinner together, and when he finally got there around eight, he pretty much said hello, grabbed a sandwich, and started in on this pile of files he brought home. I'm not even sure he was aware when I left. He called later to say good night."

"That was sweet."

"It was, but I could tell his mind was elsewhere. We've texted some the past couple of days, but we haven't talked at all. Then tonight, we had dinner plans, since Bry was going to a movie with her friends, and he canceled. Said something came up. Apologized again about being so busy and said he'd make it up to me. But I can't help feeling something's not right."

"Perhaps you should come right out and ask him."

"I would, if he would give me any time. Maybe this weekend. We're supposed to go to Wyatt and Harper's for New Year's Saturday night. Wanna come?"

"Sure. Sounds like fun."

"It'll be very different than what you're used to. Probably won't even be champagne, other than the sparkling zero-proof stuff. There's always a ton of food, though, and we play games."

Delaney shook her head. "That actually sounds appealing right now. I like your friends. How real they are. That they don't have to be half-drunk to have a good time."

"They like you too. Plan on Hunter and me coming to get you, then. You can stay the night and go to church with me, if you'd like."

"Yeah, I think I would. But I can have Ernie drive me to Harper's so you guys don't have to come out here. Maybe that'll give you some of that time you need to talk."

"We'll see. I'll let you know on Saturday. At this point, I'm not sure what to expect with Hunter."

"What does that mean? That you're not sure of your relationship? It could be he's just having a busy week."

"He's had busy weeks before and hasn't shut me out. This

is … different. I can't put my finger on it, but it's like he's purposefully keeping me at arm's length. It makes me wonder …"

She shook her head and focused on her hands clasped in her lap.

"You can't leave it at that, Shan. Wonder what?"

"I'm sure he wouldn't."

"Wouldn't what?"

With a heavy sigh, she looked up at her sister. "Hunter's had this dream from the day he started at the firm. To make partner by the time he turned thirty. He said he's done nothing for the past four-plus years but work, putting in more billable hours than any other associate at the firm, making himself available for anything the partners needed so they'd know he was the guy they could count on."

"Sounds commendable."

"It is. But that was his entire life. Until Brylie had to move in with him, and suddenly he's the guardian of a teenage girl and has to make some changes. Changes that include dialing down the amount of time spent at the office. The night we talked about it, about him having to cut back for the custody suit, he told me it was like watching all his dreams shatter around him. He was crushed."

"That's sad. I feel bad for him."

"I do too. Absolutely. But now … maybe with this suit against OPD, he's been given a way to earn his partnership. Cam said he would have Legal file a Motion to Dismiss for conflict of interest based on Hunter's relationship with me. What if he was asked to distance himself from me, help bring in this settlement, then he would get his partnership? Cam told me the suit was asking for three-quarters of a million dollars. Hunter and I are only just starting out. Maybe he weighed his options and decided he had more invested in his career than he did in me."

Delaney shook her head. "Shannon, listen to me. Don't

borrow from the future what may not even be there. I'm hearing a lot of *maybe* and *what if*, but what you need to do is talk to Hunter before that over-active imagination of yours works you into a ball of tangled twine."

Kind of like her stomach at the moment. But Delaney was right. And although Dee would laugh if Shannon pointed it out to her, she was biblically correct. Jesus Himself warned against borrowing trouble from the future, worrying about something that may be complete fiction.

If Hunter should decide to choose a promotion over her, God would be there to help her pick up the pieces. Again. Fretting about it today wouldn't change the outcome, however it went.

Delaney leaned forward. "And I have to say, the man I was talking to Christmas Eve night couldn't say enough about how special you'd made their day. Something about you baking cookies for them to decorate to keep up his mother's tradition and how much that meant to him and Brylie. The look in his eyes when he told me that wasn't the look of a man planning to distance himself from you. That's a man falling in love with you. I'd bet my trust fund on it."

Nodding, she latched onto her sister's words like a lifeline tossed into churning seas. "You're right. I need to wait until I can ask Hunter outright what's going on."

Camden walked into the room. "Yes. That would be a very good question. And I'd be extremely interested in his answer. Especially about this."

Startled, she glowered at her brother. "Oh, my gravy, Cam. Eavesdrop much?"

He held out his phone, and Shannon waited a second before taking it. Her pulse skittered at the image of Hunter on the screen with another man in a parking garage.

"What am I looking at?"

"Press play."

She hit the triangle and watched as the other man offered

Hunter a bulky envelope. Hunter looked at it, back at the man, and shook his head. The man said something else and held it out a bit farther. Hunter regarded it again, took it, peered inside, and up at the man before answering. Laughing, the man patted Hunter on the shoulder and walked away. The image stilled with Hunter putting the envelope inside his briefcase. The one she gave him.

That knot in her stomach coiled tighter. "I don't understand. Who was that? With Hunter?"

"Richard Norkowski. The partner your *boyfriend* said he's never worked with before. That was taken in their office parking garage. Our PI for the Legal Department said he's seen plenty of payoffs, and this one was textbook."

Dread rippled over her skin like ice water. "Payoff? For what?"

"Probably for helping him with this bogus case. This investigation is heating up, and it appears your boy is right in the middle of it. File enough of these lawsuits and the plaintiff's attorney can rake in some big bucks. Or maybe it's to cut ties with you and, thereby, with us. If your guy is gunning for a partnership, maybe he found his way in."

Somehow, knowing Cam had eavesdropped on their conversation didn't bother her as much as what she'd just seen on that video. Was that indeed a payoff? And if so, for what? To help bring in a fraudulent settlement, or to distance himself from her family? From her?

Her head swam with too many thoughts, her eyes with too many tears. That wasn't the Hunter she knew. The one she'd fallen in love with. But could that be the Hunter she'd met in front of the fountain that day? The one who took a business call during dinner?

His faith was new. His dream was not. He'd been working toward it for years and had sacrificed much for it.

Did that now include her?

CHAPTER FORTY-SEVEN

*H*unter had never been so glad to see the end of a week as he was this one.

He walked into the condo, his gut still twisted in knots and thoughts in a jumble. After throwing his coat over a barstool and leaving his briefcase on the floor, he loosened his tie on the way to the sofa. He plopped down into the welcoming leather and laid his head back, closing his eyes and releasing a deep breath.

If only he knew he still had a job after this three-day holiday weekend, it would go a long way toward the unfurling of that twist in his stomach. A week ago, he would have never imagined his life taking this turn.

After his surprise encounter with Norkowski yesterday, he'd stood between the promise of finally realizing all he'd worked so hard for or chucking it all to save some corporation a settlement they wouldn't even feel.

He'd made his choice, but now everything—his career, his livelihood, his dream—sat at the mercy of a few powerful men he'd chosen to trust with his future.

His phone pinged with an incoming text, and he pulled it from his shirt pocket.

Shannon:

Can I see you when you get home from
work since I couldn't catch you last
night? It's important.

He winced. She'd been beyond patient with him this entire abysmal week. Even when he canceled last night's dinner plans, she'd been kind about it, but he could tell she was confused. If only he could tell her what was happening.

He hadn't intended to be distant this week, but circumstances dictated his actions, and, unfortunately, his time with Shannon had been the cost.

She had the ConnectUP girls all-area lock-in tonight at the Arlington rec center, and he'd told Wyatt he'd come by to go over some contracts for a new camp they wanted to launch next summer. But a few minutes with her would brighten his outlook. It always did. Besides the fact he missed her like he would his right arm.

Sure thing. On my way up now.

He knocked on Brylie's bedroom door. "Hey, I'm going up to say hi to Shannon before you guys head out for the evening. Back in a few."

"Okay," came her voice from the other side of the door. "Tell her I'll be up to meet her at eight."

After locking the deadbolt, he took the stairs to Shannon's apartment, surprised when she opened the door as he reached up to knock.

"Hey, Sunshine." His smile waned at the starkness in her eyes. "What happened?"

Standing with her arms crossed, she could barely look him in the eye. "I was actually hoping you could tell me."

He walked in and closed the door behind him. "If this is about this week, it honestly couldn't be helped. And I'm sorry about canceling last night."

"It's not just the working late or canceling dinner. I know something else is going on. Ever since Cam brought up the lawsuit last week, you've grown distant. And I was okay giving you some room if there was something you were working out. But then—"

Her voice broke, and he took a step toward her with his hand out. When she stepped back, he dropped it to his side. "Then what, Shan? What's going on?"

She rocked side to side for a second, then grabbed her phone from the table beside the sofa and tapped on the screen before thrusting it toward him. "You tell me."

Unsure what else to do, he took the phone and studied the screen. His skin crawled as he watched the scene play out in front of him. Had she been following him? Stalker behavior didn't seem like Shannon at all.

When the video stopped with him sticking the envelope in his briefcase, he handed it back to her. "Did you take that?"

"Of course not. Cam sent it to me."

"Cam's following me?"

"I think you're missing the point here, Hunter."

"Actually, *you* are, but I can't explain right now. If I'm being tailed, though, I'd like to know. Especially if your brother is out there digging up dirt on me."

"Is there dirt to dig up?"

"Shannon." Her name came out harsher than he'd intended, but in his exhausted state, his patience wore thin. With Cam and his accusations. With Shannon and her willingness to believe them.

She crossed her arms again. "It's not Cam. And it's not you. Legal has their investigators looking into the lawsuit. One of them is following Mr. Norkowski. You just happened to get caught taking that payoff. Or whatever it was."

The plea in her eyes—for him to tell her it was all fine, that he hadn't taken that money—had him itching to tell her what she wanted to hear.

But he couldn't.

"That's what you think?"

"I don't know what to think, because you've completely shut me out this week. Were you being paid to keep your distance so this lawsuit could go through? Or is it more, Hunter? Is there a partnership on the line for you?"

He bowed his head, gathering his thoughts before bringing his stinging eyes up to her, whether from unspent tears or the need for a good night's sleep. Staring at this woman he loved with every part of him, the one who'd brought joy and light into his life, who now looked at him as if he were a stranger to her. And she knew him better than anybody else.

As he stood there, his gaze searching hers for any hint she believed him, believed *in* him, his chest hollowed. A week ago, he'd held her close as they danced the night away at her parents' ball. The sheer pleasure of being with her, hearing her call him *her man,* had been enough to fill him up, knowing they were all in … together.

Then came Cam's accusations that now appeared to have burrowed their way into her mind, her heart. If she'd only waited a few more days …

With a sigh, he shook his head, the stress of the week pulling at him, weighing him down like a bag of rocks. "Shannon, I'm not sure where to go from here. I can't live with the ghosts of your past casting suspicion on me if I work late. Or if your brother questions my integrity as a lawyer, or worse, as a man. I'm not your father. My work will never be more important to me than the people I love. And I'm not Nick Trent. I don't care about your money or your name. But if you don't know me well enough by now to trust me without question, then I don't know how we can go any further with this."

He nodded toward her phone. "Yes, I did take that money. I can only tell you that because you have the proof right there. But there are things I *can't* tell you, things I can't tell Cam, because they'd get me disbarred. I won't know if anything will come of it, but in a few days, things could be very different."

"And us?"

The bleakness in her eyes tore him in two, but he was powerless to fix it.

"I don't know, Shan. I've never felt for anybody the way I feel for you. But I also know we can't build anything on a foundation of distrust."

"Distrust?" A tear trickled down her face as she thrust out her hands. "You stood there and said you took a payoff. I don't know what to do with that, Hunter."

"And I don't know what to tell you other than to wait. Give me some time, and, hopefully, this will all play out the way I'm hoping."

When she said nothing but continued to stare at him with eyes filled with questions, with doubt, he walked over to the door and paused, head bowed and eyes shut. How had things come to this? If only she'd given him a little more time, maybe he wouldn't be on the verge of losing her along with everything else.

Opening his eyes, he faced her again. "I know you've been hurt. In ways I could never imagine hurting you. And I know those wounds go deep, and maybe they haven't completely healed. But that's something only you can decide. I only know I can't keep paying for the transgressions of other men."

"Hunter … I … I want to believe you."

"Then do. The choice is yours."

Her gaze penetrated deep into his for a long moment, then strayed to the image on the phone she held in her hand.

His heart disintegrating in his chest, he turned and let himself out.

CHAPTER FORTY-EIGHT

*S*hannon slipped out onto the McCowans' deck as the countdown to the New Year began. Crossing her arms over her sweater, she brought one hand to clasp the pendant she'd worn around her neck since Hunter had given it to her exactly one week ago. Except her fingers came up empty after she'd removed the necklace yesterday. She thought she'd be ringing in the new year with him, in his arms and sharing a kiss.

But the necklace now mocked her with things that apparently couldn't be. An unbreakable bond, a forging of hearts that couldn't be undone.

A cheer sounded from inside, and she closed her eyes against the ache in her chest that hadn't eased from the moment he'd left her last night, without a word.

How could he have just left? Why couldn't he tell her what was going on? What she was missing?

Because the only thing she knew for sure was he'd taken that money. He'd even confessed to it, which confused her even more.

There are things I can't tell you, Shan ... because they'd get me disbarred. I won't know if anything will come of it, but by this time next week, things could be very different.

Different how? Because he'd have his dream job?

When the door opened and closed behind her, she swiped a finger under her eye and turned, flashing a shaky smile at her sister hobbling outside on her crutches. "Hey, Dee."

"You missed the ball drop. Or was that the point?"

"Just getting some air."

Delaney pulled out a chair at the patio table and lowered herself into it. "Harper and her sister shouldn't be on the same team for charades. They use the same brain."

"Right? Totally not fair."

"We gave them a run, though. Maybe next year, the O'Connor sisters will prevail over the Townsend sisters."

Delaney stared at her, probably waiting for a response. But Shannon was still back on *next year.* What a blessing that Delaney saw all the good—and the fun—in these people Shannon adored. And she prayed her sister would be here next year, with a heart softened toward God.

"Sorry Hunter couldn't make it. Is he okay?"

Hunter. She wondered when Delaney would finally ask. When she'd shown up in her little Mini to pick up Dee for the New Year's Eve party, she only said Hunter couldn't make it, and they used one of their dad's SUVs to drive to the McCowans'. But she suspected her sister had been curious, even though she let the matter drop. Apparently, Delaney's patience only stretched so far.

Sighing, Shannon joined her at the table. "Honestly? I'm not sure. I haven't seen him since last night. Or talked to him. Other than his text to let me know he wouldn't make it tonight."

"That doesn't sound good. Is something going on?"

"That's what I was hoping he would tell me when he came by after work last night. But he wouldn't. Or said he couldn't. Then he left."

Her sister's eyes narrowed. "I'm thinking there had to be more than that."

Shannon lifted her hands and let them fall. "The money, Dee. He said he took that money, but he couldn't tell me any more. Just that if I couldn't trust him, then we shouldn't be together."

"Oh, tell me you didn't show him that stupid video."

Shannon snapped her mouth closed.

Dee's eyes widened. "You did? Why would you do that?"

"Wouldn't you want to know if it were *your* boyfriend on video accepting what appears to be a payoff?"

"Yes, because all of my boyfriends have been idiots. I couldn't trust a one of them as far as I could throw them. Your boyfriend, on the other hand, is the real deal. Has integrity in spades. Even before he was into the church stuff like you are, he was a good guy."

Church stuff. Yes, Hunter had certainly jumped full bore into his faith. Hadn't missed a Sunday, discipling with Wyatt, memorizing scripture, spending time in the Word every morning. Had prayed with Zach's dad. And had prayed with her almost daily since they'd started dating.

All of which was at complete odds with what she saw on that screen.

Delaney leaned toward her. "I should know, Shan. Remember I told you I made a fool of myself with him at that club?"

Shannon nodded, gooseflesh rising on her skin as if in warning. What hadn't she been told about that night?

"He saw some bozo pawing at me and came over to help me out. And what did I do? Practically flung myself at him and asked him to take me home. To *his* home. I was his for the taking, and he walked away. Oh, he was polite about it. But he made it clear he wasn't interested in what I was offering. You get what I'm saying?"

"I get the picture." Her stomach pitched. The idea of

Delaney hanging on Hunter, making herself available to him without even knowing his name … it made her sick.

Delaney sat back in her chair. "So, there. You know the whole sordid, ugly truth. If Hunter had been like 'most every other guy in that place, I can guarantee you he wouldn't be with you now, because he wouldn't be able to look at you knowing he'd already been with me. Intimately.

"And that he didn't tell you about it to save me the embarrassment or to spare your feelings, either way, says a lot about him. He's a good guy. You know what I mean? *Good.* If he said there was a reason he did what he did but he couldn't explain right then, your next words should've been *I believe in you, and I'll wait until you can.* You have a one-in-a-million guy, sis."

She glanced over her shoulder at the partygoers mingling inside and back with a grin. "Well, with this group, he's with a pack of one-in-a-million guys, from what I've seen. So, don't lump him in with a miscreant like Nick Trent. And don't let Cam's voice drown out Hunter's."

Her expression softened. "Or God's. I've heard you say many times how you've had to listen for God's voice over the noise of your life. I never got that. But being with your friends some over the last few weeks, listening to the pastor talk at your Christmas Eve service, I think I'm starting to see why your faith is so important to you. How it gives you strength and peace. And guidance. Don't back off of that now, with Hunter. Not when he's never given you any other reason to doubt him."

A tear slipped down Shannon's cheek, and she swiped it away. "How'd you get so wise all of a sudden?"

Delaney shrugged. "I think my big sis is rubbing off on me. You've always been there for me, trying to help me find my way, giving me advice and direction I've mostly ignored. Ignored but not forgotten. If only I'd listened sooner, maybe my leg wouldn't be held together by pins right now, and I wouldn't be looking at a court appearance in two weeks for a DUI. Maybe I'd still be pure instead of used goods, and I'd have genuine friends like yours."

Pausing, Delaney chewed on her bottom lip for a second, her blue eyes searching. "Your God ... can He really love someone like me? With all my baggage?"

Shannon reached out and took her sister's hands in hers. "He can, and He already does. Jesus gave His life for you as much as He did for any of us."

"That's hard for me to wrap my head around. But maybe if I hang with you and your friends, I'll learn?"

"You're always welcome to hang with us. Any time. I would love to see more of you."

Something Shannon could only describe as relief softened the apprehension in Dee's eyes. "I'd love to be with you more too. It's been fun. But, see, this is what I'm talking about. I haven't been a good person. A person of integrity. I've made awful decisions, fully understanding they were wrong. And you're not keeping me at arm's length, even knowing tomorrow, flighty me could change my mind and return to my old ways.

"But Hunter? Maybe you haven't known him that long, but I do believe you *know* him. Listen to your heart. Have you once ever seen anything in him that would cause you to doubt him?"

Shannon shook her head. "Not until that video."

"Ugh." Delaney rolled her eyes. "That video. Seriously, Shan. Don't measure Hunter against Nick. Or even Daddy. I don't doubt for a second there's an explanation for why he took that money. A good, *honest* explanation. I think if you take your past out of this equation, you'd believe that too."

A static sensation ran up Shannon's spine. Take her past out of the equation. Don't measure Hunter against Nick or her father.

I can't live with the ghosts of your past ... I can't keep paying for the transgressions of other men.

She thought she'd left all that heartache behind. But had she instead been letting her past keep her from moving forward? From falling in love?

Until Hunter Kavanaugh had walked into her life and broken down all of those walls. All of those barriers she'd erected under the guise of *finding herself*.

Then the past crept up on her again with Cam's accusations. And she'd allowed it to push away a man who hadn't deserved the judgment she passed on him based on the wrongs of others. Her father's disinterest, her husband's abandonment. Nick Trent had been her way out from under her father's roof, a way to shed his name.

But Hunter was …

Hunter was her person. The one who'd only ever believed in her, encouraged her, laughed with her, prayed with her.

But one thing I do: Forgetting what is behind and straining toward what is ahead …

Paul's words to the Philippians, but appropriate for her too?

Yes. The time to leave all of that behind was long overdue. The past had taken too much from her already. She wouldn't let it take Hunter.

If it wasn't too late.

CHAPTER FORTY-NINE

Getting called into the office on a Sunday morning didn't bode well.

Hunter disconnected, put his phone on the nightstand, and laid back to stare at the ceiling. He'd missed ringing in the New Year with Shannon, instead deciding to stay home so she could enjoy the evening without the awkwardness his presence would've undoubtedly caused her.

When he told Bry he'd be watching the ball drop from the comfort of their couch, she'd surprised him by staying home instead of going to Samantha's party. And twenty minutes after the start of the new year, when he should've been snuggling with Shannon, he found himself in bed. Staring up at the dark. Thinking over the past year and how much had changed. Wondering what the next might hold.

With a sigh, he sat up on the edge of the bed. Alden's call had awoken him minutes before his alarm would've gone off in time for Brylie and him to get ready for church. His plans had changed, but that didn't mean hers had to.

He looked at his phone for a moment before grabbing it and pressing the familiar icon.

After four rings, he was about to disconnect when she picked up.

"Hunter?" His name in Shannon's sleep-husky voice caused a warm ripple along his skin.

"I'm sorry I woke you. You probably got in late from the party."

She cleared her throat. "No problem." Rustling on her end had him picturing her sitting up in bed, hair tousled, eyes puffy from sleep. Looking as adorable as she had the evening he'd shown up at her door with his hot chocolate peace offering. An image he needed to quash. "I was go—"

"Can Brylie ride to church with you today? I assumed you were planning to go."

"Uh, yeah. Sure. You're not going today?"

"I'd planned to until Alden called me in."

"On Sunday? New Year's Day?"

Probably another nail in the coffin of their relationship, but what could he do? "I know. It's unusual, but there's some stuff going on I can't get into right now."

She was silent for a moment. "Of course. I understand. Go do what you need to do. Brylie's good with Delaney and me for the day. Don't worry about anything."

"Dee's going with you to church? Do you need my car to make it easier for her?"

"We have one of Dad's SUVs. But I appreciate the offer."

"Yeah, any time." All this politeness made him want to scream. But at least they could still be cordial with one another. That was something. If he couldn't have her heart, he'd still take her friendship over not having her in his life at all.

"I hope everything's okay at the office. Should I be praying?"

His gut twisted. "Yes. I could definitely use some of that."

"Then count on it."

"Thanks." More silence stretched between them. He didn't want to sever this tenuous connection, but he only had an hour before he needed to report to the general conference room. "I'll talk to you later."

"Okay."

He clicked to disconnect, his gut clenching. He'd hoped to start the New Year ushering in a clean slate upon which he and Shannon could write their future.

Now, he had no idea what his future held. Only that God was already there, even if Shannon wasn't.

Weary to the bone, Hunter walked into his dark condo late Monday night. The past two days had been grueling, fielding question after question posed to him by the senior partners—minus Rick Norkowski, who had no idea they'd been meeting without him. After scouring all of Rick's cases from the past five years, thankfully, they'd only discovered eight that were fraudulent.

His cell pinged with an incoming text, and he pulled it out of his pocket.

Julia

are you done yet? can you talk?

> just got home. it's after 11. u should be asleep.

Instead of a return text, the phone rang in his hand. He clicked on the green button. "Go to bed, Jules."

"I did, but I can't sleep from wondering what's happened since your text yesterday. So, what's happened?"

"Yeah, sorry I didn't get in touch earlier. It's been an interesting couple of days." Sighing, he draped his coat over a barstool and took the one next to it. "You should have seen the expression on Alden's face this afternoon when the final decision came down. Utter desolation."

Something Hunter would remember for a long time. The devastation that came with the knowledge one of their own had put a dark stain on the name of this long-established, well-respected legal powerhouse.

"I can imagine. His grandfather started this firm, and, until now, there's never been a whisper of scandal. What happens next?"

With his elbow braced on the counter, he scrubbed a hand down his face. His eyes burned as if he'd spent the day on the beach in gale force winds. "Well, at this very moment, Alden's assistant and three others are drafting documents to file charges against Rick and his cohorts—all the named plaintiffs, along with the witnesses and experts who provided false records. They want to file tomorrow morning, so I'm sure they'll be pulling an all-nighter."

"Oh, my. That's sure to hit the news."

"No doubt. PR is preparing press releases, and Human Resources is working on the severance documents releasing Rick, effective immediately, including his forfeiture of all benefits and seven-figure annual income."

Not that he'd need it in federal prison, where he'd most likely end up.

"That's going to be tragic for his family. I can't imagine what they'll be put through with all of this."

"It's unfortunate. His sons are both in college out of state. His wife, though, will have to weather quite the storm, I'm sure."

He'd only met Rick's wife once, but she was kind and demure, a devoted homemaker who doted on her boys. What would she do once everything was gone?

Julia yawned. "And I assume the firm would also file suit against his personal property to recoup the settlements they'll have to pay back, right?"

"Right. With a hefty punitive fee on top of it."

"I'll be praying for the family." A stifled yawn came from the other end, prompting his own. "Are you okay?"

"I will be." Eventually. Once he knew where things might go with Shannon. If anywhere.

"They don't blame you for any of this, do they?"

"It doesn't appear they do." He walked to the refrigerator by the light cast from the lamp Brylie had left on for him. "I wasn't so sure yesterday when they grilled me for the better part of the day. I honestly thought there for a while I was going to be sent packing. And then all the questions about Shannon."

"Shannon? How'd she come up?"

He pulled a water bottle from the door. "I had to tell them how I got wind something might be sketchy about these cases. Thankfully, I could show there was nothing tying Shannon or myself to O'Connor Property Development, aside from the fact it's her father's company. Good thing they believed me, because one partner hinted I might be involved but was now trying to get Rick out of the way for my own gain."

"You're joking."

"Wish I was." Leaning against the counter, he took a sip from the bottle. "Just grasping at straws to keep from coming to the conclusion they finally did. That Rick had knowingly committed fraud right under their noses."

"That's a bitter pill, to say the least."

"Tomorrow's going to be an interesting day. I don't know what to expect."

"Expect about … our jobs? The firm?"

"All of it, although I didn't get the feeling our jobs were in jeopardy. As for the firm, we won't know for a few weeks if there will be sanctions. There's certain to be an independent investigation."

His gut churned thinking about it.

"I wonder what'll happen when Rick shows up in the morning. Does Joan have any clue what's coming?"

He took a hefty swallow of water, screwed the top back on the bottle, and set it aside. "Not that I know of. Once they've dealt with Rick, they'll talk to anybody who's even possibly involved. Including his assistant."

"I can guarantee Joan had no idea what he was doing. She'll be devastated."

"Yeah, if that's the case, I feel bad for her. But there might be collateral damage from all of this that can't be helped."

Including him, if the partners decided he'd crossed a line there was no coming back from. Even if it did uncover a plot that, left over time, could've erupted into something much worse.

"I'll let you go. I just couldn't help wondering what happened over the past couple of days. I was praying for you."

"Appreciate it. And I could tell. I had peace even when I thought I might be looking at my own severance from the firm. God knew the truth even if the partners weren't so sure at first. I just rested in that."

"He is good indeed. See you in the morning, Hunter."

"Good night, Jules."

After disconnecting, he put the water bottle in the fridge. And that's when he saw it. A piece of paper slipped under the red mug Shannon always sipped her hot chocolate from, sitting on the counter next to the gas range. His pulse hitched as he pulled it out and flipped on the stove light.

> *Hunter,*
>
> *Brylie's staying the night with me and Emily will pick her up tomorrow to spend the day and tomorrow night with them. If there's anything else you need, please let me know. I've been praying for you like you asked. I may not know the words, but God does and He's with you through whatever is happening. Maybe we can talk tomorrow? Whatever works for you.*
>
> *Love,*
>
> *Shannon*

P.S. I believe in you. (It is right for me to feel this way about you, since I have you in my heart ... Phil 1:7a)

His own heart in his throat, he read it again and glanced at the clock. Eleven fifty. If it wasn't so late, he'd run up there. Close this distance between them with an overdue New Year's kiss.

She believed in him. What had changed since Friday? No way could she know what had been happening over the past two days. She must have come to her decision on her own.

His gaze fell on the Bible he'd left on the island after this morning's reading. No. Not on her own. Knowing Shannon, she'd gone to the Lord to find what she needed. The strength or the peace, whatever had allowed her to trust. Not only in him but in God, who had put them together. He had no doubt about that.

When he called Brylie earlier this evening, she only said she and Shannon had gone out to lunch before taking in a movie, not that she'd be staying the night. But he should've expected Shannon would take care of Bry, like she always took care of the people she loved.

With Brylie covered, he could head to the office early tomorrow. It could be another long, trying day, but hopefully, he and Shannon could finish it together. He didn't know when, though, as he fully expected to be kept late at the office once again. To make up for the lost time with Gail, if nothing else.

Ellie's mom texted him earlier and offered to take Brylie to counseling, since she'd already be with them, but he hadn't known Shannon had helped with those arrangements. What a blessing they all were to his and Brylie's lives. Truly a gift from God.

He turned off the light above the stove and made his way to the bedroom, his thoughts swirling. He'd regretted his hasty exit Friday night a million times in the following days.

Especially after talking with Wyatt later that evening while reviewing the campground contract.

"Could she have been questioning her place in your life more than she was questioning you? You and she haven't been together that long. Maybe she isn't as sure of your investment in her as she is of your investment in your career. Could that be what she was asking?"

His friend's words resonated in his head, even throughout the past two soul-trying days. Had he expected too much of her, knowing the pain of her past? That she could simply put it aside for him and blindly trust when every other significant man in her life had let her down?

He didn't know. But if Shannon had come this far to reach out, he would definitely meet her there, between his heart and hers.

Because these last three days without her had been the longest he'd ever endured.

CHAPTER FIFTY

The only bad thing about being on winter break was having too much time on her hands.

Shannon rearranged the books and knick-knacks on the built-in shelves next to the fireplace for the third time. She and Brylie packed away all her Christmas decorations last night while she tried not to think about what might be happening with Hunter, whose presence had once again been required at the office. On a holiday.

When it became clear getting any talking done by the time he might finally come in the door would be difficult at best, she decided to have Brylie stay the night with her. While waiting for the teen to grab overnight stuff down at their condo, she scribbled him that short note and left it under the red mug she always used for cocoa. She didn't know what he would think of it but prayed he would see her heart in the words.

Her workday had crept along, checking her phone every time it pinged after receiving Hunter's simple *Thanks for taking care of Bry. And, yes, I'd love to talk. I'll call you when I'm home* text early that morning. She stayed after work until Emily and Ellie arrived at the office with Brylie so she could attend her session and visited with them while they waited.

Home now for over an hour, she had nothing else to do but sit and wonder how he was, what might be going on after his intense weekend of … well, whatever he'd been dealing with. Nothing except rearrange knick-knacks.

Maybe tonight, he'd be home early enough they could find some time to talk. So she could tell him face to face what she saw in him. A man of integrity. A man of moral character. A godly man. That regardless of what her eyes had seen, she chose to believe what her heart already knew about him.

She prayed it wasn't too late. That her lack of faith in him the other day hadn't pushed him away for good. His text that morning hadn't given her much of a clue, but she'd latched onto the hope it brought her as if it were the last ticket home after a two-day layover.

She jumped when a knock sounded at the door, and she glanced at the clock. Five-fifteen. Maybe he'd been able to get away earlier than he had the past two nights. On her way to answer, she smoothed her hands down her hips over her jeans and adjusted the hem of her sweater. But when she pulled open the door, her smile died on her lips.

"Cam. What—"

"Is Kavanaugh here?" Holding yet another document in his right hand, he strode in the door like he owned the place. Of course, in essence, he did—or more accurately, the company did—but basic etiquette would dictate that one should wait for an invitation.

"No." She shut the door behind him. "Why?"

"I need to talk to him. Left a couple of messages for him at the office he never returned. Figured he was home, but he's not answering."

"Okay, look." She waited until he turned to her. "I'm done with this, Cam. Done with your accusations and your suspicions. Despite what you may have there, you need to hear me. I stand with Hunter. I believe whatever happened on that video was for a good reason. That he would never do anything unethical. So, until something happens to prove otherwise, nothing you say will sway me. I stand with him. I stand *by* him."

Cam stared at her for several seconds while she listened to her pulse thrum in her ears. "Wow. I'm a little proud right now."

"Don't patronize me."

He put his hand up. "Not trying to do that. I apologize. Sincerely. And I'm not here to cause problems between you and your bo—between you and Kavanaugh. In fact, I was hoping he could shed light on this."

She stared at the paper he held out before reaching out to take it. "What is this?"

"A Motion to Dismiss."

"That you filed based on conflict of interest?"

"We never filed our motion. We decided to wait to see what we could find out first. Williamson, Sheffield, and Moore filed that. This morning. They're withdrawing their suit against OPD. And what's really weird, according to our guys in Legal, is they're asking for it to be dismissed with prejudice, which means it can never be refiled. That's unheard of, for a plaintiff's attorneys to file a dismissal with prejudice before a case is settled. And it's not signed by Norkowski. It's signed by an Alden Sheffield, third-generation partner of that firm. It doesn't go any higher than that."

Gooseflesh crawled along her skin. "Something's going on."

"My thoughts exactly. I think what I said the other day is true, that your guy is in the middle of all this. But I may have been wrong about which side."

Slowly, she sank down onto her sofa. "That could get him into hot water with his own people, couldn't it?"

"It certainly could have, if they didn't believe him. But they dismissed the suit, so it appears they did. Still, if Kavanaugh put this all in motion, it took some chutzpah."

"That could explain it, then."

"Explain what?"

Her gaze floated from the paper in her hand up to her brother. "He got called into the office Sunday morning. Was there until late that night and again yesterday. A holiday weekend. Sounds like something big. Doesn't it?"

"It does. And you haven't talked to him today?"

She shook her head. "We're not ... well ... I showed him that video, asked him about it. Last Friday. He said yes, he took the money, but it's not what it seems. Only he couldn't explain because I'm connected to OPD, and the lawsuit was still active. I didn't take well to that. Thought he was hedging."

Bowing her head, her fingers drifted to the pendant she'd clasped around her neck that morning, hoping there would be no reason to put it away for good. "I said some things. Things I regret. He left, and I haven't seen him since."

Cam walked over and sat in the chair, leaning with his forearms braced on his thighs. "I guess I should take some of that blame. I put that bug in your ear. And it may have all been for no reason."

She studied him. "But, why, Cam? Why do you always think the worst of me? After all these years? After how far I've come with my life? I don't understand why you can't let my past be that—the past. Like I'm trying to do. With the Lord's help, I'm learning more about myself every day. About who He made me to be, not who I was before I let Him into my life. But you don't seem to be able to let any of it go."

With a grimace, he nodded. "You're right. And I'm sorry, Shan. Truly. It's just ..." He expelled a frustrated breath. "Nick. What he did to you. Leaving you like that. And then with the baby ... What kind of man doesn't step up when he knows he's going to be a father? I don't want somebody else hurting you like that."

Her heart clutched in her chest. Was all of Cam's posturing his way of showing his love for her? Had she been just as guilty of misunderstanding him as he'd been of her?

"But it appears I might've misjudged Kavanaugh. Misjudged you. You don't need your big brother fighting your battles for you. You're smart. Responsible. You've put a good life together for yourself after everything you went through. I don't understand all of this religious stuff, but it's working for you. And I'm proud of you."

Uncertain whether she'd heard him right, Shannon could only stare at her brother seated at an angle to her, his expression solemn, almost contrite.

After a moment, he cleared his throat. "My only question is, why are you still here? Shouldn't you be hunting this guy down to tell him you're crazy about him and you told your bully big brother where to get off?"

Her pulse quickened. "Go … now?"

"Absolutely. He's probably still at the office. Go. Make this right. And I'll do the same next time I see him. Hopefully, with you."

A smile spread on her face. The Camden she once adored had shown up at her door today, and she thanked the Lord she finally had him back.

She stood and picked up her cell phone. After confirming with Julia that Hunter was still at the office but had been upstairs with Mr. Sheffield the last couple of hours, she decided to go wait him out. Since the receptionist had already left for the day, Julia said she'd leave Shannon's name with the security desk in the lobby so she could enter the office after hours.

Forgetting to grab a jacket and leaving her brother seated where he was, she didn't even wait for the elevator, instead racing down the stairs to her car in the garage.

There was so much she needed to say. Face to face. That she was sorry for ever doubting him, that he had her utmost trust. That her heart was his.

If he still wanted it.

CHAPTER FIFTY-ONE

Hunter walked into Julia's office on his way to his own, not even sure how he got there. Didn't recall getting into the elevator from the top floor or pushing the number fourteen. He must've exited on his floor out of sheer habit.

Julia's eyes widened. "Oh, my. What is that look? Please tell me you're still employed. That *I'm* still employed."

He didn't stop on his way into his office, where he walked around the desk and lowered himself into his chair.

She followed him in and took one opposite him, staring at him across the desk. "Well?"

"Yes. We're still employed."

She slumped in the chair. "That's a relief."

He cocked his head. "Why are you here? They told everybody not to stay tonight, to be out of here before any press could show up. I've never seen this place so empty at six o'clock."

"I couldn't leave until I knew what was going on. You were up there for so long, and after all the drama this morning, with Rick being escorted out, I wondered if maybe I'd missed something. But when nobody came for me, I was hoping all was well."

He sat up and crossed his arms on his desk. "Be prepared for an onslaught of press here in the morning, if they're not already camping out downstairs. The partners are beefing up security from the parking garage to escort employees in and out of the building. They don't want anybody talking to reporters outside of the press conference scheduled for tomorrow morning."

"The press release is already out?"

"Should be on the news right now. It's going to get bad, Jules."

"Are you named? As the whistleblower?"

He shook his head. "I told them I prefer to be an anonymous source. I'll be named only as '*the senior associate who stumbled upon this unfortunate situation and brought it to the attention of the executive managing partner.*'"

"They should give you a huge bonus for this, Hunter. Rick could have brought this whole place down if this had gone on for years before it was discovered."

His gaze wandered from Julia to his hands and back. "Funny you should mention that."

Her eyes rounded again. "You got a bonus? A raise? What?"

"They offered me a junior partnership. Gail's, actually, since they're moving her up to senior partner to replace Rick."

Her jaw fell open. "You got your partnership? Are you kidding me? At twenty-eight, you'll be the youngest partner this firm has ever had. That's incredible."

He nodded, but the knot in his stomach remained. He hadn't expected the offer made to him a little over an hour ago. And while the HR manager and Alden went over the benefits and income package with him, his heart rate increased and gut roiled.

The dream he'd held and nourished and sacrificed for the

last four-and-a-half years, finally realized. All that remained was the addition of his signature at the bottom of the page.

With pen in hand, he'd hesitated, finally laying it down and asking for some time. Time to think, to pray. To consider his options. His life.

Four months ago, he'd have scribbled his name across that line as soon as they put the offer in front of him.

But now …

Now he had Brylie. Now he had school programs to attend, dinners he wanted to be home to share with her, weekends he wanted to spend hanging out with her, socializing with good friends, or helping with ConnectUP.

He had a lady who believed in him, and if they could find a minute—or thirty—to talk, maybe they could get back on track to the future he'd been imagining might include sharing a last name and a home.

Before Brylie, before coming to know the Lord, before Shannon, his whole life had been his career, which worked perfectly with the goal of becoming a partner. He'd been here many evenings working with Alden when the older man should've been at his grandson's football games. Or watching his granddaughter cheer. Working with Gail when she should've been home with her husband and two teenage daughters.

Six of the ten senior partners had been married more than once, and two junior partners were currently going through divorce proceedings. The pay was exceptional. The benefits beyond mere health insurance, a retirement package, and vacation time.

He'd get his pick of a luxury vehicle, and an office with a budget generous enough to allow him to hire a designer to outfit. He'd get a clothing allowance, a travel stipend, access to the firm's boxes at the Cowboys' and Rangers' games, prime seats at the best Dallas/Fort Worth theaters for plays and musicals, and concert halls for orchestra, ballet, and opera performances.

And in exchange, he would live and breathe for nothing but the firm.

Julia studied him. "You turned them down."

"I asked for some time. But I think all the time I needed was the elevator ride down here. Jules, this isn't what I want anymore. I can't believe I'm saying that, but I've seen the lives these guys live. The things they sacrifice to have this big life they think they're living. Their million-dollar homes and all the toys. Dressing their wives in designer clothes and taking lavish vacations to make up for all the other things they've missed.

"But you know what I want now? I want to go home at a decent hour every night, have dinner with my sister. And Shannon. I want to be available to help with homework or work with ConnectUP. I want to be a husband who's there to help with the kids, coach Little League or soccer. I want to do volunteer work and help spread the gospel. I want a *life*, Jules. Not just a career."

Julia's smile lit her Irish green eyes. "I couldn't agree more, with all of that. So, what's your plan?"

"You said you'd go with me if I decided to hang my own shingle?"

"Yes! Are we doing that?"

He sat back in the chair and regarded her for a moment. "I met a man, another lawyer. The father of one of Shannon's CU kids. He started out like this, part of a big firm. The hamster wheel, he called it. Until he decided to get off because he was missing too much with his family. Started his own practice a few years ago and has more than he can handle. He said to call him if I ever thought I might want to take my foot off the gas a bit."

"And?"

"And I think I'm ready to get out of the fast lane. This job has given me a great foundation, a lot of experience I can build on in my own practice. And I can do *pro bono* work, help non-profits like ConnectUP who can't yet afford their own in-house counsel. I believe God gave me this career, but I don't want to just use it to make a living. I want to serve."

"Hunter, I love that. And I'm on board. When do we put in our notice?"

He chuckled but couldn't deny the prospect excited him too. A complete one-eighty change in perspective from only a few months ago. "I'll call Tim and see when he thinks he can bring us on board, then we'll put a plan together. It's going to be a big change, Jules. A huge pay cut for me. And probably for you, depending on how much I can afford to pay you. But I'll make sure you have insurance and a 401k."

She flipped her hand toward him. "I don't care if I take a pay cut. And Jeff won't either. We're okay, he and I. To be honest, he's been on me the past couple of years to get off this hamster wheel myself. But I love working for you, and he knows it. So, this will be the best of both worlds."

A petite woman appeared in the doorway of his office, and he sprang to his feet. "Shannon."

Julia glanced over her shoulder and back at him. "Oh, yeah. I forgot. Shannon called and said she was on her way down, so I left her name with Gus." She looked back and forth between them and stood. "Okay, so I'll be on my way."

"Uh, yeah." He pulled his attention from Shannon to his assistant. "Thanks, Jules. For everything."

"Have a good night, you two."

When Julia disappeared through the door, Shannon crossed slowly toward him. "Hunter—"

"Shannon—" he said at the same time. He smiled and walked around his desk to meet her. "Sorry. I'm just surprised to see you here. Go ahead."

"I'm not sure where to start. I know I shouldn't have, but I heard most of that. I think. This is all … wow. You're, like, the hero of the day."

"Not even close. I saw something wrong and spoke up."

"Sounds like more than that." She cocked her head to the side. "They offered you a partnership? And you don't want it? That's been your dream."

He shrugged. "Dreams change. *I've* changed. I want different things now. More important things."

"And that alleged payoff was … what?"

"Short story is something sounded off about that lawsuit against OPD, so Julia and I did some covert investigating. Turns out Norkowski was filing fraudulent suits and pocketing the bulk of the settlements.

"Guess my detective skills aren't that great because Rick got wind of it and tried to buy me off. I was afraid if I turned him down, he'd start getting rid of evidence. If he thought I was on his side, he had nothing to hide. I gave the money to Alden along with all the other information we discovered."

"Delaney was right, then."

"Delaney?"

"She reminded me who you are. Who you've always been. That if you took that money, there had to be a good, honest reason for it, and I was an idiot for ever doubting you. She was right."

"Shannon, I can understand why you were uncertain. And if I hadn't been so exhausted the other night, maybe I would have handled that better."

"But you were right too. I shouldn't have measured you against anybody else. I'm truly sorry for that, and I hope you can forgive me."

He stepped closer and took her hands in his. "Your note. If I'd been home earlier last night, I'd have been up at your place in a heartbeat. But it was almost midnight, and I was about to drop. Didn't want to wake you up just to tell you how much that meant to me."

"I didn't know what was happening, but I needed you to

know I did believe in you. That I was *choosing* to believe in you."

He squeezed her hands. "Maybe it wasn't me you were doubting but your place with me. Every significant man in your life put you too far down on their priority list. And I'm sorry if I gave you even a moment's doubt about where you stand with me.

"So, let me be very clear. Shannon Elizabeth Trent, I am one hundred percent, head over heels, heart and soul in love with you. I choose you over every other woman on the face of this earth. If you're willing to give this a go with me, I will strive with everything I am, in God's strength and grace, to be a man deserving of you. A man who prioritizes you over all others, who you can trust without question."

A tear escaped and trailed down her cheek. "I'm one hundred percent, head over heels, heart and soul in love with you, too, Hunter Kavanaugh." Her brow creased. "I don't know your middle name. How do I not know that by now?"

He chuckled. "Actually, you do. My full name is William Hunter Kavanaugh. William after my grandfather, Hunter after my father. His surname."

Her smile was just the thing that unraveled the last of that knot in his midsection. "Well, William Hunter Kavanaugh, I choose you. I trust you. And I believe in you. You have my unwavering faith, and you did even before Camden showed me the dismissal y'all filed today."

"Wait. Camden?"

"He showed up at my door looking for you. I thought he wanted to stir up more trouble, so I told him I stood with you no matter what he thought. No matter what I saw on that video. That my heart knew the man you are, and I believed you would explain it to me in time."

He couldn't hold back his grin. "You told him all that?"

"I did. And he actually said he was proud of me. I think Cam and I built a bit of a bridge today. He's the one who told me I needed to get over here, tell you I'm crazy about you, and that I told my bully big brother where to get off."

Drawing her into his arms, he tipped her face up with his finger under her chin. "My girl stood up for me today. That means more to me than being offered a promotion."

"I'll always have your back."

"And I'll always have yours."

"I love you, Mr. Kavanaugh."

"I love you, Miss Shannon Trent."

He brushed her nose with his, then took his time kissing her as he savored the feel of her lips fitted against his, her body pressed close. The silkiness of her hair as it fell over his hands, her fingers pressing into his back. When they parted, he didn't let her go but stared down into those intense baby blue eyes.

"This is the only partnership that matters to me. You, me, and God. And I can't wait to see where He takes us next."

EPILOGUE

THREE YEARS LATER

"Sleeping babies are so adorable." Harper stood gazing down at the sweet bundle in Shannon's arms. "Until you realize they're in charging mode and you're about to be hit with all that energy again."

"So true, my friend." Shannon peered down at her daughter from where she sat on a stool at their breakfast bar, little five-month-old Sylvia snoozing soundly after gulping down her lunch twenty minutes ago.

Looking up, she locked eyes with her husband across the family room, where the guys gathered in front of the football game. Hunter's smile quickened her pulse as it always had, even more so watching him sway side to side in an effort to lull Sylvie's twin brother Liam to sleep. Sylvia, named for her grandmother, and Liam, after his father and great-grandfather, were her double blessings from God. As if He'd given her two angels for the one she'd gifted to another mother.

Shannon's gaze roamed her bustling home. With two little ones on the way a year ago, and Brylie preferring to live at home while attending Dallas Heritage University next year, they'd needed something bigger than the loft condo. When this two-story, five-bedroom went on the market in the Brants' gated subdivision, they'd snatched it up and moved in ten months ago.

Hunter's partnership with Tim had been the stuff of dreams from the day they hung their *Brant, Kavanaugh, and Associates* shingle outside the office. Home almost every day by five-thirty and taking two weeks off when the babies were born, Hunter hadn't missed any quality time with his family.

He served as counsel for ConnectUP, all for free, and had also assumed co-captainship of the club Shannon started four years ago. One of five now in Fort Worth alone, with nearly three hundred clubs serving teens throughout Texas, and a healthy presence in thirty-two of the fifty states. Wyatt had expressed numerous times he'd never envisioned all it had become but was so grateful for it. Even though he'd had to finally leave his counseling practice to run the ministry full-time.

Brylie walked up to her brother and reached for the baby, her nephew burrowing against her when Hunter relinquished him.

Two shrieking whirlwinds ran by, and Shannon grinned when Harper sighed before going after three-year-old Gracie and her bestie, Renee Carlysle. Wyatt and Zane shared the sofa, the McCowans' four-month-old son dozing against his dad's chest while Zane tried to get his two-year-old "mini-me" to finish his last chicken tender.

Gracie and Renee finally settled on the rug on either side of the golden retriever Hunter had surprised Shannon with on their first wedding anniversary two years ago, and Zane let the wiggly boy off his lap to join them. Buddy was the most patient dog ever and didn't mind all the noise or the kids hugging and lying on him.

Chuckling, Shannon shook her head as she watched Ally, sitting at the kitchen table with Yolanda, down her second piece of pie. "You must be blessed with perfect blood sugar numbers. My doctor put me on a strict no sugar, low sodium diet my last month because of my blood pressure. Longest four weeks of my life."

Ally held up crossed fingers. "So far, so good. And considering I'm due in about two hours, this is probably my last hoorah until I'm done breastfeeding. Plus, there's only one in there, not two. You're a hero in my eyes."

Hunter walked over and placed a kiss on Shannon's cheek. "I couldn't agree more." He reached for his sleeping daughter. "Here, let me go put her down. Bry just headed up there with Liam, so you should have some time to visit."

Smiling, she let him take the baby girl, little Sylvie hardly stirring as he nestled her against his chest. "And you can watch the game."

"A perfect day."

It certainly was a perfect day. The men settled around the television, their wives gathered at the breakfast bar or table, scheduling meal deliveries for the Carpenters once their second son arrived. Delaney now had the three toddlers engrossed in a story, and Harper rejoined the ladies in the kitchen.

Watching Dee entertain the littles, Shannon's heart soared. Her sister had been saved nearly three years now, since shortly before accepting a plea deal for a hefty fine, community service, and completion of a mandatory alcohol awareness program. Now graduated from college, she worked with ConnectUP as both a club team member and on staff with Shannon's North Texas crisis pregnancy team.

Having witnessed the life-altering changes in both her and Dee, Cam started coming to church and accepted Christ almost two years ago. Mom followed a few months later, although, at that point, their father had yet to set foot anywhere near church. With all of them—including their CU family—praying for him, though, he hadn't stood much chance. Once he relented and started coming with their mother, it didn't take long for him to realize the truth for himself.

The day her father walked the aisle, Shannon sank into her seat, her hands over her face as sobs consumed her. Crying out her gratitude and praise to the Lord for the miracle she'd prayed for all those years.

Hunter returned and took the empty barstool next to her. "They're both out cold up there, and Bry's in her room FaceTiming with Zach."

"Those two are the cutest."

"At least she picked a good guy."

"She absolutely did."

"Where are Cam and Kennedy today?"

"Checking out a wedding venue. I got a text from Kennedy about a half hour ago that it's the one, so they're working on setting a date now. Probably early May. Oh, and Cam found four properties that could work for clubs in Louisiana. He's going to meet with Wyatt this week and was wondering if you could be there to go over the contracts. As usual, Dad will purchase them, then sign them over to CU."

"Your dad and Cam have been over-the-top generous with these buildings. I'll reach out to find out when and where they want to meet."

Gazing at the man next to her, Shannon's soul felt full to overflowing.

This was her happily ever after. Husband of her dreams, two beautiful babies, a sister-in-law in Brylie she adored, closer to her own brother and sister than ever, not to mention the new relationship she shared with her parents. Working with ConnectUP and these amazing friends.

All of it orchestrated by God the day she sat on a bench for what she thought would be her last sunset, and He brought her an angel named Nadine.

"For I know the plans I have for you," declares the Lord, "plans to prosper you and not to harm you, plans to give you hope and a future ... Then you will call on me ... and I will listen to you. You will seek me and find me when you seek me with all your heart."

ACKNOWLEDGMENTS

Saying goodbye is never easy, especially to folks you truly care about. That's how I feel about the characters who have populated the pages of my True Calling Series, from Wyatt and Harper in *Love's True Calling*, Zane and Ally in *Love's True Home*, Hunter and Shannon in *Love's True Measure*, and all of their friends, family, and kids from their ConnectUP Student Ministry.

Shannon was always a particular favorite of mine. I loved her quirkiness, her upbeat personality, and the rosy way she looked at the world. So I was excited to delve into her more deeply as I prepared to write her story. And what I found was a truly sweet soul who's been deeply wounded by her powerful father's indifference, a broken relationship she thought would be forever, and a loss for which she still grieves.

As she journeyed through her story, I hope you, my dear reader, found your own hope, redemption, or ability to forgive —even if it's yourself, as it was for Shannon. And that you found, as both she and Hunter did, the grace of God that covers all our pain, all our mistakes, all our flaws. What peace and comfort that brings me!

As always, a book never comes to life without a lot of help. I'm so thankful for my husband, Eric, who has been so supportive of this dream of mine, even if he doesn't understand the voices and ideas constantly swirling around in my head. And my daughter, Michaela, my biggest cheerleader, not to mention my tech help desk. And my mother, Pat Thorp, who believed I could achieve whatever I set my mind to and has supported and encouraged my writing from the beginning.

I could never show my gratitude enough for my incredible critique partners—Kristi Woods, Wendy Klopfenstein, and Lori Altebaumer. Their feedback, willingness to brainstorm with me, and encouragement is priceless. And for my huddle-mates, Teresa Wells and Liana George, a constant source of knowledge, support, and love.

Thank you to soon-to-be physician, Cale Perry, who provided excellent information and articles to address my many medical questions for this book. I'm praying for this young man as he completes his medical school studies and prepares for residency. Another huge thanks to real estate agent, Jeremy Smith, of the Smith Team in Dallas/Fort Worth, for all the information about downtown Fort Worth condominiums.

Writing can be a solitary endeavor, so my writers' groups are gold to me. To the CenTex Christian Writers, ACFW National, ACFW Dallas/Fort Worth, Novel Academy/My Book Therapy, Faith, Hope, and Love Christian Writers, 540 Community, and Inkers Mastermind, I extend my heartfelt thanks.

I am beyond blessed to be part of the Scrivenings Press family, and this novel is what it is only because of the amazing editing help of Amy Anguish (content editor) and K. Banks (line editor).

To my readers, THANK YOU for picking up this book and spending time with Hunter, Shannon, Brylie, and the others who occupy these pages. My dream is made possible because of you, and I am so grateful. If you're not yet part of my community, I would love to have you along on my journey. You can find the sign-up for my monthly newsletter at https://loridejongwrites.com/.

Above all else, I am thankful to my heavenly Father, that

He's allowed me to pursue this passion and has shown me so much more of Himself as I've researched my novels and the truths I seek to impart on their pages. My prayer is that He'll make the work of my fingers a blessing to any who would read this humble book of mine.

FROM THE AUTHOR

Hey there, y'all! I find writing about my fictional characters much more fun and exciting than writing about myself, but here goes.

First of all, I love Jesus and the Bible and writing stories full of grace and the redemptive power of God's love that inspire others to get to know Him better. I couldn't ask for any more than that from the words I put to paper. Nothing else matters.

I was born and raised in Phoenix, Arizona, but arrived in Texas in 2005, and dug those roots right in. I do love me some Texas, especially here in beautiful Georgetown, where my husband and I live in our empty nest (except for our two fur-babies, Buddy and Lily). We have one daughter, Michaela, and our son-in-love, Wilson, who live up in Dallas, so not too far, thankfully.

I love to write about love and romance and all that fun stuff, with a firm foundation of faith. Clean but sassy, sparkly, and even goose-bumpy romance is a *thing*, y'all! With God in the middle, and with characters seeking and learning and changing, nothing could be more heartwarming or spine-tingly.

My debut novel, *Love's True Calling*, was the 2020 winner of the Scrivenings Press Novel Starts Contest, the 2022 winner of the ACFW Genesis Award for Romance, 2023 Scrivenings Press Contemporary Book of the Year, and a double-finalist in the 2024 Selah Awards. It was published by Scrivenings Press in June 2023, and *Love's True Home*, Book Two of the series, released in 2024.

ALSO BY LORI DEJONG

Love's True Calling

True Calling Series — Book One

After years of jumping through other people's hoops to be all they thought she should be, and enduring a tragedy no mother should, self-described "newbie" Christian, Harper Townsend, has finally found her true calling … and her true love. Until it appears that to follow one may mean leaving the other behind.

Adolescent Psychologist, Wyatt McCowan, is beyond delighted to have *the-girl-who-got-away* back in his life — and his heart. But even as they fall more in love, he realizes that being obedient to God's calling on each of their lives may pull them apart. She rejected him once in favor of another, which left him hurt and angry. But this time, he can't fault her for following hard after the God she loves with all her heart, even if it means leaving him once again.

Get your copy here:

https://scrivenings.link/lovestruecalling

Love's True Home

True Calling Series — Book Two

Allyson Kincaid needs roots. Born and raised on the foreign mission field, all she wants is home and hearth on American soil. Finally past the break-up with the man she'd thought was the love of her life, she's ready to put herself back out there. Too bad the first guy who's made her pulse skip in nearly two years dreams of a life spent in foreign missions. She's been there, done that, and, although she supports him in his calling, knows his choice means she'll be laying even more broken dreams, and a newly shattered heart, at the feet of Jesus.

When Zane Carpenter relocates to Arlington, Texas, his seventh move in thirteen years, his only thought is to meet his obligation with Becker Ministries in a few months, then take a foreign mission assignment, his dream for the past several years. But working so closely with Ally in student ministry has him feeling things he's never experienced. He's ready for a future with her, until he accepts an opportunity to work on foreign soil and Ally stays behind. He knows God put him there for a reason, although his heart still longs for the girl back home.

Get your copy here:

https://scrivenings.link/lovestruehome

Stay up-to-date on your favorite books and authors with our free e-newsletters.

ScriveningsPress.com

www.ingramcontent.com/pod-product-compliance
Lightning Source LLC
Chambersburg PA
CBHW060619100726
47907CB00006B/1686